ALTERED SEASONS

MONSOONRISE

ALTERED SEASONS
MONSOONRISE

PAUL BRIGGS

SECANT
PUBLISHING

Altered Seasons: Monsoonrise
Copyright ©2018 by Paul Briggs
Published 2018

Cover art & interior design by Molly Phipps of www.wegotyoucoveredbookdesign.com

Author photo by Sara Grantham

Secant Publishing, LLC
615 N. Pinehurst Ave.
Salisbury MD 21801

www.secantpublishing.com

ISBN: 978-1-944962-48-7

Library of Congress Control Number: 2018931871

To Evan and Jonah.

May the world they grow up in be better than I could imagine.

To a season of political and social upheaval was added a strange and brooding apprehension of hideous physical danger; a danger widespread and all-embracing, such a danger as may be imagined only in the most terrible phantasms of the night. I recall that the people went about with pale and worried faces, and whispered warnings and prophecies which no one dared consciously repeat or acknowledge to himself that he had heard. A sense of monstrous guilt was upon the land, and out of the abysses between the stars swept chill currents that made men shiver in dark and lonely places. There was a daemoniac alteration in the sequence of the seasons—the autumn heat lingered fearsomely, and everyone felt that the world and perhaps the universe had passed from the control of known gods or forces to that of gods or forces which were unknown.

H.P. Lovecraft, "Nyarlathotep"

YEAR ZERO

THE DAY THE ICE CAP DIED

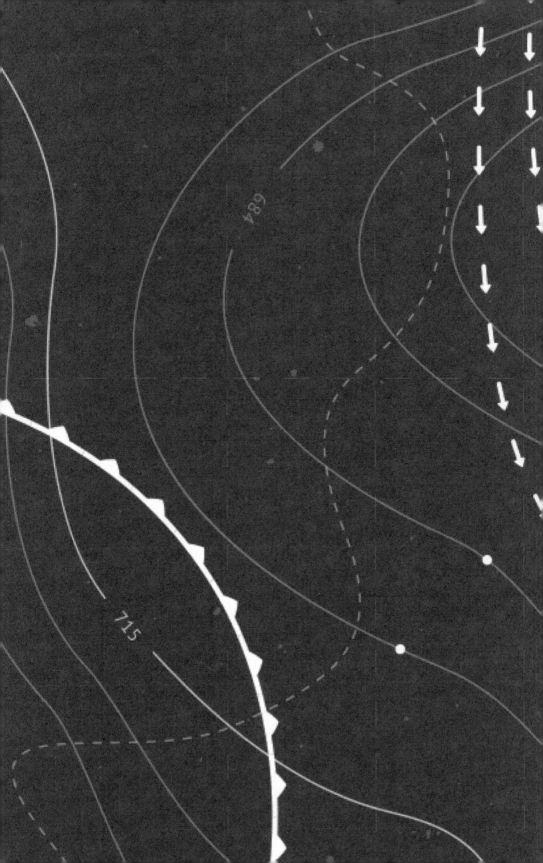

GOING BY AVERAGE GLOBAL TEMPERATURES, *this was only the second-hottest year on record—the previous year had been the hottest. It was warm enough, however, to complete a process that had begun many years earlier and which last year had nearly finished.*

When spring came to the eastern United States, it brought with it the worst tornado outbreak since 2011. This was followed by a succession of polar vortexes that flowed out of the northwest, bringing cool weather as far south as Tennessee and North Carolina. The Rockies and the West Coast, on the other hand, were dominated by a searing heat wave that began in April and continued for most of the year. In Barrow, Alaska, temperatures in the summer went into the seventies.

In Europe, March was so warm it was described as "May come two months early." Strong south winds in May and June brought Sahara-like conditions to the Mediterranean lowlands and flooding to the southern slopes of the Alps and Pyrenees, even as the pleasant weather that Spain, Italy, and Greece should have been enjoying held sway from Ireland to Karelia.

In Asia, heat waves and drought sent forest fires raging through Siberia from the end of March all through the summer. In August and September, typhoons hit the Philippines, Taiwan and southern Japan, even as the monsoon failed in India.

But the real story was what happened up north.

In a typical year, the polar ice cap in the Arctic Ocean spends the six months from April through September shrinking, then grows again from October to March. Last year was so terribly hot that the ice cap shrank to less than one million square miles in area—smaller than it had ever been in recorded history. That year the major news organizations issued a series of tongue-in-cheek stories for the benefit of small children, to the effect that Santa Claus was moving himself and his workshop to the South Pole, where the ice was still good and solid.

By April of this year, the ice cap had rebounded to 5.35 million square miles of sea ice, with a volume of 5100 cubic miles—more than anyone had hoped for, but still much smaller than it had been this time last year. An unfortunate combination of circumstances—bright, sunny weather in May and June, warm water from the North Atlantic flowing under the ice, and warmer air from Eurasia flowing over it—combined to shrink it further. Arctic cyclones in July and August created waves that broke off tracts of ice the size of states, exposing the interior of the ice cap and speeding the melting process. Meanwhile, the prevailing winds blew warm air from northern Alaska eastward over the Canadian Archipelago, melting the ice in the labyrinth of channels between the islands.

The more the ice cap shrank, the thinner it became, raising its surface-area-to-volume ratio and exposing an even greater percentage of its mass to the air and water. By the beginning of September, there was nothing left but a tiny remnant clinging to the northern coasts of Greenland and Ellesmere Island. And then, in less than two weeks, it vanished entirely.

Nobody saw the precise moment it happened—clouds and low-lying mists had obscured that stretch of ocean for more than a week. Then, on September 11, the weather cleared, and a satellite overflying the poles recorded that the last traces of sea ice in the Nares Strait and the Lincoln Sea were gone. The Arctic Ocean was finally ice-free.

ALL ON THAT DAY:

IN A DORM ROOM IN College Park, Maryland, a new student was getting in her daily twenty minutes of exercise. She was heavily built and basically okay with it, but she didn't want to get any heavier than necessary.

The room, lived in for three weeks, was half alarmingly neat and half messy to the point where it interfered with navigation. Isabel was in the neat half, where there was room on the floor for a yoga mat. Her face turned pink as she curled her fingers behind her head and pulled herself up into a sitting position. Her light-brown hair was pulled back and threaded through an O-ring to keep it out of her face.

As she exercised, Isabel cast an occasional guilty glance at her school reader, which had all her textbooks downloaded onto it. Her guidance counselor had made it very clear to her that in the field of STEM, the more options you had, the better. So, at age eighteen in a week or so, she was pursuing dual degrees in engineering and meteorology.

At least, that was what she was doing this *semester*. Right at this moment she was just doing sit-ups while listening to Rodomontade's "The Two." Later this afternoon she would be working at Celebrazione, an Italian restaurant just south of the Beltway.

While we're waiting for something to happen, let's get her backstory out of the way. Isabel Bradshaw grew up on Tilghman Island in the Chesapeake Bay, daughter of one of the few remaining full-time watermen. Her father worked very hard, earned a good living, and had done his best to impress upon all his children the importance of working hard and earning a good living doing *something else entirely*. Those children were, in birth order, Chelsey, Isabel, Kristen, and Scott. We'll learn more about them as they appear. At the moment, Isabel was at College Park, Kristen was in high school, Scott was in middle school and Chelsey was… Chelsey. As a child, Isabel suffered from a potentially fatal allergy, but after a few years of treatment she got over it. This will come up later, but for now, just forget about it.

Isabel's cell phone rang. "It's Chelsey," said the phone over the ringtone. She turned off the music.

"Hey, blondie," said Isabel.

"Hey, chunkybutt," said Chelsey. "Guess what?"

"What?"

"I'm pregnant."

What.

"Um…" Before she started congratulating Chelsey, she wanted to hear a few more details, but there wasn't any good way to ask *is this something you and Rod had intended, or did you just get careless?* Chelsey sounded excited about it, but that was not necessarily a good sign—Pop-pop had always called Chelsey an "outdoor cat." Exciting things happened to outdoor cats. Often these were bad things.

"Surprised?"

"Well… yeah," said Isabel.

"I'm gonna give Rod the good news tonight." Isabel mentally translated the phrase "the good news" to mean *yes, we actually meant this to happen and we have a plan for what to do next, so you can stop worrying.* At this point a little voice inside her head piped up and told her she was a horrible person for being so suspicious of her older sister. The rest of Isabel told herself it wasn't like Chelsey had ever given her any great reason to be confident.

"That's great! When's the baby due?"

"The doctor said April."

"Cool."

"I think Rod can get some time off by then," said Chelsey. "He's going to be really busy the next few months—the company's buying up a huge load of property."

"What about you?"

"I'm gonna hang on till the Christmas rush is over. Rod's making pretty good money, so I think I can take some time off." Isabel didn't quite trust Rod, mostly because he was a thirty-two-year-old business school graduate and he was dating a twenty-year-old woman with a GED. Since Chelsey was that twenty-year-old woman with the GED, Isabel had a hard time finding a good way to express her suspicions.

Then Chelsey changed the subject. "Hey, how's your girlfriend?"

"Jezi? Still kinda clingy. Told her yesterday she didn't have to call me every day and she got that hurt look."

"You should dump her."

"I can't."

From there, the conversation moved into smaller matters. Mostly they talked about their friends. It will come as no surprise to learn that Chelsey's friends got into much more interesting scrapes than Isabel's.

Truth to tell, it kind of annoyed Isabel that she had been typecast in her family as the studious, diligent, responsible sister—the "indoor cat," as Pop-pop put it—while Chelsey had been typecast as the wild child who went out and had fun. There was a good deal of truth in all this typecasting, of course, and it was kind of flattering that other people expected more of her, but sometimes it rankled a little. Isabel had read that introverts actually enjoyed themselves more during their non-partying hours, which after all were most of a normal person's life, but Chelsey still managed to *look* like she was having more fun.

By the time they were done talking, it was almost time for Isabel to go to work. First, she checked the news to see if there was anything interesting. Every single news story seemed to be about the 9/11 commemorations. Isabel checked a sea-ice monitoring site she visited often.

What she found… *You knew it was going to happen sooner or later*, she told herself.

Yes, but not today, she replied.

She logged in and posted a link to the news on her blog. She added only three words:

This. Changes. Everything.

Then she logged out, strapped the phone to her arm and started changing into her waitress outfit. It wouldn't do to show up late for work.

IN A LOFT APARTMENT IN Denver, Walter Yuschak, age twenty-nine, stood in the bathroom and took a long last look at his reflection.

He was a big, heavyset man with a red face and dark, thinning hair. The key word there is "thinning." His bald spot was getting harder to hide every day. As a teenager, his father's comb-over had been the laughingstock of all his friends. At the time, he had sworn he'd never let that happen to him. But the spot had been so small at first—no bigger than a quarter. Surely, he'd thought, he could cover it up for a little while.

But the spot was now an inch and a half wide and two inches long, and it was only going to get bigger. And his hair was dark. And his scalp was pale. And his public profile was rising. His biweekly podcasts had been discovered by a wider audience. A cable news station was showing interest in him. Soon his face would be as famous as his voice… as would the hairline above it, if he didn't act right now. Today.

"Say cheese."

Walt turned. Susie was standing in the doorway, holding up her phone.

"I just want one more picture of how you used to look," said his girlfriend.

"In case it turns out I look awful?" He'd heard of a guy who'd shaved his scalp after a lifetime of long hair, and had immediately screamed, "Dear God, my head's shaped like a *gourd*!"

"Don't be ridiculous. I'm sure you'll look fine." Judging by the expression

5

on her face, she thought he was making a big deal about nothing. Sensitivity to women wasn't Walt's strong point, but it occurred to him that what she was thinking right now might be the same thing he thought when he saw her spending ten or fifteen minutes making infinitesimal adjustments to her hair and makeup—*do you really think it makes that much difference?*

One she'd taken the picture, he set to work. He started with the scissors, trimming his hair away in careless chunks until it was less than an inch long and looked like it had been chewed on by goats. Then he got out the electric razor and ran it over everywhere, enjoying the buzz against his head as it reduced his hair to stubble. Finally, he lathered up the stubble with shaving cream and scraped it away. He managed it without nicking himself. Then he ran a wet washcloth over his now-naked scalp, and that was all.

Walt's head was surprisingly shiny. It gleamed with authority. He hoped people would think so, anyway. It was hard to tell right now—he was still in his pajamas, which kind of spoiled the effect.

"Missed a spot," said Susie, tapping behind his left ear. It was a little hard for him to see properly in the mirror, so he handed her the razor. With a few strokes, she finished the job.

"You look… ageless," she said, and kissed him.

Walt decided she was right. At first glance, he might have been twenty-five or forty-five. He looked just old enough that you couldn't quite dismiss him as a kid, anyway.

While Susan was getting a couple of beers for them to toast his new look, Walt checked the job postings on his smartphone—just in case the cable news deal fell through. His source of income, in addition to his podcast which some people did actually pay to listen to, was voice acting for radio announcements and the occasional animated production. But there were no job openings listed today.

Then he checked the news feed for something he could talk about in his podcast. He scrolled past the blurbs about 9/11 commemorations—he'd already recorded his thoughts on the anniversary yesterday. And there was plenty of good material in the news today for the next few days.

Here was some prisoner's advocate responding to the news that an audit of the New York State prison system had shown them spending over $21,000 apiece per year feeding the prisoners. The advocate was saying that from what he knew, the meals they were getting were somewhere near dog-food quality. A lot of Walt's followers wouldn't be inclined to believe it, but with the right words, maybe he could convince them: *Either these goons in there are eating like kings, or—and here's my theory—most of that money is going right into somebody's pocket. This is what happens with the state! They wait until you're scared half to death, then they ask for bigger prisons, bigger budgets, less oversight... and when you give it to them, you get this! If you're lucky!*

Also, the FBI was trying to gain more power to investigate online rape threats... or at least, that was what they said their motive was. That one practically wrote itself: *Some sad little troll in his mom's basement goes on the Internet and says to a man "ooh I'm a big scary tough guy and I got kicked out of the SEALs for unnecessary roughness and I'm gonna come over to your house and kick your ass" and everybody laughs at him. That same bag of hair goes online, tells a woman "ooh I'm a big scary rapist and I'm gonna come over there and rape you" and all hell breaks loose! Talk about your bad incentives!*

There was another blurb—something about Arctic sea ice—but he ignored it. He'd made the transition from "global warming is a myth" to "it's a natural phenomenon and has nothing to do with us" years ago, and he was not a man to look back.

ON I-64 ABOUT THIRTY MILES east of Richmond, a new Lexus hybrid followed the highway as it turned southeast. It was royal blue, with a **CAMBERG for Governor** bumper sticker on the back, because if you didn't support yourself, who would?

The big woman in the front passenger seat had a broad, pleasant face, a streak of gray in her dark hair and a default expression of cheerfulness that didn't quite go with her somber black pantsuit. She would be forty-three in another month. Her husband sat in the driver's seat, his head nearly touching the ceiling. Small, neat spectacles perched on what Carrie thought of as a ruggedly handsome face. He was almost a full year younger than Carrie, and a few weeks under the hard white sun of the Himalayas three years ago had turned his red hair permanently blond, hiding the silver threads in it.

Roger had been quiet, but this wasn't a bad sign. He was taciturn by nature— it had taken Carrie a long time to get used to it. And even after fourteen years of marriage, Carrie's circle of friends didn't have a lot of overlap with his, and it would be her friends at this commemoration ceremony. Also, he took to suit and tie like a duck to… suit and tie.

"I think I'm getting used to this car," said Roger.

"Sort of like riding a good horse, isn't it?"

"Not really. You don't have to worry about falling off."

"I meant the way it's under your control up to a point, but it sort of filters your actions. You can't make it do anything dangerous."

"I'm just glad I can finally parallel park without scraping the hubcaps."

Carolyn Camberg turned to look at her daughter in the rear driver's seat, sitting next to the suit jackets the three of them had draped neatly over the back seat. Eleven-year-old Thel was lucky enough to get most of her looks from Roger—freckled complexion, blue-gray eyes and a face that was trending toward beautiful, not just "good-natured" or "handsome" as people kept calling Carrie. She was wearing a smaller version of her mother's pantsuit, and had managed to avoid crumpling or mussing it so far. The only thing in disarray was her hair, which was coppery red and formed such tangled curls that no mere human strength could get a comb all the way through it in one sweep. Thel occasionally glanced out the window before returning her attention to her phone.

"Remember, this is not a campaign stop," said Carrie.

"I know, Mom. You said that already."

Carrie nodded. Her daughter was already making the smooth transition from the stage where if you told her anything less than three times she'd forget it instantly to the stage where if you told her anything more than once she'd lose all patience.

"Don't ask people to vote for you, don't mention that you're running for governor… I got all that," said Thel. "What do I do if somebody else brings it up?"

"Probably won't happen. If it does, you can talk about what it's like going back and forth between school and campaign appearances." She smiled at her daughter. "You've been doing so well. I want you to know I really appreciate it."

Thel blushed. "Thanks, Mom."

Even when I'm not campaigning, I'm still using you as a campaign prop, she thought. *You're not even mad at me yet, and already I'm hoping you'll forgive me one day.* All Thel wanted was to help her family. Carrie had been the same way at that age. And then, at a slightly later age, she had been completely different.

But for today at least, Thel and Roger were all right with putting in a required appearance. The big 9/11 ceremonies, of course, were around the Pentagon and Arlington National Cemetery, but the Navy was quietly holding its own commemoration down in Norfolk, and a lot of Carrie's old friends would be there. She'd spent four years in the Navy and had run a company that provided the naval base with a lot of its supplies. If she belonged anywhere today, it was there. Even with the election less than two months away, she wasn't going to push for her political advantage on a day like this.

Also, she was a good seven to ten points over McAllister in last week's polls. And while her opponent was doing his best to cultivate a conservative-but-not-one-of-the-crazy-ones image, a tape had surfaced this week of him speaking to a church group, explaining to them that the problems with U.S. education policy stemmed from it being unduly influenced at the federal level by a demon named "Baphomet." In an odd way, Carrie was disappointed. There was something unsatisfying about beating an opponent who sabotaged himself like this. But it assured her that even if staying off the campaign trail today was a mistake, it was a mistake she would survive.

And she could make some use of this time. Carrie dialed Jerome Ross, her campaign coordinator in Fairfax County. The good news was, he was young, brilliant, and loaded with energy. The bad news was, he was, well, Jerome Ross.

"Hello, Rome," she said.

"Hi, boss."

"I've received an email from our software providers," she said. "They say you verbally abused the people they sent. You do know they had the meeting recorded?"

"I knew that when I spoke up. I wanted to make sure my complaints were on the record." Carrie mentally translated this as *I couldn't yell at you and I couldn't yell at Horner, but I really needed to get in some quality yelling.*

And Rome had a point. Horner was a good campaign manager when it came to organizing volunteers and raising money, but he was one of those people for whom the phrase "penny-wise and pound foolish" had been invented. Nothing made him happier than finding some small way to save a piddling amount of money. But even for him, buying cheap half-tested software to run the campaign database had been a little extreme. That said, the way Rome Ross had treated the company reps from Copenhagen had also been... a little extreme.

"Yes, apparently you had a number of complaints. You asked," Carrie checked the notes on her smartphone, "'Why is it every expletive time you hit a tab key, a file closes? Why does the whole thing slow to a crawl if the file has photos in it? Why does it crash if there's an apostrophe in the text? Why are all the error messages in Danish?' Did they have any answers?"

"They said it was still in beta test and there were bugs to be worked out. They kept promising it was gonna be awesome if we could just wait six months. I had to explain to them we're in the middle of an election here."

"And then you interjected by saying 'Even when this expletive works, it doesn't work. Why can't we use runes* or passphrases instead of expletive passwords? What is this, 20-expletive-10?' You also complained that everyone had to log out and log back in again to use internal messaging, which I must admit is a pretty serious flaw. I gather the answers didn't satisfy you?"

"No. They just said they were going to review our complaints back in the home office in Denmark."

Carrie nodded. "As I understand it, it was at this point that you stood up and shouted at the representatives…" As she read the transcript, she carefully did not raise her voice, but kept it soft and pleasant. "'Expletive Denmark, I hope your country gets nuked, I hope an asteroid falls on it, I hope it gets hit by all the plagues of Egypt including the stupid one with the frogs, expletive everything Danish, expletive your language, expletive your culture, expletive your history, expletive your big ugly dogs, expletive your godawful expletive little hotel Continental breakfast pastries that taste like frosted cardboard, expletive your depressing expletive movies that make people want to slit their expletive wrists, expletive Hans Christian Andersen, expletive the Little Mermaid, I'm not even sure she has an expletive but expletive her anyway,' and, then, very loud, 'Expletive… Denmark.' Do I have that right?"

"Pretty much, yeah." At this point, Roger had his jaws clamped shut, straining to keep from laughing out loud. Thel wasn't even trying not to laugh.

"Some might consider that hate speech, young man."

"You gotta understand, everybody in tech—Leo and Daphne and Raúl, everybody who's been trying to work with this new system—they're angry.

---

* Runes are personalized images—usually watermarked photographs—that serve the same function as a password. They have the disadvantage that they can't be input manually and need to be carried in an external keydrive, but the advantage that the amount of computing power that would be required to crack them does not yet exist on Earth.

Really, really angry. As they see it, they've been working their asses off trying to do a job they can't do because management got sold a bill of goods with this software and they're gonna get blamed for everything and nobody gives a damn. They need to know that their issues are being taken seriously and somebody in authority is on their side."

"Spoken like a man with a future in politics. Although if you ever become president, I hope you'll refrain from declaring war on Denmark. Just to change the subject, what's McAllister up to right now?" Carrie expected there to be a delay of several seconds as Rome jumped to the monitor to find out what he should have been keeping track of already.

She was wrong—Rome replied instantly. "He's parked himself as close to the Pentagon as they'll let him get," he said, "and he's got a bunch of cameras in front of him. He's telling everybody as governor he'll use all the resources at his command to combat terrorism. Oh, and some people are coming forward and saying they've heard him say some racist stuff."

"Worse than the stuff you said about Denmark?"

"Not worse, but about as bad."

"Oh, dear. Is there a tape?"

"No, we just have their word for it."

"Baphomet declined to comment?"

Rome laughed. "Yep."

Carrie nodded. "Don't issue a statement on it just yet. Let it play out a little."

"Anything else?"

"That's about it. I'll let you go. Behave yourself, Rome."

"Thanks for calling, boss."

Carrie ended the call and put the phone down. Then she had a good, long laugh.

"Really, Mom," said Thel. "'Expletive expletive expletive'? Are you sure you used to be in the Navy? You know you can cuss in front of me, right?"

"Call me old-fashioned."

Thel turned back to her own smartphone and started looking things up. Carrie turned back to the road. Seeing that their lane had been blocked off up ahead by an accident, Roger hit the turn signal. Two seconds later, the car changed lanes of its own accord.

"Holy shit!"

"Thel!"

"Mom, you gotta check this out. The ice cap. It's *gone*, Mom."

"What!?" Carrie was pretty sure that neither of the world's polar ice caps could have just disappeared.

"Not the whole thing. Just the sea ice. And only at the North Pole, not, you know…"

Antarctica. If you made a list of all the things a husband and wife could have a painful, long-standing argument about, Antarctica probably wouldn't show up on it anywhere.

Dr. Roger Camberg was a glaciologist. Until two years ago, he would leave just after Christmas to spend January through March in Antarctica, monitoring the ice flow around the edge of the continent. Thel—God only knew why—had always wanted to go with him on one of those trips when she was old enough. Carrie had hated being separated from her husband, but Antarctica had a prominent place on her private list of Places You Didn't Go Unless You Were Personally Needed There, right underneath the world's war zones.

It was dangerous work. Much of it was in unexplored territory—territory that had been flown over or mapped by satellites, but that wasn't the same thing as exploring it. There were places where thin crusts of snow concealed deep crevasses in the ice that no one knew about. Blinding snowstorms could appear in a moment and last for hours. And of course the parts of the ice cap Roger was visiting were the parts where all the melting was, the parts that were least stable and most treacherous… and were usually a minimum of twenty-four hours away from anyone who could help if he got in trouble out there.

But it wasn't the ice that had almost killed him. It was the "shrieking sixties"—the notorious ring of high winds around the continent, with its frequent cyclones. He had been returning from a survey of East Antarctica through a stretch of what had been relatively clear weather… until, very suddenly, it wasn't. His plane's radio had failed, and Carrie and Thel had spent one long, horrible night waiting before word had come that he was all right.

After that, Carrie had told him enough was enough. *No more fieldwork. Take a desk job. I can't lose you. I can't raise our daughter alone.*

Roger had argued every step of the way, but Carrie had learned how to press an issue in the Virginia House of Delegates, and she had been relentless. And, after weeks of shouting and tears and long silences at the dinner table, she'd had her way.

These days, Roger was a teacher. He'd shaved his wiry beard—Carrie missed the feel of that beard against her cheeks—lost his tan and gained a little weight. But even now, those great shining sheets of ice called to him. It was a part of him that after all these years Carrie still couldn't understand.

IN A RESIDENTIAL NEIGHBORHOOD WEST of Syracuse, New York, a fifteen-year-old Kia pulled into a driveway. It had no self-driving capacity, wasn't a hybrid, was missing two hubcaps and had one side mirror held on with duct tape. Still, it had managed the five-and-a-half-hour drive from Boston, which was all its owner had asked of it.

A small, skinny young woman in jeans and a knobbly sweater stepped out of the car. Her face was pale and girlish, with thick glasses and no makeup. Her hair was a shade somewhere between ash-blond and mouse-brown, and was held in a glossy ponytail that flowed down to just past the small of her back.

She pulled two suitcases from the front passenger seat and gritted her teeth as she hauled them to the door, the loose heel on her right sneaker slapping against the bottom of her foot with every step. Between them, the suitcases weighed about half what she did.

Her name was Sandra Symcox. Nine years ago, she'd been accepted to college at the age of fourteen with great fanfare and a good deal of sponsorship. Her IQ test results, the tutoring she'd received, her calculus scores and her "intuitive grasp of chemistry" had been the stuff of local news posts. So off she had gone, visions of technological breakthroughs and Nobel Prizes dancing in her head.

She had just turned twenty-three. Her bank account was a four-digit number, and two of those digits were on the wrong side of the decimal point. She was here because she had nowhere else to go. Not that she was out of ideas—she had a few possible breakthroughs rattling around in her skull—but any one of them would have needed research funding in the hundreds of millions to find out if it was practical. And after her experience with Verdissimus, she was a little reluctant to take on another business partner.

A tall, black-haired woman of about thirty answered the door. Marty had said he'd be home by now, but it looked like he was as reliable as ever.

"Hi," said Sandy.

"You must be Sandy," the woman said with a smile that didn't quite reach her eyes. Or her cheeks. Or her lips. Actually, it wasn't so much a smile as an expression of undisguised loathing and hostility.

13

"Mmm-hmm," said Sandy with a smile that was as authentic as she could force it to look. "You're Nora, right?" She was tempted to say *You're Kendra, right?* Or *You're Michelle, right?*—those being the names of two of her father's ex-wives. But she decided that this time she'd try the diplomatic approach before she got unpleasant.

"Marty said I should expect you."

"He did say I could stay." Sandy spent two and a half seconds on the doorstep waiting for Nora to suddenly sprout a hospitality, then gave up and pushed past her into the living room. She dropped the suitcases on the floor, collapsed on the couch, then took off her sweater and mopped her forehead with it.

Sandy took a moment to look at the sweater. She'd knitted it herself a few years ago, after completing a course in advanced topological mathematics. She'd done it more as an intellectual exercise than anything else, but it did keep her warm. It consisted of two layers—a charcoal-gray layer on top and a mauve layer underneath—the strands of which were intertwined together in hundreds of complex little knots. Like the one-hoss shay in the old poem, it might suddenly collapse into a cloud of dust one day a hundred years from now, but it would never, ever unravel. It was a good sweater, and she was proud to have made it... but Sandy doubted she could make a living from knitting.

She looked around the room. It was plain her father was getting by financially. The furniture might not match, but everything was clean and in good shape... unlike the apartment she'd had to vacate, which was furnished in Early Modern Curbside. There was a nice big screen, currently tuned to a news channel. The anchor was talking about the 9/11 anniversary and various commemorations of the attacks. A message scrolling across the bottom said that according to scientists, there was no more sea ice in the Arctic Ocean. Yet another thing wrong with the world.

"How long do you plan on staying?" said Nora in what she probably thought was a diplomatic tone.

"I don't really have plans right now."

"I'm having a baby."

"I heard. Congratulations."

"It's due in six months."

"Mmm-hmm."

"We'll be turning the guest bedroom into the baby's room."

"Not a problem. I can sleep on the couch."

Nora put her hands on her hips. "To be perfectly frank," she said, sounding more and more irritated, "I would expect you to have found other living arrangements by then."

To be equally frank, you're Martin's fifth wife. So far. I wouldn't bet on YOU being here six months from now. "I hope so. We'll just have to see."

Nora glowered at her, then strode into the kitchen.

Several minutes later, Sandy heard a car pulling into the driveway. She considered greeting her father at the door and throwing her arms around him, then decided that would be too obviously fake.

The last time she'd seen Martin Clearwater had been at Mom's funeral, six years ago. He hadn't changed much since then—he was in his late forties and still looked about thirty-five. If there was more gray in his blond hair, it was hard to see. He was a short man, not quite as tall as Nora.

"Sandy," he said.

She blinked a couple of times while they just stood there and looked at each other. Then Martin smiled and spread his arms. Sandy hugged him, slipping her arms under his sport coat. The corner of her glasses pressed against his cheek.

"You look just the same," he said. To Sandy, this felt less like a compliment than a reminder that her body had gotten about a quarter of the way through puberty and then given up, but it was a compliment she could return honestly.

"Sandy, this is my wife, Nora," he said.

"We've met," said Sandy, smiling at Nora like they'd hit it off at first sight. She'd discovered over the past few years that even social skills could be learned by rote if you worked at it. Right now she calculated that if she acted like she and Nora were getting along great, Nora would lose a lot of points if she showed any sign of hostility.

A few minutes later, she was sitting on the couch again. Martin was next to her. The conversation had turned, inevitably, to Verdissimus.

"I'm sure it wasn't anything you did," he said.

"You're right—it wasn't. One or two of my friends who shall remain nameless tried to get around the patent laws for some of the tools we were using. I told them that was gonna bite us in the ass."

Martin nodded, then put a hand on her arm.

"Let me ask you something," he said. "When was the last time you really, completely failed at something? Until this year, I mean?"

Sandy had to think for a few moments. It wasn't so much that she hadn't had failures, it was that most of them had been in the area of romance or interpersonal relations. Come to think of it, the failure at Verdissimus could be thought of that way. If you knew your friends and coworkers in a start-up were making a bad move, didn't you owe it to whatever you were trying to accomplish to try harder to talk them out of it?

"That long silence kind of says it all," he said. "Everybody does it sometimes. God knows I've done it often enough."

Sandy nodded. She'd known she wasn't going to succeed at everything, but... this was not supposed to have been the failure. *We were going to do great things. We were going to change the world.*

"You are so incredibly young," he said. "You've already accomplished more than most people, and you've still got practically your whole life ahead of you."

Sandy nodded again.

"Don't give up."

"Dad, I'm not contemplating suicide, if that's what you mean. I'm just... tired and I need a little break. That's all."

"I understand." He paused. "How are things between you and—what's his name—Trevor?"

Sandy winced. Another subject she didn't want to discuss.

"We broke up," she said.

"Sorry to hear that. What happened?"

"Stop and think, Dad. How much do you actually want to know about my sex life?"

"Not much," he said. "I guess it's enough to know you have one."

Yes, it is something of a minor miracle, isn't it? I have the body of an anorexic thirteen-year-old. I keep hearing how this is what our culture thinks is beautiful, but every guy I meet treats me like his little sister.

Well, not every guy. There is a certain kind of guy who thinks I'm one smokin' hot piece of ass. But they're not much fun to date.

Martin rested a hand on her shoulders. "You know, you really are an extraordinary human being," he said. "I hate myself for not having been there for you as a child. I really missed out on a lot. I just..." He shook his head. "Twenty years ago I was a different person. A complete man-child. I wasn't ready to be a dad. I couldn't handle the responsibility."

16

I, I, I, I, I, thought Sandy.

"Anyway, I'm ready now," he said. "If you need a father, I'm here."

Dad, that ship has sailed. It is far beyond the horizon. But he was the only parent she had left now. *He wants a second chance. You need a place to crash. This will work if you let it. Don't let your drama get in the way.* She smiled at him.

"Do you have a basement?" she said.

"We can keep you in the spare room."

"That's not what I meant. There's a machine in the trunk of my car and I'd like to set it up somewhere it won't get in anybody's way."

"What is it?"

"Just a little something I slapped together while I was working for Verdissimus. Don't worry—my contract let me keep the patent myself."

"What's it do?"

"It turns raw carbon into some basic diamondoid materials. It's kind of limited in what it can do, but it's more energy-efficient than other machines that do the same thing."

"Are you going to sell it?"

"I don't even know if there's a market for it. I want to try and make some money with it myself before I do anything else."

"A start-up in my garage," said Marty. "I like the idea."

"We can't afford to support this," said Nora.

"I'm not asking you to," said Sandy. "I know a good crowdfunding site." She took off her shoes and spent a moment fingering the loose sole.

"Where do you keep the epoxy?" she said.

AS IN EVERY YEAR, WITH the passing of the autumnal equinox polar twilight and polar night descended over the Arctic Ocean in expanding concentric circles of darkness. The ocean surface, never very far above freezing to begin with, lost its heat to the cooling air.

In early October, the first traces of grease ice appeared. The ice spread, forming a slushy layer over the surface of the ocean that gradually hardened into glittering chunks. The ice chunks thickened and merged. By December, the Arctic Ocean was again covered—mostly—by a reassuring white blanket that reflected the sun's radiation back into the emptiness of space, even as it held in what remained of the ocean's heat.

But the damage was done.

YEAR ONE
WAR GAMES

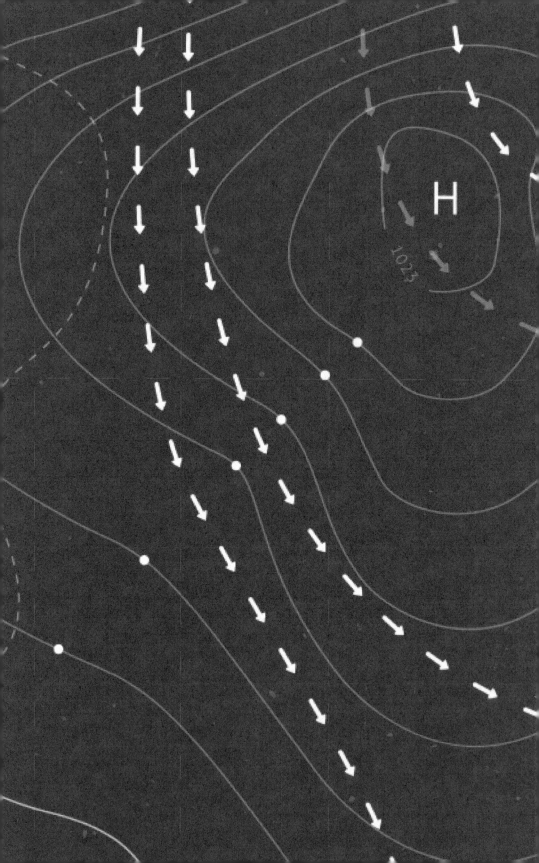

WINTER THAT YEAR, WHILE WARMER *than average worldwide, was not too far outside what had come to be accepted as normal. In North America, the jet stream flowed just south of the U.S.-Canada border. There were still snowstorms, although not generally south of the Ohio Valley and the lower Missouri unless you were in the Rockies, where small amounts of snow fell as far south as Flagstaff and Albuquerque. In February, a severe ice storm hit the Carolinas.*

The story elsewhere was much the same. Record warm temperatures in France, the Balkans and Iran, record snowfall in Japan and Korea... but overall, not a winter to ring alarm bells. Not compared to those the world had already gone through. And spring, when it came, was if anything slightly cooler than it had been last year, particularly in North American and western Europe.

THAT SPRING:

ONE OF THE COURSES ISABEL was taking this semester was called "Wargaming the Apocalypse." It was taught by a Dr. Tanaka, who grew his graying hair down to his shoulders and kept his shirtsleeves permanently rolled up as if to say *Look at me! I'm cool!*

It was one of those gut courses whose only purpose was to provide a break from the stress of real work, but it did pose a certain amount of intellectual challenge. Using powerful computers and their own imagination, Isabel and her fellow students spent the semester simulating various disasters and their effect on society and debating the best possible response by the government. They discussed large-scale and small-scale nuclear war, asteroid strikes on land and sea, a miniature black hole that had half the mass of the moon dropping through Earth and out the other side, a solar storm taking out most of the world's electronics, and the eruption of the Yellowstone supervolcano. They tried to model the effects of epidemics destroying 30 percent, 60 percent and 95 percent of the human population. Those "war games" went fairly well, unlike the famine war game, which broke down completely over the question of whether the unskilled, the elderly, or those with criminal records should be eaten first.

During the last month, they moved into more exotic threats. First, they gamed out two different kinds of zombie outbreak. They found that an epidemic of sprinting rage-monster zombies would be a definite existential threat under any circumstances, whereas the slow-but-relentless variety of zombies would only pose a public hazard in an environment where order had already broken down due to war or natural disaster. This was the sort of discussion that made Isabel wonder if this class was really the best use of her tuition money.

Then it was infertility plagues—diseases that didn't kill anyone but left men, women, or both unable to conceive or bear children. At first, more than half the class thought this sounded like a good thing—a painless long-term solution to the problem of overpopulation. Isabel was inclined to agree, but she kept her mouth shut. Knowing Dr. Tanaka, there had to be a catch.

Sure enough… "What happens when more than half the population is over seventy-five?" said Dr. Tanaka. "When a third of the country is physically too old to work? Who takes care of them? Who pays into the programs that support them?"

"Who cares?" Gregg in the front row said. "Let 'em die."

"We can't," Isabel said.

"Sure we can."

"No, we *can't*. Because they vote. And they've got us outnumbered." Isabel was already imagining herself conscripted by the government to work sixteen-hour days caring for the elderly at some gigantic nursing home/concentration camp. It would just be bedpan after bedpan after bedpan… As if it were already happening, she thought to herself *How dare they force me to do this?* Then she thought **How many people have to die of untreated bedsores so you can spend your time reading books and surfing the Internet, you selfish cow?** Then she thought *You're beating yourself up over nothing again! Stop it!* There were people in mental hospitals with fewer voices in their heads than Isabel Bradshaw.

So the class divided into small groups and went to the computers. What they found was that sperm and egg banks, plus financial incentives for fertile individuals to have extra children, worked well enough to prevent a major demographic imbalance as long as at least 10 percent of the population was still fertile. Below that, however, you just couldn't find enough fertile people who were willing to have that many more children.

It was at this point that the phrase "captive breeding program" entered the conversation. Some of the more outspoken feminists demanded that it exit the conversation immediately, along with anyone who thought of it as an option. Isabel couldn't blame them—now she was haunted by the mental image of herself strapped naked to a hospital bed while strangers stood around her with turkey basters in their hand and expressions of sorrow on their faces, explaining that they didn't want to do this, but it was for the sake of Social Security. This was probably somebody's sexual fantasy, but it didn't do anything for her.

Fortunately, the next week the subject was a little more cheerful; what if aliens started abducting people *en masse*? Nadia, who sat right behind Isabel, calculated that if the aliens were interested in sustainable harvesting, they could take as many as five million humans per month. Just to be conservative, Dr. Tanaka lowered this to one million a week. "We're assuming here," he said, "that they're concentrating on major cities, where the largest numbers of people are, and that they come to a different city at every visit."

Deon raised his hand. "How are they abducting people?" he asked. "Are they teleporting people, or just sort of levitating them up with tractor beams?"

"What difference does it make?" said Dr. Tanaka.

"See, if they're just beaming people up, presumably they could do that whether we're inside or outside. But if they need a clear shot at us, so to speak, then they'd have to start knocking holes in buildings. Otherwise we could just all go inside when they show up, and boom, the aliens are defeated.

"So let's say they just need to beam people up. The flying saucers show up over New York City, a million people just disappear, and then off they go.

"What happens to the city? It's not like a plague. Lots of people are gone, but the people left behind know they're safe until the next time the aliens hit New York. So businesses put out a bunch of 'Now Hiring' signs, lots of apartments are for rent, a whole bunch of cars end up on the black market, and that's about it."

"You're forgetting the economic effect of removing that many consumers."

"Right. But if they have to open up the buildings to get at the people inside, that's a whole different thing. Then when the aliens are gone, there's still people missing and now the city is all smashed up. There's a lot of work that needs to be done and fewer people to do it."

"Okay, let's assume the aliens can't just beam people out," said Dr. Tanaka.

"Wouldn't people start moving out of the cities after a while?" said Isabel.

"Indeed they would," said the professor, "I certainly would. And how would the aliens respond to that?"

"By… breaking up into smaller groups and going after people everywhere, I guess."

The last week was devoted to an equally theoretical threat—weaponized cognitohazards. Brown notes. Things that you could be hurt, or possibly killed, by just seeing or hearing them… and what would happen if they got on the Internet. How would people protect themselves? What would this do to freedom of speech? They started by reading some of David Langford's stories.

At the end of the semester, Dr. Tanaka gave a little speech.

"If you've learned anything from me," he said, "then what I hope you've learned is that the one prerequisite for coping with any sort of disaster is knowledge. We don't need to know exactly what the future holds. It's enough to understand what it *might* hold. That gives us the power to plan ahead.

"Our whole society is built on this. It's not this way in every country in the world, but here in America, and in most First World countries, you can drive through a town a year after a hurricane or an earthquake hit and hardly know anything happened. The whole place has bounced back. Everything's been rebuilt and repaired.

"There's a reason for that, and it's not just the economy. The economy's just money. What we have in the First World is lots and lots of ways of getting the money where it needs to go. We've got the federal government, state government, local government, we've got the Red Cross, we've got all kinds of construction firms to do the work, we've got banks of every size to finance it, we've got insurance, we've got reinsurance… seems like we're ready for anything, right?

"But all these things are built around certain assumptions. *Actuarial* assumptions, based on previous experience. How much damage is Mother Nature going to do in any given year? How many things are likely to go wrong, and how much are they likely to cost? How likely is any one kind of catastrophe?

"You see, if you can estimate the answers to these questions, then even if the news is bad you can still get ready for it. Change the estimate, and the institutions change to reflect it. Take away the ability to estimate, the ability to predict even in the vaguest way… and we're at the mercy of whatever the universe throws at us."

THE ARCTIC ICE CAP IN mid-April was a little over five million square miles in area—the smallest on record for that time of year, but surprisingly large considering it had disappeared without trace six months ago. Some wondered if they had gotten worried over nothing.

Although the area of the cap was much easier to measure, looking at the volume would have given a clearer picture of the situation. Comparing the current thin scab of ice to the massive floating layer that had once existed was like comparing a Hollywood backdrop to a brick wall—its volume was barely a third of what had existed at this time last year. If by some miracle the Earth's temperature had suddenly dropped enough to allow some trace of it to survive the summer, it might have formed the core of a new multi-year ice cap… but this did not happen.

In May, the same forces that had destroyed the ice cap in the first place got to work on its replacement. By the middle of July, there was open water at the North Pole. By August 19, the ice was gone once again.

Deep ocean water has a much lower albedo than ice. Even the weak sunlight of the high latitudes, absorbed by the water, was enough to warm the Arctic Ocean slightly—and when it warmed, there was no more sea ice to melt and cool it again. A slow but irreversible feedback loop had begun.

THE LAST WEEK OF AUGUST:

CARRIE, NOW GOVERNOR CAMBERG, SPENT the last ten days of August inflicting psychological torture on state emergency management personnel. It was in a good cause.

Mimicane was a complex program commissioned by the National Guard to simulate a hurricane hitting any part of the East or Gulf Coast. It was like an MMORPG with a more detailed map but much cheaper graphics. Carrie was using it to drill the Department of Emergency Management—and, of course, herself—in hurricane response.

The storm was being planned by Josh Jacobson, their consultant from Mimicane. Carrie had told him to hit Virginia with the worst possible hurricane, and he had exceeded all sane expectations. Jacobson had instructed the computer program to model the cyclone after Hurricane Allen of 1980, which had had winds of up to 190 mph and a 39-foot storm surge. The program had sent the eye of the storm heading straight for Hog Island with only four days' warning. Just to be evil, Jacobson had also planted an unexplained high-pressure system over northeastern U.S. and Canada, forcing the storm due west in violation of all historical precedent for storm tracks.

At this point, every single county in Virginia had either had its share of simulated damage or was in the process of getting it. Anything built on the coast was gone. The eye of the storm had passed over Richmond last night. Yes, the eye was the calm part—the trouble was that immediately before and after it passed overhead, the most violent part of the storm would do the same. So as far as the computer was concerned, Richmond was a field of drenched rubble, shell-shocked survivors and quite a few non-survivors.

It has to be said, at this point, that Carrie was cheating. In her capacity as governor during this hypothetical storm, she wasn't supposed to know any more about what was going on than the Department was telling her. In her capacity as governor during this actual test, she knew what was happening long before they figured it out. Jacobson was in the office with her right now, pointing out the finer points of the catastrophe.

The Department wasn't so lucky. The players could communicate with each other—that also was something of a cheat—but enough cell phone towers and landlines had been destroyed that their ability to assess the damage was limited. As for getting to where the damage was and looking at it, parts of the roads had washed away while other parts were blocked by fallen trees and debris from buildings.

And with the storm now hitting western Virginia, the fun wasn't over yet. "The hurricane has started spawning tornadoes where it hit the high-pressure system," said Jacobson. "About six of them are crossing northern Virginia right now."

The players, few of whom had gotten even one full night's sleep this week, were reacting to this new development with a mixture of weary resignation and shrieking madness. Carrie could see what was being said on the message board, but not who was saying it. This feature was intended to "encourage everyone to communicate freely" and it was achieving this goal.

> : And here come the tornadoes.
>
> : GOD KILL ME NOW
>
> : If you're in Loudun Fairfax or PW get everything valuable inside a shelter
>
> : WHAT shelter?!? There's nothing left standing!
>
> : CARIE YOU PSYCO BITCH

"Really command their loyalty, don't I?" said Carrie cheerfully. At the start of this simulation, everyone had been polite and professional and posting messages in complete sentences. It had been a rough ten days.

Carrie also wanted to see how the commonwealth managed given a minimum of federal assistance. The plan was for FEMA to be "paralyzed by scandal" and unable to help.

> : WTF HOW CAN FEMA BE APARLYZED BY SCANDL WAS EVERBODY CAUGT BANGIN SHEEP AT THE SAME TIME
>
> THERE ARENT THAT MANY SHEEP IN THE WHOL CITY
>
> : Camberg's just making shit up now.
>
> : What next? Locusts?
>
> : maybe the huricane will turn around come back this way
>
> : SHUTUPSHUTUPDONTGIVEHERIDEAS

"Just out of curiosity, why's the power still out in Northern Virginia?" said Carrie. "Don't a lot of places there have solar?"

"When the grid goes down, everything connected to it goes down," said Jacobson. "That way, the people trying to fix it don't get electrocuted. Some systems can cut themselves off from the grid, but not all of them—and we don't have exact numbers on how many, so it's simpler to assume the worst. Not to mention all the solar panels that got blown off by the storm."

Carrie nodded, then turned back to the simulation. The flash flooding in the mountains had reached the Potomac. She could hardly wait to read the comments when it hit Arlington.

IT TOOK A LITTLE LONGER this year for the surface of the ocean to cool enough for ice to form. It had, after all, been naked to the sun for three weeks more than it had by this time last year, and had grown somewhat warmer as a result. And when the ice appeared, it expanded more slowly. At the end of the year, the ice cap was even smaller and thinner than it had been last December.

The change in the ocean was already affecting the climate. Beginning in November, snowfall north of the Arctic Circle was heavier than it had ever been in recorded history, with the heaviest snow on the northern slopes of the Brooks Range in Alaska and in Norway east of Narvik. On December 29, there was a major avalanche near Hammerfest that killed thirty-seven people. At the time, however, this was seen as an isolated incident.

YEAR TWO

MEN WHO WILL NOT SELF-DESTRUCT

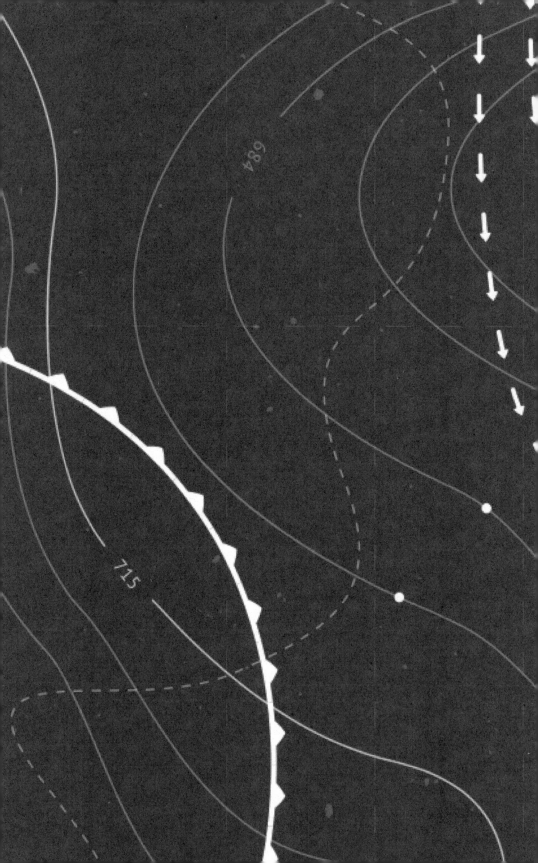

THROUGHOUT THE NORTHERN HEMISPHERE, THE winter was, on average, warmer than it had been last year. But through most of the Northwest Territories, and everywhere north of the Arctic Circle, at least one to two feet of snow fell— more in some places. This might not sound like a lot for such a notoriously cold climate, but until very recently, these places had been desert-dry, seeing not much precipitation of any kind… especially in the winter.

But every now and then, for a week or so, the jet stream weakened, and a polar vortex descended from the north, bringing freezing temperatures to the northeastern U.S. or central Asia. At these times, only a few people ever stopped to reflect that every time arctic air intruded into a part of the temperate zones, it meant that somewhere else, air from the temperate zones was intruding into the Arctic, further slowing the growth of sea ice.

MAY 6:

FOR WALT YUSCHAK, BEING LIVE on camera with no idea what he was going to say was literally the stuff of nightmares, in much the same way that college students sometimes have bad dreams about taking exams they haven't prepared for. So during his waking hours, he took pains to make sure this never happened. His writing staff was instructed to give him two different opening monologues every week, so that he could choose between them. They didn't always manage this, but he had eight opening monologues already prewritten months ago in case his staff came up completely dry. Of course, these monologues were just general statements of opinion and had nothing to do with whatever was in the news this week, but in a pinch they would get him through until it was time for the first guest.

As he sat listening to his writing staff, he thought *thank God I've got those prewrites*. They'd given him two different monologues—both about the exact same thing, neither of which he could use.

"We've finally gotten proof global warming is a hoax," said Skyler. "Check it out." He gestured at the computer monitor.

"Glaciers in three different parts of the world are bigger than they were this time last year!" said Adam, unwilling to wait for Walt. "Norway, Alaska, Elliesomething Island—they've all grown!"

Sure enough, as Walt read the report it did indeed seem that several glaciers in those places had increased in volume over the course of the winter just past. Of course, there was also a quote from some scientist or other saying the reason the glaciers had grown was that snowfall in those areas had been way above normal that winter, and the real test would be if the glaciers were still bigger than they were supposed to be six months from now.

The hell of it was, he probably could deliver one of these monologues, and it would be... good enough. They were exactly the sort of thing his listeners wanted to hear, especially with the flooding on the lower Mississippi getting the alarmists all preachy again. But Walter Yuschak hadn't gotten where he was today by aspiring to be "good enough." His name was his brand, and he wanted it to stand for something.

"Lisa!" he said. "Go down to that place on the corner and bring me back a twenty-piece box of fried chicken." Lisa scowled at him as she left. She was a committed vegan. Hopefully she'd learn a lesson here even if nobody else did. And the place at the corner did make excellent fried chicken.

Walt checked the news feed. Nothing terribly useful there. And his guest this week was a man who had a new e-book out arguing that hyperinflation was coming in six months. According to his staff, this guy had been saying the same thing for the past fifteen years. Walt personally liked the guy's politics, but this was the sort of thing that made it hard to be respectful.

So today looked like a good day to start off with the chicken rant.

AS THE CAMERA ZOOMED IN, Walt sat at his desk, a napkin tucked under his chin and the box of chicken in front of him. Fortunately, it was a plain white box, so there would be no problem with accidental product placement. "Good evening, ladies and gentlemen, and welcome to *This Week in Freedom*," he said. "I'm Walt Yuschak, and tonight I'm here… to eat some chicken!" He picked up a drumstick. "Why? Because I'm hungry and chicken is delicious!"

He took a bite, chewed it, and swallowed it. "You know, I've read that chicken used to be something people only ate on special occasions, back when chickens were all being raised on tiny little farms. Thanks to modern factory farms, now it's so cheap that anybody can afford it! According to the USDA, over ten billion chickens are slaughtered in the United States every year! Capitalism and American agribusiness—making the world a better place, one billion chicken dinners at a time!

"And yes, I know, chickens are being raised in horrible and inhumane conditions! They're all jammed together into tiny little cages ankle-deep in their own shit! They're going so crazy in there they have their beaks and claws clipped so they don't eat each other! They're forced to eat crappy food and listen to Charr Sutherland!* It's a chicken concentration camp, people!"

He took another bite. This was really good chicken. The skin was crisp and crunchy, and the guys at the corner place had a way of getting a little of the spice and salt underneath the skin before they cooked it, so the meat actually tasted like something.

"And when it's time to slaughter them, they're trucked to the processing plant in those tiny little cages and hung up by their ankles and scalded with hot water until their feathers fall off and decapitated by razor-sharp blades while USDA inspectors point at them and laugh! They *laugh*!" Walt put down the drumstick and picked up a chicken breast.

"And they've really been messed up by selective breeding. They've been bred to grow so fast and have such giant breasts that they can barely stand up under their own weight." During his podcast days, he would have added a joke like *too bad we can't do that to girls, right, fellas?*—not so much out of personal conviction as to reassure his mostly male listeners that he wasn't an SJW and would never try to make them feel bad about themselves or their desires. These days, he had to tone down his act a little for a wider audience. He pulled a chunk of meat off the breast and popped it into his mouth.

"So knowing all that, why am I eating this?" he said as soon as he was done

---

* Charles "Charr" Sutherland, a seventeen-year-old pop star adored by millions of teenage girls and loathed by everyone else on Earth.

chewing. "Because *I don't give a damn,* that's why. You want to know why I don't give a damn? Because I have *no respect* for *chickens!*

"Listen to this," he said. "Once upon a time, thousands and thousands of years ago, chickens roamed wild in the forests of… wherever the hell it was they came from. Somebody look it up online." It wasn't central to his point.

"They soared through the trees, they hunted for bugs and worms and whatever else they ate. They lived free and called no man master. Well, obviously they didn't call anybody master, because they couldn't talk, they were chickens, but the point is they were *free.*

"But it was hard out there in the woods. There was wind and rain. It got cold in the winter—unless it was some place like Central Africa, in which case it didn't. And there were all these other animals out there that wanted to eat them—foxes, eagles, wild cats, big freakin' snakes.

"I don't think any wild chickens ever died of old age. Even if they lived long enough, as soon as the arthritis set in and they started to slow down, sure enough something would get them. With so many of 'em getting scarfed down it was a struggle pumping out enough baby chicks to keep their numbers up. But hey, that's what evolution is all about.

"Then one day, somebody made them an offer they should've refused. Some human came along and said 'Hey, chickens, why don't you come to our farm? We got a special house built just for you, so you don't have to be outside in the rain. We're gonna feed you and take care of you and keep you safe from predators.' And the chickens said, 'Sure, why not? What's the worst that could happen?' Okay, that's probably not exactly how it went down—like I said, chickens can't talk—but you get the gist of it, right?

"So they did. And at first it was great—they were safe and warm, they didn't have to watch their backs all the time, they got to watch their chicks grow up instead of getting snatched by hawks. And hey—free food every day!

"And then one day the chickens started to notice that their eggs were disappearing almost as fast as they laid them. And then they noticed that *they* were disappearing one by one. It probably took a while, 'cause, you know, they're chickens. They can't count too good. And finally, finally the chickens wised up and realized the truth—them and their eggs were being eaten by the humans who had promised to keep them safe! And the chickens said to the human, 'Hey, we had a deal! You were supposed to protect us from *all* predators! That includes you!' And the human said 'I am altering the deal.

Pray I don't alter it any further.' Thank you, George Lucas.

"See, when the chickens decided to abandon self-reliance and hard work, when they let us feed them and take care of them, that was when their fate was sealed. That was when they forfeited the right to complain if it turned out their caretakers had an agenda of their own. And—listen carefully, this is the important part—now they've been farmed and bred for so long they couldn't take care of themselves if they wanted to! If a chicken truck overturned in the woods, how long do you think it would be before they all died? There's no way they can survive in the wild!

"This is the part where some dumbass says 'but there are a million times as many chickens as there are any other bird that size, so really, they're an evolutionary success story.' So what? If instead of there being eight billion humans on Earth, there were eight *million* billion humans all stuck in Martian people farms from *War of the Worlds*, getting ready to have their blood sucked out, would you really call that a better world?

"So I don't know about these individual chickens," he said, gesturing at the box, "whether they personally were good chickens or bad chickens—but as far as I'm concerned, chickens as a species got what they deserved. We'll be right back."

IT WAS LATER. WALT'S WRITERS sat around the staffroom, looking up at Walt as he glowered down on them. They seemed to know they'd done something wrong, but they didn't know what.

"Let me remind you people," he said, "that your employment here is strictly a convenience. It is not a necessity. I used to write two 15-minute podcasts a week all by myself. If I had to, I could do so again.

"First of all, two monologues about the same thing? Don't I always ask for two completely different monologues?"

"We didn't think, with this in the news, you'd want to talk about anything else," said Caitlin.

"Come on. What have I always said about global warming?"

"You've always said it's a natural phenomenon," said Skyler.

"Exactly. And I'm going to keep on saying that."

"We just thought today we had a chance to say something better than that," said Lisa.

Walt shook his head. "I can say it's not happening, or I can say it is happening but it's totally natural," he said. "But if I try and say both of those things, or say different things on different days, I'm going to sound like a bullshitter. I have to be consistent here."

Adam laughed. "With all due respect, Walt, your viewers are morons," he said. "You could tell them the president was a closet Rastafarian and they'd believe you. Your trying to be consistent is completely wasted on them because they can't remember what…" Adam's voice trailed off as he noticed the look on his boss's face. It was an expression of utter contempt. Walt glared at him until he lowered his gaze to the table in front of him.

"Adam," said Walt flatly, "don't ever talk that way about my audience again, or you're gone."

Adam nodded, not meeting Walt's eyes.

"Those people could listen to anybody or nobody, and they choose to listen to *me*. I owe them my respect. And as long as I pay your salary, so do you."

Adam nodded again. The hell of it was, some days Walt suspected the same thing about the people who tuned in to listen to him, but he knew he couldn't afford to think that way. If you didn't respect your fans, then no matter how hard you tried to hide it, it would come out in your performance in one form or another. The fans would see it, and they would be furious. And they would be right to be furious. If they wanted to listen to people who thought they were stupid, there were plenty of liberals who'd be happy to oblige.

"I get what you're saying," said Skyler. "It just seems to me we're throwing away a chance here and it might never come our way again."

"Exactly," said Walt. "It might never come our way again. And you know why, don't you?"

Skyler blinked at him and said nothing.

"Think about it. If it really were a hoax, it wouldn't matter if we missed out on a piece of evidence today. There'd be more evidence coming tomorrow or next week. Because that's how reality works." He shook his head.

"Listen to me. What's happening up there is real. I'm not saying it's us doing it, but it's real. And it's going to get worse, and worse, and worse. And there's going to come a day when it hits people where they live, and they're going to be like 'Why doesn't somebody do something? There oughta be a law!' And when that day comes, the world's going to need—more than ever before—somebody to remind them how awesome freedom really is and how they don't want to throw it all away. And it can't be somebody who spent the last few years with his feet in his mouth and his head up his ass." As a conciliatory gesture, he dropped the box of chicken on the break room table. "Enjoy."

THE SLOW FEEDBACK LOOP IN *the Arctic Ocean continued its work. This year, there was open water at the North Pole by the end of June, and the last of the sea ice disappeared on July 24. The snow that had caused the glaciers to grow by the end of spring had all melted before the middle of summer.*

Like a gear in the clockwork of the ocean currents, the Beaufort Gyre rotates endlessly between the Bering Strait and the North Pole. The seawater spent nearly three months turning and turning under the midnight sun, growing warmer and warmer. Where its waters met the colder waters coming from the North Pacific, vast fogbanks arose. The fog blew over the Canadian Archipelago in waves the size of nations. Several older planes crashed when visibility dropped to zero not only at their intended landing site, but at every other landing site within range—no small matter in a region as dependent on the airplane as Los Angeles is on the automobile. Only those planes equipped with modern guidance systems aided by infrared cameras were safe.

AUGUST 7:

JEROME ROSS AND FOUR OTHER younger members of Camberg's political team were gathered around a computer in the Richmond Democratic Party headquarters, listening to Henry Pratt's press conference. You didn't even need to have the sound on to figure out what he was saying. The former businessman already looked like a generic president out of Central Casting, circa 1990 or so. He was tall—either six-two or six-three, Rome made a mental note to look it up. His hair was iron-gray frosted with white around the ears—possibly the most presidential hair of any of this year's contenders. His face was equally skilled at stern expressions and reassuring smiles. He was wearing a navy-blue wool suit, which had been tailored to fit him but was otherwise identical to what every other man in politics was wearing. His one concession to personality was the reading glasses on a string around his neck, with a bronze frame that matched his tie.

Just listening to Pratt made Rome nervous. He knew how not to make it obvious that he was glancing at the teleprompter, and he had a real orator's voice—deep, calm, and certain. A bit leaden, maybe, but that just gave it more punch. It was hard to doubt anything he said while he was saying it. The contents of his speech were more just-the-facts than fire-and-brimstone, to the extent that they *were* facts—Rome planned on doing some serious fact-checking, but his manner made the material effective.

"As president," he was saying, "I will not engage in reckless interventionism. I will carefully weigh the risks inherent in any military intervention against the risk involved in failing to act." *If he said he WOULD engage in reckless interventionism*, thought Rome, *that would be newsworthy.* "And I absolutely will not send one ship, plane, or soldier into the territory or airspace of a sovereign nation without first consulting with Congress."

"Don't ask about drones," said Lexi, sitting to Rome's left. She ran her fingers through her red-dyed hair.

Rome nodded. Still, at least the man had made one promise that you could check to see if he was keeping.

Pratt was also promising budget reform. "My staff and I will go through the budget ourselves, and we will find and root out all waste, fraud, and abuse," he said.

Rome rolled his eyes. Every presidential candidate in living memory, Democrat or Republican, had made this promise. Every single one of them had acted as though there were some vast hidden treasure of unnecessary spending buried somewhere in the federal budget, if only someone were willing to sit down and read the damn thing. Every single one of them had claimed they would be the one to find that Lost City of Pork and bring back its wealth for the taxpayers. And every single one of them had failed to mention something very important. Would Pratt be the one to speak of the elephant in the room?

"Yes, the federal budget is over twenty-six hundred pages long. It seems impossible to comprehend, let alone control, but for twenty good staffers that's a week's work."

Rome rolled his eyes again, harder this time. No, the indoor pachyderm—Congress—would remain safely under the carpet of silence.

Sure enough, Pratt moved to the safer subject of deregulation. "Not only have our business regulations failed to protect consumers and the environment, most of them were never written for that purpose in the first place," he said. "They were written by business lobbyists to protect business from competition, at the expense of American consumers and American entrepreneurs."

He was a little more interesting on drug policy. "The time has come to end the so-called 'war on drugs,'" he said. "Make no mistake—when individual Americans choose to destroy themselves through poor lifestyle choices, it hurts us all. It costs us all. But not nearly as much as it costs us to try to stop them by force."

"Lifestyle choices?" said Lexi. "Somewhere a neurologist is crying." They shushed her.

When he got to the Q&A, the first question was about his drug policy and whether it meant he was going to be legalizing drugs.

"No. I am not advocating full legalization. As I said earlier, drug abuse costs society. As I see it, society has every right to reclaim those costs through fines or community service. But it makes no sense for society to impose further costs on itself through mass imprisonment."

The reporter, who had apparently done her homework, followed that up with a question about whether this was compatible with international drug conventions. "I believe it is," said Pratt. "If the U.N. should rule otherwise, then I will instruct the State Department and our representative at the U.N. to make it a priority to renegotiate those agreements. I absolutely will not let them restrain me from doing what needs to be done."

"Where do you stand on the proposals for Universal Basic Income?" asked another reporter.

"Where do I stand on it? It's welfare. 'UBI' is just another kind of welfare. I see welfare as a necessary evil. There may be people who need it, but I have zero interest in giving it to people who neither need nor want it. Personally, if I got a check for it, I'd send it back." No surprise there. Pratt gestured to another reporter.

"As president, what actions will you take against global climate change?"

This'll be good, thought Ross.

"The scientific consensus is that climate change is happening, and that it is due to human activity," he said. "I am not a scientist, and am not qualified to dispute their conclusions." Rome mentally translated this as *Don't blame me, folks, blame the scientists! They're the ones who brought us all this bad news!*

Still, he was a little disappointed. A Republican had said "I am not a scientist" and had failed to follow up by saying something gloriously stupid.

"Now the question becomes what to do about it," said Pratt. "The federal government is already doing many things to reduce fossil fuel consumption. We are not in a position to organize or bankroll any major efforts to adapt to coming changes, still less to attempt to prevent them—especially since we don't have any clear idea what it is we would be adapting *to*. Fortunately, many states, communities, and businesses are developing plans of their own to cope with climate change. As president, I would be willing to consider tax breaks to support these efforts."

"Don't strain your ass," said Rome.

"What about a carbon tax? Or a fee and dividend?"

"Those would not be not a part of my plan. I believe a healthy economy is the best defense."

THE NEXT MORNING, CAMBERG CALLED a meeting of her closest political advisers.

Rome wasn't there. He was out having coffee with Alexandra Casas and Gabrielle Stone, on the principle that you should keep your friends close, your enemies closer, and your frenemies within easy choking distance.

They were in their early twenties and less than five feet tall. Lexi's hair was dyed ruby red, and her shorts and tank top revealed that her arms and legs were covered in tattoos of roses on winding, thorny branches. Gabrielle was wearing beige slacks and a white T-shirt, which was as casual as she normally got. As far as Rome knew, she had no tattoos at all. He'd nicknamed the two of them Rosencrantz and Guildenstern, mostly because they were always together and he didn't trust them. He was quietly pleased by the fact that even though "Guildenstern" tried so hard to convey professionalism in dress and manner, Camberg had banished her to the same metaphorical kids' table as "Rosencrantz" and himself.

"What'd you think of Pratt?" said Guildenstern casually as she cleaned her horn-rimmed glasses.

"I read up on him last night," said Rome. "His history reveals a disturbing lack of glue-sniffing. No insane beliefs, no silly ass remarks, no bad behavior… we can't count on him to pull a McAllister and self-destruct just to make our jobs easier."

"When they asked him about abortion, he didn't even say anything creepy about rape," said Guildenstern. "I thought that was some kind of rite of initiation for those guys."

"Poor Baphomet isn't going to get any press time," said Rosencrantz. They all chuckled.

"Think he can get elected?" said Guildenstern.

"No, because I don't think he can get nominated," said Rome. "This is the GOP we're talking about. If he could, it'd be a different story."

"You planning to vote for him?" said Rosencrantz.

"Hell, no. First, the only things he'd be good at are things any Democrat would be better at—not that I'm too impressed with the crew likely to run this time. Second, he's still gotta get through the primary. By the time he's done making promises to the bottomless pit of howling madness, he's gonna be just as scary as the rest of 'em."

"So is Camberg gonna run this time?"

"It'll make her look bad if she does," said Rome. "How many times has she said it? On camera? 'I'm going to finish my term, I didn't become governor of Virginia just as a stepping stone, I wouldn't do that to this sta—excuse me, commonwealth,' blah blah blah. I'm not saying she'd never go back on all that, just that it wouldn't be like her." The problem was, the presidential election was next year. She wouldn't get another chance until five years from now.

"Even if she has to wait nine years," said Guildenstern, "she'll be what—in her fifties? Not exactly ready for the boneyard. Hell, Pratt's over sixty. She can always run for the Senate in the meantime, just to stay relevant."

"Unless things get so bad in five years everybody wants a change," said Rome.

"If that happens, will she still want the job?" said Rosencrantz.

"I think she would," said Rome. "She's always said to me, 'Don't run for office if you don't think you can handle a crisis.'" Here followed several minutes of Rome and Gabrielle trying to one-up each other in personal anecdotes proving their closeness to the governor. Finally, Lexi pointed out that the reason they were here was that Camberg hadn't invited any of them to the meeting, and they shut up.

When they finally got the text message from the governor confirming that she wouldn't be running for president this time, it was a group message that reached all three of them at the same moment. So nobody had bragging rights.

NOVEMBER 16:

SANDY PUSHED A COUPLE OF buttons on her armphone, and Martin's face appeared on the big screen on the wall. He was in the living room of that nice house in Syracuse.

Mozart was playing in the background. Nora was sitting next to Martin, trying to get Patrick to pay attention to a set of flash cards. She seemed to have developed the ambition to raise a genius of her own, possibly because it made her feel insecure to be outdone in any way by a previous wife of Martin's, even one who was already dead. Patrick, at the moment, only had eyes for his toy truck and stuffed dinosaur.

Sandy was a little surprised that Martin was still married to Nora. Maybe he was trying to turn over a new leaf. Maybe he couldn't bring himself to abandon another child. Maybe, having been in a state of midlife crisis since he was twenty, he was too damn tired to keep moving.

"Hi, Dad," said Sandy. "How's it going?"

"Pretty good. You have any plans for Thanksgiving?"

"I'm throwing a party for my employees on Tuesday." *What else would I do? You and Patrick are the only family I've got, and my friends are not that close.* "How about you?"

"We're going to Chicago to visit Nora's family," said Martin. *So much for getting an invitation.*

Sandy nodded. "Did you get my e-mail?"

"I'll look for it," said Martin.

"The paperwork is attached," said Sandy. "It's pretty straightforward. I get your share of the company. You get ten million, direct deposit."

Martin nodded. "My brother-in-law's a lawyer," he said. "He's going to look over it first. I mean, I trust you, but… you know, it's the principle of the thing." *Nora doesn't trust you.*

"Of course."

"I mean, you don't want to look a gift horse in the mouth, but you gotta make sure there's no strings attached."

"Mixed metaphor, but yeah." Nora looked up into the screen and smiled a little, as if letting Sandy know she was the one who'd talked Martin into asking for this. Sandy's goat was ungot. One thing she'd learned was that life would give you reasons enough to lie awake at night without letting yourself get bothered because somebody else thought she'd won something.

And even if it was motivated by spite or resentment, as far as Sandy was concerned it was a perfectly reasonable request. As cool as it was being able to say she'd founded her company in her dad's garage, she hadn't been able to keep it there more than a month. It was the sort of business that attracted not just criminals, but organized, competent criminals, the kind who were more than a match for the security system of your average middle-class house. Besides, Martin's neighborhood wasn't zoned for manufacturing.

So she'd moved to an industrial park in Maryland, near a nuclear power plant. Her business used a lot of electricity, and making sure it wasn't coming from fossil fuels was kind of important… although nuclear power was only a slight improvement.

The fact remained that she'd needed his help to get the company set up. If he wanted to sell her his share of it, if he felt safer having ten million right now than half of something that might be worth a hundred million or diddly-squat next year, that was his right. *And he put his own home at risk to give me a place to get started, if only for a little while. I owe him for that. This is the right thing to do for him and Patrick.*

Especially Patrick. Sandy's feelings for her father were complicated and she and Nora still despised each other, but for the baby she had nothing but warmth and affection. *My little half bro will never want for anything money can buy. I've done that much for him, whatever else happens.* And if that meant Nora would be better off too, well, you couldn't have everything.

The one downside was that all the financial risk was now on Sandy's shoulders. Worse, she'd had to take out a loan to gather all the money together. If things went smoothly, she'd be able to pay it back in a few months, but there was no guarantee of that.

Even so, with the greater risk came greater potential reward. If her plans for the next few years worked out—the new plant in New York and so on—Sandy would have more money than she'd ever imagined. And if they didn't… at least now, her father would be able to provide her with a much better grade of couch to crash on until she came up with something else.

ALL THROUGH THE FALL, HEAVY *rains had come to the Arctic, eroding millions of tons of ice from the glaciers. By the time of the first snows, the glaciers were smaller than they had ever been. Northern Norway saw six feet of rain over the course of that fall, followed by two feet of snow in November and early December.*

YEAR THREE

NOVUS ORDO SECLORUM

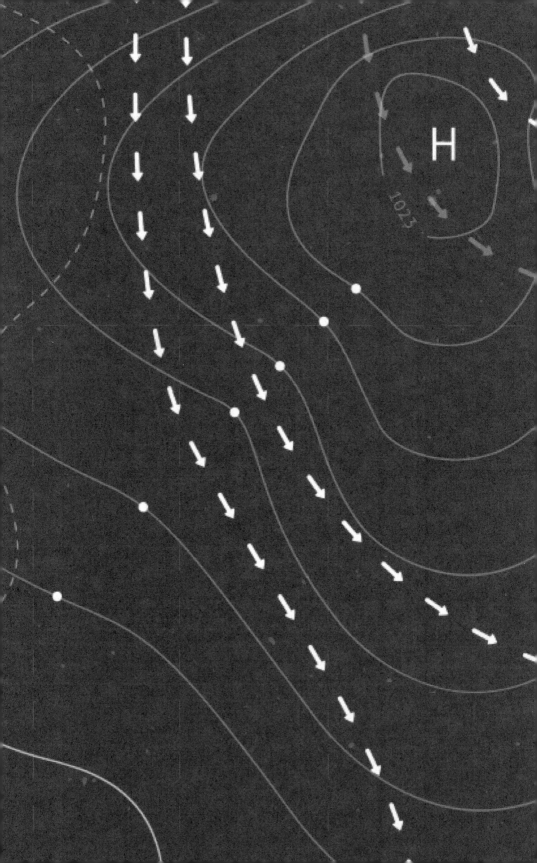

IN JANUARY, SIX FEET OF snow fell in northern Norway. The rest of the country was not quite as bad off, but in no state to take in refugees. A quarter of the population of the country had to be evacuated to southern Sweden and Denmark. Similar precipitation was seen in less inhabited areas, in Novaya Zemlya, on the northern slopes of the mountains of Alaska and Yukon, and—in another moment of false hope—in northern Greenland.

JANUARY 9:

ROME WAS NORMALLY A BIG believer in eye contact, but sitting in front of Governor Camberg's desk tested his faith. Her eyes were warm and brown and gave him the sense that they were watching his thoughts put themselves together before he could even open his mouth. She was like his mom, only smarter. And she had that little smile on her face.

"As I recall, your office in Fairfax was one of the more effective ones," she said.

"I was blessed with a good staff," said Rome as offhandedly as he could. "Lexi Casas and Gabrielle Stone, for example. They're passionate. Diligent. Good at getting out the college vote."

"Yes, I've spoken with them. They said you 'worked them like dogs and took all the credit.'"

"I'm sorry to hear they felt that way." *And if I hadn't already known those little bitches would try and shiv me, I would be seriously pissed off right now.*

"Well, obviously they were wrong about you." *And Operation Magnanimity is a resounding success. Rosencrantz and Guildenstern can suck it.* "In any case, I need people who can work hard and inspire others to their best efforts."

"I don't know who's been saying it was all me—I make a point of not taking credit for team efforts." *See, I'm humble, but everybody thinks I'm—*

"So… you're humble, but everybody thinks you're awesome?" said Carrie, smiling.

Rome's response software locked up for a moment.

"Rome, let's get something straight between us. You use your skills for me. You do not try to use them on me. Clear?"

Rome decided to skip contrition and go straight to sincerity. "Yes, ma'am."

"With that in mind, I'd like to hear your thoughts on the politics around this organ donation bill."

Rome drew a deep breath.

"Here's how I see it," he said. "The biggest bias the news media has is their need to look unbiased. No matter what the story is, there's always, I mean always, got to be two sides. And the truth has always got to be somewhere in between. They can't ever say 'so-and-so is right and so-and-so is wrong' because that would be being partisan. So if you step up and say 'Opt-out organ donation is a good idea' and some idiot screams 'OH MY GOD THE GOVERNOR'S TRYING TO STEAL OUR GIBLETS' then you're just one of two sides.

"So what I'd do is get two different people to object to it—one of them saying you're trying to get rid of organ donation, because that's what 'opt-out' sounds like to anybody dumb enough, and the other one saying…"

"That I'm out to steal their giblets?"

"Yeah. Then you get to step up and present yourself as the reasonable middle ground while the crazies cancel each other out."

The governor nodded. "I don't remember you being quite this devious as part of my campaign," she said. "Where did you learn it?"

"Working for Morgan in New York a couple years ago. Let me tell you—that woman is smart."

BY THE END OF THE *winter, four to seven feet of snow lay over nearly all the lands of the Arctic. Over the course of the spring, all that snow melted—sometimes* *in as little as ten days. Flooding was widespread. When the people driven from the northern half of Norway in December were finally able to return home, they found they had little to return to.*

In early April, the lakes of the Northwest Territories swelled until their waters met in places. The soil was quickly waterlogged all the way down to the layer of permafrost. In north-central Canada, where the soil and permafrost were spread thin over the ancient bedrock of the Canadian Shield, this happened within hours.

And gradually, inevitably, the permafrost began to melt. Like ice cubes dropped into a glass of water, it cracked as bubbles of gas within it expanded from the relative warmth. Water trickled into the cracks, speeding the melting. And wherever the permafrost melted, the frozen vegetation that had been trapped within it for up to one hundred thousand years thawed out and began to decay, releasing carbon dioxide and methane... and generating heat like a well-fed compost heap, which did even more to melt the permafrost.

As it melted, it collapsed. Hundreds of new sinkholes appeared in Siberia, Alaska, and northern Canada. A satellite captured the moment when a stretch of ground northwest of the Great Slave Lake caved in and turned into a vast, muddy depression the size of two football fields side by side, which a herd of astonished caribou had to scramble to escape.

APRIL 26:

ISABEL HAD PROMISED HERSELF THAT at this party, she wouldn't end up standing in the corner holding a drink and trying to look like she was part of the scene without talking to anybody. She had been here fifteen minutes and was already breaking that promise.

She had already chatted with the one or two people she knew here, had gone into the little kitchen of the basement apartment to get a hard cider, and had returned to find that everyone in sight had clustered into impenetrable little circles of personal acquaintances. Whichever way Isabel looked, she saw solid, curving walls of other people's backs and shoulders.

Maybe this was to be expected. Not too sociable by nature, Isabel had developed only a small circle of friends in three years at College Park, and she'd stepped outside it to come here tonight. Hanging out with her friends was a lot more awkward these days. Laurie was sure to be among them.

It would take another whole novel, or at least a novella, to do justice to the story of Isabel's love life. Suffice it to say that although she swung both ways, since high school she had mostly dated other women... which unfortunately had for the past year meant Laurie. Laurie, the guilt-tripper. Laurie, who got upset if you sat with her for more than fifteen seconds without saying anything even when you'd already explained you weren't much of a conversationalist. Laurie, the rich girl who always paid for dinner and never let you forget it. Laurie, the suburban chick who called your family "white trash" and was offended when you told her there might be people who were entitled to use those words, but she wasn't one of them. Laurie, the guilt-tripper (it bears repeating—she did it a lot). Laurie, the... person about whom enough has been said, because at this point she was out of Isabel's life and good riddance.

She thought about going into the other room, but the music was too loud in there. Was it not already painful enough to make small talk without having to shout out every casual remark like an order on a battlefield? For people who seemed like they wanted to spend most of their lives partying, extroverts were amazingly bad at it.

I could stand around some more, she thought. *Hope somebody else I know shows up. Hope I don't get hit on by somebody I can't stand. Hope I don't look too pathetic. Or I could give up and go back to my dorm and feel like a social failure.*

Or maybe there's a third option here. I can't be the only one in this position. I could find somebody else who looks kind of alone and go talk to them.

She looked around for a moment. Ignoring the girl who hadn't stopped texting since she got here and the guy who was obviously waiting to use the bathroom, the only one who looked like he needed someone to talk with was the big guy by the stairs, the one with the long dark hair and a narrow, precisely trimmed fringe of beard that was trying to impose a jawline on his round face.

Isabel considered him for a moment. He wasn't bad-looking. He was wearing a black Fear of the Onyx T-shirt. Good band. Since he was on the heavy side himself, he might not be inclined to make an issue about her weight. Then again, he might.

He noticed her looking at him. They made eye contact. He smiled. It wasn't a big smile, but it was a smile. Isabel smiled back. Nothing had gone wrong yet, so she took a few steps in his direction and made a little 'come here' movement with her eyes. Slowly, carefully, he approached.

"Hi."

"Hi."

So far, so good.

"I'm Isabel."

"I'm Sophomore. I'm a hunter. Aw shit, no, sorry, my name's Hunter, and I'm a sophomore." Hunter the sophomore and not the other way around turned aside and started biting his lip.

"I'm a junior." *Think of something to talk about. Think of something to talk about.* "What kind of music do you listen to?"

In addition to Fear of the Onyx, Hunter was into Rodomontade, Dark Incentive, Jared Behr, and Laura Bronzino, more or less in that order. Nothing objectionable there. Isabel's faves were Rodomontade, Epifania, The Kattle, Laura Bronzino and Yvain Alexander. This gave them something to talk about for another minute or so.

"Laura Bronzino's touring this summer," said Hunter. "I'm going to try to get a ticket to a show in August." He looked at her as if to say *I could get more than one ticket*.

"Unfortunately," said Isabel, "I already have plans for August, and you're not going to believe what they are." She began describing the planned expedition to the Arctic Ocean to learn what was happening up there. The little voices in her head started screaming *Look out! You're boring him! You really think he wants to hear about salinity and phytoplankton growth?* But Hunter looked like he was paying attention.

It was only after about five minutes of this she realized he'd hardly said anything about himself. To Isabel, the art of conversation was mostly the art of getting the other person to do most of the talking and providing just enough feedback to keep them going. Here, the opposite had happened. Apparently, Hunter's conversational jujitsu was stronger than hers.

"So what do you do for fun?" she said.

"I'm a gamer. Mostly Enginquest."

"I've heard of Enginquest, but I've never played it. What's it about?"

If she'd wanted to get him talking, that was the right question. Enginquest was an MMORPG with a steampunk/fantasy theme. Hunter was chief engineer on an airship belonging to a mercenary fleet, hired by the frontier republic of Albemarla to defend them from centaur and wildkin raids while launching privateer attacks on the shipping of rival states. He'd only started playing this year, and already he'd taken seventeen levels in Engineering and eleven in Combat, killed eight snallygasters, captured two jackalopes, fought a sasquatch to a draw, and helped recover treasure from the Lost Temple of Huazoatl. So he had that going for him.

When considering a possible romantic partner, Isabel had always trusted her instincts, and so far they had failed her every time. She was about ready to start going out with whoever she was least attracted to, male or female. Unfortunately, her instincts seemed to have caught on to this plan and weren't telling her anything about Hunter one way or another.

Isabel heard a noise and looked down. From the looks of things, the host's dog was quite convinced that Hunter, or at least his ankle, was one sexy beast.

"I can't stand those things," said Hunter.

"Hmm?"

Hunter waved at the pug. "They're supposed to be all cute and adorable, but they freak me out. It's the giant bulging eyeballs that do it."

Isabel nodded. This was not a subject on which she had strong opinions. "I like retrievers," she said. "Border collies, German shepherds… basically any working breed. Only you gotta have something for them to do. They can't just sit around."

"Do you have a dog?"

"No. Pop had a chocolate Lab named Major. Died last year."

"Sorry to hear that. What happened?"

"Just age. He was twelve and a half. You have a dog?"

"Nope." They looked into each other's eyes for a second or so. Then, as one, they both started laughing at the sheer pointlessness of the conversation. Hunter had a very strange laugh—almost silent, with only a slight hiss of escaping air. That by itself was almost enough to make Isabel start edging away. Then she thought *Seriously? You're that shallow? You're judging him by the way he laughs?*

At that moment, whoever was in charge of the music decided—God only knew why—to put on a Charr Sutherland song.

"Let's move further away," said Isabel as she recognized the opening bars.

"Out of the blast radius," said Hunter.

JUNE 10:

THIS FELT WEIRDLY LIKE A conflict of interest.

It wasn't, because the Cambergs had sold all their property on the Chesapeake waterfront years ago. Her brother Mike still owned property there, but he hadn't been inclined to listen to IPCC warnings before and wasn't likely to start just because they had been made by bigger computers. The house where Carrie and her brothers had grown up, where Mom and Drew still lived, was on what passed for high ground in the area. There wasn't really any way she could profit personally from this.

It was just that although every governor of a coastal state was or should have been getting a briefing on the latest IPCC projections of sea level rise, she was the only one getting it from her husband. Dr. Roger Camberg had helped the International Panel on Climate Change model future ice losses. Now he was here, talking Carrie and a handful of key legislators through their findings.

"We're pretty sure about the projections for the first twenty years," he said. The screen behind him showed a map of eastern Virginia. He moved a few controls, and it zoomed in until individual houses were visible as postage-stamp-sized blocks.

"Different shades of blue indicate the size of the storm surge you'd need to flood this area," he said. There were five shades, indicating surges of 1.5, 3, 6, 9 and 12 meters. Roger clicked something, and the colors moved a little as it switched to 5, 10, 20, 30 or 45 feet. "You'll notice we're not talking about 100-year or 500-year events. That's because we no longer believe we can make that kind of prediction.

"Purple indicates land that would be subject to flooding in the event of a perigean spring tide or heavy rains. Technically habitable, but we don't actually recommend anybody try to live there." Carrie nodded. Norfolk had been dealing with that sort of thing for years now. "Black indicates land that just isn't land any more. It's either right in the regular tidal zone or permanently underwater."

As Roger ran the simulation, black and purple expanded very slowly, nibbling at the edges of the land—a dock here, part of a street there. The varying shades of blue, on the other hand, engulfed Norfolk, Portsmouth, Hampton, and Virginia Beach.

"So we're looking at… what?" said Carrie.

"Between eleven and twelve inches in twenty years," said Roger.

"That's a good deal worse than any of us were told before," said Woodson, the leading Republican in the House of Delegates.

"We're seeing heavier precipitation in the Greenland area—rain and mist. Glaciers can't survive that sort of thing. It would be faster, if not for the fact that central Antarctica is seeing a slight increase in snow.

"We can't be as precise about the next segment—the twenty-to-fifty-year projections. Here, blue indicates a twenty-foot storm surge. The uncertainty isn't the odds of the surge happening, it's the odds of this area being in the zone." He brought up a new map, in which the blue, purple, and black had a misty-edged quality, blending smoothly into one another. At the end, looking at the projection for fifty years in the future, he said, "The area in black is between seventeen and twenty inches above the twenty-year mark. The area in purple is forty to forty-eight inches above that." The black still wasn't much, but whole neighborhoods were now covered in purple.

"And what happens after that?" said Carrie.

"Sea level rise continues to accelerate, but the exact rate becomes harder to predict," said Roger. "You understand, the next fifty years—they're not just predictable, they're pretty much locked in at this point. If we bring down the CO_2 and methane levels in the next ten years, sixty years from now is when we'll start to see the benefit."

AFTER THE PRESENTATION WAS OVER, Carrie looked at the various legislators. "So," she said, "how do we want to do this?"

"You understand I can't admit any of this in public." Woodson pretended to be a "skeptic" in public, but was willing to admit reality in private. Or possibly he was pretending to go along with the Great Big Conspiracy in private, but said what he really thought in public. Either way, Carrie didn't trust him.

"Pratt doesn't seem to have a problem with it." At the mention of his party's leading candidate, Woodson made a face.

"Pratt's a RINO. He doesn't speak for a majority, and if the majority could have just settled on one candidate, we'd have a real Republican running."

"He's the only one who doesn't remind everybody of Trump," put in Sedgwick, one of Carrie's allies.

"We're getting sidetracked," said Carrie. "The question is, how do we prepare the commonwealth for this?"

"Do we even need to?" said Woodson. "Storm surges don't happen every year. As for the tide problem, people down there have been elevating their houses for years. It seems to work."

"Yeah, if you have a hundred fifty thousand dollars you don't need," said Sedgwick.

"And if you're in one of those houses, and you're hurt, and the ambulance can't get there because the streets are flooded?" said Carrie. "Or if the house is on fire, and the fire truck can't get through? You really want to wait for the tide to go out?"

"What do you suggest?" said Woodson. "Do we buy every property that these people say is doomed? There isn't money enough in the budget for that."

"You're right about that, at least," said Carrie. "We can't buy everything. We need a real plan."

ALL THROUGH THE SUMMER, THE Arctic lands would be plagued by mosquitoes.

This was not directly caused by climate change. A plague of mosquitoes was normal for the Arctic summer. For a few weeks of every year, they would emerge by the billions in vast sky-darkening clouds, feeding off everything warm-blooded. Weaker animals and birds would be drained literally to the point of death. The rest would be forced onto the few patches of snow and ice that remained, too cold for mosquitoes to fly over.

This year, roused by the early warmth and heavy rains, they came early and stayed much longer. They were no more numerous than in any other year, but remaining active for so long meant that they needed to feed far more—and with the snow and ice melted, there was nowhere for the animals to run. Wolves, foxes, and caribou all suffered heavy losses, especially among their young.

In places where humans lived, the governments of Canada and Russia shipped in mosquito netting in bulk, along with huge quantities of mosquito repellent. Sometimes it was enough. Sometimes not. Where there were no humans, Russia carpet-bombed the swamps with insecticides. This killed more of the mosquitoes' predators than it did the mosquitoes themselves. Canada released male and female dragonflies into the far north against the mosquito clouds, which for them were an immeasurable feast. One day their descendants would bring down the numbers of mosquitoes, but not this year.

The last of the Arctic sea ice disappeared on July 9, nearly three weeks earlier than the previous year. The North Pole had been ice-free for the past month.

AUGUST 27:

THE SKY WAS IRON-GRAY AND overcast, the Lincoln Sea a much darker gray. Even here, twenty miles north of the Greenland coast, the katabatic winds that blew from the ice sheet scoured the surface of the ocean. As the cold, dry air whipped over the warmer water, it cooled the moisture in the air into tendrils of mist that blew due north in hundreds of ruler-straight lines. On the horizon, the lines of fog blurred into a gray haze that melted the edges of sea and sky.

It was an alien, monochrome seascape. The only assurances that Isabel hadn't gone color-blind were the absurdly bright yellow of the weather buoy she was perched on and the light brown of her own hair, a few strands of which had escaped the O-ring and were being whipped into her own face by the wind. Even her wetsuit was black and gray. It could not be said that she was blissfully unaware of the danger she was in, unless repairing a broken salinometer while crouched down on a violently swaying platform is your idea of bliss, but it had been a while since she'd looked behind her.

The weather buoy was about six feet wide, with a tripod frame above it that held the transmitter. The legs of the frame were connected by crossbars. Isabel was down on her hands and knees, with her shoulders pressed against one of the crossbars to help hold her in place.

Between ten and fifteen yards away, the *S.S. Kotick* floated. Before Isabel had joined this mission, the only boat she'd ever operated was the *Mary Lynn*, her father's old skipjack. The *Kotick* was as different from the *Mary Lynn* as it could possibly be and still float. It was over one hundred feet long, visibly brand new and—apart from the solar panels—gleaming white. Its hull was wide, but tapered to a narrow wedge just before it reached the water. Its cockpit stuck out above a broad, flat expanse of solar panels like the deck of a miniature aircraft carrier. Its engines were housed in wing-like nacelles under the lip of the hull on either side. Overall, the *Kotick* looked more like a spaceship than anything intended for sea travel… which was appropriate, considering how much Isabel's surroundings looked like an ocean on some other planet.

Over three hundred weather buoys, both moored and drifting, had been deployed in the Arctic Ocean over the past two years. The buoys themselves were all still in excellent condition—and well they might be, since they had originally been built to withstand almost anything the ocean could throw at them. But the salinometers hadn't been part of the original structure. They were mounted on the buoys for this particular job, and in any kind of rough weather they tended to break or fall off. In addition to just trying to figure out what the hell was going on in the Arctic, part of the *Kotick's* mission was to repair or replace these where necessary.

Strictly speaking, three different rules were being broken here. Isabel should not have been out here by herself, the *Kotick* should not have been out of arm's reach, and someone on deck should have been keeping an eye on her—or an eye on them, if the first rule were being followed. But two days ago her coworker, Brad, had gotten his hand in between the side of the buoy and one of the *Kotick's* nacelles, and three of his fingers had been badly broken. They'd had to send in a helicopter to fly him to the nearest hospital… which luckily for him was only fifty miles away, in a town called "Alert," as in "What You Should Have Been, Brad."

The other two-person team was asleep right now. One of the perks of working in the Arctic in the summer was that there was no need for everyone to wake up and go to sleep at the same time. It was much more efficient to do everything in shifts, taking full advantage of the twenty-four-hour daylight.

Isabel had assured everyone that she was perfectly capable of doing the job on her own. What she didn't say was that she liked it better that way, because (a) the buoy was only barely large enough for one, and (b) Brad seemed to be incapable of being within ten feet of a woman and not trying to hit on her. (That was an odd phrase for it—"hit on"—but at moments like those, when you were close enough to smell a guy's breath and he just wouldn't let up and wouldn't take a hint and his eyes kept drifting all over your erogenous zones, it did start to feel like a kind of violence. Especially when you, unlike him, were trying to concentrate on your work and not let your hands get anywhere they could be damaged.)

Isabel was a good swimmer, and the water right here was over fifty degrees

Fahrenheit, nothing her wetsuit couldn't handle. (And not what anyone thought of as normal for the Arctic, which was part of the reason they were here. Further north it was actually much warmer.) So the *Kotick's* pilot had agreed to keep the ship a few yards away so as not to risk any other accidents. Since then the constant wind had pushed the boat a little farther away than they'd intended, but she could still swim it easily.

Nikki Erhardt, the videographer for this little expedition, was supposed to be out on the deck watching Isabel work. But when last seen, she had been going back inside. Possibly she was bored, or had work to do, or unlike Brad took no great pleasure in staring endlessly at Isabel's neoprene-wrapped body. Or perhaps, like most people, she just trusted Isabel to look after herself.

The salinometer looked like a large syringe on the end of a robot arm. It had to take a small sample of the water to test it. The arm was all right, and the connection to the solar panel was intact, but the salinometer hadn't sent any data in two weeks. So Isabel had taken it apart and was squatting on her hands and knees, with her back turned to the south to keep the wind out of her face, trying to work out what the problem was without letting any of the important parts fall overboard.

As best Isabel could tell, looking at it under these awkward conditions, the problem was the seal between the pipette and the pump. When the arm stuck the end of the pipette in the water, the pump was supposed to suck the water up the length of the pipette to the electrodes. Then the arm would lift the pipette out of the water, the electrodes would measure the water's conductivity, and the pump would use a stream of air to squirt the water out so as not to contaminate the next sample. But if the rubber gasket that connected the pipette to the pump was damaged or misaligned, it would be like trying to drink through a straw that had holes in the sides. Nothing would happen.

Isabel had to examine it with a penlight to be sure, but she finally spotted some corrosion on the inside of the gasket. Fortunately, she had a spare in her kit. She took it out, then turned around to reach for the pipette, which had rolled somewhere behind her.

That was when she saw the polar bear. It was a streamlined white shape just under the surface, water rippling over its back and head as it swam toward her, its path straight as the wake of a torpedo. Isabel had no idea what had driven it to swim out this far in the first place, but while she had been concentrating on fixing the salinometer, the bear had been dog-paddling in her direction while staring at her hindquarters with a fixation that even Brad would have said was a little too low-class.

Over the course of the past three years, according to the International Union for the Conservation of Nature, the polar bear—like Isabel herself at this particular moment—had gone from "vulnerable" to "endangered." The northern population, accustomed to having good solid platforms of ice to hunt seals and beluga whales from, was worst off. Many of them had lost whatever fear of humans they'd had—in Barrow, on her way to the dock to join the crew of the *Kotick*, someone had gotten way too much enjoyment out of telling Isabel the story of a local man who had been cornered in his truck, killed, and partly eaten by a polar bear, three days earlier. "If the strap from the rifle hadn't got caught on the gearshift, he'd still be alive today."

For a moment, Isabel froze in place, staring, unable to move or turn away. Then the bear's head emerged from the water. It reminded her, strangely, of a gigantic white retriever—almost like Major, paddling back to Pop with a fat duck or goose in its jaws. It was looking right at her. There was a tag in its ear— it must have encountered humans before. There was nothing Isabel could read in its expression other than a simple, happy eagerness. (According to Isabel's friend in Barrow, a polar bear could put away up to one hundred fifty pounds at one sitting. Coincidentally, that was just about how much Isabel weighed minus the bigger chunks of bone.)

Isabel had already dropped everything, launched herself into the water and started doing the front crawl back to the boat by the time she thought to ask herself if this was the best way to escape. Then she decided that it was. Better than calling the pilot and hoping he could get the boat started in time to come back and get her. Especially since she could swim two and a half knots, which was already half the *Kotick's* cruising speed. No doubt the bear could swim faster, but she had a head start and it wasn't that far to the boat.

She didn't look back. She was already swimming as fast as she knew how, and looking back would have slowed her down. If the bear caught up with her before she reached it, she'd know right away without having to see it.

There was a rope ladder from the deck to the surface. Isabel grabbed the lowest rung and scrambled up it. Once she had her feet on the deck, she turned and started pulling up the ladder.

And then it got yanked down hard, so violently that if Isabel hadn't let go right away, she would have been pulled over the side. The boat tilted, slightly but suddenly.

Isabel turned and ran for the door to the cockpit. She wasn't a natural sprinter, but she was feeling highly motivated right now. She didn't know if the bear could climb the ladder, but if it could, she had even less chance of outrunning it than outswimming it.

She almost tripped over her own feet going down the half-dozen stairs to the cockpit door. Just as she reached the door, it opened, and Nikki stepped out. Isabel shoved her back through and slammed the door behind them. She locked it just in time to hear the crash of the bear's shoulder against the door.

Dr. Vohringer, the head of the expedition, was in the cockpit along with Estebán Basco, the pilot. All of them had gotten up and were staring, paralyzed with fear, at the bear.

Isabel elbowed her way past them. There was a tranquilizer gun stored under the dashboard for just such an emergency. She distinctly remembered putting it there when she'd helped load the boat. She didn't remember everything she'd brought on board, but weapons had a way of sticking in your mind.

Isabel pulled out the gun. She'd gone hunting with Pop a few times, but she'd never fired a rifle at a living thing. This wasn't exactly like a hunting rifle, but it was close enough that she could load it. Dr. Vohringer was already opening the trapdoor. Estebán was right behind him. Nikki was just standing there filming everything like a character in a found-footage horror movie. The bear was examining the windows.

With a swipe of its paw, it smashed the window next to the door. Grains of toughened glass flew in all directions. Nikki yelped and ran for the trapdoor.

The bear rested its paws on the windowsill, pushed its head through and tried to get its shoulders in. There was a moment when it was pressing its head against the ceiling. *Now*, thought Isabel, and opened fire. With two pops of compressed air, darts embedded themselves into the bear's neck just under the jaw.

And nothing happened. The bear was still trying to get through the window. Isabel looked at the rifle in bewilderment. That was supposed to have worked. They had specifically said two darts was enough for a polar bear.

"I don't think it kicks in right away," said Nikki, staring up at her through the trapdoor, holding up her camera.

Oh. That would have been a useful thing to mention when they gave us this. The bear's shoulders squeezed through the window. Nikki stood aside just in time for Isabel to head down the ladder and slam the door over her head.

"Get me the fire extinguisher," she said to Ian Jacob and Chris Yuan. She had already dropped the gun. Isabel had no further interest in a weapon that was guaranteed to make a dangerous animal fall asleep ten minutes after it had finished ripping out her liver.

Isabel looked up at the trapdoor. It was fiberglass. So was the deck. Against a bear's claws, she wouldn't bet on it.

Chris handed her the fire extinguisher. It was the kind that sprayed liquid CO_2. Even for a polar bear, cold like that would have to be uncomfortable. She hoped.

The bear tore the trapdoor aside. Isabel aimed the extinguisher up in the direction of the hole, waiting for it to stick its face in. She wished hopelessly for another gun, one with actual bullets in it. Or a bow and arrow. Or, hell, a really sharp pair of toenail clippers. Just *something* she could hold in her hands that would make her feel less like a walking sirloin.

And then… nothing happened.

And then more nothing.

And more nothing. Had the tranq darts taken effect? Wouldn't they have heard it falling down? Isabel almost went up the ladder to see.

Then she had another thought. *It's not unconscious yet. It's in a place it can't understand, so it's doing what it knows how to do—waiting by the hole for the seal to come up. It thinks time is on its side. It's wrong. Unless of course you stick your head up through the hole like an idiot. Which you were almost about to do.*

She looked around the lower deck, where her fellow scientists and engineers were huddled together, staring at her. The front half of it was crowded with the galley, the head, and half a dozen workstations where samples of seawater were under microscopes and fresh-caught fish were being examined against databases of marine life.

"I've called for help," said Dr. Vohringer. "An animal control team is on its way."

From where exactly? How long will it take them to get here? thought Isabel. But since the bear didn't seem to be in any great hurry to succumb to the tranquilizers, there wasn't much point dwelling on the question.

"You know what?" said Chris.

"What?" said Isabel.

"It's a good thing the bathroom is down here."

Nervous laughter ran through the group. Isabel thought she could hear the bear lie down on the floor above, but she wasn't sure.

After ten more minutes, Isabel decided she was done waiting. She borrowed a selfie stick, put her armphone on the end of it, set the camera to record, stuck it up through the trapdoor and slowly rotated it 360 degrees. Nothing took a swipe at it.

Looking at the recording, the bear was lying unconscious in front of the trapdoor. Or possibly just playing possum—did bears do that while waiting for seals? Isabel wasn't about to go upstairs, but at least the animal control team would be reasonably safe when they came to save the day.

Eventually, of course, the animal control team did show up. They were Greenlanders, but spoke English reasonably well. They put plastic cuffs on the bear's paws and got a muzzle on it. Then Nikki got a few shots of Isabel next to the bear in something that was as close to a mighty-hunter pose as Isabel was willing to get. *In the words of the old meme, you had one job, Nikki, one job—keep an eye out for anything dangerous. Like, say, a polar bear trying to swim up and grab me. Seriously, if I had looked up from my work ten seconds later... on second thought, I think I'm going to try not to think about that.* Isabel somehow kept smiling while this was going through her head.

As bears went, it wasn't even that big. Bigger than a black bear, but not much. They said it was female. Isabel could just barely make out its ribs and hipbones... under a heavy layer of wet fur. That was kind of horrifying. *No wonder it came after me. No wonder it wouldn't stop. This thing was just about at the end of its tether.* From the tag, the bear had been caught two years ago while chasing a dog in an Inuit village in Quebec, and had been transported here... to what they had thought was the last place on Earth where it could live the way polar bears were meant to live, without interference from *Homo sapiens*.

The fact that the bear weighed less than four hundred pounds made it a lot easier for the animal control team to load it into their net. Someone said something about trying to find a zoo that would take it. Isabel watched as they flew off to the south with the net hanging under the helicopter—a good twenty feet under, just in case. *Nothing personal*, she thought.

Up until now, the trip had been informative, but not that exciting. Temperatures in Alaska had been in the high seventies, and hadn't gotten below fifty until they passed within range of the winds off the Greenland ice cap. That was just wrong. The first thing they'd seen at sea was the surface of the ocean bubbling off the coast of Barrow as bits of undersea clathrate dissolved into methane. (Ian and Chris had turned into regular comedians at this point. "Bubble bubble toil and trouble, something something something bubble." "Ee-ah, ee-ah, Cthulhu is fartin'." "Anybody else have the urge to light up a smoke?")

The most important thing they'd learned was that the Arctic biome was changing as fast as the climate. They'd gone through clouds of plankton thicker and greener than a sick man's phlegm, and had caught Atlantic herring at the North Pole. Isabel had personally gutted and fried some of them for the crew, and had felt no compunction about doing so. Technically, herring was an invasive species here... if that even meant anything anymore. They'd seen a pod of killer whales further north than the species had ever been seen before. It really was too bad that the first time they encountered an animal that was exactly where it was supposed to be was what happened today.

Before the *Kotick* left, Isabel went back and finished fixing the salinometer.

AUGUST 28:

ISABEL WOKE UP THE NEXT morning—yes, yes, midnight sun and all that, but she'd just slept for eight hours, so it was morning to her—to the news that she had become world-famous. Nikki was supposed to have edited her video clips into a coherent package before uploading them anywhere, but she hadn't been able to resist the urge to post a compilation of the more dramatic moments of the bear encounter online. By the time Isabel got to the computer to look at it, she was the 16,943,805th viewer of her own adventure. Judging by the comments, most viewers rooted for her rather than the bear. This slightly restored her faith in humanity.

It was with a sense of dread that Isabel checked her inboxes. Sure enough, she now had thousands of phone and email messages to sort through.

"Maybe you should take today off," said Dr. Vohringer, looking over her shoulder.

Isabel shook her head. "We still have a lot to do. We're already down one since Brad got hurt."

"Chris and I can take care of it," said Ian.

Isabel started with a short public message: I didn't want to worry anybody. But yeah, things did get a little intense there yesterday. Just to confirm that she still had her sense of humor, she then sent another one—Note to self: stop using Old Bay as deodorant, along with the "this is snark" symbol for the benefit of the thinking impaired.

She sent more personal responses to Hunter, a few close friends, her brothers and sisters, and various aunts, uncles, and cousins from both sides of the family. She also sent a personal note to her old babysitter Sandy, who despite being in the middle of some sort of business battle with the entire diamond industry, had taken time to ask about her.

Finally, she took a deep breath and called her parents. The conversation, if recorded in full, would be six or seven single-spaced pages of Isabel asserting repeatedly that she was doing fine and would be home in a couple of weeks, and her mother asking if she was sure, and wouldn't she like to come home now, to which Isabel would reply that that wasn't really possible under the circumstances. In a desperate attempt to change the subject, Isabel pointed out that right now she was worried about her parents, since there was an Atlantic hurricane headed for the East Coast. "They're saying it's going to make landfall somewhere between the Outer Banks and northern New Jersey," said Isabel. "You're keeping an eye on it, right?"

"Of course," said her mother. "Chelsey and Rod are coming over on Saturday to help get the first-floor furniture up the stairs."

"I hope that's high enough," said Isabel.

SOME THINGS STILL HAPPENED NORMALLY. What happened in the waters off Cape Verde, for example, might have happened in any year. That part of the Atlantic has always been a natural birthplace for hurricanes.

Hurricane Gordon began as an area of high evaporation and low pressure moving from east to west over the ocean. Winds flowing into it were deflected by the Coriolis force into the counterclockwise spiral so familiar to meteorologists. By August 23, it had organized itself into a tropical depression centered around 14°N, 33°W. But it didn't stay there. It moved roughly west by northwest at a speed of ten to twelve knots.

Near the end of August, when it was north of Puerto Rico and east of the Florida Keys, the storm's course changed to north by northwest. By now it was a Category 4 hurricane.

SEPTEMBER 2:

THEL GRITTED HER TEETH AND made a little noise of frustration. "Mom, I don't know if you noticed," she said, "but I'm not a little kid anymore."

"I'm the one who buys your clothes, young lady," said Carrie. "So, yes. I've noticed." Thel was fourteen. Thanks to a growth spurt this year, she was now an inch taller than her mother—another gift from Roger's DNA. "But we're moving everything irreplaceable out of the governor's mansion, and that includes you."

"And unlike the glassware, you're not likely to get damaged in shipment," said Roger. Thel rolled her eyes.

"You are a fairly mature young woman," said Carrie in defiance of the immediate evidence. "On a normal day, I can look after you and Virginia at the same time. This is not a normal day. You know what's coming."

"Yes. I know. I was kind of hoping to get some good storm footage." Thel harbored ambitions of becoming a movie director.

"Come back when it's over and you can collect footage of the aftermath to your heart's content." From the look on Thel's face, that wasn't going to do it, but she couldn't find a way to admit that she was really only interested in the cool part of the chaos and destruction.

"But do I have to spend three days in the middle of nowhere with Mike and Samantha? Not to mention the no-neck monsters?" (Two weeks ago, Roger had taken Thel to see *Cat on a Hot Tin Roof.*) "With school starting next week?"

"Grandma and Drew are going to be there too," said Roger. "That help any?"

"Now go back upstairs and finish packing," said Carrie.

IT WAS MONDAY AT NOON. Hurricane Gordon was expected to arrive in a little over thirty-six hours. This morning, the President had authorized emergency declarations for North Carolina, Virginia, Maryland, Delaware,

D.C. and—just to be on the safe side—Pennsylvania. Carrie, who had declared a state of emergency three days ago, had spent half the morning in teleconference with the head of FEMA and the governors of Maryland and North Carolina.

Carrie had also finished shutting down every part of the executive branch that could be done without for a week and instructed the employees to get their families together and seek shelter. The legislators had adjourned. Courts were cancelled over much of the commonwealth. Schools were closed today—even those out of harm's way might be needed to handle evacuees. The National Guard had taken charge of the buses, and was using them to evacuate people who couldn't otherwise leave. Police and fire departments had stocked up on extra supplies. The hospitals were all swearing they were ready.

Her brain was trying to juggle the information of a dozen briefings—the condition of the power grid in eastern Virginia, location and readiness of potential shelters in the rest of the commonwealth, sociocultural data on the Tidewater communities with information from previous hurricanes on who was most and least likely to be willing to evacuate, and who might be willing but need help... it was like cramming for a test, only a lot of people would die if she got less than an A.

But she'd sent help to those who needed it and were willing, and the evacuation of the low-lying areas was going well. The fact that the Navy had pulled its assets out of Norfolk over the weekend had sent a pretty strong message: *if we can't fight this thing, what chance have you got?* Everywhere else, there were the usual holdouts—people too stubborn to retreat in the face of the elements, people worried about looters, and probably some would-be looters. To these people, Carrie gave the usual last-minute advice: "If you feel you must stay in the area, please write your Social Security number on your arm or leg in permanent marker so that rescue workers can easily identify your remains."

This afternoon, she was going to be reading reports from every county in Gordon's path, trying to guess ahead of time which of the counties that all swore they were ready really were ready. One of the things Carrie had learned from the Mimicane simulation was that trying to reinforce a county government didn't work if that government was completely overwhelmed.

Which could happen. The Commonwealth of Virginia was divided into ninety-five counties—more than California, New York, or Florida. A lot of them were tiny little places with limited resources. And some of the smallest and poorest counties were the ones Gordon was most likely to hit. Carrie began planning a task force to help them get the lights back on and personnel back in their offices… or somewhere that could serve the same function if those offices were no longer standing.

FIVE HOURS LATER, THE TASK force finally set up, Carrie got a message on her computer. It was from her mother. She clicked on ACCEPT.

Judging from the angle, Mama was holding her tablet in her lap, allowing her to look down upon her daughter with an expression of affection and good cheer that was completely unlike anything Carrie remembered from her during childhood. In her early seventies, she was as wiry and healthy as ever, but her moods had mellowed out a lot. Behind her was the interior of Papa's old vacation home in the Blue Ridge Mountains.

"Is this a bad time?" said Mama.

"Actually, this might be the only free moment I have today," said Carrie.

"I'm just calling to say I can hear Roger's car coming up the driveway."

"Thank you." Of course it would be Mama who called, rather than Roger or Thel. Both were still miffed at her for moving them as far as possible from anything that looked like danger, although Roger would never say so. Naturally they'd neglect to tell her when they'd arrived and make her worry even more. "Is the rest of the family there?"

"All present and accounted for." She turned her tablet to give Carrie a good look at the living room. Her brother Mike and his son Liam were seated nearby. Mike looked like a smaller and less cheerful version of their father in his prime, a portly man with a heavy-jowled face and dark hair just starting to go gray. Liam, almost twelve, stuck his fat little face and hand out from behind his father to wave at his aunt on the screen.

Her other remaining brother, Drew, was leaning against the windowsill, gazing out onto the front lawn. Despite this, Samantha, Mike's wife and business partner—to the extent that they still had a business after the fiasco in January—was trying to keep her short, fat self interposed between her two little daughters and Drew's indifferent back. *One day, Samantha*, thought Carrie, *you will learn that just because somebody is single and lives with his mother doesn't mean he's a pervert. You can figure it out. I believe in you.*

You've already learned that racist tweets on the company Twitter account are a bad idea. Having to publicly repudiate her sister-in-law's comments had not been the high point of Carrie's political career.

Just before Roger and Thel came in, Drew turned away from the window. Unlike Mike, he didn't look like anybody else at all, which was good news for anybody else. After sixteen years, the patchwork of burn scars and skin grafts on his face had faded and weathered into something that was still unpleasant to look at, but at least wouldn't be a source of nightmares.

Thel strode up to Drew, wrapped her arms around him and kissed a spot to the left of his mouth where there were some functioning nerve endings. "How's my creepy uncle?" she said.

"Doing all right," he said, hugging her awkwardly with the heels of his palms pressed against her spine. Samantha glowered at Thel as if the girl were doing this just to mess with her, which was probably true. *That's our family*, thought Carrie.

SEPTEMBER 3:

IT WAS NOON. IN RICHMOND, there was already a gray carpet over the sky. Carrie could hear the thirty mph wind driving the rain against the mansion's eastern windows, but she couldn't see it—sheets of plywood and heavy blankets were over the inside of the windows. The eye of the hurricane was still three hundred miles away, off the coast of North Carolina, but Virginia Beach was already getting damaged.

And the worst was yet to come. Not long after midnight, Gordon's eye would be coming ashore right at the border with North Carolina. The Newport News and Norfolk areas would get the worst of it. Carrie had moved fleets of bulldozers into Richmond and Petersburg, ready to go down there as soon as the weather allowed and clear away the remains of the houses, boats, and trees that would be littering the streets.

Richmond and Petersburg… that had been the toughest call, whether or not to stay here. This area was the heart of the commonwealth, and withdrawing from it would add days to her government's response time. But if the storm turned out to be too powerful, if it destroyed everything she'd put here for safekeeping… not only would her career be over, it would deserve to be over.

No point second-guessing herself now. Carrie was as certain as she could be that she had done everything in her power to protect lives and property in Virginia. The time had come to make one last call to FEMA.

To Carrie's surprise, it wasn't a FEMA representative who appeared on the screen. It was Congressman Darling, R-OH. His cleft-chinned, perfect Hollywood face was easy to recognize.

Carrie didn't know the names of everybody in Congress, but this guy she'd heard of. John Lyman Darling was one of those politicians who had a way of drawing attention to themselves that was all out of proportion to their actual power. He had started out as a generic right-wing Republican from rural Ohio. When his district was redistricted out from under him a few years ago, everybody thought that would be the end of him. Instead he'd changed a bunch of his positions, reinvented himself as a political maverick and, to the astonishment of all, won the election—and with very little help from the national party. You couldn't be sure any more where he would come down on any particular issue, but he was good at both PR and constituent service.

"You're still there?" said Carrie.

"Myself and a half-dozen others," said Darling. "Not enough to get any business done, but it didn't feel right to desert the nation's capital." Carrie mentally translated this to *we all want to be seen boldly standing our ground even though there's no sane reason for us to be here.* This was an election year, after all. "We're all just trying to stay out of the way of the professionals."

"Are you sure you're safe where you are?"

"There's a reason FEMA set up the JFO here," said Darling. "The Capitol is probably the safest building in D.C. right now. After all, we're on a hill—we're not going to be flooded out. And this place was built back when they knew how to build *strong*. No storm is going to knock down these walls, I promise you."

"Glad to hear it," said Carrie. "Speaking of staying out of the way of the professionals…" Darling took the hint and signaled for somebody from FEMA.

THE EYE OF THE STORM, *thirty miles wide, passed over northern Cape Hatteras,*

Nags Head, and Kill Devil Hills. This was little help to the few remaining residents, as it was immediately preceded and followed by winds blowing at 140 mph.

As predicted, the eye came ashore not long after midnight. Fortunately, the meteotsunami—the dome of water formed by low air pressure—entered the Bay just as the tide was going out, or the damage would have been even worse. As it was, a twenty-two-foot storm surge passed between—and over—the Virginia Capes. From there it spread out, losing much of its height, only to regain some of it in narrow places where the storm forced the water inland.

The eyewall moved north by northwest, over Norfolk, Newport News, and Hampton, before moving over the York River. Fragile frame houses were quickly destroyed—the wind forced its way in through drafts and popped them like balloons, or simply tore them apart. The pieces were propelled like shrapnel into the sides of other houses, creating a chain reaction of devastation. The storm surge forced its way through the lightless streets, carrying boats, cars, and trucks with equal indifference.

At dawn, the eyewall's course turned more to the north, on a course that would carry it midway between Richmond and Washington. At 11 a.m. Gordon's eye passed over Reston, Virginia. By this time its strongest sustained winds were down to 110 mph. Like a Confederate army, Hurricane Gordon crossed the Potomac into western Maryland and the hills of Pennsylvania where, late in the afternoon, it would die.

But even its death throes were a force to be reckoned with. Its rains flooded the Potomac, the Patuxent, the Patapsco, the Gunpowder, and the Susquehanna— all of which flowed into the Chesapeake Bay, where the storm surge was only just beginning to recede.

SEPTEMBER 10:

THE FLIGHT FROM SVALBARD TO BWI via Reykjavik and Boston had been long, slow, and full of terrible weather. The drive through Maryland had been an obstacle course of downed trees and power lines, not all of them surrounded by traffic cones. All the way to Tilghman Island, over the old bridge and down the island's main street, with every mile of terrain showing more signs of damage than the last, Isabel kept herself happy by looking forward to the moment when she could walk through her parents' front door and collapse onto the comfy old couch in the living room.

So of course, no sooner had she turned onto the little side street where her parents lived than she saw that old couch out on the curb. When she pulled into the driveway and opened her car door, she got a good whiff of the mildew that had taken hold in its upholstery. Mom and Pop must not have been able to get it up the stairs, and the floodwaters from Gordon must have gotten into the house. It was like looking at the corpse of a family pet.

Isabel could easily see how high the storm surge had gone. The evidence was painted on the walls of every home, the trunk and branches of every tree, on every streetlight and road sign—a layer of silt that the rain from Gordon's trailing edge had been unable to wash away, now dried by the sun to the color of cardboard. When Isabel stood on the front lawn of the house, the high-water mark was about level with her eyes. Suddenly, she didn't want to go inside and see how bad things were. She did it anyway.

The living room looked like a room in an abandoned building. The rest of the furniture was still upstairs, and the pictures hadn't been put back on the wall. The old carpet was gone. Kristen, home until Chesapeake College reopened, was scrubbing the naked floorboards by the light of a solitary lamp, so at least the power was back on. Her platinum-blond hair was crammed under a hairnet to keep it off the floor. With only the briefest of pauses for greetings, Isabel tucked her ponytail into the back of her T-shirt, got down on the floor and joined her, glad she wasn't wearing good clothes.

When Isabel went to refill the bucket, she saw the kitchen was already clean. Dad had moved the fridge and freezer downstairs again. Mom was lining up dishes on the counter. She turned to look at Isabel.

"Shouldn't you be in school, young lady?" she said with a smile.

"I'm supposed to be back in class on Monday," said Isabel. "How are things here?"

"Oven's not working. We're going to polish off the last of the leftovers tonight. Tomorrow… well, we'll have to think of something."

DINNER TURNED OUT TO BE a little bit of chili, cauliflower, and vegetable soup. The good news was that the vegetable soup had been made with that wonderful crab broth. Just tasting it took Isabel back to a dozen and more afternoons spent helping her mother in the kitchen, cracking open the crab legs joint by joint, collecting the bigger chunks of caked-on Old Bay from the bodies of crabs, putting them in the slow cooker with lemon and garlic and water to simmer overnight until all the flavor and protein from those tiny little bits of rich dark crabmeat had gone into the broth.

"So how bad off is the island?" Isabel finally asked.

"I'll put it this way," said Pop. "I've seen Tilghmans and Misters working together cleaning stuff up." Isabel was glad she had Pop to keep track of the complicated feuds on this island. It was the sort of thing she wasn't much good at herself.

"I know at least three people who had to have dead deer hauled off the front porch," said Kristen. "Poor things drowned trying to take shelter."

"A couple of deer got up on the roof of the Comegys place and couldn't get back down," said Dad.

"What'd they do about it?"

"Held a cookout," said Kristen, grinning. "Probably not legal, but…"

"Wish I'd been there. I could've helped get rid of the evidence."

"You might want to spend the weekend with Chelsey and Rod," Mom said to Isabel. "We're a little short of good rooms here."

"It's too bad the house is such a mess," said Pop. "I've been hoping to meet this Hunter fella."

Isabel tried to will her face not to turn pink, but it didn't work. There was no possible way for her to say that she and Hunter weren't quite at that stage of the relationship yet, especially since her parents took her boyfriends a lot more seriously than they took her girlfriends. And for them to approve of Hunter would be a miracle on par with Jesus personally appearing on their front lawn to heal the old couch.

"He's very busy," she said. "I'll try and bring him by before the holidays." She wasn't lying. Between schoolwork and Enginquest, Hunter really was very busy. Her parents didn't need that much detail.

Rummaging through her brain for a quick change of subject, Isabel suddenly remembered an important piece of news she'd forgotten to tell.

"I've been invited on the Walt Yuschak Show," she said. (On some level, she knew that wasn't its official name. It was called "This Week in Freedom with Walt Yuschak" or "This Week with Freedom in Walt Yuschak" or something like that. But everybody called it "The Walt Yuschak Show" or just "Walt Yuschak.")

Everybody at the table needed a moment to take this in.

"It's not just because of that thing with the bear," Isabel added. "Well, it's partly that. But they also want me to talk about what we found up there, with the change in sea temperature."

"I've listened to him a few times," said Kristen, "and I honestly think he's kind of a jerk." She said it with a touch of sorrow, as if it hurt her a little to make such a harsh judgment. Which it probably did. If Kristen thought you were "kind of a jerk," you'd reached a point in life where your best bet was to run around your house weeping and smashing all the mirrors.

"From what I've heard, he'd agree with you," said Isabel. "But if he's actually going to see reason on climate change, that's a good thing."

"Clark also has some news," said Mom. "Pretty big news, too." She looked happy.

"I got a letter from the bank," said Pop. "They said to help me cover the damage to the house, they've decided to give me something called 'mortgage forgiveness.'"

Isabel blinked. "What do you mean, forgiveness?"

"It means I own the house now. The deed's in my name—they moved it to my safe-deposit box themselves. I don't have to make any more payments."

"What, just like that?"

"Just like that. I'm not the only one, either. Bob Tilghman, Jerry Anthony, Paul Mister—same thing happened to them. No warning. They just got everything handed over. Jerry's a happy guy—he bought the house just last year."

"Are you sure there isn't a catch?"

"There probably is, girl, but what am I supposed to do about it? They gave me the deed. I can't exactly march into the bank and make 'em take it back."

AFTER DINNER, ISABEL CALLED SANDY and reassured her that her family was basically okay. Isabel's family, that is, not Sandy's. Since the death of her mother, Sandy had no family left on Tilghman Island.

"How are things going with business?"

"We had to shut down the plant in Lusby for a few days, but we're back on track. The real problem was getting everything locked up somewhere secure and making sure nobody found out where." Most warehouses didn't have the kind of security that was good enough for Sandy's stock-in-trade. "Of course, right now I'm more worried about what the Supreme Court says. Or doesn't say."

ABOUT 6.7 PERCENT OF EARTH'S surface is more than 60° north of the equator, and by the beginning of September all of it was clouded over. From space, it looked like a white skullcap on the world, frayed around the edges but still growing. In three places in particular, the sea of clouds expanded southward and brought rain. Meteorologists described the weather in these places as "precipitation anomalies."

The change in the weather came slowly in eastern Siberia. In the third week of September, a little over an inch of rain fell on the Taymyr Peninsula and the hills east of the lower Lena. In the next week, two to five inches fell over the land between the Kotuy and the Kolyma—a stretch of tundra and forest roughly twelve hundred miles wide. In the week after that, more than a foot of rain fell over the entire basin of the Lena, which would not normally receive so much precipitation in a whole year.

The city of Yakutsk, in the heart of the basin, was no stranger to flooding. It was a natural risk of living in Siberia—the rivers flow south to north, so when spring comes the upper parts of the rivers always thaw before the lower parts. In recent years the melting of record snowfalls had caused some particularly bad floods.

But nothing like this. Computer simulations made it clear that the levees would not hold. The Red Cross recommended that at least a quarter of the city's three hundred thousand people be evacuated. But the few roads of Siberia had been washed out in many places, and the nearest unaffected settlement was three hundred miles to the south.

In western Canada, the change came suddenly and without warning. In the fourth week of September, a knife-blade of storm cloud slid south along the eastern edge of the Rockies as far as Lethbridge. The three worst hailstorms in the history of Calgary all happened within a space of eleven days, accompanied by fifteen inches of rain.

It was the western edge of a triangular precipitation anomaly stretching from the Mackenzie Delta to the Melville Peninsula. Further east, the rain was still abnormal, but not so extreme. As far as conditions on the ground went, this mattered less than the fact that the rivers flowed southwest to northeast, carrying the downpour along the edge of the Rockies into northern Manitoba. With its paper-thin coating of soil, the Canadian Shield was less able to cope with flooding than almost any other place on Earth.

The worst anomaly, however, was the one that began stretching over northern Europe in the second half of September. It encompassed all Scandinavia, the Baltic nations, most of the British Isles, the Netherlands and northern Belgium, Germany, and Poland, along with a swath of northeastern Russia that included St. Petersburg and Archangel. Within the first three weeks, Hamburg had been evacuated and Oslo, Berlin, Stockholm, and Copenhagen were suffering under more than two feet of rain.

And it was getting worse...

OCTOBER 5:

THE KNOCK ON THE GREENROOM door came just as Lisa was about to start applying makeup to Isabel's face.

"Who is it?" said Lisa.

"It's me." No name. No need. That high-pitched rasp was well known. Even Isabel, who wasn't a regular viewer, could recognize it. Anyway, this was his show.

"Come in," said Lisa. Isabel was about to get up, but Lisa had a hand on her shoulder.

This was the first time Isabel had ever been alone face to face with a genuine celebrity. Up close, he didn't seem like that big of a deal—a bald guy in a black turtleneck who just happened to look exactly like that guy with the libertarian show.

"Mr. Yuschak... Hi."

"You can call me Walt." He sat down in front of her. "How're you feeling?"

"Little nervous."

"Yeah, most people are when it's their first time... damn, this conversation is turning into accidental innuendo. Sorry about that."

Isabel chuckled. Her appearance had been delayed by two weeks—the first week because a documentary filmmaker wanted to promote a movie he'd just made about next-generation psychoactive drugs and all their wonderful and terrifying possibilities, the second week because Henry Pratt had chosen to put in an appearance on *This Week in Freedom*. Well, okay, Isabel had to admit Pratt was a bigger deal than she was. So was the documentary guy, now that she thought about it. Actually, lots of things were bigger deals than she was. Her chief claim to fame, at the moment, was not being in the stomach of a polar bear—something most people managed with far less effort. Right now, she was in the fourteenth minute of her allotted fame and the clock was ticking.

Which was a relief, really. The past few weeks had been a real pain, between her trying to get back to her schoolwork and make sure her family and friends were still doing okay while everybody and their grandmother wanted to interview her.

"Anyway, let me talk you through this," Walt said. "First, you tell us a little bit about yourself. Nothing too personal, just who you are, where you're from, how you came to be on that boat in the middle of the Arctic. Then we run the tape again and you tell us what it was like. And what happened to the bear. People really care about that—I mean, no offense, you're important too, but we can *see* you're doing okay. That should get us to the first commercial break.

"After that, we talk about some of this crazy weather we're having. I understand you're a meteorologist and I've read some of your blog, so I figure you can explain it to my viewers better than a lot of people could. Try not to cuss, don't look into the cameras... you've got notes, right?"

"Yes," said Isabel. "I'm going to have to talk about global warming. You okay with that?"

"Sure. I never denied it. Well, maybe when I was a teenager, but not lately. So, any questions?"

"Why is this called a greenroom?" Isabel waved her hand to take in the room and its furnishings, none of which were green.

"I don't know," said Walt. "That's just what these places are called. Ever do any acting?"

"Hmm? No."

"I used to do a little community theater," said Walt. "Every theater's got a room like this. They usually aren't green either."

Isabel nodded. "Why'd you stop?"

"Two reasons. One, once I hit big-time this show kind of took up all my energy. Two, just between you and me, I was a shit actor. I couldn't play a corpse if you cut off my head… So, you're still in school?" There was barely any pause between topics—he just jumped from one to the other. The conversation turned to her schoolwork, and then with equal abruptness to her father's work and the skipjack that was his pride and joy. Then he left, letting Lisa get back to helping Isabel with her makeup.

By the time Lisa was done, Yuschak had begun his opening monologue, and his voice was coming over the comm system. He seemed to be bellowing about foreign aid today. To the surprise of no one, he was against it. "Canada? Britain? Germany? Ireland? Sweden? Denmark?" he shouted. "These are not poor countries! The Netherlands? They've been holding off flooding for years! They're famous for it! Russia? Even if those guys needed our help they'd die before they asked for it! I mean, come on! The last time the Russians admitted they could use a hand with something, panzers were looking for parking spaces *right outside Moscow!*

"Listen to me! This is not about saving the world! This is not about helping people who actually need help! This is about our government—our State Department, our USAID—*needing to be needed!* Not just by us, but by everybody in the whole world! They just can't stand the thought that somebody somewhere has a problem and is solving it on their own!" At this point Isabel managed to block him out enough to give her notes one last go-over.

"Don't worry," said Lisa. "He's mellowed out a lot. He hasn't called a woman a crotchburger in years. I kinda miss it." Isabel wasn't sure how to respond to this.

"Well," said Isabel, smiling a little, "I could call you one, if it would help."

"No thanks. Wouldn't be the same."

"TONIGHT, LADIES AND GENTLEMEN, OUR special guest is that girl who took down the world's last polar bear!" *I'm pretty sure that wasn't literally the last one,* thought Isabel. "An Arctic explorer, a meteorologist, and the author of… well, nothing yet, but you know it's just a matter of time. Ladies and gentlemen, please give a warm welcome to Isabel Bradshaw!"

Isabel stepped out onto the soundstage, looking as good as she ever had in her life. Her makeup was perfect, her hair styled in such a way as to fall fetchingly over one shoulder instead of its usual ponytail. Her dress was a shade of blue that was, she hoped, just dark enough to be conservative while still being bright enough to bring out her eyes.

Walter Yuschak presided over the set from behind his polished black faux-anchorman desk. In addition to his usual charcoal blazer and black sweater, today he was proping in a keffiyeh. ("Proping"—short for "appropriating"—was a new trend. To do it, you simply put on a piece of clothing that came from some other culture, preferably a culture you knew absolutely nothing about, just to show how little you cared if you offended anybody. It was an easy way to establish yourself as a Bad Boy or Bad Girl without doing any harm. In Isabel's opinion, it was also an easy way to make a complete fool of yourself—surprisingly few guys could pull off a feathered war bonnet, for instance—but Yuschak's keffiyeh looked kind of good on him.) Isabel gave what she hoped was a friendly-looking smile as she waved to the studio audience, then sat down in her appointed place.

"First of all, girl," he said, "I gotta take off my hat to you." Yuschak doffed his keffiyeh. He was wearing a yarmulke under it. *Should've seen that coming*, thought Isabel. As far as she knew, he was as Jewish as he was Arabic. She was almost impressed. *What would you call that? Multi-proping?*

The first part of the interview went smoothly. Isabel told them about where she was from, spending her childhood indoors or working on Pop's boat because of her bee allergy, and added some fun facts about crabbing and oystering ("Let me give you a little advice—if you think there might be a chunk of sea nettle on your glove, don't rub your eyes."). She gave a little shout-out to Hunter, and then it was time to watch the bear tape.

Isabel had seen Nikki's tape before, but never on such a big screen. The strange thing was that she couldn't read the expression on her own face. Anyone looking at it would have thought it was a look of annoyance rather than terror. It was a look that said *Crap, there's this stupid polar bear and now I have to drop everything and run away and rummage around for a weapon and DAMMIT THERE ARE SALINOMETERS TO FIX.*

They showed the photo of her doing that stupid pose next to the unconscious bear. Then she reported that the bear was currently in a zoo in Reykjavik, and was getting its weight back without violently subtracting from anyone else's. The audience did sound happy about that.

The commercial break gave Isabel a chance to take a discreet peek at herself in the mirror and make sure there wasn't something horribly wrong with her appearance. It was amazing how calm you could be if you just concentrated on saying what you came to say and looking good while saying it and didn't think about the fact that millions of people were watching you.

Now it was time for Part Two of the interview. "Isabel, you're a weather expert, right?"

"It's one of my fields, yeah."

"Maybe you could help my viewers understand what the hell is going on out there."

Yuschak pressed a button. A screen behind the desk showed a highway clogged with traffic, headlights and taillights shining under a gunmetal-gray sky. According to the caption, this was somewhere east of Calgary. Police were trying to shepherd the vehicles around a dozen or more accidents. Hailstones bigger than gravel were pelting everything in sight. "They're evacuating just under a million people from western Canada," said Yuschak.

"And that's in a country of forty million," said Isabel, "so this is a pretty big deal for them."

"And here's the latest from Siberia," said Yuschak, turning on another screen. "Sucks to be in Yakutsk right now. I mean, more than usual." Isabel nodded. Normally nobody in the U.S. spent much time thinking about Yakutsk unless they were playing Risk, but suddenly the place was in the news. Satellite photos showed water up to the second-floor windows and thousands of people huddled on the roofs.

"Okay, let's look at Europe." The screen showed a weather map of Europe. This was no neat triangle-shaped anomaly, but a vast disorganized mass of cloud that covered pretty much everything south of the Arctic Circle and north of Brussels, Berlin, Warsaw, and Minsk. It reached west of Ireland and tapered off in the east over northern Russia.

Another screen showed the consequences. Knee-deep or hip-deep water in the streets of twenty cities in the Scandinavian countries, the Netherlands, and Germany. Lines of sandbags along the Thames in London. The huge Lough Neagh in Northern Ireland swelling its banks. Endless pumps set up along the dikes of the Netherlands to keep the sunken land from being flooded not by the sea but by the sky.

"Yeah, that's pretty bad," said Yuschak. "So, can you tell us why all this is happening?"

"I can," said Isabel. "but I gotta warn you, you might not like it. You know how we always say you can't attribute any one weather phenomenon to global climate change?"

"Yeah."

"Well, this time you can. This weather pattern is absolutely a direct consequence of the changes that have been taking place in the Arctic. Let me explain.

"The sea ice in the Arctic Ocean has been melting earlier every year for the past three years. This year, for example, the last of it melted on July 9, and the North Pole was ice-free three weeks before that."

"And how is that causing all this rain?"

"Imagine you put a pot of water on the stove, set the heat on the lowest setting, and then wandered off and forgot about it for the rest of the day," said Isabel. "The water would be pretty warm after a while. That's what happened to the Arctic Ocean this year. During the summer, insolation at the North Pole is higher than anywhere else on Earth."

"Hang on—insulation?"

Isabel shook her head. "Insolation. Meaning it gets more sunlight."

"What, more than the tropics?"

"Believe it or not, yes. Could we see the Arctic up there?"

Yuschak pushed a button. The central screen showed a globe, centered more or less on Canada.

"Let me go up and show everybody what I'm talking about."

"Sure." Isabel got up, went over to the screen, and pointed at the Arctic. "You see, the sun is low on the horizon, but it *never sets*. With no sea ice to reflect the light, or to melt into the water and cool it, the ocean just spends the whole summer getting warmer and warmer and warmer. Especially here." She pointed at a part of the ocean between the North Pole and Alaska. "This is the Beaufort Gyre. It mixes a little with water out of the Bering Strait, but mostly it just turns in place under constant sunlight. And as it heats up, you get evaporation. You get clouds. Lots and lots of clouds.

"Now let's talk about why it's getting out of the Arctic. This"—she pointed at a ring of wavy arrows circling the pole—"this is the polar jet stream. Normally, it acts like a barrier—Arctic air stays on one side and temperate air stays on the other, and the greater the difference in temperature between the Arctic and the temperate zones, the stronger the barrier is.

"What's happening right now, this fall, is that the Arctic Ocean is still transferring heat to the air—mostly by evaporating. So the Arctic is still getting warmer at the same time the rest of the hemisphere is getting cooler… and the jet stream is getting weaker. It's distorting." Isabel brushed her finger against the screen. The display rotated the planet until it centered on California. "Whoops." She brushed her finger against the screen again. The display rotated the planet until it centered on the North Pole. *Whew. Quick save.*

"Normally this would be more of a circle," said Isabel, pointing at the jet stream. It was closer to a triangle than a circle. "Here, here, and here"—Isabel indicated the points of the triangle—"is where the flooding is."

"But why is the one in Europe so much worse than the others?"

"Two reasons. First, Europe normally gets more rain, because of moisture from the North Atlantic. Especially heavy storms. We've actually had an above-average hurricane season this year—it doesn't seem that way because only three of them made landfall in the U.S. Most of them stayed out over the ocean until they lost force and the prevailing winds pushed what was left of them into this mess.

"Second, meltwater from Greenland is being carried into the North Atlantic through the Denmark Strait, where it's hitting warm water from the Gulf Stream. At the same time, we're getting cold air from off the ice cap hitting warm air from further south. So this whole part of the ocean has turned into a giant storm factory, and most of what it's making is heading east… for now. But I wouldn't be surprised if we see some bad weather on this side of the Atlantic later this year."

Yuschak nodded. "What about next year?"

"Next year I would expect all this to happen again," she said. "There's nothing to stop it. I wouldn't expect it to always happen in the same parts of the world. The reason it's happening in these particular places is that that's where the polar jet stream is breaking down this year, but next year it may happen in different places.

"But I would expect this… monsoon season or whatever you want to call it… to become a regular feature of the weather in the northern hemisphere. In fact, most years I would expect it to be either more intense or more widespread, and to hit places further south."

"Why is that?"

"The Arctic Ocean isn't through changing. Next year, the ice-free moment is likely to be even earlier. At some point in the next few years it should stabilize, but we don't know exactly when."

"So… this isn't even its final form?"

"'Fraid not. And I have to mention that even if it stabilizes, it won't stay stable as long as greenhouse gas levels stay out of balance."

"I had a feeling you were going to bring that up."

"There isn't really a way to avoid it. I mean, not only do we have to bring down our own carbon emissions, we have to bring them down even more to compensate for all the outgassing from the Arctic clathrates."

"Yeah, I meant to ask you about those. How do you know that all this outgassing hasn't been going on for centuries? How do we know that's not what's really behind all this?"

Isabel was stunned for a moment. Then she remembered that Yuschak had promised not to claim it wasn't happening. He'd never said anything about admitting it was caused by humans.

"I mean, it's not like the Arctic is heavily explored," he added.

"Well," said Isabel, "we have testimony from the Inuit, who've lived there for thousands of years. They say the ocean never used to belch at them before. And coastlines that have been there for the whole of recorded history are eroding now because the permafrost is collapsing."

"But doesn't the level of CO_2 normally go up and down anyway? If you look at the fossil record, haven't there been other periods of warming, caused by volcanoes and changes in the sun?"

"You might be thinking of the Paleocene-Eocene Thermal Maximum," Isabel said. In fact, she suspected Yuschak had never heard of the Paleocene-Eocene Thermal Maximum and was only vaguely aware that Earth's temperature had gone up and down in the geologic past, but since he'd raised the subject, she was ready.

"Explain that for our viewers," he said, instead of *what the hell are you talking about?*

"The PETM, as we call it"—*pet-em*, that was one embarrassing acronym—"is the closest thing in the fossil record to modern climate change. At least, the earliest part of it is. It happened about fifty-five and a half million years ago. Average global temperatures rose about six degrees centigrade over the course of—"

"How much is that in real degrees?"

"Eleven degrees Fahrenheit."

"So it's like what's happening now."

"Not exactly. The big difference is, the temperature rise during the PETM took place over about twenty thousand years. The increase in global temperatures we've already measured is equivalent to about forty-five hundred years' worth of the PETM increase, and it happened in less than a century and a half. So to answer your question, we know it's not natural because we know what natural climate change would look like, and this isn't it. It is much, much, too fast.

"Oh, and here's an interesting statistic about volcanoes. In 2010, there was a volcanic eruption in Iceland that released 150,000 tons of CO_2 every day— and yet it caused a net decrease in carbon emissions for that year. You know why? Because the air traffic that was cancelled due to the eruption would have released more than twice as much.

"And about the sun—yes, it does go through cycles. However, there haven't been any significant correlation between changes in solar irradiance and changes in global temperature since around 1980. So… not volcanoes this time. Or the sun. Sorry."

"I feel like you guys want it to be our fault somehow," said Yuschak. "Like you enjoy being all gloom-and-doom."

"Seems to me you're being a lot more gloom-and-doom than I am."

"*What?*" Yuschak looked genuinely shocked. Probably no one had ever accused him of that before.

Isabel pressed on. "We're already agreed this is happening, right? We're not going to pretend it isn't?" Yuschak nodded. "So if it turns out you're right, if it's a natural phenomenon and human civilization can't affect the climate at all… we're screwed. Our food and water supplies are going to be yanked out from under us and rearranged God knows how, and big parts of the world are going to become too hot for humans to survive in, and there's nothing we can do about it.

"But what I'm saying is, to the extent that we're still causing it, we have the power to change it. The damage we're doing right now—we can stop doing that. We can fix this."

"Whoa!"

"Or at least keep it from being any worse than it has to be."

"Wait. Slow down. Hang on here. You keep saying *we*. *We* can stop. *We* have the power. Who's this 'we'? Who specifically are you referring to that's going to do all this?"

It took Isabel a moment to think of a reply.

"I was thinking... humanity in general," she said. "I wasn't thinking of anybody in particular."

"Well, you should," said Yuschak. "Or maybe not you, but somebody should. 'Cause—listen to me, this is important—*humanity in general* isn't all going to get its shit together and start doing the same thing at the same time. Just not going to happen. Humanity in general is just a big bunch of people all looking after their own needs. You can talk some individuals into changing their habits, but if it turns out that's not enough and you keep saying 'we gotta do something' it's going to end up being the government that does it. That's what scares me."

"I don't really care who solves the problem. If somebody invented a machine tomorrow that could fix the air, that would be great. We could just turn it on and be done with it."

"There's that 'we' again."

"My point is, it doesn't have to be the government."

"But it's going to be," said Yuschak. "No matter what you intend, that's what's going to happen. People aren't all on the same page, nonprofits are too small, and corporations are busy making money—it's going to be the government.

"What I'm saying is, I'm more afraid of the government than I am of the weather. People you can tell to get lost, corporations you can refuse to do business with, but the government can tell you what to do. It is fundamentally... an instrument... of coercion." He tapped his desk as he spoke, to punctuate his words. They were almost out of time. Isabel tried desperately to think of some simple way to get her point across.

"Seems to me," she finally said, "the more people step up and do what needs doing of their own free will, the less we'll need any kind of coercion."

Yuschak shook his head. "'Do what needs doing of your own free will, and we won't need any coercion.' Sure hope you never hear that on a date. Isabel Bradshaw, ladies and gentlemen."

ISABEL'S FACE MIGHT HAVE BEEN turning a malevolent shade of pink, but she kept her composure until she was off the set and well away from the cameras. Then she stomped into the greenroom, yanked her jacket off the coat rack and picked up her purse. The only person who was even trying to meet her eyes was Lisa.

"Um… don't forget your gift bag," said Lisa, holding it out nervously. Isabel snatched it out of her hand and glared inside. There were a couple of books, a T-shirt, a hat, a pot brownie, and a couple of bottles of liquor that were just the right weight to smash over somebody's head. Or to drink from until she blacked out. Either would feel pretty good right now.

Lisa was biting her lip again, looking at Isabel as if she wanted to apologize for having been in the building at the time. "Is there something else?" Isabel said, trying to keep her voice neutral.

"Yeah. Um… I'm sorry that ended like it did, but… the thing about Walt…" Lisa bit her lip again. There was a long silence.

"What about him?" Isabel finally asked.

"He wouldn't have said that if he didn't… um… if he didn't think you could handle it."

"Yeah, he's only nice to people he doesn't respect," said Adam from the corner.

"Thank you," said Isabel flatly. "I have to go." Lisa stepped out of her way as she left the greenroom.

BACK IN THE HOTEL ROOM, bearing in mind that Walt's show had agreed to pay her hotel and travel expenses, Isabel was vengefully raiding the minibar. She took a moment to look in her gift bag at the books, which turned out to be Ayn Rand's *The Fountainhead* and *Atlas Shrugged*, because of course they were.

Even though Yuschak had suddenly turned skeptic or denialist or whatever it was you wanted to call somebody who kept resurrecting every single discredited talking point that anybody had ever made in the last few decades, Isabel thought she'd been doing pretty well. Until the conversation had gone to the question of what to do about it. She had to admit that public policy was not her strong point. And that little parting shot of his had been… unnecessary. Not to mention just plain yecch.

Of course, now that she was well away from the studio, she thought of all sorts of things she should have said to him. For example: *Hey, you know what else is coercive? Two feet of floodwater in your living room. Coerces you right out of house and home. And unlike the government, when nature declares eminent domain over your property it doesn't even try to compensate you.* Or: *So, your entire argument is basically "global warming can't be our fault, and it can't be anything we have the power to affect, because if it were we'd have to do something about it and that would be terrible." I have news for you—the laws of physics are not going to rewrite themselves to accommodate your political preferences.* Or better yet: *So government regulation is like date rape? Tell you what. Tomorrow I'll visit the DMV, and you can visit the prison shower, and afterward we'll compare notes and see who had the worse day.*

But that was why Walter Yuschak had a show and she didn't. He was one of those rare people who could come up with everything he needed to say right on the spot.

Her phone rang. The ringtone was Epifania's "I Won't Forget," which meant it was somebody in her immediate family calling. "It's Chelsey," said the phone, just as her older sister's face appeared on the screen.

"Hey."

"How're you feeling, chunkybutt?"

"Not so great."

"Yeah, I saw you on the screen. Pop's gonna lose his shit when he finds out."

"Let's not tell him about this, okay?"

"Yeah… for what it's worth, I thought you came out ahead on points."

"Thank you."

"Rod said, 'He's a dick, but I respect his principles.'"

"Well, that's his opinion, I guess." Isabel had always looked at national problems with the same pragmatism she looked at her own problems with. If the toilet was clogged, you unclogged it. You didn't pretend it wasn't really clogged, or that being clogged was part of the natural cycle of toilets and you shouldn't try to interfere with it. You grabbed a toilet plunger and got to work. What Yuschak seemed to have been saying was that you shouldn't be allowed to do that, because with that plunger you should have power too great and terrible, and over you the plunger would gain a power still greater and more deadly… or something like that. It was an interesting point, and she made a mental note to think about it some more when she was less pissed off at him, which ("Sure hope you never hear that on a date") would probably take a while.

No sooner had the conversation ended than her phone rang again. This time the ringtone was Rodomontade's "Peligro," which was reserved for just one person.

"Hi, Hunter."

"Hey… you all right?"

"Fine. Just… kinda humiliated." There was a tightness in her throat. Isabel hadn't cried since she was a child, but she was suddenly very close to it.

"I'm so sorry. I wish I was there in person."

"I kinda need to punch something right now."

"Okay, then I wish I was there in person wearing one of those padded suits they use in self-defense classes."

Isabel managed a chuckle. Then there was a catch in her throat, and the tears came. She didn't make much noise, but she knew Hunter knew.

"Oh my god," she said, "I'm using up all your airtime listening to me cry."

"You're more than welcome to cry all over my airtime."

Isabel blew her nose.

"But I'm gonna have to charge you for blowing your nose on it. Hey, if it makes you feel any better, some congressman is saying Yuschak needs to apologize on air."

"Really? Is it my congressman?"

"Nah, it's somebody named Darling from Ohio. He says, quote, 'My parents always taught me to treat women with courtesy and respect. My teachers taught me to treat women as equals. Yuschak didn't do either one of those things.'"

"Oh, *darling*."

"Uh… me or him?"

"Ain't tellin'."

"Oh, hey—I know you're not into games, but I've got my own airship now and I could really use a first mate. How about it? Just you, me and a bunch of NPCs helping the Republic of Clovia fight off a chthonid attack?"

Joining an MMORPG as a noob seemed more likely to be a cause of humiliation than a cure for it. But if her boyfriend was going to be the only one watching until she got the hang of it… that might not be so bad.

CLIMATOLOGISTS WERE DIVIDED ON WHETHER to call it the Autumnal Subarctic Extreme Precipitation Event or the Northern Monsoon. The first name implied that it was a unique disaster that would not be repeated, while the second implied that it was the first occurrence of a new annual event.

By whatever name, it came to an end in early November. The bands of rain retreated north, around the Arctic Circle, and turned to sleet and freezing rain, then to snow. In Germany, the Netherlands, and the Scandinavian states, nine million people had been rendered homeless by flooding. They would need to spend the winter somewhere warmer, until their homes could be rebuilt. The northern countries sent emergency funds to France, Spain, Portugal, Italy, and Greece to help those countries look after their people.

NOVEMBER 6:

IT WAS THE DAY AFTER Election Day across the nation, but for Carrie in Virginia it was just another day at the office. Right now she was talking with a congressman and a naval official. The congressman was doing most of the talking, which gave her an excuse to let her mind wander.

Last night she had considered staying up until she was sure who the next president was going to be, but it still hadn't been resolved at 1 a.m. and forty-five was too old to be pulling an all-nighter when you had to work the next day, especially if all you were going to do was sit there and watch events unfold that you had no power to alter. Anyway, watching Virginia's results was a nail-biter for any Democrat—results from the northern counties always came in last.

Just as well she'd gotten some sleep. The morning's news wasn't great. They were going to recount the votes in Ohio and Florida one more time, but it looked like Pratt had won.

The system was what it was. The Founding Fathers might never have intended a permanent two-party duopoly for the nation, but if they had, they would have done nothing different. The White House was the biggest prize in politics, and in the race for it there was no silver medal. *We keep waiting for the Demographics Fairy to just hand us the nation wrapped up with a bow,* thought Carrie, *and it keeps... almost happening. And meanwhile we keep tripping over our own feet, or each other's feet.*

Unlike George W. Bush or Donald Trump, Pratt seemed like a real administrator. You couldn't count on him to turn everything he touched into shit. That might not be good news for the Democratic Party—or for her specifically if she was going to be running against him in four years—but at least it was good news for the country. Anyway, with the Democrats holding a one-seat majority in the Senate and the GOP holding a fourteen-seat majority in the House, it was an open question how much of his agenda Pratt would actually be able to get through Congress… especially since a lot of Republicans didn't like him all that much.

As it happened, Steven Radcliffe, R-VA, was one of those Republicans. He had run unopposed this year, which meant he didn't have to spend today recuperating. He was maybe thirty, with a glossy head of blond hair, and looked fresh out of college. Carrie felt old just looking at him.

Finally deciding to let somebody else get a word in edgewise, Radcliffe turned to the naval officer with an ingratiating smile on his face. "So what's the good word, Admiral?" Bryan Kovalchuk commanded Naval Station Norfolk, but he was a captain, not an admiral. Neither he nor Carrie bothered pointing this out.

"Weather permitting, we can have the base rebuilt by June of next year," said Kovalchuk. "But there's a problem."

"What's the problem?"

"Have you looked at the latest projections from the IPCC?"

Carrie nodded. Radcliffe rolled his eyes.

"Then you know that fifty years from now, we're not expecting there to be much left of the base—or the city of Norfolk, for that matter."

"Even if we accept that, fifty years is a long time," put in Radcliffe.

"Yes, but between now and then, it's going to cost more and more money just to keep the base operational. We've been asking Congress for years to allow us to prepare for sea level rise, but responses have been negative. And we're not just worried about rising sea level any more—or rather, not just the direct effect of sea level on the base itself. We're also anticipating an indirect effect, where the city will be less and less able to support the facility. Essential services are going to start disappearing."

"So what's your recommendation?"

"Shut it down now."

"Shut down what?"

"Naval Station Norfolk."

"*What??!?*" said Radcliffe. If you listened close enough, you could actually hear the extra punctuation marks.

"Seriously, that's my advice," said Kovalchuk. "Abandon it. Use the money you save on it to get some of the other bases ready."

Carrie blinked.

"We're the U.S. Navy," he said. "We can fight any other power on the sea and win, but we can't fight the sea itself. There are port facilities we can reconstruct to cope with sea level rise, but Norfolk isn't one of them. It's too low."

"Out of the question," said Radcliffe. "Do you have any idea how many local jobs depend on the base? Pull out of Norfolk and you basically kill the city."

"Speaking as someone who used to have one of those jobs, I'm not crazy about the idea myself," said Carrie. "But from the sound of things, the city is doomed anyway. If we had a better idea of where sea level is going to end up a hundred years from now, we could find a location for a new city and move everything there."

"I'm sorry, Admiral," said Radcliffe. "I represent my constituents. I don't represent the Navy. We can't let you do this."

NOVEMBER 28:

RODRICK FREITAG'S HOUSE HAD MADE it through Gordon undamaged. It was too far north for the wind and too high up for the storm surge. Which made it the perfect place for the Bradshaws and both sets of their grandparents to spend Thanksgiving. Except for the fact that it was a small house, and not really built to accommodate nine extra people. Even getting the various cars and vans in the driveway was a complicated sliding-tiles game.

So of course, out of all possible ways to prepare the turkeys, Rod and Chelsey had chosen the one most likely to set the crowded little house on fire. They were deep-frying both of them.

In the interests of life and property, Isabel was overseeing the process. First, when the turkeys were taken out of the beer brine she measured the remaining brine and used a little Archimedean logic to estimate their volume, so she knew exactly how much oil would go in the fryer. Then she spent a full hour drying them, inside and out, at one point using a hair dryer.

The sun was setting, and Isabel was outside, finally getting the second turkey ready to lower into the fryer. She'd turned off the burner and added a little more peanut oil to replace whatever had evaporated.

Just as she had it on the hanger, Rod came out. He spent a few moments checking the first turkey to make sure it had cooled enough, then sidled over to Isabel.

She had to admit that he was a good-looking guy. Tall, reasonably fit, blue eyes, dark hair, conventionally attractive features. At some point he'd gotten a spray-on tan, but he'd had the sense not to repeat the procedure and it was steadily fading. And he'd agreed to host Thanksgiving this year. Possibly he had other good qualities as well, but Isabel didn't know what they were.

"Smells good," said Rod.

Isabel nodded.

Rod patted her on the back. "You're doing great," he said, in case Isabel needed his reassurance.

Then his hand began fingering its way down her spine toward her butt. Using one hand to keep the hanger with the fifteen-pound bird on it up in the air, Isabel removed his hand from her back with the other and inserted it into his coat pocket with a little shake of her head, just enough to let him know *I'm going to keep things civil, but don't do that again.*

Rod stepped back a pace, smirked and shrugged as if to say *can't fault a guy for trying.* Isabel gave him a look that said *if you try that on Kristen I will personally rip off your dick, staple it to your forehead and sell you to a sideshow as the Human Unicorn.* Or at least that was the message she was going for. Some of the nuances may have been lost. Whatever message it did send was enough to convince Rod to take the cooked turkey and go back inside.

Didn't see that coming, she thought. Isabel had already disliked Rod on general principles. She felt a little better knowing her dislike was fully justified. And what had he been thinking? She had never shown him anything but basic politeness, and to be honest, not much of that. She wasn't as good-looking as either of her sisters, nor as blonde, nor as big-breasted. Her butt was bigger, for what that was worth. Had the thing with the bear and being on Yuschak's stupid show made her seem like more of a catch? Was Rod getting bored with Chelsey? Or did he get off on making women uncomfortable? Or did he just always have to try?

He better not try it again. At least Brad of the North had kept his hands to himself, except when he'd stuck one of them in harm's way by mistake.

Speaking of Chelsey, her sister came out. She wasn't wearing her usual heels, but the mass of dark blond curls on her head added a couple inches to her height all by itself. She took a cigarette out of her pocket.

"Don't even think about it," said Isabel. "We got aerosolized peanut oil over here. The last thing you want to be doing is lighting up."

Chelsey muttered a curse and put it away.

"I thought you quit," said Isabel.

"I had to quit when I had Jourdain," she said. "It's staying quit that's a problem."

"I still say if you need it that bad, you should vape."

"And I still say vaping is birdseed*." Chelsey sighed. "I'm thinking of getting a Jellicoe treatment."

"I've heard those work pretty well," said Isabel. "I think they're really expensive, though. Like, ten to fifteen thousand dollars, and insurance doesn't cover them. I mean, you would eventually make the money back just from not buying cigarettes, but it'd take a couple years."

"What are you talking about?" said Chelsey. "I get people trying to sell me discount Jellicoes every time I look at my email. They're five or six thousand at the most."

Emailed discount offers of medical services. Yep. Chelsey was Chelseying again.

"Chelsey?"

"Yeah?"

"You know how I've pretty much given up trying to talk you out of doing stupid things?"

"Yeah... what, you think this is stupid?"

"Having a change made to your brain would be risky, but it might be worth it. Having it done by the lowest bidder—that would be stupid. Also, Pratt's been talking about grants or tax breaks or something for addiction therapy. If you can wait till next year, you might be able to get some of the costs covered."

---

* "Birdseed" is an adjective meaning "hip, urban and somewhat snobbish." It refers to pearl millet, tef, and wattleseeds, which have replaced arugula and quinoa as the fashionable purchases of upscale grocery shoppers, mostly because they're things that still grow well in California despite the persistent droughts.

ISABEL HAD TO ADMIT, DEEP-FRIED turkey was delicious. And her mom's homemade cranberry relish was always good.

All the same, there had been one topic everybody had been avoiding all through dinner. Finally, as the pumpkin pie was being served, Isabel bit the bullet.

"What's the situation with the house?"

Her father put his fork down, shut his eyes and rubbed his forehead for a few moments.

"It's bad," he said. "Flood insurance might—might—cover the lost furniture… if I ever get the check, that is. I'm not holding my breath. I paid for the car and truck repairs myself. But if I want to get the house fixed up properly, I'll need to take out a loan. And that's going to mean collateral. The only thing I could use for that is the *Mary Lynn*."

"Why don't you just take out another mortgage?" said Isabel.

"I tried that," said her father. "Turns out I can't. The house isn't mortgageable any more. Rod calls it 'bluelining.'" Rod nodded his head. "Means they won't accept it as collateral."

"Have you gone to another bank?"

Pop rolled his eyes. "Would I be sitting here bellyaching if I hadn't?" he said. "I've been to seven different banks. Nobody wants to touch the place."

"It shouldn't be legal," said Mom. "It's discrimination."

Pop shook his head. "If they just did it to the blacks, that'd be discrimination and there'd be hell to pay. But they're doing it to everybody who lives right on the water, so I guess that makes it all right."

Mom nodded. "The Shermans in McDaniel have the same problem," she said.

"Who else?"

It turned out Pop knew a lot of people in this situation. As Isabel listened to him, a picture formed in her mind.

Suppose you were a banker. One day, someone came in and asked to take out a mortgage on a nice little house on the Bay like Pop's. Problem was, when you looked it up online it turned out that according to IPCC projections, in forty or fifty years the ocean waves would be getting into the crawlspace at high tide, undermining the foundations, rotting the floorboards, and generally bringing new meaning to the phrase "underwater mortgage." That was assuming, of course, that another storm surge didn't come along and get the job done early.

In theory, this shouldn't be a problem. After all, the house would still have decades of use in it. Isabel's car was certain to be worthless in twenty years and might be totaled tomorrow, but she still drove it. And unless you were a very young banker, by the time it washed into the ocean you'd have long since retired. The only thing that had really changed was that the house wasn't a long-term investment any more. You'd want to make sure the borrower finished paying for it while it was still habitable, of course.

But there was a problem after all. With a normal mortgage, the worst thing that could happen was that the borrower would be unable or unwilling to pay and you'd have to foreclose on the property and sell it to recoup your losses. In this case, if you had to take the house it was an open question whether you'd ever be able to sell it again. Your bank could easily get stuck holding the bag while the value of the house dropped to zero. Normally, the way to deal with a high-risk investment was to raise the interest rate—but you wouldn't want to do that here. That would make foreclosure more likely, not less.

And with every passing year, the risk would grow greater. With every fraction of an inch the ocean rose, the house would be harder to sell, and the temptation would grow for the borrower to stop sinking money into it and walk away, leaving you once again the proud owner of a worthless property… especially since the borrower could access the same projections you could and knew just as much as you did about how much time the house had left.

Suddenly, all that "mortgage forgiveness" right after Hurricane Gordon made a lot more sense. That wasn't forgiveness—it was abandonment.

Chelsey turned to Rod. "Honey, haven't you managed to sell some beach houses even with this ICP whatever thing?"

"I have," he said. "Mostly to retirees. I'm very upfront with them. 'You know, this house probably isn't going to be around in thirty years.' 'Me either. What's your point?'" He laughed. "Of course, even there it helps if the property isn't already damaged."

"So just use the *Mary Lynn*," Chelsey said, turning to Pop. "I don't see the problem."

Pop shook his head. "You haven't heard?"

"Oh boy. What else is wrong?"

"Algae bloom," he said flatly. "It's already outside Rock Hall, it's spreading and we're seeing a lot of dead fish along with it. Last time they said it was pfiesteria—this time they're not even pretending to know. See, when the rains from Gordon hit Pennsylvania, they had to open all the gates on the Conowingo. A lot of silt got into the upper Bay. A lot of nutrients."

"How bad is it?"

"We can kiss the rest of crab season goodbye, and at least half the oyster season. Depends on what DNR says… which means we're probably screwed." Her father had a waterman's ingrained distrust of the Department of Natural Resources. He also had a total inability to say anything stronger than "screwed" while his daughters were in the room. "Bottom line is, if I take out a loan I might not be able to meet the interest in the next twelve months. And if the skipjack is my collateral…"

"I wish I could help out more," said Mom, "but by the time we got the shop repaired, half our customers had gotten their boats fixed somewhere else. And with this algae bloom, it'll be a while before anybody needs repairs."

Nobody had much of an appetite at this point. Of course, they were all stuffed to the gills, so no harm done. Isabel spent the rest of the evening helping Chelsey rein in little Jourdain, who had all a two-year-old's crazy energy.

THAT NIGHT, EVEN THE TRYPTOPHAN in the turkey wasn't helping Isabel sleep. Also not helping was the fact that she was lying on the living room floor, next to her paternal grandparents, both of whom snored like legendary beasts.

And not helping most of all was the situation with Pop's house. And the Shermans' house. And most of the other houses right on the Bay. And… actually everything built less than four feet above the local high-tide line on every coastline on Earth. Those had once been among the most desirable locations in the world. How many trillions of dollars' worth of equity had been tied up in all that property? And what would happen when that money no longer existed even potentially?

The more Isabel tried to see the big picture, the more it scared her. Civilization, led by the banks, was beginning its retreat from the coasts. Like climate change itself, the process would be well underway by the time anyone could see it happening.

OVER THE FIRST THREE WEEKS of December, a series of nor'easters hit the East Coast from Labrador down to Cape Cod, with a force equal to some tropical storms. One of the worst storms managed a direct hit on the city of Boston, although Winthrop Bank and Logan Airport took the brunt of the assault.

Then the weather began to ease. By Christmas, the storm factory in the North Atlantic had ceased production... for the moment.

YEAR FOUR

WATER ALWAYS WINS

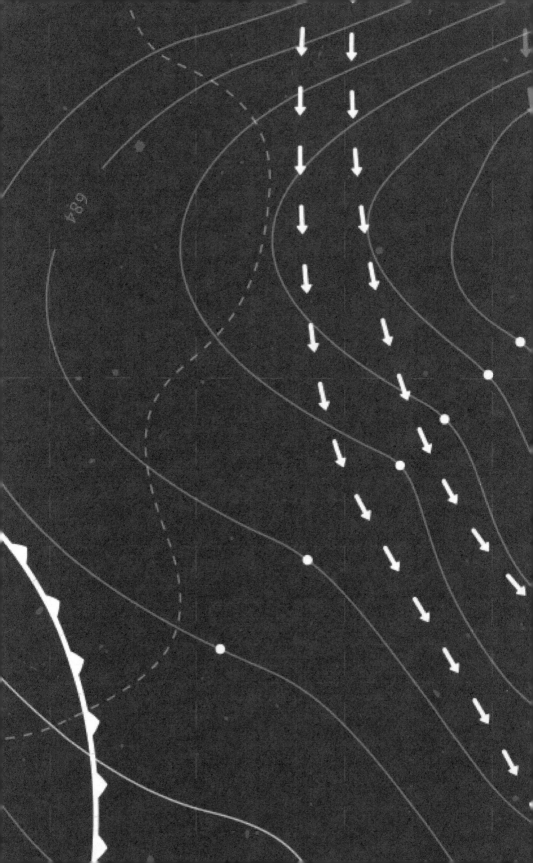

THE GOOD NEWS WAS THAT *many cities and towns in northern Norway had been rebuilt with roofs over the streets and sidewalks, to allow them to cope with a snowfall of eight or nine feet, and with larger sewers to cope with all that snow melting in a couple of weeks during the spring. The bad news was that the heavy snow was going further south this year, over all Scandinavia, Scotland, and northern Russia and Canada.*

In the Antarctic summer, the last traces of the Larsen Ice Shelf broke up and drifted out to sea at the beginning of the year. This was thrown into the shade a few weeks later by news from the other side of the continent. Since the end of November, warm seawater had been flowing under the Totten Glacier through deep troughs in the sea floor, slipping between the ice and the bedrock, unmooring, and lubricating it at the edge. On January 15, with almost no warning, the seaward end of the glacier broke up and flowed out to sea.

This caused a chain reaction for hundreds of miles inland. Over the course of the next two weeks, more than ten billion tons of ice slid into the Southern Ocean. It was only a tenth of a percent of the glacier's true mass, but it was enough to raise sea levels by just over an inch.

MARCH 24:

IT WAS TOO EARLY IN the morning, after a long, late night of work. Carrie poured herself a cup of fresh-brewed chyq,* sipped and made a face. The stuff

---

* Pronounced "chick." Genetically modified chicory, engineered in response to declining coffee harvests worldwide.

tasted like coffee with too much sugar and had the texture of coffee with too much creamer. But it had plenty of caffeine, and it wouldn't do to be gouging the taxpayers over the small stuff at an event like this.

First, she checked the news feed from yesterday evening, which she hadn't had time to do yesterday. As it happened, there was nothing about global warming or sea level rise yesterday. Apart from Pratt's efforts to wind down the drug war—which was a pretty big deal in itself—the biggest story was that Vice President Quillen had just tested positive for Huntington's disease. He seemed to be confident that it wouldn't be a problem. "FDR was confined to a wheelchair," he said. "JFK had Addison's disease. They could manage the duties of the presidency. If necessary, I will endeavor to live up to the example they set. In the meantime, I'm quite sure I can handle the duties of the vice-presidency." The other news item of the moment was that the Supreme Court had at long last completed its judicial review, and had concluded that De L'Air diamonds were indeed diamonds and could be marketed as such, and that it would be a violation of the First Amendment for Congress to try to stop them from doing this.

Then she checked her messages from various parts of the government, to make sure there wasn't anything she was missing. Trying to manage a conference and the Commonwealth of Virginia at the same time was not a job for people who were into sleep.

Then she checked the news from her friends and family. Thel wanted to bring a boy named Ethan to the governor's mansion this weekend. *Well, she is getting to be about that age.*

Then she took a shower and got dressed. The officers' quarters of what was left of Naval Station Norfolk were not exactly luxurious, but she could do without for a little while.

CARRIE COULDN'T TAKE ALL THE credit for the Norfolk Conference. It had been her idea, but the Navy was doing most of the work involved in hosting it—and that was a lot of work, considering they were holding it in what was supposed to be a working facility that Congress would neither let them close nor give them the money to adequately fix. The money had come from several different foundations and rich donors.

The point of the conference was to develop a nationwide plan for dealing with sea level rise. To that end, she and the Navy had invited engineers, environmentalists, accountants, lawyers, and anybody else whose expertise might come in handy. More than half of them were participating remotely, which saved a lot of money and a certain amount of fossil fuels and eased the strain on the battered facilities. Now the second week of the Conference had begun, everyone was sorted into their respective committees, and things were going... well, they were *going*, but not very fast.

The trouble with committees wasn't that they were all slow and inefficient by nature. The trouble was that no two committees ever worked at the same speed, which made them very hard to coordinate. The Committee on Ports and Shipping was a little ahead of schedule, with some fairly realistic-looking plans for rebuilding the nation's port facilities to allow for future rises in sea level. The Committee on Seawalls wasn't far behind. The Committee on Wildlife and Wild Lands Preservation, which Carrie had been counting on to help the Seawalls Committee by setting aside new areas for wetlands, had deadlocked over the question of how much to help animals and plants moving north. The Water and Sewer Committee was... experiencing some sort of blockage. The Committee on Taxation and Bond Sales Planning couldn't even start work until the other committees started giving them estimates of how much all this was going to cost. And if the Property Law Committee didn't get off its ass and *do something*, the rest of the conference was just going to turn pirate and start ravaging the coasts... on paper, at least.

And then there was the Environmental Justice Committee... emphasis on "was." Their goal had been to make sure that whatever steps the Conference agreed on wouldn't disadvantage those who were already disadvantaged enough. To that end, one of them produced a map of the U.S. coasts which showed, at the voting-precinct level, the percentages of people in each community living below the poverty line. Another one produced a similar map which showed the percentages of minorities living in those communities. Then they tried to decide which one to use. After about three hours of intense discussion, they all agreed to stomp out of the room in tears and vow never to speak to each other again.

Carrie was determined that in whatever solutions they came up with here, some thought would be given to those who most needed help or were most likely to be shortchanged. From the looks of things, she was going to have do that all by herself.

MARCH 25:

IT WAS JUST THE RIGHT time in the afternoon to make the evening news. The auditorium was one of the few parts of the base that had been fully refurbished, which was a good thing under the circumstances.

This wasn't going to be the worst press conference Carrie had ever held. That honor still belonged to the one where she'd had to explain to a bewildered press corps that she and her racist sister-in-law were *two different people*. Once you'd been through something like that, nothing else was ever quite as bad.

This one was going to be pretty rough, though. Ports and Shipping and Seawalls had completed their work ahead of schedule, and, in the spirit of openness and transparency, put it online for public comment. Now Carrie was going to have to explain it to the reporters. Some of them hadn't even looked at it, but wouldn't let that stop them from asking what they thought were keen and penetrating questions. Others had already looked at it more carefully than she had.

"Before I start taking questions," she said, "I'd like to start by showing you what we've come up with." Carrie gestured toward the giant screen that took up a quarter of the stage. It was the most detailed topographic map she'd ever seen—if anybody ever tried to print it out, it would stretch for dozens of miles. From the mouth of the Rio Grande to the mouth of the St. Croix, every beach and marsh, every creek and culvert, every subtle rise and dip in the land was represented here somewhere. There were similar maps of the West Coast, Hawaii, and the more inhabited parts of Alaska.

Carrie adjusted a control, and the display zoomed in on the cluster of cities around the mouth of the Chesapeake. Parts of the cities, a little back from the shoreline and three to five feet above sea level, were protected by seawalls. "So this is what we have planned for Norfolk, Newport News, the beaches, the whole area," she said. "The rebuilding of the ports should keep them operational through at least seven feet of sea level rise, which is more than we're expecting for the next fifty years or so. That will give our grandchildren time to decide what to do next, based on—yes?" A woman in the front row had her hand up.

"Jane Fuentes, American News and Media Foundation*," she said. "What

---

* Since it is (or at least could theoretically be) of great benefit to the public, increasingly hard to monetize effectively, and nobody really wants it to be run by the government, the American news

are the seawalls for?"

"For one thing, we have to worry about storm surges… like the one that pretty much flattened this city last fall. More importantly, we don't know how accurate the IPCC estimates are going to turn out to be. We've already had one nasty surprise this year when the Totten Glacier started slipping. Think of these walls as an insurance policy." What Carrie didn't say was that their real purpose was to draw a line and send a message—*that which is within these walls is worth protecting. If it is destroyed, we will rebuild it. We will not abandon it this year, this decade, or this century. We definitely won't pull that "mortgage forgiveness" crap the banks pulled in Virginia Beach and here in Norfolk.* Wind and wave would never get that message, of course, but the real estate market just might… and if it did, the walls would pay for themselves long before they were ever needed.

"If I might follow up, it seems like the walls are protecting ground that will be in danger forty to sixty years from now, not ground that's in danger right now. Why is that?"

"First of all, we need a buffer zone. Everything at the edge of the land right now, everything the coast is made of—rocks, sand, salt marsh, mangrove swamp—all of it is resistant to erosion. Not perfectly resistant, you understand—anybody who's looked at beach erosion knows that—but a lot more so than plain old dirt. Unfortunately, rising sea level means that in a lot of places, plain old dirt is what's going to be exposed to the ocean. Eventually, of course, the soluble stuff will get washed away and what's left will be more rocks and marshes and such, but most of us are not prepared to wait that long. We'll need to consult with local wildlife experts to develop plans for new wetlands—planting the right marsh grasses and so on—but the bottom line is that the shoreline is going to have to be reconstructed every ten years or so to respond to the rising ocean.

"Second, we can't protect everything. We've spent a lot of time thinking about what can be protected, what most needs to be protected and how long it's going to take. Now, how many of you can visualize a four-dimensional matrix of sea level rise, construction time, and land value estimates?"

There was a silence as deep as the tomb.

Carrie smiled. "Me either. That's why I brought in all these experts in the first place."

---

media has largely been taken over by nonprofit foundations.

"There are several fairly important cities that don't appear to be protected at all," said another reporter. "Why is that?"

"You'd have to ask the experts about that," she said. "Do we have one here? Let's see…" Carrie activated a connection to the Committee on Seawalls. A young woman with blue eyes and a light-brown ponytail was sitting at the computer. She was probably one of the students working with the engineering team.

"You're following this, right?" The student nodded. "How does your team answer the question?"

The student sighed. "I'm afraid the answer is that some cities can't be saved," she said. "Miami, for instance. It's built on limestone, and limestone is porous. You can build walls a thousand feet high, but the water's just going to flow right under them. And in the case of New Orleans, you'd have to build the walls on top of silt… which would be compacted by the weight, which would cause the walls to sink and you'd be back where you started. I'm sorry." She glanced in Carrie's direction with a slightly aggrieved look on her face, as if to say *there, I just pronounced a death sentence on two major cities in front of half the D.C. press corps. Anything else you'd like me to do on your behalf?*

Another reporter stood up. "Brentwood Smith, TKB Foundation," he said. "Do you think it's the job of the federal government to implement this plan?"

"Who said anything about the feds?" said Carrie, smiling a little. "The idea here was just to put together the best plan we can come up with. Who implements it, at what level, isn't a question we're looking at. That said, some states would be better able to do this on their own than others. Louisiana, for example, has 7,721 miles of tidal shoreline. Pennsylvania has eighty-nine miles and a slightly larger state budget. Now let's take a question from online." She went through a list of online reporters and independent bloggers until she found someone who seemed less likely than most to throw her a gotcha question.

"Taylor Pagonis of *Inside the Street*. Whoever does this, it's still going to involve buying an enormous amount of land. How do you do that at a price that won't either bankrupt the buyer or the sellers?"

"That's a good question. The honest answer is that we don't have an answer to it yet. This plan is still a work in progress." The really honest answer was that Carrie strongly suspected there wasn't an answer. Either everybody who owned property along the coast was going to go bankrupt, or the rest of the planet was going to go bankrupt trying to bail them out. Or both.

IN THE PACIFIC OCEAN, THE cool phase of the ENSO—the phase called La Niña— was underway. This brought some extra rainfall to the Pacific Northwest, but California, Nevada, and Arizona still suffered from lower-than-"normal" precipitation.

Between the Sierras and the Rockies, wildfires raged over the land. Eastward as far as the 95th meridian, crop-killing drought conditions held sway from Canada to the Gulf of Mexico.

In the southeast, rain was lower than average, but adequate. That wasn't the problem. The problem was the heat. By mid-May, everything from Texas to the Carolinas was experiencing highs in the mid-90s, and things got worse as May turned into June.

There was still rain—but when the air was dry, it was very dry. In the Ozarks and the southern Appalachians, forest fires started easily and spread rapidly.

MAY 23:

COMMENCEMENT WAS OVER. ISABEL WAS, officially, a college graduate. With honors and everything.

She gave one last hug to Ian and Chris, another one to Deon, and to Ikuko, Zoshia, and Mei, exchanged an awkwardly polite nod with Laurie, and… that was it. Isabel had a feeling she was supposed to have made more friends than this during her time here. On the other hand, the whole family had showed up—Mom, Pop, Chelsey, Scott, Kristen, Jourdain, and all four grandparents.

Well, almost the whole family. "Rod sends hugs and kisses, but he's trying to close a big deal this weekend," said Chelsey. Isabel nodded. She had no problem with Rod's absence, and she liked his hugs and kisses better in verbal form and relayed via someone else.

Speaking of hugs and kisses, Jourdain got things started by wrapping her little arms around Isabel's waist. "Ann-Is-Bell!" she said, that being as far as she could go toward "Aunt Isabel" at age three. It was hard to tell at this point, but the little lady seemed to be inheriting a lot of her father's looks. Isabel just hoped she didn't inherit his personality, and maybe not too much of her mother's.

Then she was in a clump of her family's embraces—Mom, who was all choked up and had actual tears streaming down her cheeks, Pop, who squeezed her around the shoulders with arms hardened by decades of heavy use and said, "You always could do anything you set your mind to," Kristen who at some point had turned into the beauty of the family, and Scott, who was now about as tall as Pop—wait, when had that happened? And the grandparents, all in their seventies but still healthy enough to give Isabel a certain amount of confidence in her own genes.

"Ready to start adulting?" said Kristen.

"I think so," said Isabel.

"I should hope so," said Chelsey. "You've been adulting since you were about nine, chunkybutt."

Isabel rode in the back seat of Mom's minivan, with Jourdain snuggled between her and Chelsey. Everyone else in the family had tried to dress up at least a little, but her older sister was wearing a T-shirt and fanning her belly with the bottom of it, as if trying to get some air flowing between her outsized boobs. She gave a little sigh of contentment.

"You're in a good mood," said Isabel.

"Oh yeah," said Chelsey. "I just want you to know… don't take this the wrong way, but I'm really, really glad I didn't take your advice."

"Um… what advice was that?"

"On Jellicoe treatments," she said. "Turns out the government's not gonna pay you to get Jellicoed unless you've got a serious hard-drug problem. So I went ahead and got a discount treatment. It's supposed to take at least three weeks to get the full effect, but it's already been two weeks and I feel great!"

"Well, I'm glad it worked."

There was an awkward silence—or not quite a silence, since Pop had the radio on. As always in the Bradshaw household, it was tuned to whichever NOAA weather channel had the best reception in this area. That was what radios were for if you worked on the water and your retirement plans included being alive.

"So when do we get to meet this Hunter?" said Pop.

"He'll be meeting us at the restaurant," said Isabel, hoping Hunter wouldn't be late. "Turn left up ahead."

YOU COULD HAVE A DECENT meal at Celebrazione alone or with a date, but, as the name implied, the place really specialized in big gatherings. Knowing that the Bradshaws wouldn't be the only family in town celebrating graduation right now, Isabel had made this reservation three months in advance. The minute Pop opened the door and she was greeted by the smell coming from the kitchen—a combination of simmering tomato sauce, baking bread, wine, sharp cheese, garlic, fennel, and rosemary—she was glad she'd chosen this place.

Isabel was seated at the head of a long table, with Pop on her right and Hunter on her left. Scott sat at the far end, surrounded by grandparents. She and Hunter were both having the appetizer, wattle noodles and steamed Swiss chard in a heavy cream sauce.

"They didn't have this when I worked here," said Isabel, swirling the coffee-colored noodles onto her fork.

"God, that's birdseed," said Chelsey, seated on the other side of Hunter. "Literally. Remember when wattles were those things hanging on old people's necks?" She turned to Jourdain, who was sitting in a high chair, and playfully rubbed the pink skin under her daughter's chin.

"Don't knock it," said Isabel. "Pound for pound, wattleseed flour's got more protein than steak."

"Please tell me you're not turning vegan on us."

"Not until they can make soft-shelled crabs out of tofu, I'm not."

"What's good here?" said Hunter.

"I'm having the linguini with house mussels, but for you I'd recommend the veal marsala." Hunter had a shellfish allergy. He could be in the same room with it, but couldn't eat it. That was going to be a problem if she ever brought him home—her parents would hardly know how to be hospitable if they couldn't throw a crab feast.

Isabel was hoping Pop wouldn't start questioning Hunter on his future plans. What happened instead while they were waiting for the food was almost as depressing—the conversation turned to the situation on Smith Island, where Mom had grown up and her parents still lived.

That community had the same set of problems as everybody else on low-lying ground, plus the additional problems of subsidence and erosion that had been plaguing them long before sea level rise became a concern. For a lot of people, Hurricane Gordon and "mortgage forgiveness" had been the last straw. Mom-mom and Pop-pop Horton were sticking around as long as they could, but a lot of other people were trying to do what the people of Holland Island had done just over a century ago—move the whole community to the mainland, one home at a time.

Nobody was happy about this, and they were right not to be happy. Smith Island had been settled for four hundred years, plus however long the Native Americans had lived there. The state had put a lot of money into restoration efforts. The idea of abandoning it…

You calmly told Governor Camberg that Miami and New Orleans were lost causes. Now you're shedding tears over a place whose whole population could fit into one housing project in either of those cities. Parochial much?

Smith Island is different. It literally has its own accent. Last time Mom and I got to talking about Sandy, Mom slipped and said "billionahrr." If we lose it, we've lost something irreplaceable.

Right. Unlike New Orleans, which is of no cultural importance whatsoever. Especially when it comes to music or cuisine.

What about the Smith Island cake? It's the official state dessert. And it's delicious, I might add.

It's a stack of pancakes glued together with frosting.

No, it's not. You have to bake it.

Which is why Mom stopped making them—having to wash ten baking pans at once was a ridiculous amount of work. On a good day, Isabel could deal with her inner critic by getting it sidetracked.

About this time, the food arrived. The mussels came first. They were quite simple—smoked mussels in olive oil with garlic, rosemary, and sea salt.

Hunter took a sniff. "There's rosemary, that's for remembrance, there's garlic, that's for vampires," he said. Chelsey laughed out loud at this, although it wasn't the kind of joke she usually liked.

They managed to make it until dessert before the inevitable happened.

"So, Hunter," said Pop, "what are your plans for the fall? Besides college?"

Hunter stared into his brownie for a few seconds.

"Um… I'm… not… going back in the fall," he finally said.

"You're dropping out?"

"Not dropping out. My folks… their 401(k) lost a lot of money. I think it was the property values crashing along the coast that did it… Anyway, they can't afford to keep paying my way through college. I might be able to get into a tech school in a few years and finish my degree."

"Nothing wrong with that," Isabel said quickly. "Kristen's going to nursing school."

"So do you have a job lined up?"

"Uh…" Hunter glanced around as if looking for a cue card.

"There's a consulting firm down in Louisiana that does a lot of work for the Army," said Isabel. "I've already got a position with them starting this summer. There should be something available for Hunter in the area."

"Excuse me," said Hunter. "Gotta go to the bathroom." As he left, Pop stared at his back, then turned to Isabel as if to say *Really? Him? You're telling me that's the best you could do?*

Rather than respond, Isabel sat in silence eating for the next few minutes. This was what drove her nuts about her parents sometimes—they expected her to be an independent young woman *and* to find a man who could take care of her. You'd think one or the other would be good enough.

Speaking of people who'd found men to take care of them, Chelsey was quieter than usual as she ate her gelato, nodding her head as if listening to something slow and pleasant on her earpiece. She wasn't wearing an earpiece.

Out the corner of her eye, Isabel saw Hunter peek his head around the corner. He beckoned her closer.

"What is it?" said Isabel as soon as she was close enough to him and out of earshot of her family.

"I got a question," said Hunter, looking more like a guy who had to deliver bad news than a guy who had a question. "About Chelsey…"

"What about her?"

"Does she have a drug problem or something?"

"Not that I know of," said Isabel. "Why?"

"My brother had a heroin problem for a while," he said. "That's what he looked like when he was high. Exactly like that."

Isabel glanced at Chelsey again. She did have kind of a blissed-out look to her, but…

"Um… she's eating gelato."

"Yeah."

"I kind of doubt this place is putting heroin in their gelato," said Isabel. "Also, Kristen's having the same thing and she seems perfectly normal."

"I'm just telling you what I'm seeing. I can't explain it."

Just at that moment, Chelsey got up to go to the bathroom. Mom had always said girls ought to go to the bathroom in pairs, just to be safe. Isabel didn't often follow this rule, but there was definitely something strange happening with her older sister right now. This didn't seem like the best time to leave her alone. "Excuse me," said Isabel.

As soon as she was in the bathroom, Isabel realized something was wrong, but it wasn't quite what she was expecting. There was a distinct sound of groaning and gasping and grunting coming from one of the stalls. It was definitely Chelsey's voice, and it sounded as if she were in pain, or making some colossal effort... had she not been eating enough fiber?

"You okay in there?" said Isabel.

There was a long, anxious moment before Chelsey gasped out, "Fine... fine."

Not wanting to waste a perfectly good trip to the bathroom, Isabel started washing her hands. While she was halfway through this, Chelsey came out of the toilet stall looking... well, flushed. And also rather pleased with herself. And she was sweating, which was strange because the bathroom, like the rest of the restaurant, was air-conditioned.

"You're not going to believe this," she said. Then she leaned in and whispered: *"I just had an orgasm while I was taking a shit!"*

Then Chelsey started laughing.

She was still laughing five minutes later.

WHAT ISABEL KNEW ABOUT THE Jellicoe treatment was what everyone knew. It blocked the brain from releasing dopamine in response to certain stimuli—nicotine, say—while at the same time encouraging the brain to rebuild the reward pathways that were damaged by the process of addiction. Doing a little online research on the subject later that night, she learned three more things.

The first thing she learned was that the Jellicoe treatment was only ever meant to be used for otherwise untreatable and life-threatening addictions, not the occasional cigarette craving. Given its 70 percent success rate, of course, it was too much in demand for that.

The second thing she learned was that that 70 percent success rate only applied if the procedure was performed by trained neurochemists. With the kind of discount treatment Chelsey had been fool enough to get, the success rate was about half that. In 40 percent of such cases, the rebuilding of the brain's reward pathways was only partly successful, leaving the patient in a state of cold, gray dysphoria that their drug of choice could no longer free them from. That left the one in four cases where the treatment worked too well—those pathways became so strong that the brain magnified every simple pleasure into something overwhelming, so that, for example, one could literally get high on a good dessert. While obviously enjoyable, this made it very hard for the patient to function on a day-to-day basis.

The third thing she learned was that it was irreversible.

THROUGHOUT THAT SUMMER, IT WAS common for the daily highs in the Deep South to be well over a hundred. In many plants—including corn, wheat, rice, soybeans, and other major food crops—when the temperature gets that high, and especially when it goes above 104° Fahrenheit (40° centigrade) things start to go wrong. Pollination fails. Photosynthesis stops. In dry conditions, the soil loses its moisture and the plant dehydrates.

Agriculture reporters were calling it "heat kill," but that wasn't quite accurate. The crops weren't dying. But every week they were losing hours—sometimes days—of growth.

JULY 19:

IT WAS WITH WELL-CONCEALED ANNOYANCE that Carrie watched Gov. Vince Lofton leave the hotel. He was chairing the National Governors Association this year, but that wasn't going to stop him from going back to Oklahoma City in time for church the next morning. Because apparently, Springfield, Illinois didn't have churches. Or something. Anyway, now Carrie would be running this little affair until tomorrow.

She headed to the cafeteria, but not to eat. A week ago she'd gotten a note from Gabrielle saying that Sandra Symcox—founder, owner, and CEO of De L'Air Diamonds—wanted to talk with her in person. Since this was someone who'd chipped in to fund the Norfolk Conference, Carrie was more than willing to do so. There were no unused conference rooms in the hotel this year—what with one thing and another, state governors had a lot on their minds—and meeting anyone in her hotel room would have raised too many eyebrows for all the wrong reasons. So… the cafeteria at three, and hopefully nothing would come up requiring her attention now she was suddenly running this show.

Just as she was about to sit down, a voice behind her said "Governor Camberg?"

Carrie turned around. There was a girl standing there with a briefcase.

"Can I help you?"

"I think so," she said, smiling. The girl… might not actually be a girl, now that Carrie got a better look at her. Although she barely came up to Carrie's chin and appeared to be no older than Thel, there was something in the look on her face that suggested a grown-up mind at work. She was also dressed like a grown-up, or possibly a very sharp high school senior applying for an internship, in taupe slacks and a white summer blouse. She had pale skin and an ash-blond ponytail, and smelled like sunscreen.

"Sandra Symcox," she said, extending a hand.

OVER COFFEE—REAL COFFEE, AND damn the expense—they talked.

"So what are your plans for next year?"

"My plan at this point is, once my term ends, to be an advocate for the Norfolk Plan. And for climate change adaptation in general." *And lose some weight. And write a book. And get ready for my run for the White House.*

"Advocacy isn't necessarily a full-time job," said Symcox, "and it doesn't come with a salary. I know you're not hurting for money, but…"

"You sound like you've got something in mind."

"I'm setting up a foundation," she said, opening her briefcase. "It's just starting out, but I'm funding it with ten percent of my earnings and dividends." She handed over a slim folder, which Carrie assumed contained a prospectus of some kind.

Carrie took the folder, glanced through it, and put it in her own briefcase. "What's it going to do?"

"Well, as I see it, there's two basic kinds of charitable work—the kind that helps people rise out of poverty, or at least to something above a subsistence level, and there's the kind that just keeps people alive. I'm going to be spending the first couple of years just keeping people alive, then start adding on more ambitious projects.

"What I need is somebody who can go abroad and find good places to spend money—people who are doing the most good, making the most efficient use of resources, and so on. As I understand it, before you went into politics you helped your company do charity evaluations."

"I did," said Carrie, "but apart from a couple of vacations, I haven't been overseas since the Navy. I don't think I have the experience you're looking for."

Symcox smiled. "Would you like some?" she said. "Something in your résumé you can point to when people ask about your foreign policy credentials?"

She knows.

Symcox smiled bigger. "It's kind of an open secret," she said. "Everybody I talk to seems to think you're going to be running for president in a couple of years. I'm all for that. I think it's great. The mind behind the Norfolk Plan is the kind of mind we need now and we'll need a lot more later."

AS CARRIE LEFT THE MEETING, she broke into a brisk jog. Two men were having a screaming argument in the middle of the hotel lobby. It sounded bad enough that somebody was going to have to step in and referee it. In this case, "somebody" meant her.

She stepped into the lobby and got a look at the arguers. One of them was Governor Gilbert Swank of Arizona—Carrie recognized him because he looked a lot like her father, huge, fat, and red-faced. But Papa had mostly been the jolly kind of fat man, and Swank looked the opposite of jolly right now.

The other was the governor of Colorado, a skinny guy who was bald right on top of his head. His name was either LaTour or LaCour. They were screaming over each other to the point where Carrie had a hard time telling what they were arguing about, except that water was involved. A much smaller man was holding Swank's right arm and trying to talk him down.

As Carrie approached the scene of the kerfuffle, she caught references to some sort of compact, dying golf courses, and failing businesses. Then the

Colorado governor raised his voice a little higher: "If they need water so bad, why don't you just tell them to come to Grand Junction?"

That, apparently, was going too far. Swank shoved the third man aside, stepped forward and took a swing. The bald man stepped back to avoid it, tripped over a phone-charging station, and landed on his back. Carrie got between them, planted the heel of her foot against the station, grabbed Swank by his wrists and pushed against him.

"What—the hell—is *wrong*—with you?" she shouted. This was the part where Swank was supposed to realize he was acting like a lunatic and get a hold of himself. She hadn't been planning on getting into a wrestling match with him. Unfortunately, Swank started trying to force her aside at this point.

"Stay out of this, lady!" he shouted. "This doesn't concern you!" Carrie opened her mouth to respond that it did, actually, but suddenly "vice-chair of the National Governors Association" didn't seem like the right kind of authority for a job like this. "Bouncer" would have been more appropriate. She could smell his breath. There was a little bit of booze on it, but not enough to account for this.

Carrie weighed two hundred and none of your business pounds, which was a lot more than necessary for most purposes but right now was just slightly less than enough. Despite her best efforts, Swank was shoving her out of the way. Then there was a *thump* and he let go of her and collapsed on the floor, revealing a slender blonde woman in a crisp black suit standing behind him holding a heavy glass ashtray.

Swank rubbed the back of his head, pushed himself up into a sitting position and turned around, just in time for the blonde to kick one of his knees aside and stand between his sprawled legs. The shoe she was aiming at his crotch must have cost as much as Carrie's whole outfit.

"Stay. Down." Her voice was clear and firm. There was no anger in it, only command.

There was a tense moment when he just sat there, weighing the odds. Then the blonde stepped back, just in time for hotel security to emerge from the crowd.

Carrie turned to the security guards. "He needs somebody to look at him and make sure he's not hurt," she said, pointing to the bald man. Then she pointed at Swank and said, "And he needs to be turned over to the local police." It felt wrong to involve the police instead of sorting out the disagreement herself, but she was on camera. She couldn't see it, but she knew somebody here had a camera pointed at her. She couldn't be seen downplaying an assault just because the perp was a politician.

As the guards were leading the two men away, Carrie turned to the blonde, who she now recognized.

"Thank you, Governor," she said.

"You're welcome," said New York Governor Morgan.

IT WAS DINNERTIME. CARRIE HAD gotten an early seat at a table with Rafaél Tejera. The governor of New Mexico was a smallish man with leathery worker's hands and a face that both genes and sunshine had helped turn brown. He was born and raised in Las Cruces, but it was easy to picture him as the peasant his parents had been before they came to America. He was the man who'd tried to restrain Swank. Carrie was determined to find out what that argument had been about.

"You can't understand, back East, just how seriously we take water rights," said Tejera. "Water is what decides whether your property is a million dollars' worth of cotton land or a thousand dollars' worth of rangeland. It's what decides which towns can grow into cities and which ones will never be more than wide spots in the road. And there *isn't enough of it*. There never was, and now there's even less." Tejera drew a breath.

"And this year Arizona's running especially low," he said. "The Phoenix area is hardest hit—the Salt River Project is almost dry. The state's supposed to be refilling the aquifers, and instead they're draining them again. But as luck would have it, this winter Utah and Colorado got some good rain and snow, so the Colorado River is fuller than usual."

"So why not take water from there?" said Carrie.

"Ever hear of the Colorado River Compact?" said Tejera.

"I've heard it mentioned, but I don't know the details."

Tejera took a deep breath. "About a century ago," he said, "the western states got together with the federal government and agreed on how to divide the water of the Colorado River. They created the Compact. It's a complicated agreement and I won't go into too much detail—the important part is that under that agreement, Arizona is entitled to only a certain percentage of the water, and no more."

"And Swank wants to renegotiate?"

"Yes. But, of course, LaCour has to answer to his own constituents, and they're going to keep every drop they're entitled to."

"Can't say I blame them," said Morgan, walking up to their table.

Carrie looked her over. Holbrooke Morgan was one of those governors who were jokingly referred to as "regional warlords." (Mostly jokingly, anyway.) Probably it was just that mixture of awe and suspicion that anybody in Washington had for an executive who seemed to be able to pass laws and implement policies without anybody else getting in the way. But in the case of Morgan, if an asteroid or something landed on D.C. and destroyed the federal government, it was easy to imagine her seizing control of New York State and the New England States within the first week, and then extending her Empire State empire further south, conquering Pittsburgh, Philadelphia, and Trenton and giving the inhabitants of the Jersey Shore the choice of slavery or death. (Again, kidding. Mostly.)

She was on the tall side—with her heels, she was as tall as Carrie—swan-necked and willowy, with blond hair that she kept in a complicated braided bun on the back of her head. She was three years older than Carrie, but looked about five years younger. Her suit, black and sharp-edged as if chiseled from obsidian, was an Arrigo Ciardi original. Carrie would never be able to wear a suit like that, because Arrigo Ciardi would commit seppuku with his own scissors before he ever agreed to design an outfit for a woman over size six.

"If it's true what I've heard, that Arizona is using what little water it has to grow cotton…" Morgan let her voice trail off.

"It's true," said Tejera. "Funny story behind that. Want to hear it?" They both nodded as Morgan sat down.

"Different places in Arizona are handling the drought in different ways. Phoenix and Tucson are rationing water. Which sounds cruel, I know, but at least that way everybody gets some. But for the state as a whole, Swank tried what was supposed to be a free-market approach—letting the price of water go up until it hits its 'natural' level.

"Then somebody else came along and threw a monkey wrench in the deal. The state cotton growers went to their congressman and asked for a subsidy, so they could buy enough water to stay in business. It takes a lot of water to grow cotton, you know."

"And the subsidy went through," said Morgan.

Tejera nodded. "So that's their situation. Families are learning to wash their dishes with sand, businesses are complaining that their employees are coming to work smelling like goats because nobody can afford to shower, golf courses are being shut down because even reclaimed water is running low or getting contaminated… and poor people are just getting on the bus and leaving. They can't afford to live there anymore. But the cotton industry? Doing great. And all Swank can say is, 'Hey, it's not my fault. I didn't ask for it.'"

"Another few years like this and they'll be growing cotton in New Jersey," said Carrie.

"Which reminds me…" Morgan took out her cell phone. "I better text my husband. Let him know if a video of me knocking that guy down turns up online, it's okay to let it trend."

"*Let* it trend?" said Tejera.

"You're familiar with the American News and Media Foundation?" said Morgan. "Lucas—my husband—is one of the cochairs."

"That seems like it might be a conflict of interest."

"I like to think of it as a family working together for the greater good." Morgan smiled in a way that was obviously trying to be sinister. "And did I notice you talking to Symcox earlier?"

Carrie told them about Symcox's proposition. "I like Sandy, but my advice would be not to get involved with her just yet," said Morgan. "She's a billionaire now, but she could be bankrupt next year. She's got the whole diamond oligarchy against her, she's got ex-coworkers suing her—suing for everything she's got, not just a cut of her profits… I think this foundation is her way of protecting herself."

"Protecting herself how?"

"Daring her enemies to steal bread from the mouths of widows and orphans or whoever. I mean, it's running on her income stream."

AFTER DINNER, CARRIE WENT BACK to her hotel room with Morgan and some wine. She wasn't sure if she liked Morgan yet. The governor of New York reminded Carrie a lot of girls she'd known in high school, girls who were the reason Carrie spent so much time hanging out with guys… but Carrie had come a long way from high school. Also, this was the first actual networking opportunity she'd had at what was supposed to be a networking event—trying to network at an event you were helping to run was like trying to get in a little swimming when you were a lifeguard.

In an hour, Carrie was a bit buzzed. Brooke—they were now on a first-name basis—was rather more so. *I never yet met a skinny bitch who could hold her liquor*, thought Carrie smugly.

Carrie had just gotten done talking about some anti-Semitic remarks she'd gotten online. "This is going to sound really insensitive, but... I can't help envying you those enemies," said Brooke. "I'd love to have somebody threaten to make soap or lampshades out of me. I could take their remarks and show them to everybody and say 'See? This is the kind of person who doesn't like me.' Not in so many words, of course."

"I just block, report, and move on," said Carrie. "Or rather, the girl who does this stuff for me does."

"That's it?" Brooke shook her head. "God, those people are wasted on you. They're cruel, they're freaks—freakish by choice, I might add, so you can laugh at them without feeling guilty—they're impotent in at least one sense and probably more, they've declared allegiance to one of the worst ideas in human history... you could do anything with enemies like that."

"Anything with them, or anything to them?"

"As far as I'm concerned, either one. The courts may feel differently, of course... but think how good it would make you look just to try to do something about them."

Carrie laughed. "First, I came for the Nazis, and you said nothing—"

"No, I said 'Good riddance!'"

"Next I came for... hmmm..."

"Cyberstalkers. Do them next."

"Good idea. Next I came for the cyberstalkers..."

"And I said 'Look, there's one over there! Let's get him!'"

"Then I came for... I don't know, some other kind of trolls..."

"And I said 'Okay, I can see where this is headed, but at this rate it'll be a while before she gets to anybody I care about.'"

"Then I came for... I came for..." Carrie hesitated.

"This is turning into the worst porno ever."

Carrie burst into spluttering laughter.

"I love your whole persona," said Brooke. "It's so... warm and safe. Obviously, it wouldn't work for me, but it seems to be working for you."

"What do you mean?"

Brooke was silent for a moment, collecting her thoughts as best she could.

"There's a saying I've heard. 'A politician is an actor who plays only one character.' When you're out there, you've got to pick a persona and stick with it. You can't be reinventing yourself all the time, or people aren't going to feel like they know you.

"And you can get away with a lot if the people feel like they know you. When Bill Clinton got caught messing around, we never really got mad at him because it never felt like a betrayal. We knew what he was like when we voted for him. It was no great surprise… The point is, whatever role you're playing, it works for you."

"I don't think of it as playing a role," said Carrie. "You've got to be yourself when you're up on the podium. The best possible version of yourself, anyway."

"Exactly. 'The best possible version of yourself.' Your persona can't be completely fake—it has to be at least based on the real you. But the audience has to be able to recognize and relate to it. In your case… you're everybody's mom. Or the mom they wish they'd had. I mean, we're both mothers but you're a *mom*. People look at me and they think 'She had a child? Let me guess—she had it mesquite-grilled and served on a bed of shiitake mushrooms and wild rice?'"

Carrie laughed.

"See, we're both archetypes," Brooke continued. "You're the earth mother. I'm the ice queen. You're that one teacher they always wanted to make happy— I'm that one teacher who always scared the hell out of them. Pundits have been writing editorials comparing me to Angela Merkel or Margaret Thatcher, but what I really am is the *dominatrix*. Sometimes I'm tempted to show up at a fundraiser in skin-tight black leather and stiletto heels and swinging a whip around, just to get the point across."

Carrie laughed some more. For an ice queen, Brooke could be fun to be around.

"And we can both use the personas we've got to get things done. You can raise taxes and people will hate it, but they'll figure it's for the best because they trust you with the money. If I raise taxes… they'll still hate it, but they'll figure I'm giving them what they deserve.

"But here's the thing. Dominatrixes… dominatrices… what's the plural of 'dominatrix'?"

"I think the plural is 'ouch.'"

"No, that's the group name. The collective name. 'An ouch of dominatri...'" Brooke hesitated for a moment. "More than one dominatrix. The point is, a dominatrix is *performing a service for money*. She acts like she's in charge, she makes you pretend she's in charge, you might even start to think of her as being in charge... but at the end of the day, she's doing what you want her to do because you're paying her to do it."

Carrie nodded. Brooke was going somewhere with this, but damned if Carrie could tell where.

"Can you keep a secret?"

"Of course."

"I mean a real secret. Don't tell *anybody*. Because this... this could kill me politically if it ever got out."

"I promise," said Carrie, her imagination already trying to picture the scandalous misdeeds Brooke was about to confess to.

Brooke took a deep breath.

"I hate the voters."

Carrie paused for a moment.

"I... can see why that would be a problem politically."

"Think about it, Carrie," she said. "This is a democracy, right?"

"Technically it's a republic."

"Conceded. The point is, the voters are the *boss*. We're just the office girls. We're the executive assistants. They hire us, they can fire us... Doesn't an office girl have the right to hate her boss?"

Carrie nodded. She personally thought "branch manager" would be a better metaphor than "executive assistant"—a certain amount of authority, not too much day-to-day oversight, but ultimately answerable to the home office—but this wasn't the time to quibble. Brooke sounded sincere in a way that Carrie hadn't heard before.

"And I don't hate them just because they're the boss," Brooke continued. "See, there are good bosses out there. I've had them, you've had them... They're the ones who pay attention. The ones who step up and accept responsibility. The ones who try to understand everything they're in charge of, because that's their job. They notice right away if you're slacking off, but they also notice if you've got problems. And when you tell them the truth, they listen, and they thank you, even if it's something they don't want to hear."

Carrie nodded. That was the sort of boss she tried to be.

"And then there's the other kind of boss—I'm sure you've had some of them too. The big spoiled children. The ones who never pay any attention to what's going on until something blows up in their faces, and then they lash out at whoever happens to be in the office at the time instead of trying to figure out what the hell just happened. They don't want to think about the consequences of their actions, so they don't. If you lie to them and flatter them, they reward you, and if you try to tell them the truth they punish you. And they never, ever accept the blame.

"Now here's my question, Carrie. If the American people were a boss, what kind of boss would they be?"

Carrie didn't have an answer to this.

Or rather, she did, but not one she wanted to say out loud. Or even inside her head.

Brooke got to her feet, slowly. "I need to get back to my room," she said. "I've had enough to drink."

She went to the door, picked up her purse, then turned. The expression on her face was strangely like loathing.

"I really do hate them, you know."

Carrie nodded.

"Look at me," Brooke said. "They turned me. Into. This. *Thing.*"

For just a moment, as Brooke was walking away, Carrie felt a moment of empathy. But then the thought crossed her mind: *You chose this life, Brooke. You chose it, and you really can give it up any time you like. You're tall, blonde, good-looking, smart, and rich as all hell—you'll get by no matter what you do. And here you are doing something you hate. Why?*

Is it just the power? Is that all? How satisfying can that be if you end up feeling like an employee? Or like the voters' plaything? Did you get into this hoping it would be more fun?

Are you doing this out of a sense of obligation? Do you really think if you don't step up, there won't be anyone who can take your place? What am I, chopped liver?

Do you even know why anymore?

After a little more thought, Carrie decided it really wasn't her concern. Her concern was finding something to do next year. And assuming Symcox's foundation would still be around then, that offer sounded pretty good.

THIS YEAR, THE NORTHERN MONSOON appeared as a continuous band of rain around the northern hemisphere, thicker in some places than in others. In the North Atlantic, the warped and weakened jet stream—described as a "negative phase in the Arctic Oscillation"—altered the courses of winds all over the ocean, drawing many storms to the north. Most of these blew themselves out over water, but in mid-September, a post-tropical depression poured its heart out onto the Vatnajökull in Iceland. Near the beginning of October, another storm hit the southern tip of Greenland. Rain can destroy a glacier like almost nothing else. By the time the season ended, vast amounts of ice had been either melted or broken off by erosion and carried into the sea. Smaller rain zones appeared, as usual, in northern Norway and northern Alaska.

But of more immediate concern were the three bands of particularly heavy rain that once again formed. One was over the eastern Pacific, but stretched west to include Japan, Korea, and parts of China and Siberia. Central Manchuria, South Korea, and the island of Honshu were hit by heavy rains and flash flooding in the mountains, but they were not completely devastated... unlike North Korea, eastern Manchuria, Hokkaido, the lower Amur, and the Vladivostok area.

The second band of rain stretched from Bavaria to the Caspian Sea. It was most extreme on the north slopes of the Alps, the Carpathians, and the Caucasus. The Elbe, the Oder, and the Vistula saw the worst flooding in their recorded history—but it looked tame next to the flooding of the Danube and the Sava. Hungarians, Croats, and Serbs by the millions had to evacuate, usually into parts of Europe where they weren't in the least welcome. Incidents of ethnic violence flared all over the sodden Balkans.

The third band of rain formed over the northern United States and southern Canada...

SEPTEMBER 22:

HENRY PRATT DIDN'T LIKE CABINET meetings, and didn't hold them unless he had no other choice. This was how he preferred to do his job:

• A Cabinet secretary or someone else he had appointed came to him and informed him of the situation.

- He listened to them and made his decision.
- That someone then went forth to implement his decision.

In theory, meetings of the full Cabinet ought to work the same way. In practice, they were a mess. Everyone listened to everything, and everyone felt entitled to contribute, interrupting and talking over each other, assuming expertise in areas well beyond their fields of specialization. The system rewarded those who were there to expand their own power and influence at the expense of those who were just there to do the jobs they'd been appointed to do.

But today there was no way around it. Too many departments were involved in the current disaster. They had to coordinate. Everybody had to know the whole plan and their part in it. And the meeting had to be held in the White House Situation Room, the only place where the disaster could be properly monitored.

Pratt glanced around the table. Commerce, Transportation, Agriculture, Treasury, HUD… all here. His press secretary was in the hospital undergoing a biopsy, so her deputy was here instead.

He looked to the woman at his right hand. The mental image most people had of a president's chief of staff, if they had one at all, was of a gnarled, hard-bitten old political operator who kept the cabinet in line by sheer force of unpleasant personality. Thirty-five-year-old Wendy Czeczelski was a short, friendly woman with thick glasses, skinny arms and legs and an almost spherical torso. She was also efficient and well-organized. And she was useful for detecting problem children—someone who would take one look at her and decide it was safe to treat her with disrespect was someone who probably needed to go.

Finally, Pratt looked at his old friend at the far end of the table. Terry Walther had shaggy gray hair, heavy eyebrows, and a face with a few deep laugh lines. He looked less like the Secretary of the Treasury than an aging rock musician trying to dress and act respectable for his daughter's wedding.

"Where's Simon?" said Terry.

Pratt gestured to Wendy, letting her answer. You couldn't show favoritism to your friends in a meeting like this.

"Swanston is in a discussion with Ahn right now," she said. "Ahn just got back from the summit, and he wanted to speak with Swanston directly en route to the White House. They'll be with us later this morning."

There was a long moment while everybody in the room digested this and got heartburn. For the past week, Secretary of State Ahn had been in an emergency summit with the heads of several Balkan states, followed the very next day by another emergency summit with the leaders of China and North Korea. Whatever had happened over there, he apparently wanted Secretary of Defense Simon Swanston to hear about it ASAP, even before the president. That could not possibly be a good sign.

Pratt raised his voice to address the room. "I'm going to start by outlining the basic questions we're here to answer," he said. Wendy stood up, went to one of the screens and tapped it. Four bullet points appeared on it:

- What is happening?
- How does it affect us?
- What do we do about it?
- How do we pay for it?

At a gesture from Pratt, Secretary of Commerce Helen Bird, a short, stout woman in a tan pantsuit, stood up and approached the screen at the end of the room with the expression of someone staring into the depths of Hell.

Pratt sympathized. Bird was an expert in international trade, not meteorology. Serving under her was the Deputy Secretary of Commerce, an expert in infrastructure development. Serving under him was the Under Secretary of Commerce for Oceans and Atmosphere*, Matthew Minsky, a business executive brought in from Wall Street for the specific purpose of overseeing the privatization of the National Weather Service. The bill authorizing that privatization had died in the Senate, quietly snuffed by senators worried about the Midwestern drought, the heat wave in the South and the wildfires out west. Serving under *him* was the director of the National Weather Service… nobody. Pratt had left that office vacant.

Which meant Bird was about to deliver a briefing in which she had no idea what she was talking about and was forced to rely on the expertise of people who had personal reasons to hate the administration. *If I'd known this was going to be the year the sky declared war on America*, thought Pratt, *I would have done things differently. The whole point was not to remind people of you-know-who.*

---

* Administrator of the National Oceanic and Atmospheric Administration.

In addition to being completely outside her area of expertise, Bird wasn't much of a public speaker. Nonetheless, she managed to get the point across, mostly using terms borrowed from the insurance industry. There were different ways to measure flooding—inches of rainfall, the height of the water—but one of the more useful ways was to classify a flood by the odds of it happening in any given year. According to Bird, the IPCC had given up on being able to do this, but the NWS hadn't. If there was a 10 percent chance of a flood that size, it was a 10-year flood. If there was only a 4 percent chance, it was a 25-year flood. So if you were building something to last 50 years, it should at least be able to handle a 50-year flood. Just to be on the safe side, it should be able to handle a 100-year flood, since there was an even chance of that happening.

But what was happening up north right now wasn't a 100-year flood.

It wasn't a 500-year or 1,000-year flood.

It was a *never* flood.

The deluge hitting the northern U.S. was of a kind that up until the last couple of years hadn't even been possible in that part of the world. The band of rain stretched from the foothills of the Rockies east clear to the foothills of the Appalachians, and from just north of Kansas City and St. Louis clear up to the Canadian border and beyond — poor Canada was taking it on the chin again this year. Going from west to east, it covered central and eastern Montana, the northeast corner of Wyoming, all of the Dakotas, about a third of Nebraska, all of Minnesota and Iowa, a slice of northern Missouri, all of Wisconsin and Michigan, the northern halves of Illinois and Indiana, the northern third of Ohio, the northwest corner of Pennsylvania and parts of upstate New York, Vermont, New Hampshire, and Maine. The Northern Monsoon had come to America.

Like last year's floods in Europe and Siberia, it had snuck up on the country—half an inch of rain on Sunday, a little more than that on Tuesday, a full inch on Wednesday night, almost as much on Friday morning… and the next week, with the ground fully saturated, the *heavy* rains began. "We're already seeing flash flooding in parts of New England and western Pennsylvania," said Bird. "That's where the worst loss of life is right now—eighty-three deaths, that we know of, so far.

"But the real bad news is that this is just the start of the third week. If it's anything like last year's Monsoon—and all the indications are that it's even worse—then we have at least a month and a half left to go. Since it's happening fairly slowly, we can make a reasonable guess as to which places are going to need evacuation, but… it's a lot of places.

"Especially around the Great Lakes. A three-foot rise in Lake Superior is considered a five-hundred-year flood, and we're past that now. And every drop of that water is going to flow down into the lower Lakes, which are already in a similar state."

"Thank you," said Pratt. "That brings us to the question of the impact, which… are we in touch with al-Harrak?"

"He's in the Kansas City field office right now," said Wendy. "I'll call him and tell him to get in front of a webcam."

"While you're doing that," said Bird, "may I make a couple of recommendations?" Knowing that the president was a stickler for protocol, she addressed this to Wendy, not Pratt.

Wendy looked at Pratt, who nodded. He hadn't planned on discussing courses of action yet, but under the circumstances a little flexibility was called for.

"First," said Bird, "we need to put somebody in charge of the NWS. Today, if possible. Second, we need somebody new at NOAA. I'll e-mail you a list of names for both positions." She handed a piece of paper over to Wendy, who handed it to Pratt.

It was a letter of resignation from Minsky. The short version was *I'll stay on if you insist on keeping me, but this isn't the job you hired me for and I have no idea how to do it and a lot of lives are at stake.* It would weaken Pratt to let Minsky go at a time like this, but under the circumstances it made sense.

"Mr. al-Harrak," said Wendy, turning on a screen next to the one Bird was standing in front of to show a man sitting at the center of his own little solar system of screens, all facing him from various angles, each displaying a different emergency. He was a medium-dark, heavyset man in a sports jacket over a plaid shirt. His beard was short but thick, and his hair had only a little gray in it.

Pratt allowed himself a moment of self-congratulation for having chosen this man to be in charge of FEMA. The Moroccan-born Muhammad al-Harrak had been dealing with large-scale refugee crises since the war in Syria, and he had become a master of logistics. A lot of Republicans had looked askance at Pratt for hiring this foreign Muslim for a job that would place him squarely in the Department of Homeland Security. A lot of overseas leftists had looked even askancer at al-Harrak for accepting the position—after years of helping displaced Third World families save their children, now he was going to be "helping fat, pampered Americans save their big screens," as some irate commentator had written in the *Guardian*. But al-Harrak had five children of his own, and knew enough about poverty to know he wanted as much money as possible between it and them… and the U.S. paid better than the U.N.

Al-Harrak wasted no time getting started. "Fifty million Americans are in the area being directly affected," he said. "Right now, I'm acting on the optimistic assumption that half of them will need to be evacuated. That doesn't include the people downstream, in places like St. Louis, Memphis, and New Orleans. It also doesn't include Canadians, many of whom may seek shelter in the United States."

"What would be a less optimistic assumption?"

"Less optimistically, we need to prepare housing for thirty million people. At minimum. I have a list of sites for emergency housing centers in areas that should be unaffected."

"What about the housing itself?"

"Right now, the agency is purchasing mobile homes and RVs."

"About how many are you buying?"

"All of them," said al-Harrak.

Pratt blinked.

"At least, all the ones being sold by distributors—I've also instructed personnel to search for RVs being sold privately. It won't be nearly enough, of course, but it will provide some housing for the first inhabitants while they build more housing. The agency is looking for contractors to supervise them while they do this."

"So far, so good," said Pratt, "but at some point, we're going to need to start rebuilding. What's the status of the National Flood Insurance Program?"

"Bankrupt," said al-Harrak. "No one is to blame. It could never have paid for more than the smallest fraction of this." The unspoken part of this sentence was *even if its coffers had been full, which they were not, because Hurricane Gordon exhausted our funds and you and Congress never bothered to replenish them.* "And before we deal with that, we need to get people out of the danger zone in the first place. A lot of people are going to need a lot of help getting out of there. We're mobilizing the National Guard, but they can't be everywhere."

"If you need more personnel, draw on the Army," said Pratt. "Coordinate with Swanston directly."

"I'll do that. As for the order of evacuations, the usual approach would be to give priority to the elderly and disabled. In this case, we'll need to start with able-bodied men and women to build the extra housing. That worries me. In Louisiana, when Katrina hit, about half the people who died were over seventy-five. Here, the same thing could happen on a much larger scale."

"Excuse me," said Wendy, "but it looks like Bradley has something to say."

The deputy press secretary was Deon Bradley, a kid fresh out of College Park, black, shaven-headed, and impeccably neat. He was lifting a hand tentatively. Pratt motioned for him to speak.

"Yes," said Bradley, his voice not quite cracking, "about that... there's another problem I don't know if everybody's aware of. You see, some news orgs have decided the Northern Monsoon isn't a thing—that last year was just a fluke. It's a part of global climate change, and if you're not willing to say for sure that that's happening, and you don't have another explanation, that makes it hard to talk about."

"So they're not reporting it at all?" said Pratt.

"They're reporting the weather, same as usual," said Bradley. "They're telling everybody about the rain. What they're not doing is tying it together or making any predictions beyond the five-day forecast."

"How much difference does that make?"

"Well, from what I've seen... if I were living in the affected area and all I had to go on was weather reports from—say—the TKB Foundation, I'd be a little skeptical if anybody told me I needed to evacuate."

"Thank you," said al-Harrak, though his expression was more one of dread than gratitude. "I'll keep my eyes open for that."

The reports from the Transportation and HUD secretaries could both be summed up in one phrase: *this will be really bad, but we don't know how bad yet.* The cities—hell, the entire metropolitan areas—of Chicago, Detroit, Cleveland, Minneapolis-St. Paul, and Milwaukee were obviously going to be hit hard, and Indianapolis and Columbus were only a little better off. Probably worst off would be Buffalo, flooded from both above and upstream.

As for transportation, many airports and uncounted miles of highway were in the disaster zone. It was all still mostly intact, but no one was expecting that to continue. Which made it even more urgent to evacuate as many people as possible now—the longer everybody waited, the harder it would get.

Then Agriculture Secretary Kyria Hammond spoke. "The news is not good," she said. "With the situation in the Plains and the South, we were really counting on the Corn Belt to come through this year. Most of the Belt is right under that monsoon, and most of the corn and soybeans haven't been harvested yet. Now I assume the farmers are out there right now trying to save as much as they can, but in my opinion, we'll be lucky to get half of it.

"Then there's winter wheat. A lot of next year's crop is going to be drowned in the fields or never planted at all. The bottom line is, we need to be prepared for serious food insecurity.

"And not just here, but abroad—*especially* abroad, in fact. The same heat-kill problem in the South has been happening in the south of China, and they've got a lot more mouths to feed. The wheat belt in the Ukraine and southern Russia is also being hit by the Monsoon."

"Thank you," said Pratt. He turned to Terry Walther. "I hate to ask you for a miracle, but…" He couldn't think of a way to finish the sentence. Somehow his old school chum was going to have to conjure a lot of money into being without causing inflation.

"I never thought I'd say this," said Terry, "but times like this are the reason deficit spending was invented. I think we should see how much the bond market is willing to finance before we talk about raising taxes."

"Can you do it without raising interest rates?"

Terry steepled his fingers and thought for a moment.

"What I'm about to say is going to sound very cynical," he said. "I mean, cynical even by D.C. standards. But if the market is really starting to think the end of civilization is coming—or even a major crisis of civilization, which is what this is starting to look like—then what's the investment of last resort? I mean, before everybody starts hoarding gold and guns and stuff?"

"Bonds?"

"That's right. U.S. government bonds. Because like it or not, we're the only outfit that can actually *make* people give us their money—well, us and the mob, but the mob doesn't sell bonds. Now we have seen about a dozen state governments take big hits to their bond rating just in the last year—mostly Florida and other states with a lot of coastline—but when the apocalypse hits, the federal government will be the last thing to go. So that's… the good news, if you want to call it that. We can sell a lot of bonds without raising rates too much."

Right at that moment, the door opened. Secretary of State Jae-oh Ahn, known to Pratt and his other close friends as "Jim," entered the Situation Room with Defense Secretary Simon Swanston right behind him. Ahn's salt-and-pepper hair seemed to have gotten a little saltier since he'd left D.C. last week, and his expression was grim.

"I gather the news is bad," said Pratt.

Jim nodded. "The situation in the Balkans isn't the problem," he said. "To the extent that it is a problem, the nations of Europe have it in hand. I have a more detailed report here"—he placed a folder on Pratt's desk—"but what we need to focus on is North Korea.

"The meeting was… slightly worse than the usual standoff. They spent several hours threatening us with an immediate nuclear attack if we didn't ship them food right now. I kept reminding them we had barely enough food for ourselves and our trading partners, but we did have a very large nuclear arsenal that we would be happy to deliver free of charge." Swanston's pinched, humorless face managed a grim smile at this. "They kept saying China would defend them."

"What did the Chinese say?"

"They were a little more reasonable. The foreign minister said—I'm paraphrasing—'Are you sure you don't have anything to spare? Because they're really losing everything in the floods this year.' That's the trouble with being an American—nobody believes you when you plead poverty. Especially when it comes to food."

"I take it China doesn't have anything to spare?"

Jim shook his head. "Normally, President Ma would like nothing better than to wrap North Korea around his finger a little tighter in exchange for a few shiploads of rice. This year the problem is coming up with those shiploads of rice. See, the problems we've been having in the South with heat kill—they've been having the same problems in their southeast, and they've got a lot more mouths to feed.

"And North Korea really is in a bad way right now. According to my sources in China, they were already closer to famine than we knew before the floods even started."

Pratt nodded. "Socialism."

"Socialism can never fail," said Jim, "it can only be failed… apparently by everyone in the world. And even a capitalist country would have had trouble coping with that kind of damage. Especially since one of the few things they export is coal, which China is trying to cut back on.

"Here's the upshot. In the event Pyongyang launches a first strike, China will stay out of it. And unless they really are suicidal, they're not going to launch that strike."

"In case they do," said Swanston, "we *will* be ready. In fact, with your permission Defense will begin developing a plan to forestall them."

Jim nodded. "But whatever happens, a lot of people in North Korea are going to die this winter. And by 'a lot' I mean somewhere between a fifth and a quarter of the population. And I can't even begin to speculate about the repercussions of this." He sighed. "Rogue states, unstable countries... at times like this, they're the first ones to fall apart. Let's just hope they're the only ones."

LIKE MOST RIVERS, THE MISSISSIPPI does not lie easy in its bed. It is in the nature of the river to flow to the sea by the shortest and steepest path, but with every ton of sand and silt it brings from the north to accumulate in its lower reaches, it gradually lengthens its own path, forming a long tongue of low-lying ground that extends into the Gulf of Mexico. One year, during a violent flood, the river breaks through somewhere along its banks and finds a shorter route to the Gulf. The old course becomes a backwater, the tongue of land is slowly eroded away by ocean waves and the story begins again.

The cycle takes about a thousand years. As it happens, the last time the Mississippi made a major change of course was about a thousand years ago. Left to itself, by now the river would probably have shifted to the Atchafalaya and entered the Gulf at Morgan City, La. But the cities and industries that have grown along the river's lower course need that river to survive.

And so, in the mid-twentieth century, the Old River Control Structure was built. The U.S. Army Corps of Engineers took on the task of holding the great river prisoner in its old bed, allowing only 30 percent of the Mississippi to flow into the Atchafalaya, preventing the Father of Waters from turning deadbeat dad on the millions who needed it right where it was.

From then to the present day, despite the worst floods Nature can send, the Corps has never failed this charge... yet.

OCTOBER 3:

ISABEL WAS JARRED AWAKE BY the sound of two hands clapping about a foot away from her left ear.

She sat up abruptly, and was rewarded with a jolt of pain from the back of her neck as she pulled her head up from the pillow on her desk. The thin, bestubbled face of Luke Roth, her supervisor for the morning shift, was looming over her.

"Sleeping on the job?"

Isabel did a triple-take. First, she was horribly embarrassed at having in fact been caught sleeping on the job. One second later, while her face was still halfway done turning red, she thought *I sleep at my desk because I can't leave my damn post! HOW DARE HE* and then she noticed the look in his eye and realized he was kidding. Figuring that witty banter was called for at this point, Isabel tried to think of some.

"I could sleep a lot better if they hadn't taken the beds out," was the best she could come up with. She gestured toward the end of the RV where the beds had been replaced by extra hard drives, giving her computer more storage space. For a moment, Isabel glared out the window at yet another beautiful, sunny Louisiana morning which had come to mock her for having to spend yet another day cooped up in this air-conditioned veal pen. Then she turned back to her computer and sent a file to Roth's smartphone.

"Here's the latest projections," said Isabel. "They're not good. We're looking at a flow rate well over 2.5 million cubic feet per second. There's a 96.2 percent chance the river crests over the top of the ORCS after midnight tonight, and a 62.5 percent chance the structure fails completely. That's up from 96.0 and 61.4 from the one a.m. data. Have you heard if they're going to open the Morganza the rest of the way?"

"Haven't heard a thing." At this point, the little microwave at the end of the table turned itself on, the light inside showing a single cup. Roth glanced at it.

"I set it to start at six minutes before seven," Isabel said. "When it's done, the alarm app goes off and wakes me up. That gives me five minutes to drink the chyq and get my brain back in gear before the data comes in."

"That's efficient." Roth glanced under the desk, where there was a wastebasket with a dozen energy-bar wrappers in it. "Have you been living on those things this whole time?"

"Since Brian left. Speaking of Brian, when's that replacement going to come?"

"It's hard finding a qualified candidate. If we're still here on Monday— which isn't looking too likely right now—and if Brian isn't back by then, we'll try to bring somebody in."

Isabel was really starting to think it had been a mistake for her to accept this job. To the task of helping the U.S. Army Corps of Engineers keep the Old River Control Structure standing, Eveland-Blades Consulting, Inc., had brought half a ton of computer hardware, two engineers, three supervisors and their in-house "social/interpersonal networking specialist," a man whose job description consisted entirely of schmoozing with Lieutenant General J.L. Martineau and any other important decision-makers who happened to be in the area. The other engineer, Brian Dalrymple, took a leave of absence two days ago so he could go back to Michigan and help his mother evacuate. He was supposed to have been replaced, but the teams in Greenville, Baton Rouge, and New Orleans swore they couldn't spare anybody. Which left Isabel subsisting on chyq, meal replacement bars and about three hours of sleep a night in 30-to-45-minute servings.

She glared out the window again. The skies were still clear and cloudless. You would never imagine that six hundred miles to the north—and nine hundred miles, and twelve hundred miles—such torrential downpours were taking place that all her efforts here were probably futile.

"Has anybody told the general about the problem with the simulation?"

"What prob—oh. That thing you keep mentioning in your e-mails. Look, Martineau knows this structure better than anyone alive. He knows how much it can take. I wouldn't worry about it." Which wasn't an answer... which *was* an answer. "You know, Isabel, you're really being a trooper about all this."

"Thank you," said Isabel, not sure if Roth was being sincere or if he was trying to convey *please don't blow it by turning whistleblower on us.*

"I mean it," he said. "I kind of wish we had a provision for overtime pay, just so we could give you time and a half."

"So do I," said Isabel. The microwave's alarm app started ringing.

THE EXTRA HARD DRIVES TAKING up so much room in the RV contained a map of the North American continent and surrounding waters—a map as detailed as the one she'd worked on during the Norfolk Conference. This was the key element of a program designed to predict the response of key pieces of infrastructure to extreme weather events.

Isabel's job was to take the updates that came every three hours from the National Weather Service, translate the relevant information into something the program could understand and feed it in. This took about twenty minutes.

The program then spent an hour and a half running simulations of the next week's weather. Depending on how much of the cloud the program had access to at any particular moment, it could run between two and five per second. With each simulation, it made a small change in some variable or other—wind speed and direction, duration and quantity of rain in various places. This would have been a good time for Isabel to take a quick nap, except that the program would invariably crash several times and need to be rebooted, so she had to keep a constant eye on it.

To keep memory demand to a minimum, the program didn't save the tens of thousands of individual simulations—only certain key results, which were autosaved as they came in. (Which, considering how often it crashed, was a good thing.) Isabel's next task, once she had an hour's worth of results, was to compile them into a brief report. This took ten to fifteen minutes. Which gave her as much as an hour to grab some exercise, food, or sleep before the next update came.

And with every update, the news got a little worse. Right now, the $64-trillion question was how much of the rain that fell in the next few weeks was going to land in the Great Lakes/St. Lawrence drainage basin and ruin everyone's day in Montreal as it flowed down to the sea, and how much was going to land in the Mississippi drainage basin, make its way down to Louisiana and add to the pressure already on the Old River Control Structure—and, more importantly, whether that pressure would be too much for the ORCS to withstand. That was the question this massive computer was trying to answer, and its answers were getting more and more pessimistic.

The Corps had done what it could, opening every floodgate on the structure, the Bonnet Carré Spillway and 50 of the Morganza Spillway's 125 gates. It was looking like it wouldn't be enough. The four to six inches of rain that had hit most of Iowa a week ago would begin making its appearance tonight.

If the ORCS failed, the Atchafalaya floodplain would be flooded—much worse than it was already. Whole towns would be washed away. Highways, bridges, and gas pipelines would be severed. The initial damage would make Hurricanes Katrina or Harvey look like scattered showers. That was the bad news.

The *really* bad news was what would happen when the Monsoon finally ended and the river returned to its usual volume. The Mississippi at New Orleans was at sea level. Only constant pressure from the flow of the river kept the ocean out. Without that pressure, the drinking water of New Orleans would become as brackish as the Chesapeake. And Louisiana wasn't California. It didn't have nearly enough desalinization plants to provide it with the water it needed. People were starting to accept that New Orleans would have to be abandoned sometime this century, but it wasn't supposed to happen this year. Baton Rouge would be a little better off—it would keep its water supply, but its branch of the river would either be reduced to a trickle or disappear entirely. And between them, dozens of petrochemical plants that needed all that fresh water to operate would have to move or shut down.

The loss of the ORCS would have been a blow to the United States at any time. If it happened now... well, it looked like they were going to find out.

NOT LONG BEFORE NOON, ISABEL was getting ready to compile the findings from the 10 a.m. report when she got a phone call.

It was Hunter. "Guess what?"

"What?" *Hunter, I love you, but if this has something to do with Enginquest...*

"I'm coming."

"What?"

"The mayor got a bus and asked every business in Marksville to send somebody to help out at the ORCS—sandbags and stuff," said Hunter. "So I mentioned to Joan that my girlfriend worked there and asked if I could go, and she said yes."

Isabel was briefly surprised that Hunter had done this, but then reflected that it made a kind of sense. Three days ago, he'd installed a new toilet seat all by himself, and he'd been feeling like a Manly Man ever since. This was the next logical step in his leveling up. No child of Clark Bradshaw would think anything of such a simple act of household maintenance, but Hunter hadn't been brought up that way, poor guy.

"Cool. What time are you going to be here?"

"We should get there about quarter after."

"I'll be done here about twenty after."

EVELAND-BLADES' RV WAS PARKED JUST off the southeast end of the Low Sill Control Structure, the oldest component of the ORCS. Louisiana Highway 15, which ran over the ORCS, was closed to most traffic at the moment—except for things like a busload of volunteers. Stepping outside, Isabel saw the bus parked at the northwest end.

It was ninety degrees outside—a bit warm for this part of Louisiana in October, but not too unreasonable compared to the weeks of hundred-degree-in-the-shade weather they'd had this summer. The water going through the structure was a constant, low rumble, like distant thunder that never died away.

The ORCS was designed to allow 620,000 cubic feet of water to flow through every second. (Just to put that into perspective, 85,000 cubic feet of water normally flowed over Niagara Falls every second—although God only knew how much was flowing through Niagara right now.) Isabel wasn't sure how much of that flowed through the Low Sill rather than the other two structures, but as soon as she stepped onto it, she felt the asphalt of the road vibrating under her sneakers. The chain-link fence to her left was also shaking. *This thing weighs 200,000 tons, and it's shaking. That's kind of scary.*

The ORCS was a product of a different America than the one Isabel had grown up in. It was planned and built in an age of big dreams and big projects—the interstate highway system, the Apollo program... the Chesapeake Bay Bridge, come to think of it. It reminded her a lot of the Bay Bridge—massive, strong, purely functional but with a kind of unintentional beauty. As she looked at it, she couldn't help thinking *Maybe we've been underestimating it. How many "hundred-year floods" has the ORCS been through in less than a century? It's survived all of them. There's a reason they call this thing "the old soldier."* But the numbers didn't lie. Well, okay, the numbers were lying, but not in a way that gave her any hope.

On her right, the river had risen so close to the top of the dam that if the fence weren't in the way, she could have reached down and touched it. On her left, the water flowing through the gates looked almost solid, like curving gray-brown buttresses that hit the "stilling basin" at the bottom in a churning white maelstrom.

Down near the river on the other side, not too close to the stilling basin, Isabel could see people at work, mostly in Army or National Guard uniforms. They were piling up sandbags in pool-sized rings on the slope. *Sand boils*, she thought. The weight of water on the upstream side was forcing itself down, into the ground underneath the ORCS, worming little paths through the seven thousand feet of clay, loam and compacted silt between the riverbed and the bedrock. That wouldn't do. The Low Sill was strong, but it could be ten times stronger and it wouldn't matter if the ground beneath it washed away. The only remedy was to build a small levee around the boil wherever the water hit the surface, so the water would form a small pool, creating just enough counterbalancing pressure to slow the flow and prevent further erosion.

When she spotted Hunter in the middle of a small group headed for a truckload of sandbags, Isabel gasped a little. She hadn't realized just how little face-to-face human contact she'd had since Monday. Without even intending to, she broke into a run.

Isabel got there just in time to see Hunter reach down to pick up a sandbag that had just been thrown off the back of the truck. "Stop!" she shouted—too late. Hunter wasn't exactly weak, but no one had ever taught him the basics of manual labor, including the rule "always lift heavy objects with your legs, not your back." Even as she was shouting, he was trying to lift the bag. With an abrupt little yelp of pain, Hunter dropped it and fell to his knees.

There was a first-aid station under a tent not far from the truck, for people who'd thrown their backs out or gotten heatstroke. Isabel escorted Hunter there. With every step, he apologized for having screwed up their reunion and for leaning on her like this.

And once he was there, Isabel barely had the chance to speak two words to him before she got another phone call.

"Hello?"

"Isabel? Where are you?"

"At the first-aid station."

"Are you hurt?"

"No."

"Then what are you—never mind, just get to the navigation lock on the double. We're meeting Martineau and the governor in half an hour."

"What?"

"General Martineau. He's called a meeting with us and Giovanni, and he specifically requested that we bring whoever was giving us these figures. That would be you. Get back here now."

THE CAR ISABEL AND HUNTER shared was back in Marksville, but Isabel had her bike. And she needed it, because the navigation lock was ten miles from the RV. By the time she got there, she was feeling a little light-headed. This might have been dehydration—she'd run out of water halfway there. The caffeine in her system wasn't helping either. Getting herself together, she stepped onto the gangplank that led to the tugboat in the lock, where Martineau's office was.

Isabel stopped to look at herself in the mirror, and wished she hadn't. She was soaked in sweat, wearing jeans, a Rodomontade T-shirt, and a total absence of makeup. As usual, her hair was threaded through an O-ring, but nobody would be able to see it because her bike helmet was still on. *Who cares? Are you planning to seduce the governor? You're here to work!* She adjusted her sweaty T-shirt in a desperate attempt to hide her bra and nipples under folds of cloth. She could already hear people talking in Martineau's office. The door was open a crack. His secretary pointed her in without a word.

As soon as Isabel stepped into the office, six people turned to face her. There was Luke Roth, her morning-shift supervisor, and Lydia Horrocks, her afternoon supervisor, both looking at her like teachers looking at a favorite student who'd just gotten a D. Worse, standing just past Horrocks was a thirtyish, somewhat pudgy man in an Oxford shirt. This was Chuck Eveland— the Eveland of Eveland-Blades Consulting. Mike Blades would probably also have been there if he hadn't been helping evacuate his own family from Omaha.

"Come in," said Joe Hickman, a reassuring look on his tanned and squarish face. He was the company's "social/interpersonal networking specialist," which sounded like a job for a world-class weasel. People who met Hickman, however, were pleasantly surprised that he came across as not only friendly but solid, honest, and reliable. With good reason—he was paid five times Isabel's salary to come across that way. And Isabel had to admit that while she could possibly be replaced by a few well-written apps, no software could ever do Hickman's job.

At the big desk, General Martineau—a tall, white-haired man who looked like he hadn't smiled in a long time—gave her a quick glance. Then he returned his attention to the man hovering beside him, who Isabel recognized as Governor Giovanni, and to the tablet computer propped upright on his desk. Judging by the screen, he was videoconferencing with four other people, but Isabel couldn't make out the faces from this angle.

"The point is, the lower the river is today, the lower it'll be when it crests tomorrow," Martineau was saying. "This is the only chance we have. I've made my decision. At three p.m. today the Morganza opens all the way. Get everybody ready." According to the briefing Isabel had gotten, only three times in its history had any of the Morganza's gates been opened—in 1973, in 2011, and during the flooding two years ago. No one had ever opened all of them at once.

Then he turned back to Isabel. "So you're the analyst," he said. "What's your name?"

"Isabel Bradshaw, sir." Her mind raced. Had Martineau called her in here because he didn't trust Eveland and the others anymore? Or was it just that the news was so bad he needed to hear it from as many different people as possible before he accepted it?

"Get over here."

Isabel stepped over to his desk, trying to ignore the unmistakable aroma of real coffee coming from the cup on his desk. Then she glanced at the computer screen and made an involuntary noise in the back of her throat that sounded like "eep." The screen was divided into four parts. The silver-haired man watching from the upper right, bronze-framed reading glasses perched on his nose... *You have got to be kidding me*, she thought. She'd just barely managed to work herself up to speak in front of the governor of Louisiana and the head of the Corps, and now they'd brought in President Pratt himself... and whoever those other three guys were? *But then, the ORCS really is this important.*

Martineau quickly introduced them. They were the secretary of the interior and the mayors of New Orleans and Baton Rouge.

"It's an honor," she said in a voice that came out a lot smaller than she'd intended. From the looks of the wall behind him, Pratt was on Air Force One right now. She thought about telling him she'd voted for him, but decided not to.

"You're the one who's been collecting the info and running the simulations?" said Martineau.

"Yessir."

"Tell everybody what the situation is."

"All right," she said. "With near one hundred percent certainty, the water will crest over the top of the Low Sill tomorrow. As of noon today, we estimate a sixty-four percent chance some part of the ORCS fails."

There was a long, long silence after that.

"This is the worst-case scenario, right?" the governor finally said.

Isabel glanced at Martineau, hoping he'd say something. He looked expectantly at her. She glanced at Roth and Horrocks. Roth kept his face neutral. Horrocks shook her head.

Crap. They hadn't told him. Isabel sighed. For her next trick, she was going to make her career disappear. At least she had a hell of an audience.

"Actually, sir, this is the best-case scenario," she said.

As one, Eveland and Hickman rose to interrupt.

"What she means is, it's an aggregate of possible—"

"Our analysts are trained to think in terms of—"

"Quiet," said Martineau, not loudly but firmly.

As one, Eveland and Hickman shut up.

Martineau stood up and clapped a hand on Isabel's shoulder. "I want everybody but this young lady out of the room now."

Roth fled at once. Eveland opened his mouth to speak, then closed it again and left, stopping only to give the young lady in question a long, vengeful glare. Hickman nodded, shrugged as if to say *no skin off mine* and stepped out as calmly as if going for a walk.

"Sit down," said Martineau, pointing at a chair right in front of his desk. When she sat down, he turned the computer screen so the President and everybody else directly faced her. Isabel could have done without that.

"When you say 'best-case scenario,'" he said, looming over her a little, "what exactly do you mean?"

Isabel took a deep breath. "Every simulation of the ORCS is based on the structure during its last inspection," she said.

Martineau nodded. "Two years ago, after the flooding."

"Exactly. So the program can project future damage, but it can't incorporate the damage that's already happened—the erosion under the foundations."

For a long second, Martineau was silent.

"And this is what we've been relying on all this time," he said in a scarily calm voice. There was a fine line between "best-case scenario" and "steaming pile of moose muffins" and when you neglected to factor in physical damage that you had already seen happening with your own eyes, you were well over that line.

And there was yet another reason this was bad—the Corps accounted for 19 of the company's 23 contracts and 92 percent of its income. Which meant the only customer Eveland-Blades Consulting, Inc., really had was J.L. Martineau… who was now standing there looking like he'd just caught their entire staff in bed with his wife. The fact that the President of the United States was also watching was just running up the score at this point. Very few people could put on their résumé that they'd personally destroyed the last company they worked for. *Maybe the escort services are hiring*, thought Isabel.

"I assume you heard I'm opening the rest of the Morganza Spillway gates at three. Can your model incorporate that?"

"Yes, sir."

"What's your best guess?" said the governor. "Is that going to help?"

Isabel hated guessing. When people asked you for your best guess, they always swore they wouldn't take it any more seriously than it deserved, and then they always treated it as Objective and Inarguable Truth brought down on stone tablets from the summit of Mount Science. And if your best guess happened to be wrong, you could make a much more accurate guess as to who'd get the blame.

"We're talking about diverting an extra"—she did some quick math in her head—"360,000 cubic feet per second. My best guess is, that would slow down the rise. Overflow would happen tomorrow afternoon, not tonight."

The governor just stood there, looking at her with a sorrowful expression on his face.

"Look, I really wish I had better news," she said. "Two inches of rain is falling on the Dakotas right now. Wisconsin is getting hit again tomorrow. And all that water—or most of it—once it's in the river it's heading straight for us. And if last year's Monsoon was any guide, we have at least another month of this to look forward to."

OCTOBER 4:

ISABEL HAD WONDERED WHAT WOULD happen when they knew for certain the ORCS would fail. She'd had a mental image of Martineau standing on the Low Sill in the middle of Highway 15 when the end came, like a captain going down with his ship, or possibly everyone in the Corps showing up dressed in their Sunday best with beer and country music, ready to reenact the deck of the *Titanic* Louisiana-style. It bears repeating that Isabel hadn't been getting enough sleep.

At 3 p.m., Isabel was right in the middle of compiling her latest report when someone knocked on the door.

It was one of the Corps personnel, a guy who barely looked eighteen. "Ma'am?" he said. "We're evacuating the structure and heading for high ground. I need you to move this vehicle about half a mile down the road."

"Thanks. Will do." The RV was on an island between the Low Sill and Auxiliary Structures. The "high ground" on this island was not all that high, compared to the hills east of the Mississippi. If that was where they were evacuating her to, it meant none of the components of the ORCS were deemed safe to drive on for long enough to get to real safety.

Also a bad sign—Horrocks wasn't here, and, now that she thought of it, she hadn't seen García last night or Roth this morning. After that little conference on the Corps tugboat, she'd thrown herself back into her work so thoroughly she hadn't noticed that all her coworkers had fled into the night—or possibly had been banished from the premises by Martineau. Still, at least they still trusted her not to drive off and sell all this very expensive equipment on the black market or something.

The only people left here were a handful of National Guard troops and Corps employees, all of whom were gathered in a little group at the bend in the road. Everyone was just sort of standing around, looking in one direction or another, watching the two structures… waiting to see which one gave way. Someone had set up a flagpole, but there was no wind. No one spoke.

Isabel parked the RV somewhere it wouldn't block their view and got out. "If anybody needs it, there's AC in there," she said out loud. The weather hadn't cooled any since yesterday, and heatstroke could happen even when people weren't working.

She noticed, at this point, that no one had a camera out. That one detail suddenly made everything clear. These men and women had zero interest in being "eyewitnesses to history." They were standing vigil at the deathbed of a loved one. They weren't going to let the old soldier die alone. Isabel suddenly felt like an intruder at a private grief. She had only been working here for the past three weeks, and had met only a handful of these people. The water had already gone over the top of the Low Sill—even from here she could see the sun shining off it as it streamed through the chain-link fence.

After about fifteen minutes, a couple of helicopters flew in. They didn't land, but hovered at a distance, slowly circling the structure. *And here's the media,* thought Isabel. She felt a sudden spike of loathing for them. The keystone of America's economy was about to collapse, and… well, to be fair, that was pretty newsworthy. Isabel suddenly felt guilty for hating them. More began to appear.

When the water over the Sill looked about a foot deep, it happened. There were cracking noises, distant but loud… a scream of overstressed steel… and then the southeast end of the Low Sill fell. It seemed to happen in slow motion, sinking rather than dropping, but that was only because Isabel was seeing it from three thousand feet away. The noise of its collapse took a little over two and a half seconds to reach her ears. She felt it through the soles of her sneakers before she heard it. Then the roar of the water drowned out everything else.

With terrifying speed, the water thundering through the breach ate into the soft silt of the island's bank. As much as fifty feet of it vanished in the first minute. In the next few minutes, another fifty feet was eroded away, including the spot where the RV had been parked. It slowed a little after that, but Isabel was deeply relieved when she saw more helicopters coming—these from the National Guard. As soon as one landed nearby, she headed straight for it, leaving behind her bicycle and the company's RV with equal indifference.

They're never going to rebuild it, thought Isabel as she got on board. *The foundations are all gouged out. And God only knows how much it would cost. And there's too much else that needs rebuilding now… like about a dozen major cities and three or four entire states. And everybody knows President Pratt would rather get a root canal than spend one dime more on infrastructure than he has to. And really, what would be the point? To force the river back into its old bed for another ten or twenty years?*

But even if it made sense, we wouldn't do it. Oh, we'd say we were going to do it—we'd promise ourselves every year that we were going to get around to it one of these days. But it'd be like those space missions we keep hearing about—back to the moon, on to Mars—the ones that never seem to get out of the planning phase. Or that nationwide high-speed rail network that's been ten years in the future for as long as I can remember. When did we become the country that's always going to do things? When did we stop being the country that actually does things? She turned and looked at the American flag hanging limp in the still air. *Old* Glory. Right now that seemed like the perfect name for it.

IN EVERY DISASTER, NO MATTER how terrible, there are always a few people who stay behind and try to ride it out. Exasperated governors have taken to advising these people to write their SSNs on their bodies somewhere to make their corpses easier to identify.

In the case of those who remained along the Atchafalaya when the ORCS failed, this would have been a waste of time. Almost none of their bodies were ever found.

For the first thirty miles or so of its new course, the Mississippi appeared in the form of an oncoming wall of water several miles wide that cut through human civilization like a windshield through a swarm of gnats. Every town from Simmesport to Krotz Springs simply vanished, scoured from the face of the land as though they had never existed. A few of the inhabitants of Krotz Springs, seeing the ORCS collapse on their screens, had just enough time to get in their cars and head for high ground.

Further south, the river spread out, losing some of its force. A stretch of I-10 several miles wide, and the levees around Morgan City by the Gulf, were undermined and collapsed instead of simply being annihilated in one blow. The heavier bits of debris—pieces of the ORCS, the Krotz Springs Bridge—found resting places and sank into the silt. Other pieces of debris lodged against their north sides, forming the foundations of new islands in the new delta.

OCTOBER 10:

IT WAS WITH SOME PLEASURE that Carrie signed the Drug Law Reform Act. Its official name was something a lot longer, but nobody cared, least of all her. Henceforth in Virginia, marijuana would be legal. Other things—heroin, cocaine, methamphetamine, black-market prescription drugs—would lead to small fines and mandatory time in a drug treatment center. Distribution of those things would lead to much bigger fines. *Distribution*, not "intent to distribute"—Pratt was right about that. All this would save the commonwealth a fair amount of money in the long run.

A pity they couldn't get an advance on that money now. Of the fifty Emergency Housing Centers that FEMA was planning to build—each capable of housing up to six hundred thousand people—one was in the Shenandoah Valley. To put that another way, for at least a few months the commonwealth would have a new city in it with over double the population of Richmond.

Which would be a good deal, if anybody in that city were going to be earning any taxable income. As it was, they were going to put a massive demand on services for as long as they were there, and Carrie wasn't sure how much help she was going to get from Washington. The one guy there who hated to spend taxpayers' money was also the one guy in the Oval Office.

This was coming at a time when half the commonwealth was tightening its belts… literally. The price of wheat, corn and soybeans was already going up in anticipation of future shortages. And food was a fungible commodity. When people started to bulk-buy rice and potatoes, within a week the price of those had gone up too.

And that didn't even include the economic problems they were having in the Tidewater, which were like the Rust Belt and the coal country rolled into one. The only people putting any money into those areas were speculators like her genius of a brother, buying up coastal property cheap and trusting in the government to restore its "true" value.

If nothing else, this would be good for the farming communities. Most of Carrie's time in Virginia had been spent in Richmond or the Norfolk area, and most of her political allies were north of the Rappahannock, but you could never neglect the rural areas—that lesson had been learned, thank you. And Virginia's farms, being too far north for the heat kill, too far east for the drought and too far south for the Monsoon, had been blessed with bountiful harvests this year. You had to take your blessings where you found them at times like this. According to Thel, who was studying in Beijing this school year, the food situation over there was worse... for the general public, if not for exchange students.

OCTOBER 22:

ISABEL STEPPED OUT OF THE shower and started scrubbing at her hair with a towel. The drier she got it doing this, the less she'd have to use the dryer. With the pipelines still cut, power bills weren't as high as they were on the other side of the Mississippi, but... she had other reasons for wanting to save money. (This would have been a great time for her to look at herself in the full-length mirror and spend a couple paragraphs admiring her naked body at various angles, but the mirror was still fogged over, so that was out. Sorry.)

Her armphone was resting on the bathroom windowsill. Just as she was about to turn on her hairdryer, it started playing "I Won't Forget" and said "It's Mom." She picked it up.

"Hi, Mom. What's up?"

"Hi, Isabel. How is everything? Are they giving you your job back?"

"Afraid not." Isabel bit her lip. It really hurt to disappoint her mother. "I got the word yesterday—they said not to bother coming back after the furlough. I've got severance pay, though. And I'm already looking."

"That's good. Is General Martineau going to be any help?"

"He didn't make any promises. I'm definitely going to be looking at the Corps."

"Well, I'm afraid I have some bad news too," said Mom. "And I think I should be the one to tell you, so Chelsey doesn't have to. Rod's left."

Isabel just stood there, blinking. There were so many bits of bad news she'd been expecting, but this wasn't any of them.

"I know you didn't like him."

"Well, yeah, but I didn't want him to disappear! Did he say why?"

"It's Chelsey. She hasn't been the same since that Jellicoe thing. She keeps forgetting to do things. Pay the bills, go shopping... I think the only reason she can still hold down her job is she doesn't like the job enough for it to mess with her mind. Anyway, Rod says he's willing to pay child support, but he doesn't feel qualified to be her caretaker."

"What about Jourdain? Did he take her?"

"No."

"It doesn't sound like Chelsey can take care of a child by herself right now."

"They're moving back in with us."

"You're kidding."

"Well, why not?"

"Because Mom-mom and Pop-pop are living there too!"

"They're helping take care of Jourdain."

"And what if things don't work out on Smith Island and you have to find room for your parents?"

"I don't think that's going to happen. Their house may be small, but it'll last as long as the island does. Speaking of people being other people's caretakers, how's Hunter?"

"Taking care of me right now," said Isabel. "He's turning out to be a pretty good cook."

"Really?"

"Really. He can do amazing things with a Crock-Pot." Which was true. In fact, at this very moment the Marksville apartment they shared was fragrant with the smell of a pot of chicken and sausage gumbo in the kitchen. He'd made it last night after he got home from work and set it to cook overnight. In a couple of hours it'd be done and they'd have dinner for breakfast, which was almost as good as having breakfast for dinner.

What Isabel didn't say was *Hunter never deviates from the recipe by so much as a teaspoon because he's too afraid of screwing up.* The story she'd heard from her friends about bachelor chefs was that most of them couldn't afford to throw away food that didn't turn out right, especially these days. So their standards went down a lot faster than their skills went up. They were eventually able to prepare meals to their own satisfaction, but not necessarily anybody else's. That made Hunter kind of a catch.

"Well, I'm glad to hear he's good at something."

"Mom," said Isabel, "did you ever criticize Rod this much?"

"Well, no, I didn't."

"And look how that turned out."

"It's not that simple, hon," she said. "I know I'm not being fair, but—how do I put this?" She paused for a moment.

"Chelsey was never going to make a smart choice," Mom finally said. "Her judgment was never as good as yours, even before… well, you know. We were all afraid she was going to end up with a bum or some criminal or something. Compared to that, Rod seemed pretty good."

Time for a complete change of subject. "What about that mildew problem in the kitchen? Has that been straightened out?" That had been a chronic issue ever since Gordon hit. Now that they had seven people in one house with frequent visits from Kristen, that seemed relevant.

"I think we need to call those guys back," said Mom. "I'm not convinced they got all the mildew."

"If you don't think they did it right the first time, why hire them the second time?"

"Addie Anthony recommended them. I don't want her to think I don't trust her."

ONCE THE CONVERSATION WAS OVER, Isabel finished drying herself off and put on her powder-blue bathrobe. She tied the sash tight around her waist, just enough to accentuate her curves. She also gave her hair an extra going-over with the dryer and combed it into something alluring.

She turned to glance at Hunter as she stepped out of the bathroom. He was awake, and quietly mustering the energy to haul himself out of bed. He worked the evening shift at a 3D print shop, which meant he got home pretty tired. On nights like last night, when he got home and fixed something for the next day, he collapsed into bed and was asleep in moments. They hadn't had sex since Sunday evening. Isabel was in a mood to rectify that, and the first step was to erectify him.

Isabel went to the kitchen, brewed a pot of chyq, poured Hunter a cup and waited. It was one of those mugs that changed color depending on the temperature of the contents. As soon as it had gone down from red to a sort of yellow-orange, the chyq would be at about the temperature Hunter liked. In the meantime, she had a cup herself.

Hunter's long hair, always messier than hers no matter what he did, was spread across the pillow. He looked much as he had in college—not obese, but heavy enough that Isabel usually preferred to be on top.

This was going to take some careful planning. Hunter was a good guy, but he had his mood swings. When he did something right, he'd do his victory dance and swagger around the apartment until there was no putting up with him. Actually, no—putting up with him at times like that was easy and fun, compared to the times when he'd collapse into a puddle of self-loathing and start beating himself up. Isabel beat herself up a lot too, but not where other people could hear her doing it.

"Good morning," she said brightly, handing him the cup.

"Good morning," said Hunter. "Gosh, you're looking… well, good, obviously, and… um…"

"I think 'frisky' is the word you're looking for."

Hunter took another sip. "Are we out of this?"

"We got enough for another pot."

"Good… I hate to worry, it's just everything's so expensive these days. The other day I spent ten bucks on a two-liter bottle of Coke and I got back three Red Rons* and change."

"That would be the high-fructose corn syrup." You never realized how much stuff had corn or soybeans in it until those crops failed big. "Chyq's still pretty cheap."

Hunter finished the cup and set it aside. "I'm really starting to worry about the shop," he said. "I think we might be in for another round of cutbacks. See, some of the chemicals we use—the plastics—they were made in those plants near New Orleans, the ones by the river. Jane's trying to get hold of another supplier, maybe a bioplastics company, but demand's pretty steep right now."

That wasn't good. As far as Isabel knew, Hunter was a good employee, but he'd only been working there four months—not exactly irreplaceable. **Maybe you should have thought about this stuff before you threw away your career.**

Oh hell no. You are NOT going to get on my case for that.

Everybody else at Eveland-Blades is going to be looking for a job too. You

---

* One of President Pratt's successes during his first hundred days in office was currency reform—eliminating the penny and the dollar bill and creating a permanent dollar coin to replace them. The dollar coin is made of the same copper-plated zinc that the U.S. penny was. On the face side, coins minted from January through April bear the image of George Washington, those minted from May through August show the image of Abraham Lincoln, and those minted from September through December show the image of Ronald Reagan. The original plan was for the U.S. Mint to begin producing and distributing the dollar coins at the beginning of next year, but they were able to do so two months early—hence the nickname "Red Rons."

ever think about them?

Okay, suppose I'd lied. Or suppose I'd just kept my mouth shut. Even if it didn't change anything, what would you be saying right now?

So you did what people are supposed to do. What do you want, a cookie?

I lost my job because I spoke up. The people I was trying to help have probably forgotten I exist. So yes, I would very much like a fucking cookie. Or at least for you to stop riding my ass. One of these days you're going to ask me to do the right thing and I'm just going to say no.

"Something the matter?" said Hunter.

"I was just thinking there's other places we could go, if you're feeling up for a big change of scenery." She smiled at him.

"Yeah?" Hunter smiled back. Encouraged by this, Isabel crept into the bed with a sinuous and sensual motion. Well, semi-sinuous. Definitely sensual though.

"Mom says they're talking about building biodiesel plants in Maryland," she said. "I'm going to see if there are any positions available." (Although from the point of view of someone who couldn't eat shellfish, Maryland wouldn't be much of an improvement over Louisiana.) "Until then… I'm just going to have to be your kept woman."

"I thought that was when you pay all your girlfriend's bills, but she doesn't live with you."

"Okay, then, your concubine." She slid the blanket off him.

"Isn't that like a really high-class hooker?"

"You're thinking of 'courtesan'."

"I thought a courtesan was somebody who worked for a king."

"That's a courtier." She unfastened his pajamas.

"Aren't those guys who make jewelry and watches and stuff?" Hunter smirked. "I can keep this up all day, you know."

"Let's see what else you can keep up." She brushed the tips of her hair back and forth over his groin, taking care to hit that particular line of nerves right… there. Yep. Hello. Worked every time.

NOVEMBER 20:

A PRESIDENT OF THE UNITED States—at least a good one—didn't get a lot of leisure time, particularly when the nation was in crisis. Henry Pratt had been working on one thing or another from 8 a.m. to 9 p.m. with only a couple of breaks for meals.

Pratt made the most of the few hours he did have. At 9:45 p.m. he was in bed with an e-reader in his left hand and Claire curled against his right arm. On the nightstand was a wineglass holding the last of a smoky '94 Oregon Pinot Noir, aged to a deep russet and mellowed to a velvety smoothness, that they'd shared over dinner.

An old Albert King and Stevie Ray Vaughan jam session, likewise mellowed to a velvety smoothness, was playing on his earpiece. Someone had once told Pratt that the Duke of Wellington had wanted to be a violinist before going into the army and making history. Pratt himself had once dreamed of being a blues guitarist and singer, but he had never been better than mediocre as a player and the same voice that served him so well at public speaking had sucked the life out of every song he'd ever tried to sing. So he'd had to settle for becoming President of the United States.

Pratt set down the book for a moment, picked up the glass and took another sip. The wine was almost perfectly balanced. Perhaps it was a little on the woody side—not enough to make it unpleasant, but enough to make him glad he and his wife had drunk it today. He tried to detect all the aromas and flavors the wine guide had promised, but, like his fingers and his voice when it came to the blues, his nose and palate could never quite capture all the notes. Not that he would ever stop trying.

The music made him feel sadder than usual. Claire had never been able to have a baby, and while they could have raised a dozen without straining their finances, they had both been so busy that it seemed wrong to seek out and adopt children that neither of them would have been able to spare the time and attention for. Listening to an older musician guiding and encouraging a younger one, Pratt felt that he'd missed out on something.

He took the earpiece out and tried concentrating on the book, but even that troubled him now. His wife stirred a little and looked up at him.

"What are you reading?"

"A biography," he said.

"Something bothering you?"

"You could say that." He tapped the screen of the e-reader. "This man I'm reading about… he was everything you could ask for in a leader. Successful engineer, successful businessman. His career took him all over the world. A war started, and he led a volunteer effort to get Americans out of the war zone. Then he started helping refugees from the war. Then the war ended, and he led a relief effort that saved millions of lives. He was in the president's cabinet when a massive flood hit the U.S., and he did a lot to help people there too.

"At this point, everybody thought… not just that he'd be president someday, but that he'd be a *great* president. I mean, if you tried to imagine the perfect man to become POTUS at a time of crisis and get the country through it, this would be the man."

"So who is this guy, and why have I never heard of him?"

"You have, actually. Herbert Clark Hoover." Pratt set the e-reader down on the nightstand, next to the wineglass and his cell phone.

"It's not that he did nothing," he said. "He did try to deal with the situation. If he'd just done a few things differently—vetoed that stupid tariff, gone off the gold standard when deflation hit, treated the Bonus Army with a little basic human decency…" Claire leaned her head on his shoulder and patted his arm. She could tell he wasn't really worried about Hoover.

"I can't fail, Claire," he said. "I can't become another failed president. Not now."

Claire squeezed his arm. "All you can do is… all you can do."

"I know." He rested one of his large, wrinkled hands on her small, wrinkled hand. Her glossy white hair was falling onto his chest. It hit Pratt how old everything in the room was—the furnishings, the wineglass, the wine, his wife, himself. Only his phone, earpiece, and e-reader belonged to the twenty-first century, and the earpiece was playing music from the 1980s while the e-reader was showing a book about a man who lived a century ago.

It felt like he was trying to take a break from this year. While he was enjoying the comforts of the White House, right now thirty million Americans were in mobile homes and tents and hastily built cabins, and most of them were likely to stay there for at least the next six months. From what NWS was telling him, north of the 45th parallel it wouldn't even be possible to start rebuilding until spring. And even though the emergency housing shelters were supposed to be for refugees from the Northern Monsoon, they were becoming magnets for others—people made homeless by wildfires in the West and South, or people from towns in Texas, Oklahoma, and New Mexico that were being gradually abandoned because their water supply had dried up… and of course plain old homeless people.

The worst thing about the Monsoon was not knowing when or where it would happen again. If it was going to hit the U.S. every ten years, or five years, or three years, they could at least plan around it, but how many years would it take to get a sense of how likely it was to hit in any given fall? And what were they supposed to do in the meantime?

What was it he'd said about climate change? *A healthy economy is the best defense.* He still believed it. Unfortunately, the economy had been washed into the Gulf of Mexico. Now people were looking for the second-best defense, and he didn't have one.

And then there was the Norfolk Plan, which was a proposed solution to an entirely different and much more long-term problem, and which had arrived on the front steps of Congress all wrapped up with a neat little bow and a note on it saying PLEASE SOMEBODY FIND A WAY TO PAY FOR THIS. The U.S. had over twelve thousand miles of coastline. The only way to buy all of it without breaking the budget would be to declare eminent domain and offer bargain-basement compensation. Not only did this go against everything Pratt believed in, but it would ruin every property owner on the coast. Which would defeat the entire purpose of the Plan.

Pratt's thoughts were interrupted when his phone began playing "Isfahan." The Secretary of Defense was calling. He reluctantly disentangled himself from Claire, got up and sat behind the desk with his head turned away from his wife. He trusted her, but need-to-know meant need-to-know, and there was nothing Swanston was likely to call at this hour to say that she needed to hear.

"Hello?"

"CASSIUS is ready, Mr. President." Pratt had never cared much for operational names like "Infinite Justice," "Enduring Freedom" or "Mighty Hand." They sounded like something a totalitarian regime with a very crude propaganda arm would come up with. He preferred names that sent the message: *this will do something, and if you can't tell what, neither can the enemy.*

"How long can we keep it at readiness?"

"Three to four months."

"Thank you, Simon."

"I'm having someone place the envelope in the football tonight," he said. "I hope to God you never need it."

"So do I."

"In case you do, remember… *the green bird.*"

"Say that again?"

"The green bird. That's the rune. Remember it."

CASSIUS. The green bird. Pratt shut his eyes and took a few minutes to commit it to memory. *CASSIUS. The green bird. CASSIUS. The green bird. CASSIUS. The green bird.*

WITH THE SNARLING OF OCEAN currents, Europe west of Helsinki, Lviv, and Istanbul experienced the worst winter in twenty years. Heavy snow alternated with subzero temperatures everywhere north of Madrid and Naples.

Some speculated that this would be the beginning of a major cooling trend for Europe, or perhaps even for the whole world. They pointed to sudden drops in temperature 8,500 and 12,000 years ago, also believed to have been caused by intrusions of glacial meltwater into the North Atlantic. But those events had happened on an immeasurably larger scale, and in a very different world—a world only just emerging from the depths of the last ice age. No one could really say what effect this would have now.

As it turned out, they weren't even asking all the right questions. An equally valid question would have been "What effect would slowing or stopping the Gulf Stream have at the other end?" After all, the only way the Gulf Stream had ever warmed Europe was by cooling the tropics. The breakdown in the North Atlantic Drift was like closing off two lanes of traffic on a busy highway. As the Gulf Stream slowed, warm tropical water backed up all along the east coast. Some of it turned east further south, to Madeira and North Africa, bringing unexpected heat to the Canary Current and heavy rains to the normally arid lands.

But most of it just stayed there, a swelling in the water that raised the high-tide mark by three to thirteen inches along the coast from the Outer Banks to Key West. The warmer water allowed tropical storms to form well past the end of November. A Category 1 hurricane hit the city of Charleston on Christmas Day.

What truly occupied the minds of world leaders was on the other side of the planet. In the last few weeks of December, U.S. and South Korean military intelligence began to receive reports of numerous incursions by the North Korean army into the Korean Demilitarized Zone. All these incursions were small-scale—sometimes whole squads, but more often pairs or trios of soldiers, bearing nothing but small arms. They didn't seem to be concentrating on any one area—the incursions were taking place all along the border. And if confronted by South Korean forces, they would always retreat at once.

Experts in Seoul and the Pentagon puzzled over this behavior, trying to determine what strategy lay behind it. Was North Korea testing for weaknesses in the American and South Korean defenses? Laying the groundwork for a major attack? Or simply trying to keep up an appearance of strength in the midst of the worst food crisis in its history?

The truth was far more mundane and less directly threatening, but more frightening in its implications. It was discovered on December 27 by a company of South Koreans who ventured into the DMZ following the sound of gunfire. They caught two malnourished North Korean soldiers carrying the carcass of a musk deer.

It was really that simple. The army—or rather, the soldiers in the army—were acting entirely without orders. The DMZ, simply by being off limits to human habitation for decades, had become one of the great wildlife refuges of the world's temperate zones. The soldiers were going into it, guns in hand, to hunt for game.

Pyongyang had always had trouble feeding its people. Now it could no longer even feed its own army.

YEAR FIVE

IF AT FIRST YOU DON'T SUCCEED...

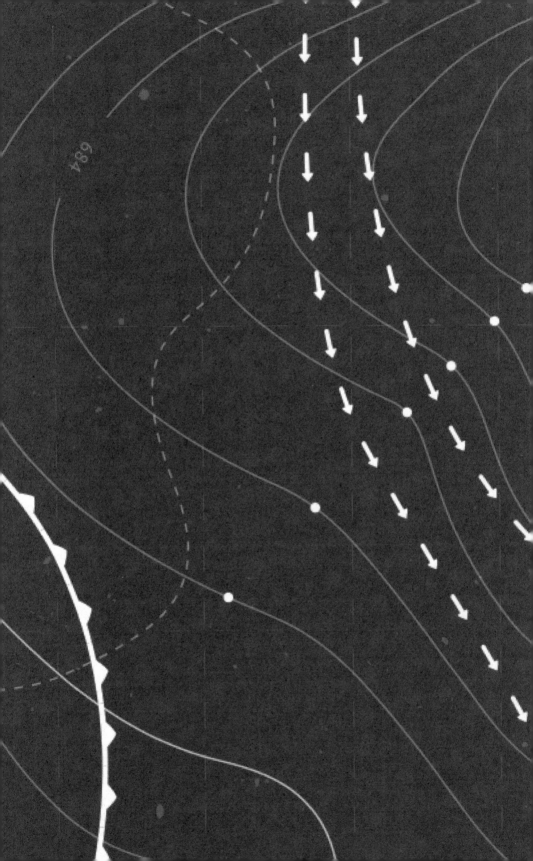

THERE ARE TWO KINDS OF *bad weather generally associated with winter—extreme subzero temperatures, and heavy snowfalls. Fortunately for the well-being of mankind, these are rarely seen in the same place at the same time. The heaviest winter storms are those that happen when the air is just above or just below freezing, and moisture-laden winds blow in from some warmer part of the world.*

By January a blanket of snow, four to seven feet thick, lay over most of Canada and the United States north of Wyoming, Nebraska, and the Great Lakes. It was widely compared to lake-effect snow, except that the "lake" in question was the Arctic Ocean and Hudson Bay. Within this blanket, the people who had stayed through the Northern Monsoon now survived as tight-knit communities, living off whatever they could salvage from empty, flooded homes and whatever meager federal aid made its way to them.

But the Gulf of Mexico was warmer than ever, and moist tropical winds came north and northeast over the United States. Where they met the blanket of snow and the pool of cold air above it, blizzards and ice storms formed. They slashed across the map like razors from the upper Midwest to New Jersey and southern New England.

The ice storms were the worst. Roads quickly became impossible and deadly to drive on. Ice built up on the power lines, the few remaining telephone landlines, and the cell phone towers. Blackouts struck the Chicago area, then Indianapolis, then a dozen places in Ohio and Pennsylvania. For forty terrible hours, New York City lost power entirely. Mayor Lopez ordered the dark and silent subways to be opened as shelters for those who had no heat at home. With salt and sand beginning to run low, FEMA had to requisition fresh supplies from Virginia, Kentucky, and North Carolina to help the northern states keep open ice-free paths between the cities.

All over the High Plains, oil pipelines ruptured in the storms. With so many places where the roads had collapsed or been buried under snow, repair crews were sent out in snowmobiles to fix the pipes before the spring thaw.

JANUARY 16:

ISABEL STOOD AT THE FRONT of the meeting room and gestured at the blueprints. "A heliotrope array and fiber optic cable are definitely the way to go," she said. "First of all, you're trying to maximize photosynthesis, and natural sunlight is the best. Second, I don't care how good solar panels get, turning sunlight into electricity and back into light again is never going to be as efficient as using sunlight directly—the laws of thermodynamics are pretty clear on this point."

The director looked a little skeptical. "What about the energy cost of the array tracking the sun?"

"That's negligible. We're talking about incremental movements over a twenty-four-hour period. Sunflowers do it without running a loss—that's where the designers got the idea."

The director, Sean Lao, steepled his fingers for a moment.

Then he nodded. "I like it," he said.

The meeting was in the office of Marshpower Biofuels, Inc., an anonymous little suite of offices in a business park near Annapolis, miles from the construction site where the plant was already being built. Marshpower was one of several companies building new stormwater-and-sewage treatment and biofuels plants up and down the East Coast. Their business plan looked something like this:

• Say what you will about them, long-chain hydrocarbons are a very effective way to store a lot of energy in a convenient package of whatever size you may need.

• Burning them, of course, releases all that carbon into the atmosphere. But in the case of biofuels, the carbon was removed from the atmosphere to make them in the first place, so no harm, no foul.

• Algae can be engineered to convert sunlight and atmospheric carbon into those helpful hydrocarbons. Since people don't often eat algae and it isn't grown on arable land, this gets rid of the problem of humans having to compete with their own machines for food.

• Up until now, this technology hasn't really been able to compete with fossil fuels in terms of the price of the fuel. However, the loss of the ORCS and the petrochemical infrastructure of the Texas-Louisiana area has boosted the price of fuel somewhat. Also, many state governments are willing to subsidize it as much as necessary.

• One good feedstock for algae is sewage.

• Everybody poops.

• Sewage flows downhill.

• A lot of low-lying land on the coast has recently become quite affordable, even near the cities. Where there are millions of people. Every single one of whom, as aforesaid, poops. And pees. That's useful too.

Most of the cash Marshpower had on hand right now was from the sale of small biodiesel plants to chicken farms around here and to pig farms in North Carolina. Isabel had helped set a few of those up. A lot of manure that might otherwise have been a nuisance to dispose of went into those things. And there were rumors that some large group of investors was trying to buy a controlling share in Marshpower, which might give the company a little more cash to work with.

WHAT WITH ONE THING AND another, Isabel didn't get out of the building until just after six. It was a pleasantly cool April evening… in the middle of January, but people were getting used to this sort of thing by now. When Isabel turned the key on her old first-generation hybrid, the car's wi-fi started playing "Darkness and Snow," one of those songs Rodomontade wrote based on an old poem from a century ago, written by T.S. Eliot or W.H. Auden… unless it was W.H. Eliot and T.S. Auden. Isabel wasn't literary enough to say. Traffic on the Bay Bridge was light, but the surface was hard on the car's suspension. Money for bridge repairs was another thing in short supply.

Dinner that evening was a rather thin soup made from a half pound of finely chopped beef hearts, whatever vegetables had been in the bargain produce*

---

* "Bargain produce" means fruits and vegetables that are deformed or unsightly, but otherwise wholesome to eat. Rising food prices have inspired many supermarket chains to offer this to their customers as a cheap and edible alternative.

section the last time Hunter had gone shopping, and enough Old Bay to cover a multitude of sins, especially blandness.

"You don't have to pretend it's any good," said Hunter, staring into his own bowl. They were having Quesch with dinner, but it didn't seem to be cheering him up any.*

"Considering what you had to work with, it's not bad."

"Thanks… nice to know I can do something right."

"I'm guessing the job interview didn't go so great."

"You could say that. I got there, and they told me they were going out of business at the end of the month."

"I can see how that would be kind of discouraging… any luck with one of those house-moving companies?" The Eastern Shore was blessed with a great many fine old colonial homes which had been built centuries ago and were good to last for centuries to come, if only they weren't so close to the waterfront. So if you were a rich guy whose McMansion had been built in the '00s and was falling apart around your ears, you could do worse than buy one of those old houses cheap and have it moved to higher ground.

"I've sent in my résumé, but I don't think I've got the job experience they're looking for."

"Have you checked the schools? I know they've gotten completely toilet, but there's got to be an opening for a science teacher."

"You think they'd hire me?"

"You were a pretty decent student, and you liked the subject," said Isabel. "You don't have a teaching degree or anything, but I don't think the schools are going to care—with this budget crisis going on, at this point they'll hire pretty much anybody. No offense."

"Could you really see me as a teacher?"

"As long as you don't start beating yourself up in front of the students… yes, I could. Of course, you wouldn't be earning much of any money, but it would be something."

---

* Quesch's main selling point, as a soft drink, is that it contains small traces of THC—not enough to get completely high on unless you drink three or four liters at one sitting, but enough for a slight effect.

JANUARY 17:

ISABEL BRADSHAW, IN HER CURRENT incarnation as Belle772505, was hanging upside down in the forward ball turret of the airship *Unsung Hero*, waiting for the centaurs to come into view. Her long white-blond hair whipped behind her as she scanned the western horizon with her spyglass. The wind stirred the mottled-silver fur of her jacket, made from the hide of a Lyncid warrior-mage who'd made the mistake of picking a fight with her during the last big quest.

They can't have gone far, she thought. *It's not like there's anywhere to hide.* This part of the world was an endless expanse of grassy plains, low hills, and occasional cottonwood-lined creeks.

The *Unsung Hero* floated in the middle of the formation, between the *Trumpeter* and the *Clockmaker's Daughter*. They were a mile and a half in the air, trying to see as far as possible.

The Republic of Alvar had hired the Hindenburger Guild to help it fight off the centaurs. The war band known as the Stinging Wasps had been seen near Fort MacLaine, westernmost outpost of Alvar. But where were they now, and what were they up to?

There was definitely a fight coming. The game was pretty reliable that way. Victory here would protect not only the people of Alvar, but the investments of their true employer, the Magnatess Astoria Kingsmark. In the long, secret war that defined this world—between steam and magic, between the engineer and the sorcerer—you never knew what might tip the balance.

Belle772505 was ready. The turret was equipped with a Gatling gun and an exquisitely crafted bronze grenade launcher, both fully loaded. In case something jammed, she had a spare oilcan tucked between her breasts—sexual harassment was forbidden by both guild law and the game admins, so she'd seen no reason to stint herself when designing her character. Although she was a lot less well-endowed than Kym_the_Sniper on the *Trumpeter*, who she suspected was a guy in real life.

There was a line of dark cloud on the horizon. It didn't quite look like the smoke from a prairie fire, and was the wrong color for a storm.

Then the lookout, Falconer66, gave the traditional cry of *"Oh shit!"* As Belle772505 looked deeper into the cloud and first caught the low, steady rumble, she understood why.

Thunderbeasts.

Millions of thunderbeasts. The herd stretched for miles to north and south, a sea of shaggy black hair and gray-brown hide, half-hidden by the cloud of dust they were raising. They looked something like bison, except that they each had two pairs of long horns on their heads and short black elephant trunks for noses… and they were the size of the extinct *Indricotherium*. And on the fringes of the herd were centaurs in full war paint, each one waving a torch.

Now they knew exactly how the Stinging Wasps were going to attack the fort. The problem was how to defend it. Thunderbeasts were afraid of nothing except fire, and in full charge even that wasn't guaranteed to stop them. This herd would crash right through the stockade of Fort MacLaine and trample it into garden mulch, along with everybody inside it.

Belle772505 looked up—down, from her POV—at the other two airships. The semaphore panels on the decks were signaling… that OnyxFan11, a.k.a. Hunter, and the other airship commanders were squabbling in a way which would have gotten any real-life military unit killed in combat.

Finally, a clear plan emerged. *Split the herd. Try to deflect most of it to the north.* Hero, Daughter, *go five miles south of here and set the grass on fire.* Trumpeter, *go to the southern edge and start picking off the centaurs.*

The *Trumpeter* carefully stayed above a thousand feet, well out of the vertical range of any rifles the Stinging Wasps were likely to possess. Getting shot down would be very bad. The centaurs of the western plains had been modeled so closely on the 19th-century Comanche that a lot of people found them offensive. You didn't want to get captured alive by them.

For this to work, the other two airships would have to go a little lower. It was a good thing thunderbeasts didn't have rifles. And they'd have to work quickly. A charging animal that weighs fifteen to twenty tons can't turn on a dime—not if its physics are being properly modeled. They'd have to start the fire well in front of the herd.

Coils of rope and sacks of coal, already on fire, fell from the decks. Isabel loaded the grenade launcher with incendiaries and fired them at the ground. With a sudden inspiration, she took out the spare oilcan, loosened the top and put it in front of the next grenade. The oil spread into the air hundreds of feet below, then erupted into a bloom of fire when the grenade went off.

Just then, Isabel heard the opening bars of "I Won't Forget" and a voice saying "It's Kristen."

Cold, wordless dread ran down her spine and along her nerves. Not only was that her family's ringtone, but her phone was on Protocol 3 screening—any caller would be sent to voicemail except for a select few, who would be asked to affirm that this was an emergency.

"Sorry, guys," she said. "RLE. Gotta bail." Her guildmates were a decent bunch. They understood real-life emergencies. Isabel took off the VR headset and picked up her armphone. Kristen would never say something was an emergency unless it damn well was.

"What's up?"

"We took Pop-pop to the ER this morning. His breathing is getting worse—he was coughing and wheezing all night."

Isabel nodded.

"We just got the word," Kristen continued. "It's definitely mildew. He'll live, but he'll need to be somewhere else for a while. The Comegys have agreed to take him in. I'll stop by and look after him when I can."

"I take it their house got cleaned up properly?"

"We think so, yeah," said Kristen. "And on top of everything else, the doctor said he'd have to report it to the state. Seems HCD is cracking down on houses with mold problems and stuff." As far as Isabel was concerned, the Department of Housing and Community Development would be welcome to personally spank the entire family if they would just pay to clean the house properly themselves.

"How's everybody else doing?"

"Nobody else is having any health problems," said Kristen. "Not yet, anyway."

ALL THROUGH JANUARY, SMALL SQUADS of North Korean soldiers began threading their way through the U.S. and South Korean lines under cover of darkness. Avoiding military outposts, they struck at civilian targets, appearing out of nowhere and vanishing in minutes. It was the oldest form of warfare in human history—the raid for plunder.

But the North Koreans hadn't come for cattle, or gold, or women. They'd crossed the DMZ for the sole purpose of looting the grocery stores. Last year had been a bad one for agriculture in the Republic of Korea, but what seemed just barely adequate to them looked like endless abundance to their northern cousins.

When these bands encountered units of the South Korean army on patrol, they sometimes fought, but far more often they fled. And thousands of them surrendered without firing a single shot. The South Korean government quickly set up an interment facility at Cheorwon to accommodate this influx of prisoners. There they fed the prisoners as best they could… which again looked good to the soldiers.

Some of the soldiers "escaped" from Cheorwon—the ROK Armed Forces made no effort to stop them—and ran back north to tell their comrades of the good treatment they'd received. But the DPRK government had spies within the ranks of its own army, and they reported what was happening back to Pyongyang.

Somewhere in the capital, somebody panicked.

FEBRUARY 3:

HANDS CLAPPED NEXT TO HIS ear. "Wake up, sir."

Pratt never woke up before 7 a.m. unless it was an emergency. It was well before that now. And it was Noreen Baxter, one of his Secret Service agents, clapping her hands. And the voice saying "Wake up, sir," belonged to John Edmondson, who only Pratt and a few others knew was the man entrusted with the nuclear football.

Edmondson—short, thickset, black, and about fifty—was much more than just a baggage handler for the world's deadliest carry-on. He was the Pentagon's emergency liaison with the President. As soon as Pratt was sitting up and had his glasses on, Edmondson handed him a tablet, already turned on.

The news was simple—North Korea had launched one short-range nuclear missile. Cheorwon was gone. No word on casualties, but a thirty-kiloton bomb had exploded right over the barracks two minutes ago.

Pratt hadn't gotten where he was today by being indecisive. "Open the briefcase," he said as he sat up. In bed behind him, he heard Claire's sharp intake of breath. None of this was for her ears, but no help for that. "Hand me the 'CASSIUS' envelope."

Ever since he'd ordered CASSIUS prepared, Pratt had been afraid of one of two things happening. One was that he would receive evidence that North Korea *might* be about to launch an attack… or might not. Then he'd have to decide whether to execute CASSIUS, and how to explain it to China afterward. The other was that North Korea would attack on a massive scale with no warning at all and the operation, which took several minutes to implement, would be too late.

Compared to that, the deaths of thousands of POWs and an unknown number of civilians was something of a best-case scenario. It was an attack South Korea would survive—but it was unquestionably, inarguably, an attack. No one could doubt that Pratt had the right to do what he was about to do.

He took the manila envelope and broke the seal. Inside the package was a cell phone, a thumb drive, and a smaller envelope.

Pratt switched on the cell phone and pushed SEND. The phone was programmed to dial only one number. A message appeared on the screen:

PLEASE SELECT RUNE

Pratt hooked the thumb drive up to the phone. A gallery of photos appeared at the bottom. One of them was of a little green bird with a red face. Pratt selected that photo, and a microphone icon appeared on the screen.

The computer at the other end of the line was programmed to recognize his voice. The Pentagon had hired three different voice actors to try to fool it. None of them had succeeded.

He opened the envelope. Inside was a single sheet of paper with four words on it. Pratt held the phone up and, in his best orator's voice, uttered the words:

"Speak, hands, for me."

It was done. Now there could be no going back. Pratt got out of bed, pulled a bathrobe off the back of a chair, and slid his feet into a pair of slippers. As he did this, he made a mental note to reread *Julius Caesar* when this was over and see if it was actually Cassius who had said that. He had a feeling it wasn't.

By the time he'd reached the Situation Room, the smell of brewing coffee was in the air. Also in the air were many cruise missiles and Nightgaunt drones launched from U.S. subs parked just outside North Korean territorial waters.

AS CARRIE WAS PUZZLING OVER how to compose the presentation, the plane whoomphed.

That really was the best word for it. It wasn't sudden or violent enough to be a thump, and it wasn't quite long enough to be a shudder. It was just enough disruption to make her glad she didn't have a glass of water on her tray. It happened a couple more times over the next five seconds.

She sighed. For as long as she could remember, the airlines had responded to every change in technology and the economy by making air travel more unpleasant. Now the flights were longer, more prone to turbulence and passengers had to bring their own food, which was especially annoying on an intercontinental flight like this one, although it did make it easier to stick to her diet.* She would have liked to take a private plane, but jet-setting around the world at Symcox's expense would do her no good come election time, especially if what she was burning was fossil fuels.

Carrie returned her attention to the presentation. She thought she had a pretty good way to begin. This podcast from an Alice Springs blogger, made on January 28 of this year, would certainly set the right tone:

Fifty degrees. Three damn weeks.

One of the little drawbacks to this job was having to re-learn the metric system. Finding out what fifty degrees centigrade was in Fahrenheit had been horrifying.

> You can't go outside during the day—not without a couple gallons of chilled water which you're supposed to be conserving. You can't drive anywhere—the streets have melted. Even when they're cool enough to be solid, they look like somebody put Salvador Dalí in charge of a road crew.
>
> So anything you have to do, you do at night, on foot. Businesses, city offices… everybody's changed their hours. I used to be the

---

* All for the same reason—thanks to the use of reinforced graphene, the planes' fuselages have gotten lighter, which means they don't need as much lift to reach the same cruising altitude and can burn less fuel even while flying slower. Unfortunately, not only is the lighter body more affected by turbulence, but longer flights need more water, which is incompressible. Eliminating in-flight meals frees up storage space for drinking water.

sort of woman who would build her plans for the day around not having to cross a parking lot alone at night. Now I go shopping at 3 a.m. and think nothing of it. It's a lot less dangerous with everybody else doing the same thing.

Anyone vulnerable to heatstroke is supposed to be evacuated to Darwin or Adelaide. There's about an 8-to-10-hour window at night when these people can go outside long enough to do this. Using small planes. Big ones can't land, because the tarmac at the airport has melted. Forget the train—the tracks are buckled in a dozen places.

Early afternoon is the worst. You're supposed to be asleep by then. Not lying awake listening to the AC running full blast and thinking "What if it breaks down? What if the power goes out? What if some vital piece of machinery turns out not to have been designed for this kind of heat?"

Once everybody had gotten an earful of this, she'd point out that all these things had happened in one of the less inhabited parts of a fairly rich country—one which could afford to put air conditioning in every home, every business, every public building. In a country where this wasn't the case, a heat wave like this one could kill millions of people in a few days. There was nothing to stop it from happening. Back in '03, a much milder heat wave had killed about seventy thousand people in the heart of Europe, simply because at the time they were used to such an even climate that not that many people bothered with AC.

Carrie started typing:

Luckily, you can turn almost any large, enclosed space into a temporary heat shelter for several hundred people. You need air conditioning—a central unit, and some window units in case the central unit fails. You need something to power it in case the grid fails—solar panels, for preference. Medical supplies. A refrigeration unit capable of holding, at minimum, 50,000 liters of water. And of course you need the water.

But if we assume this is something that's going to be needed, on and off, for the foreseeable future, then instead of retrofitting an existing space every year it makes more sense to create purpose-built shelters that will last longer with less maintenance.

The simplest way to do that is to put it underground. No matter how hot it gets on the surface, go down five to ten meters and it's maybe fifteen degrees maximum. Of course, if you've got a lot of people down there—first, you have their body heat to think about, and second, you've got to have air circulating. And if some of the people in there are sick—which is probably the case—you don't want everybody breathing the same air.

So lots of ventilation. If you run the ventilation shafts through the ground, that should cool the air and cut down on the need for AC.

As far as light goes, these shelters will mostly be in use during the daytime, so fiber-optic lighting is an option for parts of it. If somebody needs medical attention, or if you just want to put in a reading room—people are going to get bored in there—you'll want something a little brighter. And of course cell phone and Internet access are a must. If anything goes wrong in there, people have to know.

But for this summer we're concentrating on giving people the tools they need to refit existing spaces into temporary shelters. I mean, the worst thing that could happen is that we'd have ten villages in an area that need shelters and only one that has one. Then we would just have given people something to fight over.

Suddenly, she became aware that people all around her were muttering "holy shit" and "have you seen this?" A second later, she saw that the news app on her tablet was blinking red. She clicked on it.

As soon as Carrie saw the news, she forgot all about the presentation. Cheorwon—which was technically a POW camp, but actually more of a refugee camp—had just been hit by an attack from North Korea. A nuclear attack.

Even now, an ugly little part of her brain was thinking *if Pratt handles this well it might make him harder to run against in two years*, but the rest of her forced it to shut up. This wasn't the time. Roger was at a conference in New York City. Thel was in Beijing, and while China wasn't a part of this war, it could become a part in a matter of minutes. She wasn't going to worry about how this might affect her future political career until she knew exactly how much world there would be when this plane landed, or how much country and how much family she'd be coming home to.

"MR. PRESIDENT?" SAID JIM ON the State Department's screen.

"Yes?"

"We just got word from Pyongyang," he said. "They're saying that the launch at Cheorwon was strictly a 'punitive action' against 'mutineers,' not an act of aggression. They're instructing us not to respond."

"They're instructing us, are they?" said Pratt. He turned to Swanston. "How soon are our missiles going to come within range of their radar?"

"Right about... um... now."

AS SOON AS THE CRUISE missiles were detected in North Korean airspace, the government ordered its whole nuclear arsenal launched. Despite this, many of the weapons were destroyed on the ground. Many, but not all.

A missile can be hidden—a missile launch can't. The plume of fire is visible at night even to human eyes, and is unmistakable by infrared. This provided a target for the Nightgaunts, aerial drones which could be used to destroy missiles at or near their launch point. This was the old "hit a bullet with a bullet" problem, but a Nightgaunt could make course corrections much faster and more accurately than a human could, putting itself on course to intercept the missile in flight. It also had a five-kiloton warhead of its own, set to go off within fifty meters of the target. Over much of North Korea, the night was interrupted by a few seconds of daylight as the Nightgaunts exploded five to ten miles over the surface, causing no damage on the ground but blinding the unfortunates who were looking up to watch the missiles.

Of North Korea's nuclear arsenal, nine short-range missiles, two Taepodong-2 missiles and one Taepodong-3 missile survived Operation Cassius—but they were still being tracked. The Stormcrows, high-altitude surveillance drones, identified the launch sites, calculated the flight paths, and fed the data to U.S. and South Korean anti-ballistic missile systems, updating every ten seconds in case the missiles changed course.

With this data, the Americans and South Koreans were able to destroy eight of the nine short-range missiles before they could reach their target. The ninth suffered a glancing blow from a kinetic warhead, which damaged its guidance system and sent it off course. It detonated over seven miles off the coast, well away from the city of Ulsan where it had been aimed. Ironically, the only South Koreans to die in this attack were those who chose to evacuate the city by sea and happened to move their boats into the blast radius.

Far more damaging to South Korea was the artillery barrage that began at about the same time as the missile launches. Maybe half of the North Korean artillery crews were still at their posts and obeying orders, and only three quarters of their shells went off, but that was more than enough to wreak havoc on Seoul, especially in the north. Not many of the people in the city had a chance to evacuate or seek shelter before the bombardment began.

But the Americans were focused on the three Taepodongs. The Stormcrows watched them arc toward the edge of space and sent the data to the Air Force, which alerted the Missile Defense Agency. As it happened, two of the missiles were headed for Alaska and Los Angeles—almost directly at the Interceptor sites at Vandenberg and Fort Greeley.

The Ground-based Midcourse Defense, the next line of defense against missiles, had the same hit-a-bullet-with-a-bullet problem as the Nightgaunts. Their solution was lots of "bullets"—Exoatmospheric Kill Vehicles, which were intended to collide with the incoming missile while it was in space.

The missile headed for Los Angeles had the longest path—one that took it just south of the Aleutians over the Pacific, bringing it to the attention of both Fort Greeley and Vandenberg. As a result, it was the only one that was struck even a glancing blow. The missile survived, but was knocked slightly off course.

At the same time that it was calling the MDA, the Air Force relayed the information to the FCC, which activated the Emergency Alert System. In Alaska, Hawaii, and California, citizens were awakened from their sleep by the sudden terror of air raid sirens. They had less than ten minutes in which to decide how to respond. Some got into their cars and fled. Others took shelter in their basements. Others simply gathered their families together, held each other and prayed.

"WE'RE GOING TO TAKE AT least one hit, Mr. President," said Swanston. "Probably more. No way to stop it now."

Damn. Damn. It wasn't that Pratt had any doubt he'd done the right thing— you couldn't let a country set off a nuke on an ally's turf with no provocation at all and get away with it, not if you ever wanted to have another ally again—but a couple of American cities were about to be damaged or destroyed on his watch and there was nothing he could do about it. "Counterstrike options?"

"If they have any nuclear assets left, we have no way of knowing where to look. What we do have are fourteen possible locations of underground complexes in or near the capital where the government could be hiding. We can hit those sites with bunker busters… or we can respond with a large-scale attack."

Henry Pratt had never had a taste for vengeance. If you saw a threat and neutralized it, your work was done as far as he was concerned. On the other hand, he understood the logic of deterrence—sending a message to every nation that might be watching. *Strike a blow against America on her own soil, and you and everything you love will perish in fire.*

"If they do have anything left—on a submarine, say—we used all our GMD assets on those three missiles," said Swanston.

"Sir," said Barber from the NSA, "in my opinion, the government is the one thing over there you don't want to destroy. We need somebody to negotiate with when the war's over."

So I should destroy the rest of North Korea and leave the government standing? Let a handful of well-heeled sociopaths be the sole survivors of a holocaust they caused? No thank you. Besides, Russia and China had to be on a hair trigger right now. One wrong move, one misidentified attack, and this could turn into the end of the world. Best to act with precision.

181

"I'll let them know when the war's over," he said. "Bunker busters. Aimed at Pyongyang. Take out all fourteen sites."

TO LOOK AT THIS APARTMENT, you wouldn't think the occupant was worth billions. In fact, she was going to move into a ludicrously expensive place overlooking Central Park in a few months, more to finalize her status as a member of the city's elite than because she needed the space. Right now, however, she was still living in this cramped little hole. At least it had good security.

Sandra Symcox was fixing herself breakfast. Whenever time allowed, she had at least one real meal a day, preferably in the morning. This one was... not really an omelet. It was two eggs beaten with salsa and garlic salt and fried in a pan, to be served with orange juice and coffee.

As she cooked, Sandy kept one eye on the big screen in the next room. It was a business news channel. She normally watched it with the forced attention of a good student taking a dull course that she needed to pass, but right now she was watching it with a certain smug pleasure. It was a report on Suiamor abuse at certain Wall Street firms. Apparently, a number of people had taken black-market swee in the hope that it would turn them into the ruthless corporate sharks they thought everyone wanted them to be. There had been... unintended consequences.

"Normally when you hear about homicide committed under the influence of drugs," a cop was saying, "you picture somebody going crazy and biting off somebody else's face. With swee, it's always some Agatha Christie bull[*bleep*] they try and—" The screen went dark blue, with the giant red sans-serif letters EAS dominating the top half. The words IMMINENT NUCLEAR ATTACK ON ALASKA, HAWAII scrolled across the bottom.

After that, Sandy didn't give a crap about swee abuse. New York City was America's biggest target—at least as much so as the capital. And where she was right now was Manhattan, the one place on Earth every terrorist and rogue leader on the planet had wet dreams about fucking up. *How quickly can I get out of this city?* she thought. *I knew I should have gotten a helicopter.*

Suddenly, an alarm sounded, high-pitched and painful.

It was just the smoke detector. Sandy switched off the stove and the alarm, thinking *if New York were in danger, don't you think somebody would have mentioned it?* Just to be on the safe side, she turned on her phone's input mike and spoke the words "nearest fallout shelter."

The non-omelet was scorched around the edges. She ate it anyway. When it came to wasting food, old habits died hard. And on a cold morning, you needed something hot and filling in your stomach. As she ate, she kept one eye on the screen and made a note of the path to the nearest shelter from here.

THE MISSILE AIMED AT HONOLULU landed in the ocean just south of Iroquois Point. The warhead failed to detonate.

The missile which had been aimed at Los Angeles landed some two hundred miles away, between Independence and Lone Pine in the Owens Valley. The good news was that the explosion was not from a hydrogen bomb, and killed only twenty-three people. The bad news was that it severed the Los Angeles Aqueduct.

The missile aimed at Anchorage didn't fail. At 3:03 a.m. local time, a quarter of a mile out to sea, a blinding fireball, sixteen hundred feet wide appeared over the ocean as the bomb went off with the force of thirty thousand tons of TNT— also not from a hydrogen bomb, but still more than half again the size of the Hiroshima explosion.

ISABEL'S EARPIECE WAS SET TO wake her up at 7:15 a.m. giving her enough time to shower, have some breakfast and head for work. Today something woke her up nine minutes earlier.

It was her armphone, sitting on her nightstand and chiming. She'd set the phone to make that noise when it got an ANMF news alert. The American News and Media Foundation was the only news organization in America that had resisted the urge to overuse its all-platform alert system to the point of worthlessness. If they sent an alert, it wasn't because some celebrity had had a butt implant. She picked up the phone and touched the news icon.

ATTACK ON U.S.
NORTH KOREA LAUNCHES NUCLEAR STRIKE
ON ANCHORAGE, ALASKA

Casualties unknown

Holy fuck they actually did it.

The video wasn't much help—you couldn't see anything besides the skyline of a town or city lined in fire. The still photo was much more impressive. Someone had used their phone to get a shot of the airburst at the moment when it was no longer blinding but still clearly visible—a crimson ball of light over the water, illuminating the already-smoldering and collapsing western half of the city and the underside of the mushroom cloud.

POSSIBLE SECOND STRIKE AGAINST HONOLULU
CITY UNDER MANDATORY EVACUATION
COAST GUARD SEARCHES FOR POSSIBLE WARHEAD
Mayor: "All I can tell you is, we're still standing"

U.S. DEFLECTS MISSILE STRIKE AGAINST L.A.
NO WORD ON PLANNED RETALIATION BY PRATT

This called for a bigger screen. Isabel put down the phone and picked up the tablet.

It didn't take long for her to bring herself up to speed. They'd nuked a place called Cheorwon on the South Korean side of the border. Pratt had tried to take out their nuclear capability. He'd gotten… some of it. Maybe most of it. But obviously not all. Now Alaska's largest city was in flames and everybody was watching Honolulu… through several sheets of dark glass, just in case. Isabel suddenly thought of all the potential targets around—D.C., Annapolis, the Pentagon, Dover AFB.

"Hmm? What's going on?" The sudden tension in her body, lying so close to his, had done what the alert chime couldn't. It had woken up Hunter.

Isabel leaned against him. Instinctively, he wrapped his arms around her. There was no real protection there—only a little bit of comfort.

IF EVER A NUCLEAR STRIKE could be surgical, Pratt's attack on Pyongyang was it. Fourteen bunker buster nuclear weapons, each one more than thirteen times as powerful as the bomb that had destroyed Anchorage, plunged through the skin of the city and the surrounding hills like bullets and detonated deep underground within three seconds of each other. The heat of the explosions vaporized rock, soil, and concrete, and flash-boiled underground water. The force of the blasts spread outward in seismic ripples that overlapped and intersected in complex patterns, nearly canceling each other out in some places, creating far more violent convulsions in others.

A nuclear strike can't be surgical. The ground on which Pyongyang was built shook like the head of a drum. Avalanches fell from every hillside, uprooting some buildings and crushing or burying others. From the sewers, and the holes made by the warheads, geysers of steam and radioactive ash came bursting out. But most of the population of the city was inside at this point, so that wasn't their problem. Their problem was that virtually every building in Pyongyang was collapsing into rubble over their heads.

SEVERAL HOURS PASSED. THERE WERE no more missile launches. A robot sub found the Honolulu warhead and was slowly and carefully carrying it out to sea. When it was a safe distance away, someone would arrive in a boat and attempt to disarm it. Pratt made a mental note to recommend that person for a Congressional Medal of Honor when this was over.

Speaking of boats, the other unambiguous victory thus far was command of the sea. The U.S. Navy had lost one cruiser when a North Korean submarine managed to get too close and torpedo it. There would have to be an inquiry to find out how that had happened. The NK navy, by way of comparison, no longer existed. It had been obsolete, many of its ships and submarines older than Pratt himself, and in such poor shape that even in peacetime its eastern and western squadrons could not have made it around the peninsula to help each other.

Swanston was looking over reports from the battlefield. "There doesn't appear to be any coordinating strategy," he said. "Most of the NK artillery has either been taken out or… just stopped firing for some reason—they should still have ordnance. In the west, two corps between Kaesong and Yeoncheon are fighting back. In the center, there's a corps east of Pyongyang—excuse me, Pyonggang—that's also fighting. They might still be afraid of what happened at Cheorwon.

"Everywhere else, we're seeing whole divisions just surrender or desert *en masse*, we're seeing North Koreans fighting each other… and it looks like one NK corps is on the move… in the direction of Pyongyang."

"If somebody's planning a coup, he's in for a disappointment," said Pratt. He thought for a moment.

"From your description," he said, "it sounds as though all lines of communication were relayed through Pyongyang, and now they're down. At some point, fairly soon, their army is going to arrange a way of talking to each other. The question is who's going to take charge and what that person is going to decide to do. Given this state of partial collapse and the loss of the capital, I'd surrender and be done with it, but I'm not a North Korean general."

More hours passed. The sun finally got around to rising over Alaska. The best you could say, once you'd managed to see something through all that dust and smoke, was that Anchorage still existed… partly. There was almost nothing left standing between A Street and the ocean. More than half the downtown had collapsed, houses had been flattened as if stepped on by a titan, and what was left of the city was on fire. Worse, the thermal updraft of the bomb had gone, replaced by a steady breeze from the west that was blowing the flames east. The city authorities—or whoever was in charge over there right now—had fallen back across Route 1 and were trying to turn Merrill Field Airport and Lake Otis Parkway into firebreaks, to protect the hospital and the universities. A lot of lives might be saved if they succeeded. And speaking of saving lives, the bomb that fell on Honolulu was successfully disarmed.

Shortly after six p.m.—eight a.m. in Korea, where they must have had the longest night in their history—Pratt got word from the field. "It seems to be a committee of NK generals," said Swanston. "No word if any one of them is in overall command, but it doesn't matter—the important thing is, they're offering unconditional surrender."

"Excellent."

"I've just got word from Seoul," said Jim. "The Republic of Korea will be securing all government and military assets within the… 'former DPRK.'" Pratt mentally added the words *starting with the nuclear stuff*. "They're asking American forces to remain on the alert in case of rogue units that don't want to cooperate with the surrender."

Pratt nodded. Ever since he'd realized—no, *decided*—that the DPRK wasn't going to make it through the next twenty-four hours, a part of his mind had been quietly considering possible endgames. Now he had one he liked.

"Tell our forces not to come within…" He glanced at a map. "Ten miles of the border. We don't want any incidents."

FEBRUARY 7:

SEEING THAT THERE WERE CAMERAS outside, Pratt waited until his hands had stopped shaking before he stepped out through the front door. He left Alaska Regional Hospital with a hundred nightmarish images burned into his brain like pajama patterns onto skin.

When he was too young, he'd seen a movie called *The Day After*. It made dying in a nuclear attack look downright merciful—FLASH, bones, nothing. No time to feel pain.

That would probably have been the case for anyone who had been inside the fireball itself. But the people who died in Anchorage died horribly—burned over half their skin, crushed by falling houses, trapped in piles of debris, and roasted alive in the advancing flames. Those had been the lucky ones. The unlucky ones died later, or were still in the process of dying right now, of radiation poisoning.

He couldn't decide if it was a mercy or a torment that everyone seemed grateful to him. Nobody blamed him for what had happened. Everybody agreed that it was the fault of that crazy bastard in Pyongyang and Pratt had dealt with him pretty good. Three different people who wouldn't live two more days had promised to vote for him in two years.

Judging by his approval ratings, most of the rest of the country agreed. *What is wrong with people?* he thought. *Give them peace and prosperity and they find things to complain about. Lead them into a war and they feel they owe it to their country to support you.*

Not that I ever gave them prosperity…

Heather Sanchez, his science adviser, was waiting outside with Governor Hugh Keegan. A dozen cameras watched as Pratt joined them. Ignoring them, Pratt turned to her. "Any new word on the fallout situation?"

"That's the one mercy," she said. "There isn't much fallout. It was an airburst over the ocean, so the fallout is mostly from the weapon itself, plus some sea salt that got vaporized and sucked up into the fireball. The good news is, the worst elements have the shortest half-lives. Iodine-131 has a half-life of eight days. That means it's"—Sanchez did some quick work on her phone's calculator app—"29.3 percent gone already."

"You mean twenty-five percent, surely," said Keegan. Pratt had had the same immediate reaction, but he wasn't inclined to correct his science advisor's math.

"No, that would be a linear progression, and I wish it was what we were dealing with—then all the iodine would be gone in sixteen days. As it is, in a month it'll be about ninety-three percent gone, and in three months you'll never know it ever existed. The bad news is that a lot of the concrete in the eastern half of town is going to have to be replaced. The rain soaked into it, went through it and left most of the fallout behind." Considering that *everything* in the western half of town would have to be replaced, including just over fifteen thousand people, this didn't sound so bad.

And even thinking about what had happened here felt like self-indulgence. Seoul had suffered three times as many casualties from plain old non-nuclear artillery fire. And no one would ever know exactly how many people had been killed—no, how many *he* had killed—at Pyongyang, but it was more than had died at Hiroshima and Nagasaki combined… and close to fifty times as many as the death toll from Anchorage.

On the way to Anchorage, he'd gotten a report from the handful of brave souls in radiation suits who'd ventured into the ruins of the Pyongyang bunkers. The government that had troubled the world so long was gone. Even where the bunkers hadn't collapsed entirely, their walls had cracked open, letting in streams of skin-destroying superheated steam and ten-thousand-degree rock vapor that ignited everything flammable. Where the steam and vapor hadn't gotten in, the flames had sucked out the oxygen, replacing it with carbon monoxide and other poisons. All the powerful men and their families who had taken shelter down there were dead before the radiation even had a chance to take effect. That said, it would be best if nobody else disturbed their tomb for at least four thousand years.

"Mr. President?" said Keegan as they got into the back of the limo. "While I've got your ear, could I talk to you about something else?"

"All right," said Pratt, already dreading this a little.

"Somebody needs to have a talk with Japan about the tuna fishery."

Pratt gritted his teeth. People swore up and down that they didn't want Washington to have too much power, that they would never dream of giving the federal government any more control over their lives than absolutely necessary... and then *something went wrong*. There was some sort of issue with eminent domain in New York that people were asking the Justice Department to intervene in. Sen. Ramos of Florida was asking for more help from FEMA in dealing with the aftermath of the off-season storms and tidal flooding—as if FEMA didn't have enough to do. The California delegation was divided over whether to ask for money to rebuild the Los Angeles Aqueduct or to build more desalination plants. And now this.

"It's the damn *oke-maki** fleets," Keegan said. "They're always out there, like a bunch of damn shepherds. They act like they own the tuna, and Tokyo backs them up. Some of our fishermen have been shot at for trying to do their jobs. Those are international waters. We have as much right to those fish as anybody."

Pratt checked his tablet. "According to Fish and Wildlife, only about a third of the wild tuna in the Pacific is currently under supervision by the *oke-maki* industry."

"With all due respect, Fish and Wildlife is running off old data. Real tuna's getting hard to find out there—all these damn shifts in ocean temperature are screwing up the food chain, and tuna's a high-end predator. We have to charge more for the real fish, and they can undercut us. Think about what De L'Air did to the diamond industry. We could be next."

"Surely there's still a market for genuine tuna." Pratt couldn't imagine eating *oke-maki* unless he was desperately hungry.

"Rich foodies," said Keegan. "They gotta have real fish, and it's gotta be wild-caught. They'll pay any price. But there's not enough of these people to support the whole industry. Fish oil, cat food... there's a dozen markets we're gonna be priced out of if somebody doesn't do something."

"What I hear you saying," said Pratt, "is that there are not as many tuna as there used to be, and there are not as many people who want to eat tuna as there used to be, but you would very much like there to be as many tuna fishermen as there used to be. Is that about right?"

Keegan, who was apparently smarter than he sounded, didn't reply.

---

* Vat-grown tuna muscle, increasingly popular in Japan due to the rising price of tuna. The fleets accompany the schools of tuna and collect fresh tissue samples as needed.

"And do you seriously think that at a time like this I have nothing better to do than prop up one of your state's industries?"

"We help feed people," said Keegan. "Now more than ever, you need that."

Pratt shook his head. "Now more than ever, Governor, if there's someone else out there who can feed more people for less, then I'm not going to stand in their way."

FEBRUARY 23:

THE ELECTRIC LIMO WAS COMPLETELY self-driving. Without even a chauffeur to talk to, Secretary of State Ahn had nothing to do on the road from Busan to Gyeongju but go over his notes for the summit, or just look out the window. He'd memorized his notes on the flight, so he looked out the window.

Ahn had lived in the United States since before his fifth birthday—only his very earliest memories were of South Korea. This place, as beautiful as it was, didn't look like anywhere in America. Even under a foot of snow—snow that was already starting to melt—you could see the differences.

Perfect little homes with roofs of faded blue tile. Ahn had been born in a house like that.

Steep, forested hills rising like islands out of a sea of farmland, their tops hidden in gray clouds during the morning hours. The fields were even more of a wonder than the hills—South Korea was less than 30 percent arable land, but they made the most of it, growing crops on every flat stretch of ground bigger than a doormat. Even highway median strips would have vegetables planted in them come spring. *Another few years like the last one and we'll probably be doing the same thing*, thought Ahn.

And to make sure the farmers stayed in business, the government placed tariffs on food imports, although those had been relaxed during the current shortage. As much as libertarian-minded people like Pratt and Walther hated this sort of thing, it made sense under the circumstances. During a longer war than this one had turned out to be, ships from the outside world might not be able to get through, and the country would have to be ready to fall back on its own resources that very year.

Ahn shook his head. When he thought of home, he thought of the Newark neighborhood where he'd grown up. Only his family called him "Jae-oh" any more—to everyone else, he was Jim. South Korea was another country.

No. Not South Korea anymore. *Korea.* Ahn supposed it shouldn't have been too surprising how quickly the North had caved. Dictatorships were like that— while they were in power, they seemed to have no trouble stage-managing themselves. Everyone who lived under them had an incentive to parrot the party line and hide all signs of dissent. Reporters showed up, were wined and dined, given the grand tour, and came home babbling about how everybody over there was just aching to do or die for the Dear Leader. And then, when the government collapsed, the truth came out. That was why these talks would feature representatives from Seoul, Moscow, Beijing, and Washington, but not Pyongyang.

GYEONGJU—WHICH WAS KYONGJU ACCORDING to the romanization system Ahn had gotten used to, but he didn't feel like arguing with Seoul about it—had once been the capital of the Silla dynasty, which lasted for about nine hundred years in the first millennium A.D. and at its height governed most of the peninsula. These days the main industry was tourism, and late winter was the off-season. There were crowds here, but they were people who'd lost their homes to the flooding last fall or the shelling of Seoul. So it was as good a place as any to hold an emergency summit, especially if you were trying to emphasize Korea's identity as a nation and culture in its own right and not anybody's vassal state or puppet government.

Right now, Ahn and the rest of the U.S. delegation were in the Daereungwon complex on the southern edge of the city. At first glance, it looked like a park with a lot of small, smooth-sided hills covered in melting snow and dead grass. Then you noticed that the hills had doorways in them, and you realized these weren't hills at all. They were tumuli—the burial mounds of the Silla dynasty. Like the pyramids of Egypt, they seemed almost too big to be man-made.

Ahn looked toward the east, the ridge where Unification Hall stood—the place where he would be meeting today with the foreign ministers of Korea, China, and Russia. Officially, the name of that place referred to the unification of a number of small feudal states by the early Silla kings, whose achievements were celebrated in murals within the hall. This fooled no one. Especially not now, when unification was becoming a reality.

I have to make this happen just right, thought Ahn. *The whole world is watching. Not just Russia, China, and Japan. India, Pakistan, the Basra Pact... even the Second Union. They're all watching in fear. Fear of us.*

The United States had defeated the "Democratic People's Republic of Korea" in less than twenty-four hours. That wasn't the scary part.

The United States had partly thwarted a nuclear attack. That wasn't the scary part—or rather, it was only scary to Americans. If it hadn't been for the GMD, casualties would have been ten times higher. If it hadn't been for the Nightgaunts, they would have been a hundred times higher.

The scary part was that the United States had suffered a terrible blow and had kept fighting. The whole world thought of America as having a glass jaw—great power to inflict havoc and ruin, balanced by an absolute inability to withstand any pain that could be noticed. The Special Forces would be deployed against some terror group in some odd corner of the world, ten terrorists and one American would be killed in the battle, and the media would howl that the death of that one American soldier was a terrible tragedy that should never have happened. That impression of weakness, embarrassing as it was, was the only thing that allowed the U.S. to be anything less than terrifying.

Now, after Anchorage, that impression was gone. It was as if Dracula had stepped out into the sunshine and said "Gosh, what a nice day." No one knew quite what to do next.

Which made this summit crucial. The Russian government wanted to expand its influence, the Chinese government wanted the same, but both were now contemplating the threat of a U.S.-allied Republic of Korea on their borders whose GDP had been slightly higher than Russia's even while it was just South Korea.

The worst-case scenario was that Russia, China, and who knew how many other nations would start allying against the United States for no other reason than to prevent Henry Pratt from dominating the world. Yevgeni Nardin, the new Russian foreign minister, would certainly do everything he could to make that happen.

It wasn't going to happen if Ahn had anything to say about it.

IN LATE FEBRUARY, HALF THE blanket of heavy snow covering so much of the northern United States melted with warm winds coming from the south. Then a polar vortex caused it all to refreeze for three bitter days. Then it resumed melting and vanished in the first week of March. The entire process took eleven days, and caused fresh flooding in many of the places that had been hardest hit by the Northern Monsoon.

Those whose houses had been on higher ground, allowing them to remain in the affected area through the Monsoon, had experienced only intermittent contact with the outside world that winter. Many of them had been forced to raid the flooded houses for supplies to survive.

Meanwhile, all through the American South that January and February, winter had only been a word. Warm, damp air flowed northeast from the Gulf over the warm, damp land from the lower Mississippi to the coast of the Carolinas. Rain was frequent, but gentle and moderate.

In late March, a powerful upper-level trough emerged in the skies just east of the Rockies and began to move east. Its progress was slow, but carried with it the promise of violent thunderstorms when it hit the warmer air. Behind and just below it, a mid-level jet stream was coming. It was like the weather conditions that had prevailed in April of 2011, just before the largest outbreak of tornadoes in recorded history.

The result was similar.

MARCH 25:

"SO HOW BAD IS IT?"

"Not good, Mr. President," said al-Harrak. "One of the tornadoes hit Oklahoma Bravo late last night. It plowed right through the northern half of the camp."

"Casualties?"

"We don't have an exact count, but… somewhere between six and seven hundred dead."

"From a tornado? How is that possible?"

"Two reasons. First, normally—at least in the United States—any concentration of people that large would have enough big buildings in it to break up tornado winds, so such a thing would never be in danger of happening.

But our camps are just trailers and cabins and portable schoolrooms. Nothing to stop them, and nothing that could possibly withstand them.

"Second... I've done what I can with what was available, but the truth is that hospital facilities in the camps are just barely adequate to the needs of the population under normal circumstances. In the face of this kind of disaster, there was no way to help the injured quickly enough."

"Jesus Christ."

Al-Harrak nodded sorrowfully. "The news doesn't get any better, I'm afraid," he said. "Kentucky Alfa was hit by a derecho. There were fewer than a hundred casualties, but a lot more of the homes were damaged. Beyond use, often."

"Any chance of expediting their return home?"

"I've been trying to get everyone home. Anyone who's still in a camp is someone whose home didn't survive the flood and the winter intact, I'm afraid. Or they were homeless to begin with."

"Is it true that cities have started busing their homeless population into your camps and leaving them there?"

"I'm afraid so. After the ice storms, Chris Lopez admitted it openly—he said we were better able to care for them than New York City was."

"And now we're going to have an influx of people from all over the South whose homes were destroyed by tornadoes."

"Things might not be that bad," said al-Harrak. "They at least still have some insurance. Of course, if anything like this happens next year—"

Pratt raised a hand for silence. "Sufficient unto the day is the evil thereof."

"And then some. Do you want to hear the rest of the bad news?"

"I suppose I'd better."

"Two camps are suffering from measles outbreaks," said al-Harrak. "Kansas Alfa and Texas Charlie. At last report, there were over three hundred victims— people with weakened immune systems, people whose vaccines didn't take... babies too young for the shots. Two deaths so far.

"I have discovered the cause of the outbreaks. The camps bring a lot of people from all walks of life together in close quarters, and it seems not all of them chose to have their children vaccinated." Al-Harrak was silent for a moment, collecting his thoughts.

"Mr. President," he said, "I understand that you and your laws permit this. I respect this even though I don't understand why. However, a lot of people in the camps themselves—especially people who are originally from

Mexico or China—aren't prepared to tolerate this kind of risk. Given that law enforcement is in short supply in the camps, they're likely to take matters into their own hands.

"So what I'm doing is ordering immunizations of everyone. Those who refuse will be transferred to a separate camp. My original plan was to set one up in upstate New York, which doesn't have any camps yet. But when Governor Morgan found out, she said she would fight it every step of the way. I didn't understand why—she offered to help us build one last fall—but she said she wouldn't tolerate us putting a health hazard on her doorstep."

Pratt nodded. "Is there enough space in the other camps now to move everyone out of Kentucky Alfa?"

"I think so, yes."

"Good. Do that, and then turn Kentucky Alfa into the shelter for the unvaccinated. In fact..." Pratt considered for a moment how to pose the next question. "What would be the obstacles to shutting down some of these camps and consolidating their population?"

"There would be several," said al-Harrak. "For one thing, the cost reduction would be offset by the expense of dismantling the camps and moving all these people around. For another thing, a lot of what happens in the camps to keep them working depends on the people in them—the little informal networks and communities they've built among themselves. Shuffle them around, move them from one camp to another, and you destroy those networks. Most of all, we don't know what's going to happen this fall with the Monsoon. It may miss us completely, or it may hit us harder than last year. We might need all these camps as going concerns. We might even need more of them."

Pratt grimaced. "The same thing is going to be true next year, and the year after that," he said. "When are we going to be able to shut these places down?"

"Not until we've rebuilt every city and town north of the fortieth parallel with the kind of infrastructure that can keep going during the Monsoon," said al-Harrak. "I'm sorry. And even then, there's the towns losing their water supply, there's the towns on the coast..."

Pratt gritted his teeth, clenched his fists, and breathed through his nose for a few seconds. He hated the fact that these camps existed. He hated that the TKB Foundation's news outlets were spreading all kinds of horrifying rumors about them. He'd been looking forward to shutting them down once and for all. Instead, the camps would still be a going concern when he was running for re-election in two years, and probably for four years after that. Maybe they'd be calling them... Prattvilles.

ONCE AL-HARRAK WAS BACK AT work, Pratt looked at the latest reports from Jim in Gyeongju. These were a lot more encouraging. It seemed they were close to agreeing on a timetable for the withdrawal of U.S. forces from the Korean peninsula. That would be hard to get through the Senate after Anchorage, but the stated reason for keeping U.S. troops in South Korea was to protect it from North Korea, which made it a little hard to justify their presence now that there was no North Korea. Also, it seemed that Park Min-young, the ROK's foreign minister, was negotiating nonaggression pacts with Russia and China without consulting the U.S. State Department.

Which was exactly what Jim Ahn had asked Park to do. What he and Pratt really wanted was a Republic of Korea that needed very little from the United States—one strong enough that neither Russia nor China could conquer it without considerable damage to themselves, and open enough that both nations could trade freely with it. A Korea that wasn't a U.S. ally, but could become one in a day if any of its larger neighbors made any threatening gestures. This would benefit China, and Russia if they had the wit to see it, but mostly it would benefit peace and order. The tricky part was going to be getting there without looking like that was where they were planning to go.

APRIL 4:

IT WAS SATURDAY MORNING, BUT neither Isabel nor Hunter had time for Enginquest right now. Hunter was grading papers, and Isabel was still looking over the blueprints of the Conowingo Project, which she'd spent all night inspecting. Most of it was straightforward, the same sort of algae-based biofuel plant Marshpower normally designed, but on a much larger scale. Some of it—the toxic metal detectors, the phosphorus recovery system— would have to be tested before they knew how well it worked.

The only other difference was the degree of political interest, and personal interest on Isabel's part. It wasn't just that the state needed the fuel—it might save the Chesapeake Bay.

The Susquehanna River drained a huge stretch of Pennsylvania and upstate

New York, but the mouth of the river was in Maryland at the northern end of the Chesapeake. The Conowingo Dam stretched across that river about nine miles before it reached the Bay. A hundred years' worth of sediment and phosphorus were waiting behind that dam. Just a little of it had gotten into the Bay two years ago, and that had been enough to trigger a toxic bloom that put half the state seafood industry out of commission for months, including her father's business. If the Northern Monsoon hit the Susquehanna basin this year and flushed that whole monstrous load of nutrients into the Bay… just the thought of it made Isabel sick with dread. Her family and the whole Shore were having enough trouble as it was. And no wonder if Governor Alpert wanted the project done this year if possible, although that would take a miracle at this point.

A notice popped up on her tablet. It was a message from Chelsey. *Oh yeah… that's today, isn't it?* Isabel clicked on it. A new window opened to fill half the screen, occupied mostly by Jourdain's beaming face and bright blue eyes, with Chelsey in the background looking zoned out.

"Aunt Isabel hi it's my birthday!" Her dark hair was in little ringlets, and Isabel could see chains of construction-paper rings hanging on the light fixtures behind her when she moved her head.

"Hi, Jourdain," said Isabel. "Happy birthday. Tell me how old you are."

Jourdain held up four chubby fingers. The math checked out, but Isabel still felt sure she'd helped change this girl's diapers not too long ago.

"Are you having a party today?" Jourdain nodded. After another minute or so of this conversation, Jourdain went to the kitchen to get a drink of water. Another two minutes went by and she didn't return, and Chelsey didn't seem to notice. Isabel shrank the window to a much smaller size and went back to work, glancing at the window every few moments in case her niece came back or her sister woke up.

Then Isabel got the message from Marshpower. Sean Lao looked unusually grim.

"Are you sitting down?" he said.

Uh-oh. "Yes."

"Good." Sean took a breath. "The new owners are canceling the Conowingo Project. In fact, they're canceling everything."

"*What?*"

"The new owners. They're shutting everything down. I don't know why they're doing it."

"What's 'everything'?"

"Everything. Marshpower. Other companies in the same business."

"Did they say why?"

"No."

Isabel shook her head. "This is crazy."

"Tell me about it."

"Where's the governor in all this? I mean, this thing was his baby."

"We haven't heard from him. Supposedly they're trying to fight this up in New York, but here, I don't know… and I'm not even sure what anybody can do. Normally I'd say take the money and start a new company, but these guys who bought us out—they own the patents on a lot of the tech we use, and they don't seem to want us using it at all."

"There's got to be something you can replace it with."

"Maybe," he said, "but it's getting harder and harder to find investment capital. There's just too much everywhere that needs doing—everybody wants to rebuild their house or raise their house or move their house somewhere else, and that's just the homeowners."

"Fuck."

"I just wish I could tell you what's going on. It just seems like whoever owns the company is bankrupting themselves trying to shut down the whole industry and I don't know why."

"Not to be crass," said Isabel, "but is there any chance of me getting paid for the work I've done?"

Sean shook his head. "I'm sorry," he said. "If I had the money, I'd give it to you."

On that note, the conversation ended. Isabel rested her elbows on the desk and rubbed her temples in frustration. *How are we supposed to protect the Bay? And how am I supposed to get paid?* She was starting to get that blah feeling you got when you realized that the wonderful afternoon nap you'd promised yourself, in lieu of the night's sleep you hadn't gotten because you were busy doing work that had turned out to be a complete waste of time, just wasn't going to happen.

As far as employment opportunities went, oddly enough, her best bet was another engineering consultation firm. With every city, town, and county in the northern half of the U.S. and all of Canada wanting to know how to rebuild their infrastructure so it could weather the Monsoon, that was a growth industry right now. Just as long as nobody heard about what she'd done to Eveland-Blades.

Still, Isabel was strangely glad she'd already bought those tickets to the concert in June. If she had to do it now—assuming it wasn't already sold out, which it probably was—she wasn't sure she'd be able to justify spending the money.

IT WAS WARM OUT, EASILY over eighty, partly cloudy with a slight breeze. Everything smelled of rain that had just finished falling. Skies were still blue, the world was still upholstered in millions of shades of green... on days like this, you might almost think nothing much had changed from the twentieth century.

When Isabel went walking through a neighborhood in the springtime, a part of her mind always noticed the flowers. There were maybe two dozen species that she could identify by sight, but still her instincts told her to watch the flowers like a soldier in an urban battlefield scanning the rubble for snipers. It was an old habit she'd picked up in childhood. Flowers meant bees.

Even so, as she went on her walk it took her a few minutes to realize exactly what was wrong. Only when she passed by someone's lawn and noticed all the little holes in the ground near the sidewalk did it come to her.

There were no dandelions. There were only holes in the lawn where they had been dug up, roots and all. They were famously hard to uproot, but someone had done it.

And the same thing was true in the next lawn, and the next, and the next, all the way back to the front yard of the building where she and Hunter rented an apartment. And the slender blue-green stems of the little wild onions that could be seen everywhere... couldn't be seen anywhere. The violets also seemed to be missing. And when Isabel looked closely at the white clover, she saw how it had been stripped of its leaves.

Only now did the thought cross her mind that at some point in the last six months, she really should have Googled "edible wild plants in Maryland" and seen what was available in her own backyard. From the looks of things, somebody in this town, or several somebodies, had beaten her to it. "Treat it like a war" was a phrase she'd been hearing online more and more often. In wartime, people did things like this.

Isabel glanced around in a doomed attempt to figure out if there was an unusually small number of squirrels still around. Come to think of it, those pigeons that nested in the attic might be worth catching. Of course, she'd have to cook them very thoroughly before she ate them. They weren't clean birds. **So even though there are obviously other people around here hungrier than you, you have to get the pigeons first?**

On second thought, you're right. Pop is still bringing in oysters, and crab season is about to begin. I don't need animal protein that badly. Admittedly, that doesn't help Hunter and I can't make out with him after eating it, but—

How long are you going to keep sponging off Pop? You know the problems he's having lately.

MAKE. UP. YOUR. MIND.

GET. A. JOB.

I. HAD. ONE. THIS. FUCKING. MORNING.

When she opened the door to her apartment, she was greeted by an evil-sounding hiss. This cheered her up—Hunter hadn't felt much like laughing lately. Isabel still didn't get why a guy like him had a laugh that would make the Joker start edging away, but the important thing was, right now he was in a good mood.

"What's the joke?"

"It's a biology paper," he said. "One of my students has gerunds mixed up with gonads."

"I wonder if he makes that mistake on his English homework," said Isabel, feeling a little like a hypocrite—she couldn't remember what gerunds were, except that they had something to do with grammar.

Hunter laugh-hissed even harder.

"You know, you have the quietest laugh I've ever heard," she said.

"Yeah, there's… kind of a story behind that," said Hunter. "When I was a kid, I sounded completely different. I had this really loud, distinct laugh."

"What happened?"

"Well, other kids made fun of me, Mom and Dad thought it sounded fake, so… I changed it."

"Changed what? The way you laugh? You can do that?"

"It took a while, but yeah. Only it wasn't exactly something I could fine-tune. If I could, I'd have gone with something a little less creepy."

"Jeez, Hunter, that's depressing." Isabel spent much of the rest of the day looking up jokes and comedy routines online and trying to get Hunter to laugh the way he did as a child. Unfortunately, he didn't seem to be able to do it anymore. But at least it took her mind off her own problems. And Chelsey's problems. And the Bay's problems. And Hunter's other problems, the ones that weren't exactly psychological. *I brought him out of Louisiana to the Eastern Shore. As far as economic opportunity goes… there's an old saying about frying pans and fires that applies here.*

APRIL 10:

PRATT LOOKED ACROSS THE *RESOLUTE* desk at Wendy Czeczelski. He was sitting, and she was standing, which put their heads at almost the same height.

"Any progress to report on the treaty?" It would be very embarrassing if, after winning the war against North Korea, getting China to stay out of it and getting a good deal in the Treaty of Gyeongju, he lost the peace in the Senate.

"All the Democrats are on board," she said. "They don't like giving you a victory, but in a case like this they'll let it go. I'm working on the Republicans. Ten of them have committed—in person at least—to ratify. Another eleven have told me they won't. That's in addition to the three that have already denounced it in public."

"So we're close to where we need to be. Do any of the holdouts want anything in particular?"

"Mostly more aid to their states in the next budget."

"I can do that," said Pratt. "I don't like it, but I can do it." He shook his head. "These people who are against the treaty—I've heard some of them on the stump. They're always complaining about our overseas commitments and the money we spend on them. This reduces one of those commitments and saves us money without leaving us or the Koreans worse off. I don't understand what their problem is."

"Mr. President, you're thinking too much. This isn't a rational objection. This is a simple revulsion at seeing U.S. forces retreat from anywhere. Even in five years."

"Senators aren't supposed to make up their minds on that kind of reaction."

"With all due respect, Mr. President," said Wendy, "speaking as a lifelong Republican, you knew what you were getting into when you joined us. If it makes you feel any better, of the ones who haven't made up their minds there are five that I know I can talk around, and I'm pretty sure about Turgeon, Rieck, and Brearley. One vote from one of them and the treaty makes it through."

"Well, get out there and bring me that vote."

"I won't let you down, Mr. President." She looked at him like a daughter hoping for her father's approval... possibly. Pratt wasn't too sure. His knowledge of children in general was strictly theoretical. He gave her a small smile as he motioned toward the exit.

As soon as Wendy was out the door, Pratt returned his attention to the Transportation Secretary's report. Rebuilding was going slower than expected; there wasn't enough concrete and asphalt out there, and fuel for the machines kept running short. Federal projects, and state/local projects in Minnesota, Illinois, and New York, were being further slowed down by the requirement that they be designed and built to withstand another Monsoon. The same was true of the rebuilding of Anchorage. Pratt had no regrets about this. Infrastructure spending was his least favorite thing after welfare, but that was precisely why he wanted it done right the first time—so he wouldn't have to do it again next year.

Then Treasury Secretary Terry Walther entered for his appointment, his lined face looking particularly troubled. A little conversation showed why.

"On the tax front," said Terry, "I expect the usual last-minute filings, but if they follow the same pattern as what we've already seen, we're not going to see much revenue from the places the Monsoon hit. Or from Louisiana. In fact, right now the West Coast, New England, and the New York City area are basically keeping the government afloat. I'm talking about taxes and bond sales both, you understand.

"And it isn't just the damage itself—it's the secondary effects. Like the inflation." They had long since had the conversation on the different parts of the money supply, the upshot of which was that it was indeed possible for a country to suffer from inflation even while trillions of dollars in equity were disappearing.

"The people trying to get their houses back in shape," Terry said, "aren't spending any money on anything they don't urgently need right now, so they're not going out to eat at the restaurants which are having to raise their prices to cover the rising cost of food, so those restaurants are going out of business. They aren't going out and buying a new screen, or if they are they find the stores don't have any new ones because the roads are still out and they can't get resupplied. They're putting off that plastic surgery until next year, patching up their old clothes, scaling back their wedding plans, not going out to the movies… basically, if you don't happen to be in the building trades or selling something people need every day, you're more and more likely to be out of work. So we get unemployment."

Pratt closed his eyes. This was exactly the sort of problem he was afraid of. Every instinct he had said *if the economy is going to have a downturn, let it have a downturn. Trying to command it not to do that will only make things worse in the long run.* He knew, of course, that if he didn't do something, he would be voted out of office and replaced by someone who would. The support he'd been given after Anchorage was already starting to fade.

"Then there's the foreclosures. A lot of homeowners, a lot of small businesses are going into debt trying to rebuild. More debt than they can handle, in many cases. We're starting to see the first bankruptcies, and I expect to see a lot more.

"There's a bill in Congress to make it harder to declare bankruptcy. I think you should try to support it if you can do so without drawing any attention to it."

"It doesn't sound like a popular measure."

"It isn't. But… this is going to sound very cold, but banks and lenders are the heart of the economy. They direct the flow of money, get it to where it needs to be. If times get hard enough, and the heart has to cannibalize fat and muscle in order to sustain itself… well, it's better than dying."

"Except that in this case, the fat and muscle vote, and they have the heart outnumbered," said Pratt.

"That's why I'm glad I'm just a public servant," said Terry. "I just have to recommend policy. You're the one who has to make it sound good. By the way, have you talked with Helen lately?"

"She's been preoccupied with her work," said Pratt. "I was planning to touch base with her soon."

"When you do that, ask her if she's keeping track of Group 77, and the situation in New York."

Pratt wasn't one for vague hints, even from friends, and especially from subordinates. "Tell me what you know about Group 77," he said.

Terry sat on the arm of a sofa, facing the president. "The truth is, nobody knows much of anything about Group 77," he said. "That's just the name they use in transactions. It's a group of investors with an enormous amount of money. They've been buying up the whole biofuel industry, or the patents on the technology it depends on, and shutting it all down. Now the SEC is investigating them. Suspicion of criminal conspiracy, they say, but damned if I can see what they're doing that isn't legal.

"Speaking of things that might or might not be legal, Morgan declared eminent domain over the biodiesel plants in New York State and compensated Group 77 for the value of the lots, but not the plants. The theory being that the plants were worthless if they weren't in business."

"That sounds dubious."

"They might just be trying to get the group to promise in court that they're going to start the plants back up again," said Terry. "And speaking of court, something strange is happening with the lawyers. One week after Group 77's law firm—Mekaelian, Murphy, and Pilkington—filed a legal injunction, NYPD searched their offices… allegedly because they were looking for evidence in the SEC investigation. I don't know if they found anything, but a few days after that, the law firm was hacked by a group called INB4. All sorts of information about their clients got spilled to the general public. And since nobody working for Group 77 is very popular in New York, or much of anywhere else, their clients are under a lot of public pressure to find some other lawyers.

"And here's the thing. Hacking is a lot harder than it used to be, especially if the target can afford good security. A law firm like Mekaelian, Murphy, and Pilkington—you can't get into their system without a copy of their runes. Which are not easy to get. But which the police would have had."

"Wait a minute," said Pratt. "Are you suggesting that the NYPD are in collusion with this INB4 group?"

"I don't know," said Terry, "but it wouldn't be the first time INB4 has gone after somebody who pissed off Morgan."

"My impression of hacker groups is that they pride themselves on not working for anyone, least of all any sort of government."

"That's what's strange," said Terry. "And there's something else you might want to think about. I can't prove this is happening… but New York State's GDP is about as big as Russia's—well, Russia's before the oil market started going crazy. If Moscow can afford a cyberwarfare division, so can Albany."

As soon as Terry had left, Pratt made a call to Arioc Kaplan. The director of the SEC said he was "keeping an open mind" until the Group 77 investigation was complete, and didn't seem to think there was anything sinister about the Mekaelian, Murphy, and Pilkington hacking.

"I suspect runesnapping software may have been involved," he said. "Someone sneaks a program into the computer that infects the rune reader and sends copies of the runes. Nasty business. Leaves everyone wondering if they've been betrayed. There are software patches you can use to guard against it, but if somebody doesn't install one in time…"

Pratt nodded. Ari Kaplan had a reputation for honesty—which was good, because he also happened to be somebody the president couldn't fire. And now that Pratt thought of it, the NYPD answered to the mayor, not the governor… to the extent that they answered to anyone at all.

It seemed he was hearing more and more about Governor Morgan these days, and liking less and less of it. But he wasn't ready to assume the worst just yet. Especially not when he had so much else on his plate.

And who are you to judge her, sitting here thinking of ways to help the banks ruin people's lives? The Aztecs told their victims they were sacrificing them to save the universe. The most you can tell people is that you're letting them be sacrificed to save the economy.

This is the dark side of "treat it like a war." Times like this bring out the worst in governments on every level. If you don't like it, get busy bringing about better times. If you can't do it, who can?

MAY 15:

NORMALLY, POP WOULD HAVE GONE to Mr. Roberts' office in Easton, but neither he nor Mom could take a single day off work now. So Mr. Roberts had taken the unusual step of driving out to the island to visit Mom-mom and Pop-pop and discuss their legal options.

Which were not great. They were now seven people, including a small child and a teenager, living in a house that was getting less and less habitable every day. They couldn't afford to have it cleaned properly because they had to spend all their money keeping Pop-pop going despite the illness he'd contracted from... living in this house. The state was almost certainly going to condemn the building—they'd take any excuse to have one less waterfront house to worry about. Which would have been okay at this point, except that the only other place the Bradshaws had to go was Mom-mom and Pop-pop Horton's on Smith Island, a house on even lower ground. The last king tide had come within a few feet of their back door.

Mr. Roberts was a small, light-skinned African-American with a rather diffident manner. He looked about the same age as Chelsey, but in terms of legal help he was what they had. Isabel approached him while he was talking to Mom-mom.

"Hey, when you have a moment," she said, "I've got something I'd like your advice on."

"This is likely to take most of my day," he said.

"I don't know if you've had much to do with Isabel," said Mom-mom, "but if she says she's got something she'd like your advice on, what she means is she's neck-deep in angry pit bulls. You should help her."

"If you charge by the hour," said Isabel, "I can—" Mr. Roberts waved for her to stop.

"I'll make this a part of today's visit," he said. "No extra charge. Now, what can I do for you?"

"I've got this problem with the student loan company," she said. "I've been paying them twenty-five percent of my earnings, which right now is more than I can really afford. That was the deal. Now they're raising it to thirty-five percent. Can they do that?"

"I'd have to look at the paperwork," he said. "They might be able to, or they might be betting on you not wanting to fight it. Even if they can, there might be some recourse."

"I thought you might say that." Isabel handed him the file. "Why are they altering the deal?"

"Same reason Willie Sutton robbed banks," he said. "You have money. They want it. And there's a lot of other people who owe them money that they can't get it back from. People out in the Midwest who're going bankrupt, for instance. They tried to get a bill through Congress to make bankruptcy harder, but some congressman—I think his name was Darling or something—started making a lot of noise against it and got it stopped.

"Then there's the tarpies. There are about eighteen or nineteen million people still living in FEMA camps, and those places... if you walk into one of those places trying to collect on a credit card debt or a student loan debt, you're not likely to find whoever you're looking for. Or if you go in with no backup, you have some kind of tragic accident. Like you accidentally strangle yourself to death putting on your necktie or something."

Isabel considered this.

"So what I hear you saying," she said, "is if I can't pay the rent and I get kicked out of my apartment, I can move into one of these camps and they can't come after me without turning up dead in a dumpster?" Her conscience screamed at her for even suggesting as a joke that she might do such a thing, but it had already been screaming at her as loud as it could for *owing people money* and *not having paid it back yet*, so no harm done.

Roberts just sat there staring at her for a moment. Then he said, "Let's file that under 'best alternative to a negotiated agreement.'"

MAY 16:

HER GYM MEMBERSHIP WAS ONE of the few extraneous expenses Isabel allowed herself, and she kept it for days like today—days when she not only needed some hard exercise to make up for the days spent sitting in front of a computer, but also really needed to work off some steam.

Last night had come the bad news from Mr. Roberts. Yes, her loan company was entitled to raise its rates. No, there was nothing she could do about it. Yes, at some point this year her family was probably going to lose its home, although Mr. Roberts was going to drag it out as long as possible. No, there was nothing she could do about that either.

And it was once again her turn to support Hunter. School had been let out last week—earlier than Isabel had ever heard of it happening, but that was yet another thing that could be blamed on budget cuts. His meager paychecks were gone. Which meant he was likely to start going down into a spiral of self-loathing again.

Luckily, there was any amount of work for an engineer willing to look over plans for rebuilt overpasses and airports and shopping centers and assess how to make them Monsoon-proof, or just rebuild them. The problem was that they were outsourcing a lot of this work to Chinese and Indian engineers, who were willing to work for one to two thousand dollars each… which meant Americans got the same awesome deal. For something that could easily take two weeks if you did it properly. She felt like saying *If you want people voting for fascists, just say so! Don't incentivize it!* But nice girls didn't say things like that.

I suppose you think you're superior to all those Chinese and Indian engineers?

No, I think I live in a place with a higher cost of living.

And on top of everything else, there was what had happened this morning.

It wasn't your fault. There was nothing you could have done. He said so himself. Also, can we talk about the fact that we're mourning the death of an imaginary beaver-man? And Hunter can create a new character and get back in the game any time he likes?

But OnyxFan11 had been a little more than just an avatar in the world of Enginquest. The brave Castorid had captained the *Unsung Hero* for over a year now, and had been Hunter's alter ego for as long as she'd known him. He was fearless, resourceful, and equipped with a broad assortment of useful skills. In short, he was everything Hunter had ever wanted to be in real life, assuming Hunter had wanted to be six inches shorter, bucktoothed, covered with fur and equipped with a paddle-shaped tail.

And now he was gone—killed instantly in the explosion when an enemy fireball spell with +30 damage hit the *Hero*'s boiler. The surviving humans and wildkin had managed to land the *Hero* on the beaches of Macandal, where they disposed of the corpse avatar with great ceremony and… okay, they ate it, but respectfully. Besides, they needed the health points. And it wasn't technically cannibalism, since he was the only Castorid in the group.

Isabel, who had intended to spend one hour playing Enginquest and then get back to work, had spent forty minutes playing the game and two and a half hours trying to comfort Hunter. She'd never seen him so crushed.

Now Hunter was fixing dinner—reheated vegetable soup and fried eggs, but cooking or fixing something was the only thing that seemed to brighten his mood at times like this. Isabel was at the gym. She'd used the treadmill, worked on her core, and now she had her hands wrapped in cotton and was using the punching bag, picturing the faces of the student loan officers, the idiots at Housing and Community Development, the assholes who didn't seem to care about the fact that she and they were part of the same country, and most of all the face of her whiny bitch of a conscience that tried to make her feel guilty over everything and nothing.

She hit the bag again and again, with force that a lot of men would be proud of. Later tonight, when she went back to the keyboard, she'd be sorry she'd used her hands as hammers like this, but right now she couldn't make herself care. In a single fluid motion, she jumped up and forward, lashed out with a near-horizontal push kick that sent the bag halfway to the ceiling, fell on her butt, rolled to one side, got to her feet while the bag was swinging past her, stepped back into position, and blocked the bag with her shoulder.

Now she felt better.

WHAT ISABEL REALLY WANTED TO do was eat dinner as quickly as possible and then get back to work. She had two projects to design—both culvert crossings being replaced by bridges—and was behind on both. The plans for the bridge in upstate New York needed to be finished by Monday. The one in Minnesota didn't need to be done for another two weeks, but she wanted to devote as much of next week as possible to the redesign of the St. Cloud stormwater system. She had a hard-earned reputation as somebody who turned work in on time, and she was determined to live up to it come hell or high water again.

But there was Hunter. As he sat down next to her, she noticed for the first time how much weight he'd lost. He hadn't shaved since school let out, either—his face was covered with scruff. At the moment, his expression was dull and flat.

Complimenting him on dinner would sound kind of patronizing, but she had to do something. Isabel cut into one of the yolks with her fork.

"I notice you always get the eggs done so the whites are cooked all the way through but the yolk's still part runny," she said conversationally. "How do you do that?"

"I get the eggs cooked real good on one side, flip them over, and then I turn the gas off and wait a couple minutes. The residual heat does the rest." He smiled a little. "I see what you're trying to do."

"Well, yeah," she said, resting a hand on his arm.

"It's just a game. You know that."

"It mattered to you. Your character mattered to you. That's okay."

"I was playing it too much anyway. It was getting to be an addiction." Hunter sighed.

"Funny how your life can turn into this Jenga tower," he said. "It just keeps getting worse and worse and worse and you can ignore it as long as you've got this one thing, if it's going right you can forget that everything else is going wrong... and then that one thing goes and the whole thing just collapses all at once. Or maybe it collapsed a long time ago and you never noticed." Isabel waited a moment for him to say something more, but he didn't.

"Times are hard," she said at last. "They're hard for everybody. If you're going through a rough patch—"

"It's not that. It's how useless I am. I was supposed to make something of my life. I wasn't supposed to end up as a... part-time biology teacher."

"Hunter. There is no shame in being a teacher."

"They only hired me because they couldn't get a real teacher at that salary," he said. "I don't know, I just... just... I don't know what's wrong with me! It's like, I know I'm not stupid..."

"Of course you're not. You're a smart guy."

"That's just it! I've got all these brains and I can't fucking *use* them!" Hunter's voice caught. He put down his spoon and started pinching the skin between his thumb and index finger.

"What are you doing?"

"Trying to stop myself from crying." Judging by the choking sound in his voice, it was almost working.

"Your parents taught you how to do that?"

"Nah. Googled it."

Isabel looked around, found a box of tissues, and handed it to him. "The few times I've cried, I found it stopped once I blew my nose," she said. "Except for the time I got a chunk of sea nettle in my eye. That was bad."

"*Ow*," said Hunter. "That... I don't even know what a sea nettle is, but..." He blew his nose.

"Kind of jellyfish."

"Well, that puts my life in perspective." Hunter shook his head. "Maybe I have success phobia, I don't know. The whole time when I was growing up, my parents were trying to push me to succeed at everything. I'd have fun at the pool and they'd sign me up on the swim team. I'd sing a song and they'd get me singing lessons and try to get me on one of those shows. Anything I did for fun, or because I wanted to... suddenly I absolutely had to be the best at it and then it wasn't fun anymore."

Isabel nodded. That explained why the two things he was best at were online games, which nobody had ever wanted him to be good at, and cooking, which he hadn't started until well after he was out of the house.

"My point is, I had every advantage, every opportunity, and I can't *do* anything. I ended up hiding in another world because it was a world where I made a difference. I'm just this big useless load."

"Okay, now you're starting to piss me off," she said. "Seriously, Hunter, if I heard anybody else talking about you the way you're talking about yourself, I'd fucking hurt them. I *love* you."

"I know. And I love you. But..."

"But what?"

"But if you had a cat, you'd love it just as much and it would do you just as much good."

Isabel tried to think of something to say to this. Something like *cats can't cook* or *some cats catch mice* or *sex with cats is illegal in this state*. But as the awkward pause dragged on second by second, she couldn't come up with anything that would actually improve his mood.

"Have you heard what they're doing up in Canada?" said Hunter.

"What?" This was a weird conversational segue, but Isabel wasn't going to complain.

"It's amazing. They're trying to rebuild and Monsoon-proof their whole country, and they're planting whole forests up beyond the old tree line in the Arctic. They need all the help they can get."

Isabel nodded.

"I think I'd like to help."

Isabel blinked.

"Help... how?"

"Go up there. To the Northwest Territories. Help them plant trees."

"Are you serious?"

"Yeah." Hunter's expression, as best Isabel could read it, was sincere.

"Canada?"

"Yeah."

"And not like Vancouver, but *northern* Canada?"

"Yeah. What's the big deal? You've been to the North Pole."

The discussion went on until they were both finished eating, and for a good half hour afterward.

"Why northern Canada? Why not building houses in Wisconsin or helping people in the camps?"

"I used to help my mom with gardening. I know how to do this."

"What about the concert? Should I try to get a refund on the tickets?"

"I want to stick around just long enough for that. I can go afterward. It'll be a little late in the year, but I think there's still gonna be time to accomplish something."

The more Isabel looked at Hunter, the more she began to think she ought to give in. He had this light in his eyes that she hadn't seen in a while, and certainly hadn't expected to see any time recently. This idea was giving him hope.

"I wouldn't ask you to come with me," he said in a slightly hopeful tone.

"I'm glad you wouldn't," she replied in a flat tone. He couldn't quite hide the look of disappointment.

LATER THAT EVENING, ISABEL WAS at work. In the kitchen, another pot of chyq was brewing—thanks to all this drama in her life, she was going to be pulling an all-nighter. Again.

Hunter had gone to bed. *If I don't have sex with him, is he going to think I'm mad at him? If I do have sex with him, is he going to think I'm trying to persuade him? ARRRGH. The best thing about our relationship was not having to worry about unspoken psychological shit like this.*

Isabel thought about going to Canada with him. Actually, no she didn't. She had the vague feeling that she ought to be thinking about going to Canada, but that wasn't the same thing as giving it serious consideration. The idea held no attraction for her at all. It hadn't even occurred to her to go with him until he said he wouldn't ask it.

Isabel wondered why the idea seemed so alien. He'd followed her back to Maryland, and she couldn't honestly say that had worked out well—especially not for him. But this was just so weird and random that she couldn't see herself doing it.

And if she went up there, she wouldn't be able to pursue her own career in that place. The Internet connection might be good enough to let her do her work, but there wouldn't be time. She would be working more or less full time at whatever they decided her job was.

People don't always appreciate it or pay for it properly, but I'm doing something that needs to be done. Something that not everybody can do. A lot more people can plant trees than can re-engineer a combined sewer.

And what if my family needs my help?

That was the deciding factor. If Hunter went north, he'd go alone.

MAY 18:

ISABEL AND HUNTER HAD EATEN meat maybe twice in the past week, but when you picked a day out of the week and called it "Meatless Monday," that made it feel like an actual choice. Over a Meatless Monday dinner of baked potatoes topped with scrambled eggs, Isabel made a few more efforts to dissuade Hunter.

"I notice they mention the danger of 'mosquito-induced anemia.' You know what that means, right?"

"Being slowly drained of blood until you die? Yeah. I know."

"Sounds a lot worse than getting eaten by a polar bear."

"Pretend for a moment that you were the one who really wanted to go up north," said Hunter. "Would you let that stop you?"

"Well, no, but..."

"They've got ways of protecting their people. Don't worry. I'll be all right. And I'll come back. And in the meantime, won't this make things a little easier for you?"

Isabel opened her mouth to protest, and then silently closed it again. The truth was, it would. She was supporting Hunter right now. If he were up in Canada and his care and feeding were somebody else's problem, that might make it possible for her to pay the extra on her loan. Especially since, with Hunter no longer eating from the same fridge, she could take up her father on his offer to spare her a few more crabs from his catch.

Convenient, isn't it?

Fuck you, it's what he wants. And maybe it really will be good for him.

In middle school and high school, Isabel's teachers had sternly told her about experiments in which rats were put in individual cages and given two water dispensers, one with regular water and one with heroin or cocaine in it. The rats drugged themselves until they died. This, she and her fellow students were assured, was what would happen to any one of them who dared touch Demon Weed.

Years later, in college, she'd learned that other scientists had tried the same experiment with a group of rats in a much larger, more pleasant, and varied enclosure in which they were free to socialize. Given dispensers of morphine-laced water and regular water, the rats in "Rat Park" stayed away from the drugged water. Even rats who were addicted to morphine recovered when put in "Rat Park." The drug was there for the taking, but the rats apparently endured the withdrawal symptoms of their own… whatever passed for free will in a rodent's brain.

This went with some of the stories Isabel had heard of drug addicts who'd had successful Jellicoe treatments. Some of them had been able to turn their lives around, but others had just found themselves as unhappy as before and started looking for a different way to self-medicate. The problem wasn't always the drug. Sometimes it was the cage.

Likewise, Enginquest hadn't been the source of Hunter's problems, it had just distracted him from them. He didn't like himself or the way his life was going. He wanted a change. It was hard not for Isabel to take this personally, since she had been so much a part of his life, but he had never seemed to complain about her.

Set him free, I guess. Set him free and hope to God he comes back.

MAY 22:

WALT OCCUPIED A BOOTH AT the San Diego Convention Center, THC-laced beer in one hand, in the other an AutoGraff personalized stylus that let him sign electronic copies of his new book *Boundaries*. Instead of his usual turtleneck, he was wearing his favorite T-shirt, which featured a crude drawing of a man's hairy buttocks and the words I DON'T KNOW ABOUT MOHAMMED'S FACE, BUT I'M PRETTY SURE HIS ASS LOOKED LIKE THIS. Some nights, when Walt couldn't sleep, he wondered if his political views were nothing but a function of his personality and style of humor. The one time he'd tried to make an ecologically conscious statement, back in college, what had come out of his mouth was "How come Chinese guys can't get it up without a dead rhinoceros?" It hadn't gone over well.

You might think the Libertarian Party convention (theme: "Let There Be Freedom") would be the happiest place in America. The President was sympathetic to their cause. Drug law reform was happening at the federal level and in twenty states. Even sentencing reform was starting to happen in some places. And they had a record number of candidates running for local office this year. And the crowd here was pretty big for a midterm year.

But as Walt listened to the conversations of people around his table, he found they were starting to realize the truth—that successes for libertarian causes didn't necessarily translate into success for the Libertarian Party. Pratt was the closest thing to a Libertarian the Oval Office had ever seen, yes, but he was not actually a Libertarian. Likewise, the good things being done in Congress and the various State Houses were being done by Democrats and Republicans... well, mostly Democrats, but also some Republicans.

If you're a third party in America, thought Walt glumly, *this is what success looks like—your best ideas getting stolen by the Big Two... or at least your most popular ones. Which of course leaves you with nothing to offer but the parts of your agenda nobody else wants to touch. No sense complaining. Not like we can sue them for copyright infringement. Even if we could, it wouldn't be a very libertarian thing to do. And at least this is good news, for the country in general if not for us.* Which was important, because what Walt was going to be bringing them tonight was bad news. For everybody.

HAVING GONE BACK TO HIS hotel room and changed into his usual outfit, Walt was at the podium. It was just about time for him to speak. The last of the delegates were seating themselves.

He had never addressed this conference before. The crowd was predominantly, even mostly white. Walt was aware that some people might see this as a problem, or at least as vaguely embarrassing. As far as he was concerned, their philosophy was right, and if white people liked it better, that was more likely to say something good about white people than something bad about the philosophy. *Still, it'd be cool if we could find a way to broaden our appeal.*

Nobody was naked or wearing a funny costume. That was a dark and grim sign, and what he was about to say wasn't going to help.

"Ladies and gentlemen," he said, "thank you for inviting me. It is an honor to deliver the keynote address to this convention." He went on to talk about reforms in drug policy, and to talk in a rather perfunctory fashion about other good things that had happened. Once he had that out of the way… "But the truth is, I've got some bad news. I need to deliver it, and you need to hear it. The news is—war is coming.

"War is coming, because the people in power need it to come. I was going to start out with a reading from Orwell's *1984*—the 'War is Peace' section, to be precise—but that's kind of clichéd, isn't it? Let's turn to a guy we haven't heard from in a while. A great thinker who died over a hundred years ago, when he was a year younger than I am now. Let's hear from Randolph Bourne." Walt made a great show of pulling out an old-fashioned sheaf of papers.

"Randy here summed up his big idea in seven words: 'War is the health of the State.' And if you want the details, I better warn you right now—this was not a man who dumbed things down. Check it out. 'War sends the current of purpose and activity flowing down to the lowest levels of the herd, and to its remote branches. All the activities of society are linked together as fast as possible to this central purpose of making a military offensive or military defense, and the State becomes what in peacetimes it has vainly struggled to become—the inexorable arbiter and determinant of men's businesses and attitudes and opinions.'

"We know what he's talking about, don't we? We've all seen it. The morning Anchorage happened, suddenly Congress got real friendly. Democrats were like 'Today we must all stand with our President in this time of crisis. We'll get back to ripping him a new one tomorrow or next week.' The right-wing crazies were like 'Yay, Pratt! Let's go kick some North Korean ass! Wait, they already surrendered? Shit.'" Seeing the crowd nod, hearing it chuckle, Walt felt a little stronger. The whole movement was weighed down with "libertarians" who whined about taxes and moochers, but who never saw a war they couldn't cheer or police misconduct they couldn't make an excuse for. But those in this room were the genuine article. They were his people.

"Presidents are never more popular," he said, "and they never get more cooperation from the rest of the government, than when the country is at war. Talk about your bad incentives!

"And listen, this isn't a new thing. This has been going on for a lot of American history. During the Civil War, Lincoln imposed martial law on Maryland. Legislators, judges, pretty much the whole government of Baltimore, all arrested and held without charges, and when the court said he couldn't do that, our great national holy martyr basically said 'try and stop me.'

"During World War I, Woodrow Wilson beefed up the government bigger than it had ever been before, built a massive propaganda operation, cracked down on pacifists and anarchists, and the government was still at it years after the war was over. Or look at World War II—rationing, the Smith Act, the internment of Japanese-Americans. Or the Military Commissions Act of '06. Again and again, Washington has used wars of one sort or another as an excuse to increase its power, lessen its accountability, and diminish the economic or political freedom of the people!

"And the worst part? The people have been completely okay with it! They've even cheered it on! They always react the same way—'I distrust and fear my government, but *not today*. I value dissent, but *not right now*. *Now* is not the time. *Now* we all gotta stick together and get behind our leader.'

"Our friend Randy knew about this, too. He called it the 'gregarious impulse'—'the tendency to imitate, to conform, to coalesce together.' And here's the money quote. 'Animals crowd together for protection, and men become most conscious of their *collectivity* at the threat of war.'" Walt emphasized that word to get the attention of his fellow Ayn Rand fans.

"'Consciousness of collectivity brings confidence and a feeling of massed strength, which in turn arouses pugnacity, and the battle is on! In civilized man, the gregarious impulse acts not only to produce concerted action for defense, but also to produce identity of opinion. Since thought is a form of behavior, the gregarious impulse floods up into its realms and demands that sense of uniform thought which wartime produces so successfully. And it is in this flooding of the conscious life of society that gregariousness works its havoc.' Again, sound familiar? Governments love this shit. They love it when everybody's baking American flag cakes and signing up to give blood the hospitals don't need.

"And here's where the bad news comes in. Up until the last few years, all this required that the government be able to point to some kind of enemy. A *human* enemy. Foreign powers, rebels, terrorists, even drug traffickers—it had to be some person or people who were coming up with plans to ruin our day and who might actually carry out those plans. Nothing less than that was scary enough.

"Oh, they tried. Back in 1977, President Carter tried to get the nation to wage 'the moral equivalent of war' on the energy crisis. It didn't work. Nobody bought it. Nobody was *afraid* of the energy crisis.

"See, the human brain is wired to respond to threats from other humans and take them seriously—more so than we take anything else. In the average year, more Americans are killed by lightning than by terrorists, but nobody talks about waging a war on lightning. Over ten times as many Americans were killed by car crashes as by terrorists *in 2001*, and how did we respond? We sucked it up! What I'm getting at here is that there have always been limits to the ability of the government to exploit this… gregarious impulse." Dramatic pause. "Until now.

"In the Northern Monsoon, we finally have a natural disaster severe enough for people to respond to it like it was an enemy attack. This has been happening since last fall, but only this year has it gone mainstream. I think it was Anchorage that did it—we got attacked, suddenly the whole country was in that war frame of mind, and when the war was over we started looking for an excuse to hang on to it. Because it feels *good*! Let's just come out and say it—the gregarious impulse feels fucking awesome! People love it! Like Bourne said, 'consciousness of collectivity brings confidence and a feeling of massed strength'—like a drug. I wish there were a Jellicoe treatment for it.

"People love that feeling, and they're hanging on to it. 'Treat it like a war, treat it like a war'—you've all heard it. People in the suburbs turning their lawns into 'victory gardens' like this was World War Two or something.

"And, you know, in some ways, it is like a war. Not only did more Americans die in the Monsoon than died at Pearl Harbor, or 9/11, or even Anchorage, but the physical damage was comparable to a war fought on American soil. That's not my opinion—that's the Red Cross, and they have some experience there.

"I'm not the one to tell you what it's been like. I'm from Denver, and Denver got off easy. A lot of you are from places that were hit. You've seen in person what people do, right? You've seen how they react to emergencies. They don't lean out the window and yell 'WOOHOO! TOTAL MINARCHY!' They should, but they don't. They do whatever they can to survive, and to help their friends and neighbors survive, but when—not if, when—that turns out not to be enough, that's when they start calling for help from the outside world. That's when you can say 'I'm from the government and I'm here to help you' and all you'll hear is 'What kept you?'"

"And that's why the government loves, loves, loves a good state of emergency. They'd like nothing better than to declare a state of emergency that lasts for the rest of our lives. And thanks to climate change, that's pretty much what we've got."

HIS SPEECH WENT ON FOR another twenty minutes. He emphasized that he wasn't here to spread gloom and despair, but to encourage everyone to pay attention to what else was said here for the next few nights. The other speakers would outline the party's strategies for keeping the little campfire of freedom burning through the coming storm. His job was to let them know what kind of storm was coming.

After his speech, Walt would have liked to go back to his hotel room, but he had a seat on the stage and leaving would have been rude. Which was too bad, because the next speech was so depressing it made his sound downright bubbly. It was by a state party chair and economics professor. "The last couple of years, the kids I teach have gone crazy," he said. "All they want to talk about is externalities. 'How does this reduce carbon emissions?' 'How does this lower the albedo?' 'If we can't make it happen through private incentives, don't we need to get the government involved?' I'm trying to teach them how the economy works, and they just want to learn how to make the planet work no matter what happens to the economy."

Walt didn't get to go back to his hotel room until after eleven. Normally he'd be hitting the bars and seeing if any girls were interested, but tonight he wasn't in the mood. He picked up his tablet, set it to State News: California and started reading. He didn't spend a lot of time in California, but since he was here, he might as well learn what was going on.

It didn't make him any happier. A lot of Walt's viewers thought of California as a socialist hellhole—especially the ones who couldn't afford a home in it.

Once upon a time, decades ago, it had been a happy state full of tax revolts and political paralysis, the land of Nixon and Reagan. When libertarians and conservatives talked about it now, they made it sound like a lost homeland that had sunk into the ocean or been conquered by an enemy.

Actually getting a good look at the place was worse. For as long as Walt could remember, people had been predicting the imminent collapse of California due to earthquakes or immigrants or wildfires or welfare or mudslides or... *something*. And it kept not collapsing. Unless you listened to TKB or something similar, of course, in which case it was a no-go zone.

And the more you listened to the people here, the more you realized they liked their state just the way it was. They thought of the old days as a time of smog, budget crises, and racist cops. They didn't miss any of that. They were proud of their power grid, which used sun, wind, and tides to bring electricity to forty-two million people, twenty desalination plants and close to a third of the nation's electric cars with a minimum of carbon emissions. They were proud of themselves for replacing their green lawns with xeriscaping and finding drought-adapted crops to grow in the Central Valley. They didn't complain about the taxes or the regulations—not much, anyway. They weren't even complaining about water rationing in L.A. In fact, a lot of them were saying the city should double down on desalination and leave the water in Owens Valley where it was.

It made Walt feel like... he supposed, like a feminist in a room full of contented housewives. He kept wanting to scream *why are you all okay with this? Don't you see what you're giving up? If you're happy, then you're happy, but don't you realize that people will see your well-oiled machine of a state as a good example? Does it even bother you that someone might use your happiness as a weapon against mine?*

Just by existing, this whole state was a kind of threat. It said *this is what the world looks like without you, and it is beautiful.*

JUNE 10:

AS CARRIE LEFT THE CAPITOL, she saw a group of young men and women—probably pages—out on the steps. She thought one of them looked familiar, but his back was turned and impeccably dressed young white men of slender build were not exactly in short supply on Capitol Hill.

Then the young man spoke up. Not only was his voice recognizable, but... "Yeah, watching Congress in action is like watching pandas fuck," he said. "You wait forever for them to do something and then they do it wrong." Yep. That was Jerome Ross. She immediately went up to say hi. She could practically see him start to glow at having a famous politician greet him by name in front of his peers.

A few minutes later, they were in a coffee shop, waiting for their coffee to arrive. It was close to lunchtime, but Carrie wasn't going to be having lunch today. Over the course of the last fifteen months, she'd lost ninety pounds. She was finally down to her target weight. She would have lost even more weight, but she didn't want to lapse into anorexia. (And, yes, she was worried that if she lost too much weight, she'd lose her "earth mother" image along with it.)

In any case, Carrie could fit into her old outfits again, her knees didn't hurt any more, and all she had to do now was exercise, keep her calories low, and watch her weight for... the rest of her life, basically. Because those ninety pounds she'd lost were still out there somewhere, building alliances, plotting to reconquer their old homeland, holding secret meetings, and toasting each other with *next year in Carrie Camberg's caboose*. All of which meant that she couldn't really meet people for lunch anymore. She could meet them for water, or black coffee, but not lunch.

Carrie started by talking about her work. "Right now I'm on leave from the foundation so I can advocate for the Norfolk Plan," she said. "Before that, I spent a couple months in sub-Saharan Africa looking over soil-renewal plans... winged beans, *terra preta*, that sort of thing."

Rome nodded. "Are you going to stay in town till it passes?"

"I like your optimism, but no. I'm going to Korea to see if there's any big projects we can help them with. Then I'm going to Israel, and this time I'm bringing the family."

"Vacation?"

"Sort of a working vacation. Also, now that we've got Thel speaking Mandarin like a strange-looking native, I think it's time she learned a little more about her own heritage."

Rome, as usual, needed no prompting to start talking about his work. "I'm working with the DSCC," he said. "It occurred to me that all these people getting moved around by the Monsoon and FEMA has opened up some new possibilities this year—places that would normally be hopeless suddenly look a lot more competitive." Carrie knew for a fact that Rome was far from alone in having this insight, but she just smiled and listened.

"So I'm going to be heading out west in a couple weeks. Setting up campaign offices in the camps. There's gotta be some tarpies with political experience."

"Some what?"

"Tarpies. Short for 'people in emergency camps.' Okay, not really short for, but they use a lot of tarps."

"How do they feel about the name 'tarpies'?"

"Well, they call each other that, but… yeah, I better check before I call 'em that where they can hear it."

"Good idea. How's your family?"

"Clint's in trouble again," he said. "There's a new runesnapping program he says he wasn't involved in writing. Hasn't gone to trial yet, so I don't know what the evidence looks like, but I really thought he was gonna go straight after the last time."

"You think he's guilty?"

"One day he was hitting me up for money and three weeks later he was paying me back and throwing in a bottle of Tanqueray No. 10 to get laid with. I gotta wonder." He shook his head. "I hope to God he's not guilty. See, there's this place called Otterholt Lake where they send cybercriminals—repeat offenders, the kind they've given up on trying to reform. Hackers joke about lots of shit, but you never hear 'em joke about the Lake." He bit his lip, then looked up. "How's your folks doing?"

"Thel's back from China," said Carrie. "Filling the house with the siren sounds of Chinese pop music and… what's it called? Rusty?"

"Rhust. R-H-U-S-T. How'd she like it?"

"Oh, she's got lots of stories."

Rome nodded. "I saw those videos she did over there with her classmates." *Of course you did*, thought Carrie. *I posted the link every two weeks.* "Seemed like she was having a good time."

"She was. At least until she got back and found out Ethan was seeing somebody else."

"That was her boyfriend?"

"Was, yes," said Carrie. "I don't know… it's not that I want her to die an old maid, it's just when I try to picture a male I'd be comfortable with her seeing, I can't. I just remind myself of how exasperating my own mother got when I started dating."

"Yeah, every time I try to bring a girl home to Mom, she always says 'That girl isn't good enough for you!' She said the same thing to Clint before he got married."

"I knew it couldn't be just Jewish mothers."

"Yeah, but you gotta be some kind of dumbass to cheat on a governor's daughter. Or even an ex-governor's."

"Oh, if he'd turned out to be abusive in any way, I'd have brought the wrath of God down on his head—Roger and me both. But he was just unfaithful. To a girl he hadn't seen in almost a year. Part of me still wants to have him publicly flogged for that, of course, but not a part I listen to."

"All the same—and don't take this as any kind of indecent interest—if I had a woman who looked anything like her, I'd wait."

Carrie nodded. "Don't take this as any kind of intrusion into your personal life," she said, "but you've had several women who looked pretty darn good. And then you lost them because you were so wrapped up in work you didn't pay them enough attention. I'm guessing something similar has happened with Sheilynn?"

"That is a totally unfounded and unwarranted assumption," said Rome, "which happens to be true, but I'm not giving you any points for it. How's Roger?"

"Doing all right. Teaching at George Mason. Still not trying for tenure, though. I have the suspicion he really wants to get back in the field."

"The field meaning…"

"Antarctica. Or Greenland. Or someplace up in the mountains where there are still glaciers, if he can find any. I've told him—no risking your life until Thel is in college." What she had actually meant, as both of them knew very well, was *no risking your life until I'm out of the White House.* And not even then, really. Carrie's own father had been an explorer—of rich food, booze, and cigars—and she'd lost him to an aneurysm before he was sixty. There was no need for her daughter to go through that.

"And Mike's on my case about the Norfolk Plan," she said, changing the subject. "He bought up a lot of land on the coast cheap and now he's worried he'll have to sell it even cheaper. See, you're not the only one with a brother who makes terrible life choices."

"I take it you're not letting that slow you down?"

Carrie shook her head. "What's slowing me down is that I've got a bill with one version of the Plan in front of the House, and another one in front of the Senate... and the Senate one is being held up while the House one keeps getting changed."

"Changed how?"

"They're moving the seawalls." Carrie shook her head. In retrospect, she should have taken it as a warning when the bill was called the SUSTAIN Act, or Safeguarding United States Territory And Improving Navigation, a highly strained acronym that could have meant anything.

"It started out as little things," she said. "Somebody with a lot of clout wanted a specific house or their end of a street protected, so they called their congressman and made it happen. Then they had to make more changes, and more changes, and at this point it's turned into exactly the sort of giant-seawalls-on-the-beach project that we already determined wouldn't work. And now people are adding on all kinds of projects that have nothing to do with it. One of the worst is Radcliffe from Norfolk—I really thought he'd come around. Sometimes it seems like the only one besides me who wants to see the real Plan pass is Congressman Darling."

"Darling, huh? I've heard a lot about him."

"Anything interesting?"

"He might be having a tough re-election fight. District got hit hard by the Monsoon. A lot of his constituents are still in camps, and the ones who stayed behind got their own problems. More than he can help them with." Rome paused. "He doesn't play golf."

"Come again?"

"He *doesn't... play... golf.*" Rome glanced around for a moment, then sighed. "There's never a horror movie soundtrack around when you need one. Trust me, if you were in Congress, and especially if you were a man, you'd have crapped your trousers hearing that. A man who is physically capable of golfing and chooses not to do so. That's like... it's like a young dude saying no to sex. Even if it's the right call, you gotta wonder why he's making it."

"Do you golf?"

"Only socially."

"Heard anything interesting on the golf course?"

Rome paused for a moment.

"A lot of Democrats aren't sure you're serious," he said.

"Serious about what?"

"About passing the Plan this year. Or at all."

"Why wouldn't I be?"

"For one thing, we all know you want to be president, and you want it two years from now, not six. And whatever you think of Pratt's domestic policy, or lack thereof, he's still the guy who kicked North Korea's ass. Your main selling point, as a candidate, is the Norfolk Plan. So if that plan passes in anything close to its original form and the president signs it…" Rome let his voice trail off, which was not something he normally did.

"Then what am I needed for?"

"Well, I didn't want to say it, but yeah." Rome, possibly for the first time since elementary school, looked sheepish. "Don't get me wrong. Out of all the politicians in this country, I don't know anyone I'd rather see in the Oval Office than you. Not even Morgan. Don't tell her I said that."

JUNE 12:

LOBBYING MOSTLY WASN'T DONE IN lobbies. For that you went to a congressperson's office in one of the buildings near the Capitol. Depending on your status, you might get to talk with the senator or representative, or you might just get an audience with the legislative correspondent.

Tom Lazebnick represented New York's First District, the eastern half of Long Island, a district Pratt had carried pretty handily in the last election. He was in his mid-thirties, with a slight widow's peak and a cynical smile.

"I'll level with you," he said. "My constituents don't have any particular need of the Plan. They're building their own seawalls." Left unspoken was that any of his constituents who didn't live in the Hamptons and couldn't pay for their own seawalls weren't really his constituents. "Morgan lets them do it, as long as they don't interfere with the Plan elsewhere."

"Morgan lets them," said Carrie.

"Yes," said Lazebnick. "She *lets* them. You heard what happened to Group 77's lawyers? Or the ones fighting the offshore wind farms? Officially, of course, it's just a gang of hackers and they have nothing to do with her, but… Look, to get back on track, my constituents are already paying to save the state. They'd rather not have to pay to save the country. Especially the way this bill is growing."

"That's sort of why I came to you," said Carrie. "Your constituents don't have a lot of needs, beyond the basic need for a functioning society and guaranteed future. I was hoping you'd help steer the SUSTAIN Act back toward something closer to what it's supposed to be. Like the Senate version."

"I could try to do that," said Lazebnick in don't-get-your-hopes-up tones. "Truth is, though, the minute they opened the door to changing the Plan, everybody sort of went crazy. Why protect one extra street when you can protect two? If you're going to save a whole town, why not this area just outside of town?

"As for the Senate version, if you want to know who's holding that up besides the usual suspects, it's Ramos. He's convinced we can protect every last inch of soil if we just put our backs into it. He introduced a bill to outlaw bluelining last year."

"I didn't hear about that."

"You wouldn't have. Bank lobbyists shut it down pretty fast. That was one of the few times Morgan ever told me how to vote on something."

Carrie nodded. *Note to self—get Morgan on my side.*

ON HER WAY BACK FROM the meeting, Carrie found a spot to park herself out of the way of everyone else and pulled out her phone. There was a hearing in town that she wanted to catch at least some of.

It was already going on. Agriculture Secretary Kyria Hammond was testifying in front of the House Committee on Agriculture. She'd spent the spring doing the same thing for agricultural policy that Carrie had tried to do for sea level rise.

The hearing was already going on. It was Radcliffe who was talking. Somehow, he still looked like the chairman of the Young Republicans on some college campus. "You're saying you want subsidies for farmers who alter their planting schedule for some of their fields, but not others," he was saying. "And you're confining this program to the states of… let's see… Alabama, Arkansas, Georgia, Louisiana, Mississippi, North and South Carolina, and Tennessee.

Can you explain your reasoning?"

"Certainly," said Hammond. She looked something like a black version of Carrie herself—tall, fortyish, and just shy of obese. Her skin was very dark, and her expression was calm.

"According to our computer models," she said, "if farmers in these states had planted wheat and corn in the fall like they do in India, they'd be bringing in a big harvest right now. The food shortage would be over. But—there is no guarantee that the same thing's going to happen this year. If they plant in the fall and we get anything like a normal winter, we'll lose another whole crop. Which we cannot afford to have happen.

"And that's the problem—uncertainty. In any given year, we might have a winter, or we might not. This summer, we might have heat kill or we might not. So the only strategy that makes any sense is to plant some fields by the old schedule and some by a different one. That way, no matter how things turn out, we'll know we're going to get something to eat. I'd rather have the certainty of fifty percent loss than the possibility of a hundred percent loss."

"And is this the president's plan," said Radcliffe, "or is it your own?"

"The plan was developed by myself with the support of President Pratt."

"How much support exactly?" he said, in tones that suggested he was trying to resist the urge to jump up and scream *Run for your lives! The Secretary of Agriculture has gone rogue!*

"What my colleague is trying to say," said another congressman whose name Carrie didn't happen to know, "is that we have yet to hear from the President or his spokespeople on the subject of this bill, or the problem it's intended to address." Carrie mentally translated this into *you are a mere Cabinet official, and we are Lords of the Legislature, and you need putting in your place.*

Or maybe they really were worried. For the most part, Pratt was his own brain trust. There wasn't any shadowy cabal of advisors who controlled him. Whatever policy came out of the executive branch either came from Pratt himself or had been brought to him first. That was a hard thing to get used to from a Republican president.

"Henry Pratt's got a lot to keep track of right now," said Hammond. "He's not an expert in ag issues, but he's got an old boys' network that could fill this room. He could have picked anybody for this job. He picked me because he wanted somebody who would act with initiative to do what needs to be done. Well, that's what I'm here to do."

Carrie had another appointment coming up, so she put her phone away. Hammond's plan, at least, was probably going to pass in something close to its intended form. Democrats weren't going to object, and as much as Republicans disliked the concept of federal intervention in... anything, really... most of them were from rural states and districts. Helping farmers was something they could see the point of. And if they couldn't, their constituents would be happy to explain.

And of course, Hammond was right. There was too much uncertainty in the weather right now. If every farmer who guessed wrong on what the next few months would bring was allowed to go bankrupt, in a few years the United States would suffer its very first famine.

JUNE 15:

LIKE MOST OF THE WEST Coast representatives, Jared Chiang (D-CA) was a big supporter of the Norfolk Plan in its original form. In California, Oregon, and Washington, the Plan was already being implemented with state resources. The government of Hawaii wanted to, but rising aviation fuel prices had drastically reduced tourism and crashed the local economy. As for Alaska, they were rebuilding Anchorage according to the Plan—and well they might, since the waterfront was the most badly damaged part of the city—but that was about it.

"Do you want my honest opinion?" said Chiang sadly.

"All right," said Carrie.

"This isn't going to be your year. You're trying to protect the coasts from long-term damage when a big chunk of the interior has suffered short-term damage. You can't blame people from Ohio and Iowa for trying to get more rebuilding money. We really haven't done enough for them."

"What about Darling? He's from Ohio."

Chiang shrugged. "Darling does what Darling does," he said. "You really want to know how you could help?"

"How?"

"Help us pass some tax reforms that would give us a little more money to work with. I mean, Pratt... he means well, but he's got us passing laws that we were talking about ten years ago and we should have passed twenty years ago."

"Like that carbon fee and dividend?"

"Exactly. It's like, now that the hole in the dike is three feet wide and growing, he's turning to the Dutch boy and saying 'Okay, fine, you can stick your finger in.' So the taxpayers are getting some money back, which is good, but it doesn't give us anything to work with."

"Wouldn't Pratt veto anything that increased revenue?"

"He probably would." Chiang sighed. "I supported him as much as anybody after Anchorage. Now… I am so damn sorry we have to wait two years to vote for you."

"That might be the nicest thing anybody's ever said to me."

AS SHE LEFT, CARRIE ALMOST literally bumped into Gov. Tejera, who was heading down the hall with a couple of aides following. He stopped to talk.

"So what brings you to D.C.?"

"Trying to get something added to the SUSTAIN Act," he said. "Something for New Mexico. What are you up to?"

"I'm… trying to do the exact opposite of what you're trying to do. Don't take it personally."

"I don't. I know, the Norfolk Plan is your baby and you don't want to see it messed with."

Carrie nodded. "Considering the feeding frenzy it's turned into, I don't blame you for wanting a piece of the action."

"It's not really for ourselves," said Tejera. "This spring was the hottest we've ever seen, and from the looks of things it was just warming up… so to speak.

"Right now every town in New Mexico—every town that isn't abandoned, anyway—has its own heat shelter. If we start seeing sustained temperatures over one-twenty like they had in Australia, we'll be ready. The counties of southern California are still catching up, but they should be ready in a year or so."

"So why do you need help from the federal government?"

"The problem is Arizona and Texas. They have no heat shelters. They haven't even started building them. If a heat wave hits, it's not going to respect state borders. Our little state doesn't have the shelter space, water or anything for ourselves and our neighbors too. But they'll be coming, and we couldn't stop them if we wanted to."

"Couldn't the FEMA camps take them in?"

"No FEMA camps in New Mexico—we don't have enough water. Besides, Pratt's trying to get people out of those camps, not into them."

"I hate to say it," said Carrie, "but it sounds like you're doing the right thing."

IT WASN'T UNTIL CARRIE WAS in the elevator that she noticed the NameDrop app blinking on her phone. She clicked on it. Time to find out what people in the news were saying about her.

The app had gotten a one-minute clip. It was Sen. Brent Ramos (D-FL) speaking on C-SPAN. He was about sixty, a man of average height with tan skin, and hair white around the temples and black everywhere else.

"And for all the people who are complaining about 'delaying tactics,'" he was saying, "I just have one question. What is the rush? What is the goddamn hurry? 'Run for your lives, the ocean is rising, it's coming for us all'—at maybe one inch a year! Why do we have to solve the problem in this session? Or this year? Or this decade, even? Why not wait and take the time to come up with a better plan?

"In fact, why are we even discussing this? We should be debating how to protect our people and their property, not how to abandon them! The United States of America has never ceded territory to a foreign power in its history, and Carolyn Camberg wants to cede our most valuable lands to Davy Jones! She's a quisling for the fish!

"If you ask me, our colleagues in the other chamber have the right idea. We should be trying to protect as much as we possibly—" The snippet cut off there.

Well, that was a surprise. Carrie knew Ramos was an opponent, but she hadn't expected him to be so vocal about it. So far, opposition to the Plan had mostly been low-key and quiet. The Plan was being rewritten or held up, but the only people speaking against it were Republicans from High Plains states who couldn't for the life of them see why the government was going to this much trouble on behalf of people who lived on the coast.

Before Carrie could fully process this, especially the part about being a quisling for the fish, she got a text message. It was from Grant Curtis.

We need to meet some time tomorrow.

What times work for you?

Interesting. The chairman of the party wants to meet me, and tomorrow, not next week or later this year.

JUNE 18:

CARRIE HOPED CURTIS WOULD BE on time for this meeting—or better yet, early. With temperatures in the high nineties, the sun blazing off the white marble and the air stinking of heated asphalt, nobody wanted to stand around outside in D.C. any longer than necessary. Even if you'd found one of the rare shady spots near the Russell Senate Office Building.

As luck would have it, he arrived at precisely 1:15 p.m., no more nor less. Democratic Party chair Grant Curtis was black, about fifty, and had his graying hair cut to an even length of a quarter inch around his head. He was approaching Carrie with the bone-weary look of a man whose job involved dealing with obstreperous children he wasn't allowed to discipline.

Carrie followed him into the building, through a security checkpoint and into the elevator. They exchanged updates about their families, but Curtis said nothing about the meeting until they were in front of the door to an office.

It was Senator Ramos' office. Carrie turned to Curtis, drawing in a breath to ask him what the hell he thought he was doing.

"Just come inside," he said. She followed him into the back room where Ramos was seated at his desk. When he looked up and saw them, his jaw dropped. *He didn't know this was happening either.*

"You can both plot revenge against me later," said Curtis. "In fact, that would be great as long as you did it together. See, what I need you two to do right now is kiss and make up. Okay, you don't literally have to kiss, but... look, we both know how it works. Republicans could be chasing each other around D.C. with machetes and chainsaws, but the media'll take any excuse if they can report 'Democrats in Disarray.' Right now, you two are that excuse." Curtis pulled up a chair in front of Ramos' desk, and motioned for Carrie to sit in it, which she did. It should have been Ramos making the invitation, of course, but given what he'd said about her, she was entitled to a little disrespect.

"Brent, Carrie here doesn't want to destroy America," said Curtis. "Carrie, Brent doesn't want... whatever bad thing you think he wants. When you're both running for president—yes, we all know it's coming—you can tear each other down to your hearts' content. Until then, sort this shit out between yourselves and Stop. Being. Enemies." He stood over by the antique filing cabinet, arms folded, glaring down at them.

Carrie looked at the senator. "You go first," she said.

Ramos rubbed his temples. "I don't even know where to begin," he said. "This... Norfolk Plan of yours. I'm trying to understand here, I'm trying to get inside your head, and I just can't! You're proposing gutting our whole economy right now over a threat that's going to be here in fifty years! It's like we've been in the lifeboat for five minutes and you're already trying to talk us into eating somebody! Can we maybe wait a little longer?"

"What is it you think is going to happen if we wait? Who's going to save us?"

"I don't know—it could be anybody! Look at your friend Sandra Symcox with her graphene batteries! The biggest drawback to battery technology was lithium storage and mining pollution, and now suddenly we don't need lithium anymore! We're finally putting a carbon fee and dividends in place, and we don't know if it's even going to end up moving any money! All the world's most brilliant minds are working around the clock now to fight global warming! Why are you betting against them?"

"Okay, I'll play along," said Carrie. "Let's suppose—just for the sake of argument—that at some point in the next fifty years, somebody invents... I don't know, a freeze ray or something that can re-grow the glaciers and the ice caps back to where they were in the twentieth century. Do you honestly think the world's going to say 'It's too bad we can't use this thing, but we promised Carrie we wouldn't try to save the coastline?' Of course not. If they can actually solve the underlying problem, they'll make a merry bonfire out of the Plan! And if I live to see it, I'll personally light the match! It won't be needed anymore!

"You see, the point isn't to limit our options, it's to protect the present and the near future. It's to respond to what we know is coming."

"Have you ever tried seeing it from the point of view of somebody in Florida?" said Ramos. "Anybody who owns anything on the coast? The people you're supposedly trying to protect? Do you realize what the Plan means to them? You're saying millions of people have to abandon their homes and businesses—most of their net worth—and even if they were willing to do that, they can't leave because they can't sell their houses! Property values have gone through the floor, which means property taxes are down, which means no money for schools, which means even if the house is on high ground, families with kids don't want to move there! And the best part? Not only has the state's bond rating gone down to junk, but the legislature, right now, is talking about raising taxes to pay off all the assholes cashing in the bonds they've already bought!

"And go to Louisiana! Maryland! Delaware! New Jersey! North Carolina! They'll tell you the same story! Your goddamn Plan is declaring war on us just by existing! As an idea! Without anybody even trying to implement it! And you wonder why we're fighting it?"

"I notice you left Virginia out of that list," said Carrie. "I'm from Virginia. I used to live and work in Norfolk. I know at least as much about the problem as you do."

"That's just it! If you were from some godforsaken flyover state like North Dakota or something, it would make sense. You wouldn't have any way of knowing what you were destroying. But you know!"

"Yes. I do. And you know as well as I do that the Plan is not the problem. The problem is rising sea levels. Without the Plan, the problem would be worse."

"No, without the Plan, we'd have a better Plan. A Plan that protects everything. A Plan that doesn't accept excuses about why things can't be done and places can't be saved. If a wall sinks, build another one on top of it! If water gets in under it, pump it out! Or do something else!"

"Like what?"

"I don't know! That's your problem—you keep asking! You never *ask* engineers what's possible—you tell them what to do and let them figure out how!"

Carrie shook her head. "First of all, if we try to do things your way, the cost alone will break us. By the time we're ready to do things my way, we won't be able to afford the Plan because we'll be spending so much money meeting the interest on the national debt. Second—I really shouldn't have to explain this to a fellow Democrat—failure is disheartening. The government tries to do something, it doesn't get the results people are hoping for, and instead of saying 'let's try harder' people say 'let's give up.' That's been the story of so many government programs. Hope is like money—false hope drives the real thing out of circulation. And the more you try to print, the less people take it seriously."

"By the time this becomes a problem, your daughter's going to be old enough to run for president. Why are you making decisions now based on problems that *might* come up then? Why can't you trust future generations to fight their own battles?"

"Because that kind of thinking is what got us into this mess in the first place," said Carrie. "You and me—once upon a time, we were the future generations that were supposed to solve the problem. We were supposed to have the tools that would make it possible. Well, here we are. We have some of the tools, but the problem's grown enormously. Do you really want to hand things over to our children—or their children?"

"What I want," he said, "is to fight. I want to fight sea level rise on the beaches, I want to fight it in the marshes, I want to fight it everywhere like Churchill. There's a reason why I called you a 'quisling for the fish'—I want us to treat this problem the same way we'd treat a foreign invasion. I want us to cede *nothing*. If we fail, we try again. If we need more money, we get more money—tax it, borrow it, print it, whatever. If we need more hope, then we *hope*. We never, ever give up. Certainly not at this stage."

WHEN CARRIE LEFT THE MEETING, she turned on her phone. She'd gotten a text from Thel assuring her that she and her friends had arrived safely in D.C. and were on their way to see Rodomontade live at the Verizon Center. After hearing some of their music, Carrie would have been more tempted by seeing Rodomontade dead at the Verizon Center, but at least somebody in the family could come to this city and get what they wanted.

JUNE 19:

ISABEL'S CAR WAS OVER TEN years old, but she'd had a modern feature added to it recently. The windows and windshield could go into mirror mode at the press of a button. This kept the inside of the car cool on hot summer days.

It had other uses as well. To pick an example completely at random, if you and your boyfriend had just come from a concert that ended just before midnight, and your boyfriend had to catch a train at about three in the morning, leaving you with not enough time to justify the expense of a hotel room, but you had managed to find some decent overnight parking in D.C., mirror mode would allow you and him some privacy in the back seat of the vehicle while you tried to find out how much sex could be crammed into two hours and forty-five minutes.

Three rounds. The first one was quick, hot, and rough, with the fire and thunder of Rodomontade's music still echoing in them both. The second was slower, more tender, knowing this would be the last they saw of each other for months, if not a year.

After that, Isabel and Hunter just sort of snuggled together. His beard was rough against her cheek. She was glad he'd lost so much weight. There wasn't room back here for her to be on top. When his weight slipped off his elbows, as it always did at some point, having a 210-pound man on top of her was easier than having a 260-pound man.

The third round was kind of experimental—*can we do this? Yes we can!* It took a little while, and once it was done, Isabel had to get back into the front seat quickly and head for Union Station.

Restoring Amtrak to its former glory was not a high priority of the Pratt administration, but the route north to Montreal was still intact. As for the rest of the journey, somehow Canada kept its trains running on time despite Monsoon damage that made the U.S. look like it had gotten off easy.

Hunter looked at the station, then back at her. Isabel tried to read his face by the light of the dashboard and streetlights. Excited? Scared? Sad? It looked like all those things.

"This is it," he said. He didn't see Isabel pinching her own hand. For the first time in a long time, Hunter seemed happy and hopeful. She couldn't begrudge him that. But it was going to be so hard to going back to living alone.

"Let's limit ourselves to one goodbye kiss," said Isabel. "That way you won't be late."

There was one goodbye kiss. It lasted as long as they could make it.

"You... you look out for yourself out there, all right?" That hand-pinching thing was not working at all.

"You're the best girlfriend I could ask for," he said. "I'll come back to you, I swear. We'll be together again."

"I'll be waiting."

And so, he left. Isabel blinked aside a few tears and watched Hunter take his luggage out of the trunk and walk away. Maybe she was reading too much into the way he was walking and the new straightness in his back, but he seemed more confident, less apologetic. As if he knew exactly where he was going. Even though he didn't.

THE HEAT WAVE DOMINATED SOUTHERN *Arizona and New Mexico, a broad swath of west Texas and the interior of northern Mexico. It was not quite as bad as the heat wave that had plagued inland Australia six months earlier, but it was close. Daytime temperatures of 105, 110, 115 degrees held sway. At least the air was bone-dry, which made it possible to survive in the open by sweating until you could get somewhere there was water… unless of course you couldn't, in which case it was a death sentence.*

Further south, a dry period in Oaxaca and Chiapas ended dramatically with a series of microbursts and macrobursts—so-called rain bombs—in late May, heralding a summer of heavy rain. Hundreds died in the resulting floods.

Not even the Yucatán was spared. There was a brief period, from March to the middle of May, when the Gulf of Mexico and the Caribbean were too cool for hurricane formation. But they were still much warmer than usual for this time of year, so it didn't take much to push them back over the edge. In late June, a Category 2 hurricane formed in the western Caribbean and began heading for Cancun.

But Mexico had other problems besides the weather. For a long time, its drug cartels had divided its territory among themselves and shrugged off the efforts of the central government to defeat them. They had suffered the occasional disruption of a smuggling route, the loss of a refinery every now and then, the arrest of a kingpin. It had made no real difference. The one thing that could truly harm the cartels was a drop in demand for their product within the United States.

And that was exactly what was happening. With the Pratt administration's blessing, even those states that weren't legalizing drugs were giving Jellicoe treatments to the addict population as a much cheaper alternative to prison.

Many of America's functional addicts were weighing their financial options and choosing the Jellicoe route as well. And for the people who weren't really addicts at all, but just happened to like doing drugs, times were tough enough that all but the most well-off of them were cutting back on use. The cartels were now the apex predators of a collapsing food chain.

The smarter members took whatever money they could and fled. The rest, inevitably, turned on each other, fighting desperately for shares of the diminished but still substantial revenue stream. And as the cartels fought, they grew more brutal. They had kept order within their own ranks, and enforced their will on others, with a mixture of money and threats. With money in short supply, threats were all they had left. The cartels began assassinating government officials, police officers—anyone who seemed likely to turn on them at their weakest moment.

The government of Mexico—what remained of it—gathered up their families and took shelter with the armed forces, who were frantically purging their ranks of anyone who could be proven to be in league with the cartels. Once the army had secured the safety of its officers' own families, it began the slow, relentless reconquest of its own country. In this it was joined by former enemies it could never have imagined partnering with—the leftist guerrillas of the south.

JULY 11:

"TONIGHT, LADIES AND GENTLEMEN, OUR special guest is a real-life American capitalist success story. She's an inventor, a businesswoman, a certified genius, and living proof that diamonds really are a girl's best friend. On top of all that, her business is helping to save the environment. Ladies and gentlemen, please give a warm welcome to the owner and CEO of De L'Air Diamonds, Sandra Symcox!"

As Walt Yuschak watched her step up to the stage, he was struck again by how young his guest looked. If he hadn't known she was selling artificial diamonds, he would have guessed she was selling Thin Mints and Samoas. She was wearing a cream-colored pantsuit and carrying a big black briefcase with both hands.

"Welcome to the show. It's great to have you."

"It's great to be here." Her smile was pleasant, but there was something sharp and knowing behind it. Well, of course there was. And she'd demanded that he treat her with respect and courtesy. As far as Walt was concerned, she'd earned it.

"I just have to say, you are one incredible woman."

"Thank you."

"Really, you are. You're a real-life rags-to-riches story. Five years ago you were living on ramen—"

"Which was a lot cheaper back then."

"And now you're worth what? Billions? Tens of billions?"

"Let's not get too specific. What the IRS doesn't know won't hurt them."

"A buttload of money."

"Umpteen-point-six buttloads as of last quarter."

"And I love the name 'De L'Air Diamonds.' It's got that French classiness to it. Are you French, or do you have any French ancestry or heritage or anything?"

"Nope."

"Just proping, huh?"

"Yeah."

"Here's my big question. People have known ways to make artificial diamonds for a long time, but nobody's ever been able to bring them into the market before. What did you do differently?"

"Well, I had a more efficient way to make them—that was a plus—but it sounds like you're really asking about the marketing."

"Yeah."

"I did a couple of things. First, of course, there was the whole eco-friendly aspect of using artificial trees to collect carbon from the air. That was a good angle. Second, I didn't make the mistake people usually make—thinking 'I made these things cheap, why not sell them cheap?' You see, one thing I've noticed is that there are certain situations where people don't want to save money—where they actually want to spend as much money as they can afford, because that's their way of showing how much they care."

"And how much money they have."

"That too," said Symcox, "but let me give you a specific example. Coffins. They cost thousands of dollars each, and they're just boxes. You look at what they're made of, the cost of labor, the fact that we just stick them in the ground, and there's no reason they should cost more than a hundred... except that people want to spend that much on them. Nobody wants to lay their loved ones to rest in a cheap-ass plywood box. What I realized was that the same thing is true of jewelry. No matter what it's made of, or how much or little it cost to make, nobody wants to be the guy saying 'Will you marry me? I got this ring for fifty bucks!'"

Walt laughed. "Speaking of the price, I got some news reports that say De L'Air diamonds are being sold—legitimately—in India for less than a fifth of what they're selling for in the United States. How do you justify that?"

"How do I justify it?" said Symcox cheerfully. "I don't. I just do it. Again, it's what the market will bear. If anybody wants to start up a company and sell diamonds in the U.S. for a fifth of what I'm offering, I say let 'em try it and see how it works."

"A woman after my own heart," said Walt. "So how do you know how much to overcharge?"

"That's the big question, isn't it? Charge too little and people won't want to buy your stuff. Charge too much and you'll price half your customers out of the market.

"Luckily, most of the job had already been done for me. The big boys in the business put a lot of mathematicians and market analysts to work trying to find the sweet spot on the curve. What I did was to look at what they were charging, then charge just a little bit less than that and say 'And it's eco-friendly!' That way, I get more people who can afford it, and knowing you helped save the world a little bit makes up for the fact that you're buying something cheaper." Sandy gestured in the air as if pointing out words on a poster. "'For your future. For her future. For all our futures.'"

"I remember that. That was one of your early slogans, wasn't it?"

"Yep. So that was what we did the first few years. This spring we introduced colored gemstones, which we sold for about as much as our competitors were charging for clear ones. The trick was to make them better than mined diamonds—but not too much better. We didn't want it to look like costume jewelry. It took a while to get the colors right, but we could afford to use up a lot of carbon on experiments. Some of them didn't test well, like the Champagne line—focus groups said the color looked too much like pee. But anything that doesn't work out can be sold as industrial grit. Let me show you what we've done." Symcox picked up her briefcase, put it on the table and opened it up. She took out a roll of black velvet and spread it on the tabletop.

Then she started taking out diamonds of various sizes and putting them on the cloth. "First, some regular clear diamonds for comparison," she said. "Now here are the ones you've seen—the Moonlight, Snowshadow, Horizon lines. They're made with just a hint of boron. They're the ones we rolled out this spring. Notice how delicate the colors are. Very subtle shades of blue." Walt motioned for one of the cameras to zoom in on them.

"I'll level with you," he said. "I can't tell the Snowshadows and Horizons apart."

"Not everybody can. The human eye isn't really adapted to parse different shades of blue. They're both the same intensity, but the Snowshadows have just a hint of violet in them. We also created some blue-green diamonds, but the color looked a little too institutional."

Then Symcox took out some more. "And now, for the first time ever, are the colors you haven't seen before. We'll be bringing them out for the holiday season this year. Nice warm colors for winter." They were red-orange, yellow-orange and whiskey-colored. Walt could barely focus on their names, except that the red-orange ones were called "Hearthfire." Just looking at them made him want to pull off a heist.

Eventually she put them away. "Now, in addition to the diamonds you're also in the graphene and diamondoids industry, is that right?"

"Yep. In fact, they're kind of my first love."

"Really? More so than diamonds?"

"Really. I mean, diamonds have been good to me, but at the end of the day, they're just shiny objects. Sometimes I feel like an English Lit major who got rich writing 'My Stepbrother the Billionaire Weredinosaur' erotica. No complaints about the money, but I want to do more. And I keep thinking everybody's going to wake up tomorrow and say 'Wait, why are we paying thousands of dollars for tiny lumps of compressed soot?' It pays to diversify, just in case.

"And graphene—I could spend the whole rest of the show talking about the properties and applications of graphene."

"Please don't."

"But the hard part isn't finding uses for graphene, it's manufacturing it on an industrial scale without using too much energy or generating too much waste. I've found ways of doing that."

From there the conversation turned to the new materials being developed at De L'Air Graphene & Diamondoids. Symcox reached into her briefcase and pulled out a rectangle of something that looked like rigid white cardboard, only brighter than any cardboard could possibly be. Under the studio lights it was a hard, blazing white as if cut from a sheet of magnesium flame. Walt had to squint when he looked at it.

"We call this 'Point-925,' because that's the approximate albedo. That means it's literally whiter than snow."

"I believe it."

"And it extends pretty far into the infrared and ultraviolet. In fact, if you could see in ultraviolet, this would look like a mirror."

"What's it for?"

"Roofing tile. You put it on your house and it helps keep it cool in the summer. It weighs about as much as asphalt shingle and costs about twenty percent more, but you get your money back from lower AC bills."

"We also have a little treat for the aerospace industry." Symcox reached into her briefcase again—whoever packed that thing must have been a genius of organization, Walt could barely get his clothes for one weekend into one suitcase—and brought out a small net bag with a loose mesh. Something in the bag floated like a helium balloon, so she had to keep hold of the drawstring to keep it from drifting up to the ceiling. Whatever was in the bag was about six inches across, shaped like a cushion, and made of something so clear it was a little hard to see.

"This is a vacuum bubble," she said. "We call it a q-me."

"How is that spelled?"

"Q-dash-M-E. We tried spelling it C-U-U-M-I-E, but everybody kept misspelling that and it got embarrassing. Anyway, it's got a graphene skin, diamondoid reinforcement and literally nothing inside. As of now, this is the biggest one we can make, but if we made enough of them to make a balloon, it would have about the same lift as if you filled it with hydrogen. And because it's small, you can tuck them into the fuselage of a plane or a drone and shave off a little weight."

AFTER THE COMMERCIAL BREAK, WALT decided it was time to delve a little more into his guest's history. "I understand you've got an IQ of 210. Tell us what that means, exactly."

"Well, in theory what it means is that I'm 2.1 times as intelligent as the average person. In practice, it means that I'm 2.1 times as embarrassed whenever I do something stupid."

"Obviously you're doing something right. You're sure your superior intellect had nothing to do with it?"

"Actually, it did," said Sandy. "My superior intellect told me I didn't know a damn thing about managing a company and I'd better find people who did. But not MBAs, because I've noticed they have this tendency to destroy everything they touch. So I found some people who'd managed nonprofits."

"It wasn't just starting a company, it was taking on the diamond oligopoly and winning."

"That's partly because it took them a while to start taking me seriously," she said. "There was a point right near the beginning when they could have shut me down, but they ignored me. Then there was a point when they could have bought me out, but they tried to shut me down. Then there was a point when they should have started treating me as an equal, but they tried to buy me out. Now they're treating me as an equal. A lesson for us all, I think."

"Elaborate on that."

"Well, at first they treated it like a gimmick. Then, when they realized they were losing serious market share, they tried to make it illegal for us to call what we were selling 'diamonds.' In the U.S., they went to the Consumer Product Safety Commission, and the Commission said 'talk to Congress.' Then they spent God knows how much money lobbying Congress. We just asked for judicial review… and the Supremes ruled in our favor. What they said was— I'm paraphrasing—'If De L'Air were lying about where their product came from or how they made it, that would concern us. But they're putting it right there in the ads. It's free speech.'"

"Good to see the regulators losing a battle every now and then."

"I don't see regulatory agencies as the enemy," she said. "I see them as a battlefield—a strategic location you have to fight for. If your competitors take control of them, they can lock you out of the market. So you want to either control them yourself, or at the very least deny them to anyone else. Keep them as no-man's-land."

"That's an even scarier way of putting it. Thank you for that."

"No problem. After that, they started fighting back in different ways— running ads like 'Is that a real diamond?' They had guys going into their long, proud history, and traditions—'My family's been in the diamond business for generations! My great-great-great-great-grandfather burned three African villages and pulled a guinea worm out of Cecil Rhodes's taint! How can you do this to me?'—or whatever it was they said. But the more they tried, the more publicity they drew down on themselves—business practices, how they were treating diamond miners… Basically, the press said we were the underdog, the market said we were the hot new trend, and everybody said we're helping save the earth. That's a pretty good position to be in."

"Speaking of publicity, I've been meaning to ask you about the 'Wear the Air' campaign," said Walt. "Tell us something about the creative process that gave rise to it."

Symcox laughed. "That's the nicest 'What were you thinking?' I've ever heard," she said. "That had its origins in the bowels of our marketing department. The only thing I contributed to it was the suggestion that instead of hiring models, we look for celebrities who were willing to appear naked… for a given value of 'naked'—strategically placed objects and all that. Got to admit, I wasn't expecting the governor to volunteer."

"Why celebrities?"

"I wanted the nudity to be a statement of power and confidence. I didn't want them to come off as vulnerable or exploited or objectified or anything—I wanted them to look like they were there and naked because that was what they wanted. I tried it myself, but we didn't use the photo because market research said it made people uncomfortable." Walt nodded. This woman had the wrong face and body for that sort of thing. "The photo of Governor Morgan, on the other hand, went over quite well."

Walt called up the image of the ad in question. Morgan was just sitting there butt naked in some kind of upscale lounge area, cool as a rock in a stream, working on a tablet like this was completely normal, legs casually crossed, tablet just high enough to keep her nipples out of view.

"Getting back to your experiences with regulatory agencies and what you said about them," he said, "have you ever considered… I don't know, joining the Libertarians? We could use a few good candidates for office."

"I did go through a libertarian phase when I was younger," she said. "I think most really smart people do."

"Excuse me," said Walt, a little sharply. "A phase?"

"Well, yes. See, nobody likes taking orders from somebody dumber than they are, and if you're a genius, that's almost everybody. But at the same time, we don't want to rule the world, because we really are smart, and we know it would be too much work and not much fun. So we dream of a world where giving or taking orders in general just doesn't happen very much."

"Exactly! As little coercion as possible! Not forcing people to do things or pay for things against their will if there's any alternative!" Walt stopped himself before he could launch into a filibuster. "So what changed your mind?"

"When I was sixteen, I tried to write a science-fiction novel. It was set a hundred years in the future and there were all these libertarian space colonies out in the asteroid belt, collecting volatiles while looking for valuable ore to refine and ship back to Earth. All the characters were looking for this... thing that was going to make somebody rich if they could find it. A MacGuffin, basically. And they'd form these little alliances among themselves while plotting to betray each other, and my hero was this slim, sexy, nerd girl who was really into inorganic chemistry..."

"This is sounding good," said Walt. "I kinda want to read it."

"I'm sorry to disappoint you, then. I didn't get very far with the novel—I never even decided what the MacGuffin was. I spent more time designing the colonies than I did developing characters. The power, the docking facilities, the water recycling... this was the stuff I thought was interesting. Not so much the people.

"But that part—trying to design these places and figure out how they'd work—that was what really did it for me. Try to imagine a space colony run on libertarian principles. We're talking about a place where every drop of water, every breath of oxygen has to be accounted for. You'd somehow have to monetize all that stuff. Meaning that anybody who went bankrupt would have to be kicked out the airlock."

"Well, you wouldn't necessarily have to go that far," said Walt. "I mean, they'd have to leave, obviously."

"Right. On a spaceship. Which would also cost money—cubic footage, food, water, air, the energy to transport the mass... whatever you're using for money, you'd have to loan them some just to get rid of them. The more I looked at the system, the less sure I was that it could be made to work, and even if it could I wasn't sure how many people would actually want to live like this."

"But if people were expanding into space, then they'd be building new space colonies all the time," said Walt.

"They would, but every one of them would be subject to the same restrictions as the old ones. An infinite number of prison cells isn't the same thing as freedom." Walt opened his mouth to interrupt again, but couldn't think of anything to say.

"At this point," Symcox said, "I asked myself—'What's the difference between the planet Earth and a space colony?'"

"It's bigger, obviously."

"It's bigger, and things like water and air can't be monopolized, but the most important difference from a human perspective is that the margin of error on Earth is a lot wider. Wider, but not infinite—in fact, it seems like we've already exceeded it. So what kind of philosophy only works in a world with infinite margin of error?"

FOR MOST OF THAT EVENING, Walt found himself going over that conversation in his mind. He thought he'd done a passable job of defending libertarianism, but he hadn't been up to his own standards. It was hard to talk to somebody whose mind just casually made giant leaps from the concrete to the abstract and back: *Every one of them would be subject to the same restrictions as the old ones. An infinite number of prison cells isn't the same thing as freedom.* He supposed that was what an IQ of 210 got you.

And yet he couldn't help but feel that Symcox, for all her brains, had missed the point. It wasn't about trying to achieve the best possible outcomes, although obviously good outcomes were... good. Libertarianism was *right*. Walt was no anarchist. He accepted that there was a certain bare minimum of coercion without which human society wouldn't function. The object was to get as close to that minimum as possible, and never to forget that it was a necessary evil. Never to stop looking for ways to lower it just a little bit further.

Figuring out how to make this work was the job of somebody smarter than himself. And, apparently, somebody smarter than Sandra Symcox.

JULY 15:

ISABEL LOOKED AT IT ONCE again. She walked all the way around it, not wanting to lose a single detail. After today, she would never see it again.

The house where she'd grown up. The off-white walls. The faded navy shutters. The roof with its patches of shingle that Pop had laid down himself. The little path to the dock where she'd walked thousands of times, keeping an eye out for bees the whole time.

The house where she'd grown up. Where she'd hidden inside on sunny days and rainy days. The living room where she'd listened to NOAA broadcasts. The kitchen where she'd helped Mom with dinner.

The porch where she'd played with Chelsey or Kristen, or where Sandy had taught her about science. The place under the porch where Major used to sleep during the summer, back when they'd had a dog.

Wherever she had gone—College Park, the Arctic Ocean, Louisiana—she had always had this place to come back to, if only for a visit. Until today.

Condemned. From the point of view of the state of Maryland, one less place to worry about. Isabel gritted her teeth and went back inside to get another piece of furniture to put in the U-Haul.

The day had come to move everyone and everything out, and Isabel was feeling emotionally drained. Over the course of the last two weeks, she had used up all her tears. Also her profanity. She had left most of that at HCD in the form of messages that were at the absolute legal limit of what was permissible to say to another human being or institution without it constituting a threat. *God damn it, why? A little understanding. That was all we needed. Just a little patience from the fucking state after a lifetime of paying our taxes and dealing with the DNR.* She had punched the wall of her own apartment. As it turned out, she had punched the wrong part of the wall. Now there was a hole in the drywall a foot wide and she hoped her landlord didn't find out about it.

A fair amount of stuff had already been sold online or in yard sales. The last thing in the house was the chest of drawers in Mom and Pop's bedroom. Scott helped her get it down the stairs.

Or to be perfectly honest, *she* helped *him* get it down the stairs. Over the last couple of summers, the sun had tanned his skin and bleached his hair as light as Kristen's, and he was at least as strong as Pop had ever been. Isabel was having a hard time reconciling the impressive specimen in front of her with the baby whose diaper she distinctly remembered changing.

Afterward, Isabel went through the house one last time, trying to ignore the smell of mold, making sure nothing valuable was in here. With no furniture, with nothing on the walls but wallpaper and none of Jourdain's toys on the floor, the place seemed strangely impersonal. It was as if this house were an elderly relative that had forgotten she was family.

Kristen and Chelsey were in the front yard, doing a last check to make sure they had all Jourdain's toys. The one good thing about this being such an unhappy day was that it let Chelsey be a little more lucid.

"How's Hunter?" said Kristen.

"I think he's doing okay." *Better than I am. It's been almost a month—why is it so hard to get used to living alone? I'm not even that sociable.*

"Where is he right now?"

"He's in the Yukon." Seeing the blank look on Chelsey's face, Isabel added, "Just east of Alaska." This probably didn't help. Chelsey had been fifteen when she found out that Alaska was not literally in a giant box in the middle of the Pacific. One of the things Isabel appreciated about Kristen was that unlike Chelsey, she never let being book-dumb become a part of her identity.

"Are they doing that tree-planting thing?"

"Yeah. First, they have to check to see if the permafrost is gone. You can't plant trees on top of permafrost—it lowers the albedo of the ground and warms it up. So Hunter's job is using this machine like a big syringe to take samples of the ground.

"He's also gotten a job in the camp kitchen, and they're already saying good things about the food he makes. So… yeah. We kinda miss each other, but…"

"But now that he's gone, you can get yourself a real man," said Chelsey. "Or a woman." Isabel almost didn't hear that next bit. If Jourdain hadn't been watching, she might have hit Chelsey right there.

"She didn't mean it," said Kristen, seeing the look on Isabel's face.

"I know," said Isabel. "I know." She had met people—not all of them straight—who still thought bisexuals couldn't be faithful, that no one partner could give them more than half what they wanted. That wasn't true, but it rankled. Even leaving Hunter's good qualities out of consideration, she had made him a promise and she intended to keep it.

Chelsey gave her a knowing look. "Spiny*, spiny, porcupiny," she said. "Personally, I wouldn't have put up with that boy for one day."

---

* Needlessly defensive.

"Personally, you married Rod. So personally—"

Kristen held up a hand to stop Isabel, then turned to Chelsey. "If she's bringing that guy up," she said, "you're not gonna win this one."

"Probably not," said Chelsey. Then she turned to Isabel. "But don't you feel better now that you got something to be pissed off about?"

Even with mild brain damage, Chelsey wasn't dumb about everything.

ISABEL RETURNED TO HER APARTMENT, aching in muscles she hadn't known she had. Every single piece of furniture in the U-Haul was now in the storage unit. Eventually she was going to have to fix herself some dinner.

Her armphone started playing "I Won't Forget" and said, "It's Kristen." It turned out to be a video from the bow of the *Mary Lynn*, carrying Kristen and the rest of the family to the Hortons' place in Smith Island. One of the advantages of having your own boat was that you didn't have to drive down to Crisfield and wait for the ferry.

Kristen was humming something to herself as she kept her camera trained on Smith Island, a line of green between denim-colored water and the pale edge of the sky. It was beautiful. And unspoiled. And flat. And vulnerable. Moving from Tilghman Island to Smith Island was... as far as sea level rise and bluelining went, that old saying about frying pans and fires came to mind again.

One day it will be gone. And it will never come back. But not today.

And we'll always have the cake recipe.

JULY 21:

MR. WALLACHINSKY WASN'T BUILT FOR grand, sweeping gestures, but he was doing the best he could. He waved his short, stubby arms at the crystalline ceiling overhead with an expression of justified pride, then turned to Carrie.

"What do you think?" he said.

"I think we've all been thinking much too small," said Carrie, looking around.

The city of Haifa hadn't been building heat shelters. It *was* a heat shelter. On the surface, it didn't look so different, except for the slightly greater prevalence of AC and emergency vehicles, and the occasional staircase leading to the tunnels below.

Where Carrie was standing was an underground tunnel connected to the old Carmelit subway. Within the crystal panels of the ceiling were embedded the ends of fiber-optic cables that led to the outside, where their other ends were kept pointed at the sun. The panels refracted the pure sunlight into interesting patterns that illuminated the space with a soft glow.

"Is this one of the emergency elevators?"

"Certainly. Try it."

It looked like any other elevator, except for the crank attached to the wall next to it. Turning the crank, Carrie found it was surprisingly easy to raise and lower the car. Of course, it would probably be harder if the elevator was full of people—but not a lot harder. A hydraulic jack would let a much smaller woman than Carrie raise and lower a two-ton truck with her own muscles. This was not so different. And it would continue working no matter what happened to the power.

"All this is just the beginning," said Mr. Wallachinsky. "We're digging tunnels into the heart of Mount Carmel for extra storage space." There was already enough room down here to shelter the entire population of the city for several days.

Looking at the map, Carrie could see how parts of the complex could be isolated from the whole in case of a disease outbreak. No terrorist would ever take out the whole place with one virus or neurotoxin.

Some were predicting that in a later century, disastrous climate changes would make the tropics and low temperate regions uninhabitable to humans and other mammals during the daylight hours of summer. If that was the future, Haifa was almost ready for it right now.

Carrie knew of no other nation, not even Saudi Arabia, that was doing such a thorough job of preparing for whatever disasters might come. Maybe it was just the effect of having gotten used to the idea of existential threats.

THE THING ABOUT A COUNTRY the size of New Jersey is that everything is within a few hours' drive of everything else. Leah Lemel, one of the locals she'd hired as bodyguards for this trip, was sitting beside Carrie as the self-driving car took them back to the hotel in Jerusalem.

Carrie had been to Israel once before, as a child. Her memories of the trip were vague to the point of uselessness. Certainly she hadn't expected to be seeing this much farmland. It was one hundred degrees outside and bone-dry, but the crops were still alive, kept going with desalinated water injected into the soil. *Another five degrees and all the care in the world won't matter. This country is at risk like everywhere else.*

But while it lasted, it was worth appreciating. "It's beautiful," she said, forgetting she was speaking out loud.

Leah spoke up. "You could stay."

"Hmmm?"

"Why don't you stay here?" said Leah. "You and your family. In Israel."

"Are you serious?"

"Of course. Why not?" She sounded perfectly sincere.

Carrie took a long look at Leah. The woman was in her early twenties, and looked to be not long out of the army. She wasn't a big woman—about five foot four, maybe 120 lbs—but she was physically fit and had an alert and dangerous look that never quite left her. Even now, while she was talking, her hazel eyes kept glancing over Carrie's shoulder or taking sidelong looks out the windows.

"I can't just…" Carrie groped for words. "I mean, I'm an American citizen. I have some serious career plans that involve… well, being in America." *You fool, you must be the only person on the planet who doesn't know I'm planning to run for president.*

"You should move here anyway," said Leah. "For your daughter's sake. Or her children."

"I know Israel's doing as well as any country. Better than most, in fact. But I think the U.S. can do just as well. I want to help make that happen."

"It's not how well they do for themselves I'm worried about," she said. "It's how well they do for you."

"What do you mean?"

"How long has your family lived in America, anyway?"

Carrie needed a moment to think. That was an unexpected question.

"Roger's family lives in Scotland, actually," she said. "But my father's family moved to America from Russia around 1910 or so. And my mother's family traced its start in America to Providence in the late seventeenth century. So to answer your question, we've been Americans for a very long time."

"Three hundred fifty years," she said. "My ancestors lived in Amsterdam longer than that, and then… the lucky ones escaped. And there were Jews living in Spain for over a thousand years, but that didn't matter when the king decided we had to leave." She shook her head. "No. There's Israel, and then there's other people's countries. Where we live on sufferance. And sooner or later they always turn against us."

Carrie could think of three different objections to this right from the get-go. The first one was that darn it, the United States of America really was different from all those other countries. The second one was that the worst thing America was likely to do to its Jewish population was assimilate them into being indistinguishable from everyone else, and G Dash D knew there were worse ways to go. The third one was that the future had become such a strange and unimaginable place that Carrie found it easier to picture her descendants a hundred years from now being uploaded into a supercomputer than deported in an act of ethnic cleansing. But none of these arguments seemed likely to persuade Leah—who, to be fair, did have the weight of a lot of very nasty history on her side.

But she had to try. "I've lived in the U.S. for almost my whole life," she said. "We get a little crazy sometimes, but there are things we just won't do."

Leah went quiet as they drove into the hills west of Jerusalem. She had the look of somebody who hadn't changed her mind but saw no way to win the argument.

WHEN CARRIE ENTERED THE HOTEL room, she looked around in confusion.

"Grandma's taking a nap out on the balcony," said Thel. "She's got Nahida watching her."

"All right." Neither of her brothers were free right now, but Carrie couldn't have gone to Israel without her mother. She was the religious one in the family. Or perhaps religious wasn't quite the right word for it, but she was the one to whom their identity as Jews meant the most.

Roger was watching the big screen. The news was on. Watching the news in a foreign country was always interesting, if you could find an English-language version, and sometimes even if you couldn't.

"Last night in Mea Shearim, another demonstration against Terna's proposed tax on seminary exemptions for military service turned violent," said the newscaster. "Although that tax now appears unlikely to pass, Prime Minister Terna is still not backing down."

Ruth Terna was about fifty; a small, stern-faced woman with medium-brown skin from her Ethiopian mother. The joke everyone made about her, at least in English, was that her middle name was "Less." She was taking an even harder line with the Palestinians and the Basra Pact than her predecessors had, and had increased spending on the IDF by 9 percent after inflation. And right now, she was taking a hard line on people who might actually have voted for her.

"I am not compromising on defense," she was saying. "The security of Israel against all adversaries—foreign powers, terrorists, the climate itself—is paramount. And that security costs money. Those who benefit from it without taking part in it must at least be willing to pay for it." *And if the Foundation wants to do anything to help the Palestinians,* thought Carrie, *this is the person whose government I'm going to have to convince. Joy.*

Soon the show went to foreign news, which for the Cambergs turned out to be not so foreign. "Today in Washington, the political world was stunned when a Republican congressman sharply criticized Israel during a discussion of a proposed aid package to support the building of additional desalinization plants in Haifa and Elat."

The scene shifted to the floor of the House of Representatives. "A third of the people in my district are still in emergency shelters, and you're asking for an aid package?" Darling was shouting. "We already give you people 3.8 billion dollars a year! What do you want, tribute maidens? Do you have any idea what else we could be doing with all that money?"

You people. Of course, if anyone asked him, Darling would say he meant Israel, and specifically the government of Israel. Not… anybody closer to home.

"That was… harsh," said Roger.

"I want a T-shirt that says 'Tribute Maiden #799,'" said Thel, brushing her hair out of the way of her headcams.

"I want a daughter that has some taste," said Carrie. "Although I'm somewhat reassured by the implication that you're still a maiden."

"Mom!" Thel sat down on the arm of the sofa in a way that she'd really gotten too big for. Everyone else said—if they dared remark on it at all in Carrie's presence—that China had obviously agreed with the girl. From Carrie's point of view, her daughter's body had been inappropriately sexualized by its own hypothalamus, ovaries, and pituitary gland. She wasn't quite as voluptuous as Carrie had been at that age, but she was close. Combine that with her face, and Carrie was dreading the moment Thel went back to school. The boys would build an altar and start sacrificing livestock to her.

In the meantime, Carrie and Roger had bought her a new wardrobe specifically for travel in the Holy Land. Loose, long-sleeved white cotton shirts. Loose-fitting khakis with belts. Broad-brimmed hats to keep the sun off her face. All of it was designed to eliminate the risk of heatstroke, sunburn, or showing up at the Western Wall in a tight T-shirt and booty shorts, and it did those things. But it couldn't hide her shape. The only way to do that would have been to carry her around inside a large steamer trunk, and when Carrie saw men and a few women turning to look at her from two blocks away, she was tempted to try this.

Carrie smiled as she turned back to watch the screen. Several Knesset members were denouncing Darling's remarks.

"Kinda OOP to be making this much fuss over a U.S. congressman," said Thel, brushing her hair out of the way of her headcams again. They looked like a couple of very short ballpoint pens attached to a headband, pointed forward, resting against her temples. They were switched off, but keeping their field of view clear was a reflex she'd picked up.

"Oh-oh-pee?"

"You know… out of proportion."

"It's something kids say online these days," said Roger.

"Why do we give these guys all that money, anyway?" said Thel.

"We don't," said Carrie. "We give it to ourselves. It's… think of it like a gift certificate. You can only spend it in certain places. All that money is earmarked to buy product from U.S. defense contractors. So Israel gets weapons and we get our money back."

Thel nodded, her eyebrows slightly raised. "Clever."

The door to the balcony opened. Mama stepped in, a slender woman of average height who had spent much of her life dwarfed by either her husband or her children. At seventy-four, she'd finally made peace with the passage of time, but she'd done it in her own way, dyeing her hair a perfect white and buying a pair of glasses with gilded frames. She was wearing a long-sleeved white blouse and a long black skirt. She'd been well-dressed every day of this trip, as if the whole country were a special occasion.

Right at her elbow was Nahida Junbalat, the other female bodyguard. She was tall, dark, wiry, and hadn't tried to make conversation with any of them once. Her eyes were pointed at the door.

"I figured you'd be busy today," said Mama, "so I made dinner reservations at a place within walking distance. We should probably get out the door within the next few minutes."

"Thank you." It was nice to not have to be in charge of everything for once.

As they were going through the lobby, Carrie checked an app that followed various friends and former employees of hers to see if there was any news. The only news was that Jerome Ross's brother was pleading guilty in whatever it was he was on trial for—the details had escaped Carrie's mind at the moment.

JULY 22:

DEFENSE MINISTER AVNER SHAPIRA WAS maybe forty, but had already developed the beginnings of a fine set of frown and scowl lines on his forehead and around his mouth. He was looking at Carrie as if she'd come to his office to sell him life insurance and he didn't have a family.

"Before you say anything," said Carrie, "I already spoke with the Palestinian Authority, and they said this kind of construction needed to be cleared with the Israeli Defense Forces. So I went to IDF, and they said to talk to you. If you try telling me to talk to the Palestinian Authority, I'm just going to leave."

"Don't worry," said Shapira. "I'm not going to give you the runaround. I can't make any promises about what I'm going to decide, but you're in the right office."

So Carrie launched into her usual presentation. "The potential is here for a humanitarian disaster like you've never imagined," she said. "I wish we could just take a warehouse, set it up with the water and medicine and whatever else we needed, and call it a day. But an above-ground heat shelter is a perfectly good one right up until the power goes out, and then it's a death trap. And if there's one thing this part of the world is known for, it's terrorism. Not just against Israel—different factions of the Palestinians have been known to use it on each other." Some of the members of Terna's government got antsy about the use of the word "Palestinians," but Shapira seemed okay with it. "If an above-ground shelter was in use, a terrorist wouldn't need a bomb to ruin everyone's day. He'd just need to take out the power."

"Now I understand the problem. If a shelter is far enough underground to protect people from the heat without power, it could also be used as a bomb shelter."

"Or as part of a tunnel for smuggling, if it's close to the border," said Shapira.

"True. But here's the thing—no shelter we know how to build could stand up to a bunker-buster. A conventional bunker-buster, I mean." After Pyongyang, that was an important distinction. "And you have plenty of those."

"I'm glad to see you addressing our concerns," said Shapira. "Let me reassure you that the Foundation will be welcome to help build heat shelters in the... West Bank. However, we'll have to confine them to a specific set of locations." He pushed a couple of buttons on a cell phone, feeding the data to Carrie's tablet.

Carrie glanced at the list. "In the first place, this isn't close to enough locations for a population this size," she said. "In the second place..." As she spoke, she fed the list into a mapping program, then, feeling very guilty about it, brought up a second map and clicked on **Overlay**.

A second later, the guilty feeling was... still there, for some reason, but the rest of her was telling it to shut up. Her tablet had just confirmed the suspicions she'd been ashamed of having.

"In the second place," she said, "I can't help noticing that every one of these sites is in the middle of a Jewish settlement."

"Those are the most secure locations for building."

"And who's going to be put in charge of these shelters? You have to let people in according to age and medical need—who's going to decide who gets in and who doesn't?"

Shapira crossed his arms. "What exactly are you implying?"

"What do you mean, what am I implying? I'm asking questions here."

Rather than answering directly, Shapira took out a tablet of his own and looked at the screen. "Three days ago, your daughter went to a Natan Bendayan rally," he said.

"What's that got to do with anything?" All Carrie knew about Bendayan was that he was some sort of young liberal activist who'd been making a stir in Tel Aviv and Jerusalem. This conversation seemed to be going in a strange direction.

"During this rally, Bendayan made the following statement—and this is a direct quote—'The Terna government is trying to take options away from whoever comes after. Expanding the settlements, saying no to talks—everything the Prime Minister does is meant to make a lasting peace impossible. She wants to force our generation to one day expel or destroy the Palestinians, because she doesn't have the nerve to do it herself right now.'" While Shapira was going on about this, Carrie touched the query icon on her tablet and typed the words **peligro lyrics**.

"Many of us find this deeply offensive," Shapira said. "What do you have to say?"

If Shapira can bring things up at random, so can I. Carrie checked her tablet. "It's true," she said. "Thel did go to that rally. Know where else she's gone? Back in June, she and some of her friends went to a Rodomontade concert. During this concert, lead singer Jake Villanueva made the following statement, and this is a direct quote…" Carrie read the words off her tablet screen. "'I'm your wolf and I'm your tiger, and I'm rising like a shark/I'm the fear and the desire that you dream of in the dark/I'm your devil, I'm your demon of determination firm/And I'm here to fill you up with foreign sperm.' I suppose this is my fault too? Because all sorts of people find it deeply offensive."

Shapira sputtered for a moment, then said, "That's completely different."

"Darn right it is—I paid for the tickets. At least the rally was free. Look, if you're trying to get me to issue a statement on this Bendayan guy one way or another, it's not going to work. He's your problem. Yes, I'm a Jew, but I'm also an American and this is my first visit to Israel and I have no intention of wading into your politics."

"Then why does every word coming out of your mouth sound like a watered-down version of something he would say?"

Carrie sighed. There wasn't going to be any way to avoid this issue.

"Here's what I can tell you," she said. "There are governments out there—Iraq, Turkey, a few others—that are giving certain ethnic groups, certain religious communities, preferential treatment in where heat shelters go. And meanwhile, other communities aren't getting shelters at all. Kurds in Turkey, Shi'ites in Saudi Arabia—"

"And Sunnis in northern Iraq," Shapira interrupted. "Exactly. Many governments are making this sort of decision. You think Nigeria is doing anything right now for the Fulani? The Hausa? The Kanuri?"

"They're in the middle of a civil war."

"In a way, so are we. You know those people teach their children out of *Protocols of the Elders of Zion*? They give money to the families of suicide bombers! Why exactly should we go out of our way to save people who want us all dead? Why are we being held to a higher standard than other countries?"

"You're not. That's the problem. The Symcox Foundation has a policy about nations that do this sort of thing—we don't do business with them. We don't help them. The question is, are you willing to put Israel on that list?"

"The question is," said Shapira, "are *you* willing to put Israel on that list?"

It would have been easy, and truthful, for Carrie to say that it wasn't her call—that this policy was the work of Sandra Symcox, and it was mostly her money they were playing with. But that wasn't how you earned respect as a leader. Even if people hated your decision, they had to know it was you making it. Besides, Carrie was confident she could talk Sandy into making an exception for Israel, and Shapira knew it.

She could do that, yes... and what would people say when they heard about it? It was easy to predict what the usual anti-Semites would say, and she was never getting their votes anyway. Other people would be more... understanding. *Sure, there are rules, but what do you expect? She's gotta look out for her own people. If you look at their history, is it really surprising?*

That was what decided it. You couldn't afford to make your voters feel like they had to make excuses for you. Not if there was anybody else in the race who was at all acceptable.

Shapira seemed to see the decision in her eyes. "You wouldn't," he said.

"I absolutely will."

Shapira was momentarily stuck for a response. Then he managed a bitter little sneer.

"Right, I understand," he said. "There are more Muslim voters than Jewish voters in the U.S. these days. And you wouldn't want anybody accusing you of... dual loyalty."

Carrie stood up. "I think we're done here," she said. "Minister, I do love Israel, but—at the risk of repeating myself—I *am* an American. Remember that the next time you're tempted to act like I owe you a favor."

ON HER WAY BACK TO the hotel, Carrie did some more reading about Bendayan, just to see exactly what sort of people her daughter was getting herself entangled with, and to give herself something to do besides punch the dashboard of the self-driving car. It was all so stupid. There were countries the Symcox Foundation couldn't help with shelters because the only contractors the government would allow to do the work were contractors the Foundation couldn't do business with—or, it might be more accurate to say, *Carrie* couldn't do business with—without being accused of violating the Foreign Corrupt Practices Act. The Foundation was a nonprofit and Carrie never got so much as a souvenir T-shirt from the government or contractor in question, but she didn't even want the accusation out there.

That wasn't a problem in Israel. This place had standards. Here the problem was something else entirely.

And it wasn't as if they needed the Symcox Foundation. Israel, which had done more with its total lack of oil than some of its neighbors had with their abundance of it, could easily foot the bill for whatever it wanted to do. Even if it couldn't, there were other charities specifically for setting up heat shelters in Israel, which she suspected were also involved with the settlement projects. Carrie knew this because she'd sent one of them a check a month ago.

And tomorrow, when she spoke with the head of the Palestinian Authority, she was going to have to let him know what had happened. That was going to be embarrassing. Today there was something more immediate that needed taking care of.

Just outside the hotel room, she caught up with Thel and Leah. Thel's mane of hair was still wet from the shower and smelled slightly of sweat, and she looked very pleased with herself.

"You gotta try the gym," she said. "Leah's been teaching me Krav Maga. It's a little like Chinese martial arts, only a…" She looked at Carrie's face for a second or so. "Aw crap."

"It's not that bad." Carrie escorted her daughter through the hotel room and out onto the balcony. It faced the north, and was shielded from the sun by the bulk of the building. It looked out onto a vista of modern solar panels and ancient red tile, interrupted by tall, cone-like cypresses, all brought to full technicolor glory by the light of the Middle Eastern sun.

Thel sighed. "Okay, what'd I do?"

"Nothing. But I want you to stay away from any more of Bendayan's events."

"Mom!"

"It's just a precaution," Carrie said. "We all have to be careful who we interact with. Who we let ourselves be seen with. There are people out there who will try to use us for their own purposes. Especially you. You're young and idealistic and they'll think they can talk you into things."

"He's not like that," said Thel. "Bendayan, I mean. I'm not saying he's right, but he's one of the good guys. It can't hurt just to listen to him."

Carrie folded her arms. "Thel," she said, "sit down. This is going to hurt." Thel looked mulish, but she sat down.

"You think this Natan Bendayan is a good man, and you know what? You're right. He is. That's the problem. He's a man who wants to make life better for millions—or to save millions from something terrible. But do you know what a man like that sees when he looks at you? He sees a rich, beautiful, coddled teenager who lives in a world full of pain and hasn't suffered her share of it. Yet." Carrie put a finger under Thel's chin and lifted, gently drawing her daughter's face up to look her in the eye.

"You mean everything to me, but to him you're just one person. One person who, in the long run, will be okay no matter what happens."

Thel looked up at her angrily. "Tell the truth, Mom. Are you actually worried about me getting hurt? Or are you just worried that I'm gonna embarrass you?"

Carrie drew herself up to her full height.

"I *am* worried about you getting hurt," she said. "And if you're not worried about you getting hurt, then you're not nearly as smart as you think you are." *Especially since I just now barely stopped myself from smacking you in the face very hard. And one of these days you're going to meet somebody a lot less patient than me.*

The door opened. Roger and Mama were standing there looking at her, expressions of concern on their faces, not even trying to hide the fact that they'd overheard every single word.

"Yes?"

"I have an idea," said Mama. "I'll keep an eye on her while we're here."

"So you're supposed to be my chaperone now?"

"Either me or your father, dear. Take your pick."

"Fine," said Thel with an exaggerated sigh.

Roger followed Carrie back into the bedroom. Seeing the look on his face, she raised a hand in a signal for him not to start talking. *There will come a time when I'm ready to talk about what she just said. This is not that time.*

Even as a little girl, Carrie had always been ambitious—either to be President of the United States or a billionaire. At the very least she'd wanted to exceed her father, in status if not in mass. In fact, it was Papa she credited for this. He'd been an important man in his own right, and his social circle included many rich and powerful people. Through him, she'd learned that those the world called great were not fundamentally different from herself, and there was no reason she couldn't join them, or surpass them if she had it in her. The road was hard, but it was open and it went to the highest places.

But her ambition came at a cost. While the rest of her lived and loved and cried and regretted, there was always that one part of her brain that was just sitting back and quietly judging the things and people around her, determining if they were to her advantage or not. It had grown stronger as her ambitions had condensed from dreams into plans and conscious choices.

When she'd first looked at Roger—tall, remote Roger with his seeming air of hauteur—most of her had seen him as a challenge. That cold thing inside her had said *tall, smart, good-looking, should clean up well. Lots of potential social status. Yes, you can work with this.* She told herself that all successful politicians had something like this, but that was no comfort when the calls were coming from inside her head.

Carrie didn't always obey the cold thing. More than once, it had told her that Mike and Samantha were liabilities and should be cut loose. But even when she didn't, it usually found a way to rationalize her decisions—*not a good look to abandon a brother, even if he is useless.*

And sometimes that inner sociopath of hers made her sick to her stomach. Nothing was sacred to it, nothing off-limits. Looking at things like Anchorage and the Northern Monsoon and calculating how they'd play politically was the least of its sins. Her father's death? *This will win you sympathy.* George's injury and death? *When you speak to veterans' groups, tell them of this.* Drew's disfigurement and long, slow recovery? *This will come in handy during health care discussions.* She didn't like to think of the cold thing as part of herself, but it was never far away. And even if she could have had it removed or exorcised or something, she wouldn't—she was afraid she needed it.

The cold thing was very pleased with Thel. She was beautiful, brilliant, highly presentable, and idealistic without being rebellious—perfect First Daughter material. But it didn't love her, because it didn't *love*. Its approval was creepier than all the men on the street who turned to look at Thel like dogs looking at steak. Much, much creepier, because it was coming from a place where nothing like it should even exist.

And the worst part? Thel knew about the cold thing. She knew. The only thing she wasn't sure of was to what extent her mother *was* that thing. ("Are you actually worried about me getting hurt? Or are you just worried that I'm gonna embarrass you?")

And if she knew, it was a safe bet that Roger knew. And her mother. And who else among her family and friends?

As long as you never let the voters find out about me, you're all right.

JULY 23:

FOR THE PURPOSES OF THIS conversation, Carrie had gotten the hotel to separate a part of the lounge for a half hour. This was not a good time to be overheard.

President Ahmed al-Masir of the Palestinian National Authority gazed out through the screen of Carrie's tablet. His glasses were thick, and made him look like a white-bearded owl. Two of his Cabinet ministers were visible behind him.

"I can't say I'm surprised," he said in lightly accented English. "We'll have to find another source of funding, less beholden to the Zionist entity."

It's called "Israel." Can you say that? Is-ray-ell. "If you can find someone, go for it," said Carrie. "But as I see it, you're in kind of a bad spot. The only people in the world who still have money to spare for you are the Basra Pact, and how long do you think that's going to last? Their biggest export is oil, and every country on Earth is trying to get off oil."

"That is not going to happen. Not if Group 77 has anything to say about it."

"You know something about this group?"

"No. I've only seen what they've done. Along with everyone else."

You're not as good a liar as you think, thought Carrie. The Palestinian Authority couldn't possibly be involved in Group 77—it was too much of a charity case for that—but somebody in the group had told al-Masir something, possibly to soothe his anxieties over this very subject. The best-informed people Carrie had spoken to claimed that Group 77 was dominated not by oil companies, but by the governments of oil-producing nations. Which made sense. If you ran an oil company, you could diversify, invest in renewables, and sell the oil wells if necessary. If you ran a nation with large oil reserves, on the other hand, you really needed crude to be selling at a decent price.

"Have you seen what happened in China?" replied Carrie. "They tried buying the whole biofuel industry and shutting it down and the government just took it away from them. Do you think nobody else is going to try that?

"Look, we're getting off track. The point is that if you want to be able to protect your own people, then somehow or other you're going to have to work with Terna. You need to give her some kind of guarantee—something enforceable—that if she lets you build shelters, she won't be sorry later." Al-Masir didn't respond. He just looked impatient.

"And you need to do it this year," said Carrie. "Vague promises of a peace deal five years from now or ten years from now—"

"Do you seriously think the Zionist entity is going to be here ten years from now?"

Carrie just sat there looking at al-Masir. He didn't sound like someone uttering a party line nobody actually believed. He sounded like somebody stating a well-known fact. As if it were an elephant in the room that everybody had been trying to avoid and it had just become impossible. As if Carrie were the delusional one, thinking the State of Israel was a long-term proposition, and he'd just gotten tired of humoring her on this. And the two ministers were nodding their heads.

"We're winning the war," he said, his voice going into Rousing Speech Mode. "You heard what your Congressman Darling said. Even the Americans are tired of their servitude to the Zionists. And every day, more and more Jews are leaving Palestine. One day all the Gharqad trees will be uprooted. I still have the key to my father's house outside Jaffa, and I will live long enough to use it."

Carrie had to shut her eyes for a moment to keep herself from rolling them. She didn't even know what a Gharqad tree was, but it didn't matter. *Yes, a small percentage of Jews are leaving Israel. A much larger percentage are not leaving Israel. And a smaller percentage are still coming to Israel. And the ones who stay—or who actually come here—are by definition more committed to the Zionist project than the ones who abandon said project, and less inclined to negotiate with those who regard said project as illegitimate. Which explains a lot about the direction Israeli politics have been going. That's half the reason why every attempt to reach a peace settlement fails harder than the last one. The other half is that your side is full of people who've broken off diplomatic relations with reality. People like, to pick a name at random, you.*

And here's the thing. The ones who leave—whatever percentage it is—aren't taking their share of the nation's arsenal with them. Everything from small arms to nukes is staying behind in the hands of an increasingly radical government.

All this was crashingly obvious to Carrie, but she had the feeling that if she tried to explain it, she'd be met with nothing but blank stares. This guy didn't even grasp that whoever was living in his dad's old place outside Tel Aviv had probably changed the locks by now.

"Well, then, you're set," she said. "The... 'Zionist entity' is building some of the best heat shelters I've ever seen. Once you've got them nicely driven into the sea, you'll have those shelters all to yourselves." Then she broke the connection.

Carrie just sat there for a moment, shaking her head. How did you talk to people like that? How did you negotiate? Even if she could wave a magic wand and replace the Terna government with a government headed by, say, Natan Bendayan, that was only half the problem solved. Talking to al-Masir reminded her of the Ghost Dance of the 1890s, which she'd done a paper on back in college: *One day the dead will rise, the buffalo will come back, the white people will go away, everything we ever lost will be restored, we'll be free to live again as we once did...*

Carrie had once thought of delusional thinking as the privilege of life's winners, that losers were forced to face reality. Reading about the Ghost Dance, she'd realized that in the most extreme cases, this no longer held true. Somewhere on some subconscious level, people started to think: *If we engage in the clearest, most cold-eyed realism, if we discipline our minds to reject all wishful thinking and accept the situation as it is... we'll get stomped into the dirt anyway, because we have no power and no way of getting any. If we embrace wishful thinking, at least it'll make us happy every now and then. There's nothing left for us in the Desert of the Real.*

When she went back to her room, she found two of the bodyguards outside. Roger was inside alone, reading an online glaciology report.

"Where are Mama and Thel?"

"They went to some sort of women's march," he said, barely glancing up from the screen. "I didn't catch the details, but it was your mother's idea, and Leah and Nahida went with them, so it seemed all right."

The first thing Carrie did was report back to Sandra Symcox. It was early morning in New York, so Sandy was sitting at her kitchen table. She had a little bowl of what looked like shiny multicolored peas in front of her, and she was eating them with a pair of jade chopsticks which she handled as expertly as Thel. Somehow, she still looked like a student who'd been pulling too many all-nighters.

"Not your fault," she said. "I didn't want to say anything, but I had a feeling Terna and al-Masir weren't going to be reasonable."

"Don't judge Terna too harshly," said Carrie. "If you look at Israel's history… well, you know…"

"I've heard."

"And don't get me started on the Palestinians."

"I'm not judging anybody." Sandy set her chopsticks down and looked squarely into the camera. "But if we start making exceptions, we'll never be able to stop."

Part of Carrie wanted to say *no, you don't understand, this isn't some Third World country, this is a Western nation stuck in a bad neighborhood, these are good people and we should find a way to help them*. It was one thing to give Avner Shapira tough love, but in front of Sandy she just wanted to defend the nation. But… no. Not a good look.

"What are you eating?"

"Spherified fruit juices," said Sandy. She picked up a couple of orange globules. "Or reverse spherified, I should say—they mix the juice with two percent calcium lactate gluconate, bathe it in water containing sodium alginate and it reacts to… sorry. Chemistry geek. You ask me a question like that and you get way too much information.

"The bottom line is, Israel will get by without us, you did all the right things and we haven't compromised our principles. So I guess… enjoy the vacation."

Carrie didn't believe in jinxes. If she had, she might have blamed Sandy for what happened next.

JUST AFTER FIVE, CARRIE GOT a call. Her phone said "It's Mama."

It also made the three sharp chimes that meant *emergency*.

Carrie's fingers fumbled a little before they hit the right button.

"Carrie?" came her mother's voice. "Oh my god I'm so sorry, something terrible's happened and it's all my fault."

"Mama, what happened?" On the screen, Mama was sitting in some sort of cinder-block room. Alone. *"And where's Thel?"*

THE REST OF THE EVENING was a fog of fear and rage, in which occasional moments stuck in Carrie's memory like icebergs looming out of the mist.

Moments like sitting in the hospital waiting room listening to her mother's explanation of what happened. They had taken part in a women's march in Jerusalem, to protest gender separation in Orthodox neighborhoods. "What I was thinking," she said, "was that if Thel wants to get involved in a cause, it ought to be a good one. I mean, one that we can all agree on." Carrie nodded.

"Half of us were dressed well. Better than average. A lot of women were dressed casually, and a few were dressed like prostitutes... I didn't really approve of that, but I think this was on purpose. A way of saying 'As different as we look, we're all on the same side on this and we won't be divided.'" Carrie nodded again.

"We weren't even going into the Mea Shearim proper—it was just some streets where a lot of Haredim had been moving into, where there were suddenly a lot of restrictions... or maybe not restrictions, just social pressure... we were just walking down the street and singing. That's all.

"There was a crowd of men following us. Haredim. Mostly young. They were getting angrier and angrier. They were shouting at us, we were trying to drown them out with our singing..." She shook her head.

"We should have... *I* should have listened to the bodyguards. Leah said this place was getting dangerous and we needed to get out of here, Thel said, 'What about everybody else here?' and Leah said, 'I'm not here to protect them, I'm here to protect you.' She didn't want to leave, and as for me, all I could think was, 'This is ridiculous. I'm a Jew. This is Jerusalem. No one can tell me I'm not supposed to be here. Not even another Jew.' I didn't..." She shook her head. "I didn't think they'd hurt us." Carrie reached over and folded her mother's hands inside her own.

"I didn't even see it happen. I just heard something... break. And suddenly Thel was swaying, about to fall down. I caught her, but there was blood coming out from under her hair. A lot of it.

"I heard the gunshot, but I was down on the ground with Thel. I didn't see what happened. Oh, god… what have I done, Carrie?"

Then there was the moment when she saw it on the news. By then, the media had gotten footage from Thel's headcams and half a dozen phones. Forcing herself not to look away when the screen showed the incident was the hardest thing Carrie had done in a long time.

The view from the headcams wasn't much help. Thel could see over the heads of the women around her, giving the cameras a good look at the faces of the men in the crowd. They looked not only furious, but—it was a terrible thing for her to admit to herself—alien. The black hats, and the black coats in hundred-degree weather, might almost have been a uniform.

The microphones caught them shouting over the singing. The song was some bit of Israeli pop that sounded almost as innocuous as "Had Gadya," although Carrie couldn't make out the lyrics. And judging by the humming, neither could Thel. From the way the men were reacting, it might as well have been something by, say, Rodomontade.

The one thing the headcams didn't see was the rock. Instead, the image suddenly went from integrated-stereoscopic to one-camera, and went from the perspective of a girl standing erect to one who was gradually sinking to the pavement.

Someone else's camera caught the rock. It was irregular in shape, and about the size of an apple. It didn't hit her dead-on, but struck her right temple from behind and at an angle. *From behind. Somebody hit her from behind. Somebody didn't even have the nerve to confront a girl head-on.*

The good news was that Thel didn't just go limp—she sat down. Mama was under her right arm, helping lower her into a sitting position, but Thel's own legs had to be supporting at least some of her own weight. She was just too big a girl for Mama to have done that otherwise. *She can't be that badly hurt. Right?*

The footage from Leah Lemel's firearm, which was supposed to be in police custody, had also leaked. That firearm was the latest model of Uzi pistol. As per security company rules, it was equipped with a camera—if she had to fire it, she also had to be able to show everyone the reason why. When she drew the gun, the camera turned on automatically and started recording. By this time, she was already through the crowd of women and facing the rioters directly.

Red lights blinked at the corners of the screen at the instant the shot was fired. The bullet went over everybody's heads and buried itself in a sandstone block in the wall of a building across the street.

At the same instant, everyone in the image either ducked or froze.

Then Leah swept the laser sight of her pistol over the crowd at face level. For a split second, the laser went directly into the right eye of a young man holding a rock. He screamed silently and dropped the rock. *She might have scorched his retina. Not that he wouldn't have it coming.*

The record from Nahida's gun camera had also leaked, but it didn't add any new information. She hadn't fired, but she'd helped Leah hold off the rioters—if "hold off" was the right way of talking about men who were either sinking to their knees, hands in the air, or else fleeing in all directions. Carrie couldn't help imagining the smell of loosened bowels and bladders as she watched them run away.

What took most of her and Roger's time that evening was the hiring of the legal team for Leah and Nahida. Not a lawyer—a legal team. She owed them that much.

DR. ZARZIR WAS TAN, BABY-FACED and couldn't have been older than thirty. Carrie's first thought on seeing him was *who put this kid in charge of my baby?*

"I'll start with the good news," he said. "There's no skull fracture and no sign of whiplash. The rock broke the left head cam, so we had to pick some bits of it out of her scalp—there's a few cuts from that. There's a lot of bleeding under the scalp, so it'll look pretty bad. Her pupils are the same size and not dilated, but she's showing signs of dizziness, loss of coordination, slightly slurred speech… the bottom line is that this is a basic case of concussion, and we know how to treat it. I don't like making promises, but I've seen less healthy people make full recoveries from much worse injuries."

Carrie nodded. *She's going to be all right. She's going to be all right.*

"Whatever you've been told, the thing she needs right now is sleep, and lots of it. You can stay overnight if you like—I'll let you know when she's ready to see you. And I know it's not my business, but can I just say this doesn't normally happen here?"

"We know."

"I'm not with the Department of Tourism or anything, but I'm an Arab myself—my family's got a solar farm out in the Negev—and politics in Israel… it can get scary, but at least we *have* politics. That's not common in this part of the world. And every time I think about moving to New York or London, somebody over there goes and elects some lunatic and those places stop looking so good." *Ouch.* "Anyway… the best thing to do in a case like this is to let her sleep and come back in the morning."

For close to a full minute, Carrie stood there holding her mother in her arms, Roger's arms around them both. "*Barukh atah Adonai Eloheinu, melekh ha'olam,*" whispered Mama.

There had once been a time in Carrie's life when she thought of tragedy as something that happened to other people. That had ended nineteen years ago.

It happened only a few days after her honeymoon with Roger was over. A phone call, out of nowhere, with no warnings. (Well, no warnings for *her*. Her father had gotten any number of warnings from his doctor, only to laugh them off.) "Big Bill" Exter, fifty-eight years old, too much in a hurry to even wait for an elevator, had collapsed on the stairs of his own office building from an abdominal aortic aneurysm. After a few days on life support, his heart had given out. *We should have at least let them donate the organs.* That man who had seemed so much larger than life was now small enough to fit in a coffin. Well, a large coffin. He was six foot five and weighed close to four hundred pounds.

And that had been just the beginning. George's injury and death, Drew's injury, Mike's business failures… for a few years, it had seemed like there was a curse on her whole family.

And then, after immense pain and effort—*child-bearing hips, my ass*—a baby had come out of her. It was Roger's idea to name her Thel, after a character in a William Blake poem he'd read back in college. Mama had been hoping for something a little more traditional for her very first grandchild, but she'd come to like it in time.

Little Thel seemed to lift the curse off everybody just by being around. Carrie and Roger had always meant to have more children, but their jobs kept them apart so often… and Thel was such a perfect child that trying too hard for another seemed like pushing their luck.

She's going to be all right.

Why did I bring her here? What was I thinking?

She's going to be all right.

I sent her to China by herself for two semesters. She spent the war scare in Beijing wondering if she was about to get nuked by her own country. And she came out of that no worse for wear, except for the phoenix tattoo on her back. Which is actually very good as tattoos go. Even better than Lexi's roses.

She's going to be all right.

Of all the places I've been in the past year, this is the one I was willing to bring her to. This is the place she was supposed to be safe.

She's going to be all right.

JULY 24:

IT WAS MORNING. "I THINK we can release her tomorrow afternoon," said Dr. Zarzir, "but for the next few days you'll have to make sure she doesn't strain her brain too much."

"What do you mean?"

"No heavy reading. No hard puzzles. I'd say no schoolwork if this weren't summer vacation. If she watches a movie, make sure it's a dumb one." At any other time, Carrie might have responded with *that will definitely not be a problem*. Now she just nodded. "Would the three of you like to see her?"

"Yes, please."

It took Carrie a split second to recognize her daughter. For most of her sixteen years of life, Thel had been a slender shape with a big copper mop on top. Now, just when Carrie was getting used to the girl's new figure, that mass of hair was gone—cut off and stuffed into a cardboard box on her nightstand. There was nothing left but a red-gold sheen on her scalp in the morning sun. Her head looked so much smaller, and her shoulders broader, without it.

But as Thel sat up in bed, her freckled, beautiful face was still the same as ever. Seeing her mother's shocked look, she smiled a little, the familiar dimples forming on both cheeks. There were neatly stitched cuts above her left ear, and fresh, swollen bruising from there down behind her ear halfway to her neck.

"Yeah, they had to shave part of my head just to get at it," she said. "My hair wasn't... cooperating with them. I didn't want to spend three months with a chunk of my hair shorter than the rest... so I said 'take it all.'" She waved at the box on the nightstand. "They're gonna... give it to the hair donations guys.

Wigs for children in chemo or whatever."

"That sounds wonderful. How are you feeling?"

"Kinda toilet," she said. As far as Carrie could tell, "toilet" as an adjective was modern slang for "better than terrible but not as good as mediocre." "Hey... did anybody else get hurt? Nobody'll tell me."

"Just you," said Carrie. She stepped forward and brushed her fingers over the stubble on the right side of Thel's head. Then, on a sudden irresistible impulse, she pulled Thel up into a hug.

She patted her mother on the shoulders. "Uh... Mom, you know it grows back, right?"

"Yes. Yes, of course."

"Just so you know, I'm gonna do something different with it this time. Make it a little more manageable."

"That's fine, honey."

Roger got out a tablet and contacted Drew. The face of Carrie's youngest brother was hard to read, but there was a distinct look of shock on it when he saw Thel.

"Hey, Drew," she said. "This time, you're the good-looking one."

"Nah, still you. How're you feeling?"

"I'll live."

"So what's the story?"

Thel ran a hand over her scalp. "The shepherds of Israel were having trouble meeting their wool quota, so I chipped in," she said. "Please tell me it's not like... three a.m. or something over there."

"Just after midnight," he said. "I wish I'd been able to come along. I should've been there."

"It was supposed to be a women's march, but I bet we could have found a dress in your size."

Drew chuckled. "I should cut this short—I have to get to work early tomorrow."

"Tell them you were up all night talking to a sixteen-year-old girl online. They'll understand." She managed a wink. "Good night."

About this time, one of the orderlies arrived with breakfast. It was scrambled eggs with toast and orange juice. Thel drank the orange juice, then examined the pieces of toast as if trying to decide which one was closest to edible.

"I know," said Dr. Zarzir. "It's hospital food. But we need to make sure

270

you're willing to eat something. TBI cases often suffer from nausea, vomiting, and loss of appetite."

"I think I've figured out why," said Thel, poking at the scrambled eggs with her fork. "Hey, Grandma, is there a thing in kashrut where if somebody gives you burnt toast and runny eggs, you get to dump it down their shirt?"

"I'm afraid not."

"There should be. Somebody work on that."

"You know what?" said the doctor. "I think you're going to be all right. That said, you should wait a few days before undergoing air travel."

"I can't leave just yet anyway," said Mama. "The authorities need me to make a deposition first. I'm one of the witnesses." She looked down. "I am so sorry I got you into that."

"You didn't get me into anything," said Thel, spreading eggs onto toast with the air of one determined to make the best of things. "I wanted to be there."

Just then, Carrie's phone let her know she had an incoming call.

She checked it. It was from Ruth Terna. It was accompanied by check marks from two different ISPs confirming that this was indeed the prime minister and not some prankster.

THE MEETING WASN'T IN THE prime minister's office, but in a conference room somewhere in Kiryat Ben-Gurion, the main government complex. Terna, of course, was sitting at the head of the table, the expression on her face a little softer than normal. There were several tough-looking Shin Bet agents around her.

At the other end of the table was a tiny, wizened man cradling his hat in wrinkled hands. *Is that who I think it is?* No question—it was Rabbi Eliav Rubin, a well-known scholar and the most prominent leader of the ultra-Orthodox. The burly man next to him was his translator, although he looked more like a bodyguard.

"Have a seat," said Terna. Carrie took a seat in the middle, where she could see everybody.

"Once again," Terna said, "I'd like to say—and in person this time—how very, very sorry I am that someone did this to your daughter. I wish to apologize on behalf of my country. We will make every effort to track down and punish whoever did it."

"Thank you. What about Leah and Nahida?"

"Personally, I wouldn't bother pressing charges, but that decision is in the hands of the city authorities."

"I understand."

Terna gestured toward the other end of the table. "The rabbi also has something to say."

The rabbi spoke in Hebrew, sounding rather flat. Carrie's last Hebrew lessons had been some thirty years ago, but there was definitely an apology in there somewhere.

"I must apologize for what happened on behalf of my community," said the translator. Carrie nodded. Neither he nor the rabbi would look her in the eye, but Carrie happened to know that this was because they weren't supposed to look a woman in the eye unless they were married to her.

Unfortunately, the rabbi kept talking. "You must believe she was never the target," came the translation. "If we'd had any idea your family was there, we never would have allowed things to get so out of hand." Carrie's mood, which had been starting to improve, suddenly turned unpleasant. *Seriously? That's your excuse? You're going with that? Two days ago I would have considered it an honor to speak with you, Rabbi. Now here you are lying to my face.*

"How the fuck," she said, keeping her voice even, "do you look at a crowd of women and not notice the six-foot redhead?"

Terna winced. That was not the most diplomatic thing she could have said. The translator would probably soften it—if nothing else, Hebrew had been a strictly liturgical language for a long time and had to borrow most of its profanity from Arabic. Even so... *The most famous Jewish American politician since Bernie Sanders is going to be ending her first trip to Israel on a sour note. That's already bad. Don't make it worse than it needs to be.* Was that the cold thing speaking, or just her own instinct to make no needless enemies? How separate were they?

"We were all trying not to look at them too closely," said Rubin via the translator.

"Nobody should have been throwing things at anybody," said Terna, sounding like an angry kindergarten teacher.

"We didn't keep the crowd under control the way we should have. Some of our young men are... reckless. They feel that our way of life is under attack, and... well, you must admit your daughter was rather provocatively dressed."

"I must admit nothing of the sort," said Carrie. "*You* must admit you've got some animals that belong in cages."

Terna nodded. "Compared to a lot of women you see out there, she was quite modest." This remark was aimed more at Rubin.

That cold part of Carrie didn't always offer advice. Sometimes it made observations the rest of her was too upset to make. Now it was telling her this: *They're not even trying to look like a united front. Or, maybe, they're trying to look like a disunited front. Or rather, Terna is trying to look like she's keeping her distance from Rubin. Even though parties representing the ultra-Orthodox are a part of her coalition.*

And this makes sense. For all she knows, she's talking to the next president of the United States. She doesn't want you going away angry—or at least, not angry at her.

"You understand," said Terna, "that this is all strictly personal. None of it should be taken as a sign of policy changes on other matters."

"I understand," said Carrie. She hadn't really held out much hope that this incident would shame Terna into changing her government's position on underground heat shelters in the occupied territories.

At the other end of the table, the translator was sitting, eyes pointed at a spot on the table, biting his lip. As for the rabbi, Carrie had never seen a man that old fidgeting in his seat before. She clenched her teeth. *Sorry about all the girl cooties in the room. Go rinse yourself off in holy water or whatever the fuck you need to do.* With a mighty effort of will, she said nothing. At times like this she envied politicians like Rep. Darling, who'd built themselves a public persona that let them say whatever they felt like in public and get away with it.

JULY 28:

THE HOUSE WHERE CARRIE HAD grown up and Mama and Drew still lived stood on the crest of a hill northwest of Newport News. Carrie sat on the northeast side of the wraparound porch, looking out at the York River in the distance, a tall glass of homemade mint iced tea in her hand. It was the middle of the morning, and the day was already getting hot—the horrible muggy heat of Virginia, not the searing dry heat of Israel. The chair was one of the big, solid, comforting, old polished hardwood chairs that her father had bought because they could support his weight.

The house felt strange and wrong with Mama not here. She wouldn't be back until the authorities in Jerusalem made up their minds on whether they needed her as a witness.

Roger came out, a glass of homemade lemonade in his hand. He sat next to her and looked out at the water. For a long time, he was quiet, but she could tell there was something he wanted to say.

Then, finally, he spoke. "The thing about Antarctica—"

As soon as she heard the name of the continent, Carrie had to suppress a groan. "Not this again," she said, almost overlapping the second half of his sentence. "Honey, have we not talked about it enough?"

"Yes. We have. And what you said at the time was that going there was too dangerous. But the thing about Antarctica is, nobody ever tries to hurt you there."

"Of course not," said Carrie. "It's the one place on Earth where other people aren't your biggest problem. And speaking of other people, why should it be you that goes there?"

"Because in fact there are not that many people in the world who know how to collect data in Antarctica and stay alive while doing it," said Roger. "On the other hand, there are a million corporate tools out there who could do what you do just as well—in fact, the only reason you're the one doing this is so you'll be a better—"

"I think I know where you're going with this," said Carrie, "and again, I have to say no. I never meant to put anybody in danger. If I had, it would have been myself, not you, not Mama, and most of all not our daughter. Because she ended up in danger anyway, that's no reason for you to deliberately—"

"Yeah, God forbid we do anything dangerous!"

Carrie turned. Thel was standing over them. "We're the Cambergs!" she said scornfully. "Standing up and taking risks is for other people! We're just so... special!"

"Sit down, honey," said Carrie. Thel sat down, but didn't look mollified at all.

"You said it yourself, Mom. A guy who's trying to save millions of people— you didn't want me having anything to do with him because he might not care if I got hurt! And I was supposed to be okay with that!" Thel shook her head.

"What sort of person do you think I am?"

Your father's child. And a better woman than I'll ever be. And God, I wish you weren't.

It wasn't just her husband and daughter, either. George, who could have done anything with his life, joined the Army, went to Afghanistan, and came back wounded and addicted to pain meds. Drew got horribly burned in a failed attempt to save his brother.

Even Mike had a touch of whatever this was. When Carrie asked how he and Samantha had gotten together, he told her how she'd helped him save his business after the real estate bubble. When she asked him about their relationship now and what it was he loved about her, he told her... how she'd helped him save his business after the real estate bubble. Everyone who knew him had been expecting him to dump her and get a good-looking trophy wife. Instead, he stayed with a woman he didn't love out of lingering gratitude and a sense of obligation.

What is wrong with our family? Why can't any of us be selfish?

ON AUGUST 18, TYPHOON HAIYAN grazed the north of Taiwan—doing terrible damage even with its edges—and hit mainland China. The storm was considered a Category 5, but only because there is no Category 6 or 7.

The Chinese government had to arrange the evacuation, in less than a week, of about as many people as the United States government had needed to evacuate during last year's Northern Monsoon. And finding empty land to build camps is not so hard in the United States, but in China, if land is empty it's empty for a reason—usually lack of water.

Winds of over two hundred miles an hour lashed the heart of Shanghai and Ningbo, and a forty-foot wall of water followed behind. Even if every single structure in the path of the storm had been built to the most exacting codes— and quite a few structures didn't seem to have been built to any code at all—this would have been too much to withstand.

The storm was still Category 5 when it was over western Shandong. It did not die entirely until it had gone west of Beijing and spent the last of its rain and wind on the arid lands of inner Mongolia, pelting the Great Wall on both sides as it passed.

AUGUST 25:

HENRY PRATT SAT IN THE Oval Office, listening to Jim Ahn's report.

Group 77 had collapsed. In the midst of the wreckage, it had turned out that what everyone suspected was true. The Group had been a conspiracy of oil companies and oil-producing nations to keep the price of petroleum high by kneecapping the alternatives. Now there was political turmoil in a dozen countries—not counting Mexico and Nigeria, which were in a state of turmoil to begin with. Yesterday the government of Venezuela was overthrown. *And nothing of value was lost*, thought Pratt. In Saudi Arabia, civil unrest had broken out in five cities. In Kuwait and Brunei, once-trusted finance ministers and treasury officials were being tried, convicted, and executed, not always in that order. The new Russian president, Yevgeny Nardin, was making a great show of rooting out and arresting Russian officials and oligarchs involved in the Group.

And, even as the president of Iraq was demanding the resignations of half his ministers, the government of Iran had just gotten a no-confidence vote. "Any chance this will shake the Basra Pact?" Pratt asked.

"Unfortunately, no," said Jim. "The opposition in Iran is as pro-Pact as the government itself. Even if they're allowed to win, it doesn't help us.

"The good news is that we might be able to isolate the Pact. The government of China is getting a lot of mileage out of denouncing this… vast criminal conspiracy, they're calling it."

"One question," said Pratt. "In this 'vast criminal conspiracy' did anybody at any point ever actually break the law?"

"Possibly," said Ahn. "It would depend on the laws of the countries in question. A lot of oil company executives are saying they were coerced by government officials into contributing to the Group's funding."

"Are you sure they're telling the truth?" asked Terry Walther, seated on the left-hand couch.

"You suspect otherwise?"

"To be honest, yeah," said Terry. "The people in the industry, and investing in the industry, aren't the same people that were there five or ten years ago.

You know about all the people who decide to sell their stock in fossil fuel companies, right? Here's the thing we keep forgetting—every time somebody sells that stock, somebody else buys it. So the people still in the business are self-selected true believers. As far as they're concerned, if it isn't black and doesn't come out of the ground, it's not real energy." Pratt nodded. There was a time when he'd felt that way himself.

"Look at Texas," Terry said. "It wasn't just oil billionaires putting in their own money. You had state officials lining up to shove public funds into the Group's coffers. The same thing happened in Louisiana, which barely even has a budget anymore. There's a chance we could be looking at two governors going to jail over this. Not any time soon, however. This is the kind of legal mess it takes years to sort out." Ahn nodded. "And does anybody want to hear the bad news?"

"Want to? No," said Pratt. "Need to? Yes."

"Our favorite governor is claiming vindication over this. She's been the one fighting the group the hardest this whole time."

"How can she justify gutting the legal system to fight a group of investors when all she had to do was wait five months and let it fall apart of its own accord?"

"The problem with that," said Terry, "is that it didn't fall apart of its own accord. It fell apart because a lot of governments—China, India, a lot of European countries—just chose not to respect the Group's claims. And like it or not, that does include Morgan."

"So she's the fly on the wagon?"

"I'd give her a *little* more credit than that," said Terry. "There are a lot of swords sticking in this beast. Hers is one of them, but not the biggest and probably not the one that killed it. The bottom line on these people is, Group 77 destruct-tested the willingness of Western civilization to play by its own rules—at least when it comes to property and patent law."

Jim nodded. "They were desperate," he said. "It's not just the money. They're looking at a fundamental loss of importance in the world. This was a Hail Mary pass. A last-ditch attempt to stop that from happening. And now that it's failed…"

Pratt nodded. Russia weakened, the Basra Pact weakened, maybe even a chance for free elections in Venezuela… things were looking up. Mexico was still a problem, but he and Swanston had a plan to help that country restore order.

On the other hand, diminishing the importance of oil would also strengthen the hands of people like Rep. Darling—people who regarded involvement in the Mideast not as America's right, nor as America's sin, but as a curse and a burden America would be well done with. Pratt had a certain amount of sympathy with this, but having brought the country through the North Korean crisis and strengthened its hand in the world, he found himself even more reluctant than he would normally be to preside over a diminishment of American power and influence.

SEPTEMBER 4:

WITH A DEEP SENSE OF satisfaction, Isabel completed the last check on the Penobscot project and sent it to the government of Maine. They hadn't even asked for it to be able to stand up to the Northern Monsoon, but she'd designed it that way anyway. All indications were that the Monsoon would strike again this year, somewhere in North America.

Having done that, she decided for a moment to celebrate by playing Enginquest. And then she remembered. Belle772505 was dead. She had fallen in battle helping the Hindenburger Guild and their allied guild, the submarine-riding Children of Nemo, bring down an elder chthonid outside the capital of Macandal.

Isabel felt as though she'd lost a friend. Belle was awesome. She lived for adventure and battle. A day when nothing was trying to kill, eat, or enslave her was a day wasted. She'd beaten so many foes, leveled up so many times. She had all the qualities Isabel valued in herself, and a lot more in the way of beauty, style, and general badassiveness. And now she was gone—or rather, Isabel had lost the ability to pretend she existed. She could always go back, create another character, and start over again, but without Hunter it wouldn't be the same.

She checked her messages for something from Hunter. Tree-planting season was over, but he was finding other things to do. His last message had been about helping with somebody's harvest. He seemed so happy now. For the first time in his life, he knew what everybody wanted from him and he could do it.

Isabel looked around the room. Hunter's things were packed neatly away in boxes, and the apartment was impeccably clean and neat, the mess he usually made everywhere long since tidied up. There was no sign that anyone other than her had ever lived here.

Damn. I need more hobbies. I need more friends. I need... something in my life besides work.

With no other ideas about what to do with herself, Isabel decided to watch the news. This week, Congress had come back from recess and, after much debate, finally passed the SUSTAIN Act. Now...

"Money to build a new sewer system for a small town in Texas which no longer has drinking water thanks to aquifer depletion," Pratt was saying. "New cattle grazing permits on land that is no longer suitable for grazing cattle. Continued subsidies for cotton growers in Arizona to buy water that citizens can barely afford to drink. Repairs to the Los Angeles Aqueduct, and desalination plants to replace the aqueduct, *at the same time.* Those are just a few of the hundreds of examples I could cite. This is the most shameless indulgence in runaway spending I have ever seen even from Congress.

"And I haven't even told you the worst. Many of you have been following the debate over the proposed 'Latania Project'—whether to rebuild the Old River Control Structure and try to bring New Orleans back to life, or to accept that the Mississippi's course has changed and build a new seaport and deepwater channel at the former site of Krotz Springs in Louisiana. The SUSTAIN Act funds both. *Both.* Even though the completion of one would render the other useless.

"Congress has budgeted 1.1 trillion dollars—*trillion*—to pay for this. According to the CBO, that won't be nearly enough. According to the CBO, there is, quite literally, *not enough money in the world* to pay for this monstrosity.

"They sent me this bill in the apparent belief that with so much infrastructure spending attached to it, and so much infrastructure needing to be rebuilt, I wouldn't dare veto it. If that was what they thought, they don't know me very well. I am vetoing the SUSTAIN Act. If Congress wants to get anything done before they adjourn again and face the voters, they'd better bring me something I can sign."

On the one hand, Isabel couldn't argue with this. That bill had become a disaster. On the other hand... *please tell me none of the projects I worked on were on that bill.*

Isabel approved of Pratt's handling of the Korea situation earlier this year. On the other hand, she couldn't help but think he could be doing more to rebuild the country he was actually president of. And there was his annoying habit, as far back as the election, of making speeches at colleges where he told students the world didn't owe them anything and they needed to get to work. Since that was already how she was living her life, she didn't need the lecture—and from what the pundits said, he only did this to make himself more popular with older people, who were more reliable voters than the young. *If it's not aimed at you personally, then don't take it personally. In fact, you probably shouldn't be listening at all.* That was a lesson it had taken a while to learn and Isabel still didn't think she'd fully internalized.

Checking another news feed, she saw a story out of Denver. The 10th Circuit Court had ruled that residents in FEMA camps would be allowed to vote in the midterms. According to the story, this affected Wyoming, Kansas, Oklahoma—but especially Wyoming, where "tarpies" were now a majority of the state population.

Then she saw a story about some congressman named Darling who had been put on the ShameList for things he said eight or nine years ago. He was being quoted as saying "I was misled." One commentator said, "He's not the first Republican official to end up on the list—he's just the first one who doesn't sound proud of it."

Then, on the state/local news feed, something jumped out at her.

Alpert: Smith Island to be evacuated by Christmas

The governor of Maryland was speaking at a dock overlooking the Bay. "There's nothing that can be done for the land of Smith Island," he said. "This historic island is low, and getting lower every day. As the seas rise, the island sinks due to erosion. Like Holland Island in the last century, its history has come to an end, but its people will continue. We are building new housing in St. Mary's County, and my hope is that by the beginning of next year we can bring new life to this ancient community."

Isabel turned off the news feed, then sat back and sighed. *Well, you knew this was going to happen one day. And maybe it'll work out well. If everybody gets a place in this community, that solves a lot of problems right there.*

Of course, Pop-pop's health is still going to be an issue whatever happens. He'd been prescribed a very expensive medication. He was taking a cheaper Canadian version of an expensive drug—not strictly legal, but under President Pratt, the FDA tended to turn a blind eye to that sort of thing. Unfortunately, Canada had its own problems, so the cheap version wasn't always available. Which meant the family had no idea how much they'd be spending on health care in any given month.

Sandy's birthday was tomorrow. Isabel was planning to send her an e-card. *Maybe I should ask her—*

No.

Isabel hadn't heard much from Sandy in a while. She had the impression that her old friend had been very busy for the past five years, and had been mired in court battles for much of that time.

And there might be good reasons she hadn't already offered to help. She might be afraid of being deluged with calls for assistance from everybody she'd ever even as much as smiled at. She might still not be too secure in her own wealth.

Or she might just not care that much anymore.

No. She wouldn't have forgotten me completely.

Either way, hasn't she given you enough already?

Isabel didn't have an answer to that.

SEPTEMBER 19:

WALTER YUSCHAK SAT BEHIND HIS desk, not even trying not to look smug as the cameras aimed at him. For the first time in a while, his chair was framed by two American flags.

"Ladies and gentlemen, I am feeling great," he said. "I am feeling more positive, more optimistic, more hopeful about the future of this country than I ever have before! You know why? Because as I'm sure you've all heard by now, last night Congress—working late into the evening—failed to override Pratt's veto of the SUSTAIN Act! Even as I speak, they are headed back to their districts to run for re-election having accomplished precisely dick!

"America, we have dodged a bullet here. That bill would've ruined us! Just think of all the money that would have had to be spent! Taxes that would have to be raised, bonds that would have to be sold, debt that would have to be run up! One point one trillion dollars—that's *trillion*, with a *T*—and the government's *own experts* say that would have been just the beginning! Thank you, Henry Pratt!

"And seriously, did anybody actually need this thing? Not me! Do you know how much property I own along the coast? None! Because I'm not stupid! I know what's coming and I don't want to be affected any more than necessary! There was a time, yes, when I thought climate change wasn't happening—or I pretended to think it wasn't happening just to watch liberals get upset—but that was many years ago! So I don't even need the original Norfolk Plan, let alone whatever that thing was they were trying to pass. Why the hell should my tax dollars—or yours, or anybody else's—be spent on helping people with a bad case of wishful thinking?

"Anyway, it didn't pass. Because Henry Pratt remembered enough of his campaign promises not to let Congress run wild, and Congress couldn't *not* run wild! They couldn't make themselves pass a bill he would sign! Their own interest groups—their own constituents—would turn on them if they did! This is awesome! The government has tied itself into a knot that nobody knows how to untie!"

Walt shook his head. "So many people act like this is a bad thing," he said. "You hear it again and again. 'What's wrong with this country? Why can't we do the Norfolk Plan? Why can't we have high-speed rail? Why can't we rebuild the ORCS? Or how about this Latania Project? That looks cool! We need to modernize this, protect that, fix up the other thing—we used to be the country that landed guys on the moon! What happened to us?'

"Listen to me! This is important! The greatness of a society is not measured by its ability to build big huge things! Ancient Egypt built the pyramids, China built the Great Wall, but you wouldn't have wanted to live there while they were doing it! Some Americans once went to the moon, but there are parts of this country where you still can't go to a marijuana dispensary! The greatness of a society is measured by the freedom it allows!"

Walt shook his head. "You know, people keep comparing this thing we're going through to a war," he said. "'Treat it like a war,' they say. I say no! Don't treat it like a war, because it's not a war! It's just weather! There's no planning, there's no intent, there's no *will* behind it! When there's a dust storm, it's not somebody kicking sand in your face, it's just nature!" He'd wanted to say *don't rain on my leg and tell me it's peeing*, but decided at the last moment that it would sound silly.

"In this country—in the whole world, to be honest—we've lost sight of something very basic. The purpose of government is to protect you from one thing, and one thing only. *Other people*. Criminals. Invading armies. Other people that want to violate and take away your rights. It's in the Declaration of Independence. 'To secure these rights, governments are instituted among men.'

"And what are rights? Rights are *boundaries*." Walt was going to work the title of his new book into this monologue if it killed him. "Rights are rules—'don't touch me, don't touch my stuff.' We as human beings are supposed to respect these rules. But nature doesn't respect these rules. Nature doesn't *think*. Nature doesn't *care*. Nature says sooner or later we all have to die, but that does not make nature a murderer.

"And this is where people keep going wrong. We don't just want the government to protect us from each other, we want it to protect us from nature. Which is why the SUSTAIN Act turned into the monster it did. And now that monster is dead, we have, in this country, a golden opportunity.

"Right now, as we speak, people in Ohio and Illinois and Michigan and Wisconsin and a bunch of other places going through the Monsoon again—the people there are cooperating to survive, the way they did last year! They're policing their own neighborhoods, holding little informal lessons for their kids, getting their own sick and wounded to the hospitals that are still open! What if we just… let them do it? What if we stopped trying to help them and let them help themselves? Let them hang on to their dignity? What if we all just agree that whatever nature does to us, we're not going to steal from each other to fight it?"

Walt took a deep breath. "Listen to me," he said. "This part is important. The United States is uniquely blessed with its limited need for government. A lot of countries—even if they got that the only reason for government is to protect you from other people, they still need big governments because they need big armies, because they've gotta worry about their neighbors. In Europe they gotta worry about Russia, Russia's gotta worry about China, China's gotta worry about Japan… they need strong governments because their neighbors have strong governments. That's their tough luck.

"But guess what? It's not ours! Who do we have to be afraid of, really? Canada hasn't got enough people in it, Mexico can't get its shit together, and Cuba and the rest are too damn small! And for the rest of the world, generations of crazy-high defense spending have left us with all the superweapons we'll ever need, and then some. For a lot of our history, we were able to get by with one of the smallest armies in the world. It was only when Woodrow Wilson decided it was time for us to step up and become a Great Power that things started going downhill.

"The point is—we've already got everything we need. We've got the know-how. We've got the resources. As a country, we have the potential to save ourselves, naturally, if the government would just stop *trying* so hard. Just… let it happen. Stop listening to the people who say, 'Why can't we have nice things?' We can have freedom. And freedom is the nicest thing of all. We'll be right back."

THIS YEAR, THE MASSIVE BELT *of rain around the Northern Hemisphere resembled a square rather than a triangle—or perhaps a diamond centered almost exactly on the prime meridian and the International Date Line.*

One corner stretched harmlessly over a vast, empty reach of the North Pacific, south of the Aleutians. It bothered no one, and helped to cool a ridge of heated water that had built up southwest of the Queen Charlotte Islands.

Another corner struck the north-central United States, the same region that had been devastated by the previous year's Monsoon. It was not quite so severe as that flood, but it stretched from the Dakotas to upstate New York and as far south as Springfield, Illinois. Things that had been shoddily repaired, or not repaired to withstand the Monsoon, were quickly washed away again.

The third corner stretched from the Atlantic Ocean over Western Europe, covering the north coast of Spain as far as the mountains, all of France, the north slopes of Switzerland and southern Germany.

The fourth corner, in the heart of Asia, had the most dramatic impact. Over the course of that autumn, one to three feet of rain fell from Lake Balkhash to the Khingan Range. Nothing even close to that had ever happened before in all recorded history. The thin soil of Mongolia could not possibly absorb such a deluge. It all had to go somewhere.

Much of it went to the Turpan Depression. The hot, dry depression was well below sea level and had no outlet, so the water that flowed there stayed there, and the silt and debris it picked up sank to the bottom of the depression and raised its floor slightly.

Lake Turpan was born.

OCTOBER 3:

FROM WHAT ISABEL COULD SEE of Hunter on the little screen, he'd never looked better. It wasn't just that he'd lost even more weight, or that he was looking a lot fitter, or that he'd finally managed to grow a full beard. (And how had that happened? He'd never been able to build up more than a layer of scruff.) He looked self-possessed. Confident. Like somebody who'd finally grown up. *I wonder what he'll be like when he comes back. I can hardly wait to find out.*

He was sitting in what looked like a small loft apartment. Rain spattered the window behind him—western Canada wasn't getting the worst of this year's Monsoon, but nowhere along the jet stream was really safe.

"So... uh... what news from the North, tree-planters of Rohan?"

"We've all pretty much abandoned the far north for the rest of the year," said Hunter. "I'm living in Lethbridge right now."

"How are you keeping yourself together?"

"I'm a cook at Martin's. It's this sort of soup kitchen/restaurant."

"A soup-kitchen-slash-restaurant," said Isabel. "How does that work, exactly?"

"There's a very basic meal—mug of vegetable soup, a roll, glass of water— you can get that for free twice a day. Not much, I know, but it's as much as we can afford to give. If you want something more, you pay for it. Think of it like UBI, only with food instead of money. My job is making the free soup."

"They really should be paying for that."

"They are. Half our paying customers are people wanting a second mug of soup. Or a whole bowl."

"What sort of customers do you get?"

"A lot of people from southern Ontario. Refugees, basically. Martin says they'll be in town until spring and head back once the snow melts. Speaking of food, what are you eating lately?"

"I'm not as good a cook as you, but I can manage," said Isabel. "And I've been getting a dozen or so crabs a week from Pop."

"Good," said Hunter. "Right now I'm... not exactly a vegetarian, but pretty close. We don't have a lot of meat, and we save most of what we do have for winter when we really need the calories."

"So what do you make this famous soup out of?"

"To be honest, some days it's more famous than others," he said. "It kind of depends on what vegetables we can get. Today all I had was eggplant and potato and rye flour for thickening, so I toasted the flour just a tiny bit to give the whole thing kind of a roux-like flavor and I browned the eggplant a little and... I'm going into food geek mode. Sorry."

"It's okay. We're both masters of boring conversation." Isabel paused. "Seems like you're doing great."

"I am. It seems weird, but I've never been happier. This whole country is so beaten up, but everybody here... it's like we look at each other and we know we're all part of the same thing."

"You're actually making it sound kind of like a cult."

Hunter laughed his odd, hissing laugh. "Yeah, I guess you could say that," he said. "It's like this whole country is a cult, but there's no leader. Or maybe the weather is the leader."

"What about the government? Don't you have one of those?"

"Yeah, but it kinda has its hands full." Hunter sighed, and stopped smiling. "Look, Isabel, I called for a reason."

This sounded serious.

"I called to tell you I won't be coming back this fall and I don't know how long I'll be staying. It could be another year. Or two. Or... I don't know when I'll be back, and I don't want you spending too long waiting for me."

This sounded bad. This sounded very bad.

"I know you," he said. "You're faithful. You keep your promises. I'm just saying you don't have to keep this one." He took a deep breath. "And... um... well... I've met someone."

For a moment, Isabel's brain tried to interpret this sentence as *I met a total stranger the other day and he has nothing to do with any of this, but I just thought I'd mention him.* She had to force it to even consider the obvious meaning.

"Her name is Annie," he said. "Actually, no, that's not her name. Her name is… well, never mind. We call her Annie. She's not… no one could ever replace you, but… I don't know, I just feel completely in sync with her like I've never felt with anybody before. And I've… we've reached the point where I can't break things off with her without hurting her."

"Does she know about me?"

"She does. She feels bad about it, but she can't… she said she's leaving it up to me. That she trusts me to do what's right for me."

"And… this is what's right for you."

"Not just me. All of us. You, me, her. I can't keep you waiting when I don't know if I'm ever coming back. I can't keep her at arm's length when…" He paused. "We love each other. There. I said it."

Isabel just sat there, blinking.

"I love you, too," said Hunter, his voice catching a little. "That's what makes it hurt. I'm so sorry. I… you deserved better than this from me."

Isabel sighed. She could see the tears in his eyes. "So… that's it, then." Maybe later, she would get angry. Almost certainly, later she would cry. Right now, her brain was on autopilot, telling her the next thing that needed to be done.

"A lot of your stuff is still here," she said. "Where do I send it?"

Hunter gave her an address. "We'll split the cost," he said. "I've got some money now, and I know it's not as cheap as it used to be."

"Not as fast, either," said Isabel. "Especially right now. I can get it in the mail tomorrow, but I'm not making any promises about when it's coming."

Hunter nodded. "That's the great thing about you. A lot of girls would be piling my stuff up in the parking lot and setting it on fire."

"That wouldn't be very carbon-neutral."

They both laughed at that, but only a little.

"I want you to know I'm… I'm really grateful. You stood by me when I didn't deserve it. I'll never forget you."

Isabel bit her lip. The seconds ticked by. Neither of them wanted to break the connection, knowing this might be the last time they ever saw each other.

Finally Isabel spoke. "I love you. Let's end this."

Hunter nodded. "Goodbye."

The screen went black.

So now my boyfriend in Canada has a girlfriend in Canada. I suppose I should have seen that coming.

Isabel made a call. "Kristen?" she said. "At some point in the next week or so I might need a shoulder to cry on. Are you going to be available?"

"Of course," she said. "Did Hun—I mean, what's wrong?"

Is it that obvious? "Yeah, Hunter and I just broke up. Don't tell anybody just yet, okay? I want to tell them when I'm good and ready." *And in the meantime, I don't want to hear anybody saying "I told you so" or "Good riddance." Especially not Chelsey.*

After the call was done, Isabel took out her earpiece and set it to Playlist 4, which was all Epifania and Laura Bronzino instead of the rhust she usually favored. Rhust was all about staring into the face of every primal fear and dark impulse, confronting your anxieties head-on and kicking their asses. Right now, she needed the musical equivalent of a hug. ("I'll come back to you, I swear. We'll be together again." "I'll be waiting.")

While she was listening, she checked his social media for signs of this "Annie" who wasn't named "Annie." Finally, she found a photo, dated a week ago, of Hunter and a girl named "H. Gorman" with their arms around each other. The girl was petite and looked part Asian, with a heart-shaped face and a delicate, fragile sort of beauty that Isabel had never possessed in her life.

She went into the kitchen for a fresh cup of chyq. Practically everything in the kitchen reminded her of him. It had once been his domain.

It bothered him to be living off me. That's why he learned how to cook—so he could give something back.

All I ever wanted was for him to be happy, and now he is. He's turned into exactly the kind of guy I always hoped he could be. A little more than that, even. Why couldn't it have happened while he was with me? Was I doing something wrong?

Did he ever actually love me? Or did he just need me?

CANADA WAS NOT THE ONLY nation trying to help important biomes in their migration toward the poles. Off the northeast coast of Australia, only the southern quarter of the Great Barrier Reef still supported anything resembling a functioning ecosystem, and it was in a perilous state. One chemical spill, one population explosion among the crown-of-thorns starfish, and the last piece of the Reef might die.

At the same time, the waters south of the reef were now warm enough to support coral populations of their own. So this spring, the Australian government succumbed to necessity and began trying to build new reefs, setting aside stretches of shallow coastal water away from the shipping lanes. Such places were not easy to find on the more heavily populated southeast coast. New Zealand was trying the same experiment.

Of course, one can't simply plant a coral reef any more than one can plant a forest. The most the Australians and New Zealanders could do was create the first stage of the process and encourage helpful organisms to settle there while trying to keep away those that might devour it before it could properly establish itself. But even this was made more difficult by the lowered pH of the ocean.

OCTOBER 24:

IN YEARS GONE BY, THE screen over the bar in the restaurant would have been tuned to a sports channel. Now it was on the news, letting everyone know about the progress of the Monsoon and which counties needed evacuating this week. Admittedly, it was TKB news, so Isabel only trusted it so far. The Chinese weather-control device had to be bullshit, and the cannibal gangs going around on flatboats also sounded pretty dubious. But it was definitely still raining in the upper Midwest this evening. You had to take your points of common reality where you could get them.

Why am I doing this again?

There's no reason not to. An old… acquaintance is coming through the area and wants to meet. I've got the time.

It's been two years. How much could she possibly have changed?

It was 5 p.m. The dinner rush hadn't started. She was supposed to have arrived by now.

She always did run five minutes late. Never on time, but never fifteen minutes late either. Always five to ten minutes. You'd think she'd learn to do everything ten minutes sooner.

The first time they'd met, Isabel had thought she was the luckiest girl in the world. It was like a cheesy anime come to life—a girl much more beautiful and sophisticated than herself had suddenly just glommed onto her out of nowhere. Toward the end, though… "Why do you always have to be so defensive?" "How about this—you stop attacking, I'll stop defending!" "I'm trying to help you! You just can't take a little honest criticism!" "Who the fuck died and made you Pope? You act like you have this perfect moral judgment and I should just accept everything you say as God's own truth!"

I've never tolerated physical abuse. I never should have tolerated emotional abuse. I broke up with her because the alternative was me punching her in the face.

We're just meeting for dinner. That's all. If it turns out she's like she used to be, we get separate checks and go our separate ways, no real harm done.

"Isabel?"

Isabel looked up over her shoulder.

Laurie.

She did look a little different—instead of dyeing her whole head of hair, she had left it brunette and put indigo highlights at the tips. She was dressed as if for a job interview in a white blouse, dark brown jacket, and matching skirt, but Isabel couldn't focus on the clothes. She kept looking at Laurie's face.

It was the face she'd fallen in love with. It wasn't just a beautiful face, but a kind one. The brown eyes went right into you like sunlight through the windows. The little twitch in the corners of the mouth promised subtle, gentle humor. Everything about the way she looked at you said *I understand you and I love you, I have seen your soul and it isn't so bad, I can help you with your pain.* In short, Laurie's face wrote checks that bounced the minute she opened her mouth.

"You're looking great," said Laurie.

"Thanks. You… well, you always look great."

Laurie sat down with her usual smooth grace. "Let me get this out of the way right now," she said. "You were right. I was wrong. I'm sorry. End of story."

"Um… okay." At the end, even apologies had become a minefield. In fact, that was the subject of their last argument—"God damn it, Laurie, every time I apologize to you I end up regretting it! You just throw it right back in my face! It's like you hear me say 'I'm sorry' and think it's a sign of weakness!" "Well, you seem to think 'I'm sorry' means 'Shut the fuck up!'" Isabel doubted Laurie remembered what any of their arguments were about at this late date, but she couldn't very well *not* accept the apology.

"My car's running low. Are there any charging stations on the Shore?"

"They're on Route 50."

"Thanks." Laurie accepted a glass of water from the waiter, then turned back to Isabel. "So… you and Hunter really split up?"

"Yeah. It happened. And if you say anything that sounds like gloating, if you so much as smile"—Lauren hastily wiped a smile off her face—"this conversation is going to be over."

"All right. No gloating. I just have one question, though, and I want you to answer it honestly."

"Shoot." Isabel lifted a glass of water to her lips.

"Did you start dating Hunter just to get back at me?"

Isabel had never done a real spit take in her life, but she came close. "No," she said firmly as she set the cup down. "No. My reasons for dating Hunter had nothing to do with you."

"Good."

"I admit, after you I did kind of need a change of pace. But I stayed with him for two years. Does that mean anything at all to you?"

"Yes. It means you're loyal and stubborn and have the absolute worst taste in everything. And yes, I include myself in that." That got Isabel's attention. The Laurie of two years ago wasn't into self-deprecation. Sometime in the past two years, she'd grown a perspective.

Time to learn a little more about her. "So what have you been doing with yourself?"

"I'm in sales right now," she said. "I'm selling this." She pulled a small bottle out of her jacket pocket.

"You're not going to try and sell it to me, are you?"

"Not unless you have a newborn baby I don't know about. It's supposed to prevent asthma and bad allergies."

Laurie handed her the bottle. The label said it was "immunogenic baby powder" and included such advice as "apply 1/8 tsp once a week inside fresh diaper," "not for oral use" and "DO NOT USE ON INFANTS OVER 12 MONTHS OLD."

Isabel looked at the ingredients. "Hmm… active ingredients include cat, dog, and mouse dander… 'beneficial bacteria'… 'organic periplaneta product.' What is that, exactly?"

Laurie stood up, leaned over the table, brought her lips next to Isabel's ear and whispered the two words that Isabel had never fantasized about having whispered in her ear by a beautiful woman—*"Cockroach feces."*

"Oh… kay."

"I don't sell it straight to the parents. Mostly I talk to health stores."

Isabel nodded. "Before we go any further," she said, "tell me the truth. Does this—I mean this literally—does this shit actually work?"

"Legally, I can't make any promises," said Laurie. "Theoretically, it should. Studies have shown that if babies are exposed to this sort of thing at the right age, it lowers their risk. But the FDA hasn't looked at it and we've only been selling it for a year, so…" She shrugged.

"It's just that I kinda have a personal stake in this," said Isabel. "You know I used to have a really bad bee allergy, right?"

"I think you mentioned it. Was it the kind that could, um…"

"Kill me? Yep. My earliest memory is of a nurse sticking a tube down my throat to keep it from closing up and choking me to death. That was during the allergy test."

"Jesus."

"Even when I was little, I was never allowed outside on sunny days unless it was winter."

"Didn't you go out to help your dad on his boat? I remember you talking about that."

"Well, yeah, I did go outside for that. Our house was right on the Bay—the dock was just past our yard. And every step from the front door to the dock, I kept my eyes open."

Laurie nodded. "I remember that time on the quad you spotted the bee," she said. "You were all tensed up and laser-focused—it looked like you were about to whip out a gun and start shooting at it. I think that was as close as I've ever seen you come to looking scared."

"Yeah," said Isabel. "I don't think I was in any danger, but it was kind of a habit. Anyway, if this stuff works, that's awesome. And if it doesn't, I'm coming after you and I'm going to make you eat it."

Laurie chuckled. "Speaking of eating," she said as she picked up the menu, "the chicken is really cheap here."

"Yeah, this is a big chicken-farming area."* Two years ago, Laurie had been the sort of vegan who gave other vegans a bad name. Isabel had no idea what had changed, but if it meant she could order something with some meat in it and not get a lecture or a disapproving look, this was all to the good.

---

* One of the side effects of the carbon fee that passed this year is that the cost of the fuel used to

"'Non-GMO chyq.' How can chyq be non-GMO?"

"Maybe the particular company didn't modify the plant a second time. Or more likely, the FDA is staffed with Pratt appointees. The same people who let you go around selling roach poop as baby powder, so don't complain."

"Good point."

WHEN THE WAITER SHOWED UP, Laurie ordered the baked chicken with ratatouille. "Only could you replace the eggplant with extra zucchini?" As far as Isabel knew, Laurie wasn't allergic to eggplant. She just didn't like it. This was the first thing she'd said or done that reminded Isabel of the old Laurie—going out to eat and trying to micromanage the kitchen from her table. Isabel would have bet that she'd unknowingly ingested more than one pint of restaurant employee spit over the course of her life.

"I'll have the strip steak with mushrooms and scallions," said Isabel. Her first dividend check from that carbon-fee-and-dividend thing had arrived a few days ago, dated October 15—Congress had timed it on purpose, so the checks came not too long before the midterms. This was as good a thing to spend it on as any.

She spent most of the time until the food arrived telling Laurie about her family and the troubles they were having, carefully watching her reaction for any sign of the old snobbery. There was none. Either her old girlfriend had gotten a great attitude adjustment, or had taken a course in acting.

Conversation stopped when the food arrived. Isabel's dish was mostly a pile of sautéed mushrooms and green onions on a bed of mashed potatoes, slathered in gravy, with four ounces of strip steak on top. But the steak was perfectly cooked, with some of the juice and redness still inside despite the narrowness of the strips. Laurie's chicken with eggplant looked a little more meat-heavy. Watching her eat it, Isabel wasn't sure whether to feel sad or relieved. Laurie's ideals and beliefs had been real—or Isabel had always thought they'd been real—and something had happened to them. She wasn't sure how to ask what it was.

We're just meeting for dinner. That's all.

And maybe she is spending the night. So what? That would be a perfectly sensible thing to do. It would save her the cost of a hotel room.

---

transport a given foodstuff a given distance tends to be reflected in its price.

Anyway, I've been spending too much time alone. I need some conversation with somebody, even if it's her.

We are definitely not having sex.

IT WAS JUST AFTER ELEVEN. Isabel sat up in the queen-size bed, naked, stretching her arms and legs a little, enjoying the little chill as the air pulled the sweat off her skin. Laurie lay on her belly next to her, also naked, arms folded under her head, droplets of sweat still visible on her shoulders. She looked up at Isabel out of the corner of her eye, a contented smile on her face.

Isabel ran her fingers gently over the surface of Laurie's butt and down the back of her thigh. It was a butt she highly approved of, from an engineering standpoint. It was compact and efficient, with just enough convexity to draw the eye. While it lacked the raw mass and power of Isabel's behind, it made up for it in elegance of design. Isabel would have liked to tell her so, but her attempts at talking dirty had never seemed to have the right effect. She wasn't sure why.

Laurie wiggled happily under her touch. "You still have those tiny little scars on your fingertips," she said. "I love those little scars."

"You never told me that before."

"Well, it seemed like kind of an insensitive thing to say. I mean, you got them when your dad… sold you to a fish-packing plant or whatever. I forget the details."

"It was a crab-picking plant. And he got me a job there one summer because he knew the owner."

"Wow," said Laurie. "What a tragic waste of perfectly good white privilege."

A sense of humor about yourself? Laurie, I might actually learn to love you again.

She turned onto her side to face Isabel. "I never did understand—why'd he do that to you?"

"He tried to get Chelsey to do it, to teach her the value of hard work. She pitched a fit and wouldn't go. So I volunteered."

Laurie looked at her in disbelief. "Why?"

"Basically to prove I wasn't her. It was teenage rebellion, only it wasn't Mom and Pop I was rebelling against."

"Refresh my memory. Aren't you supposed to be the smart one in the family?"

"I was fifteen, okay? I was fifteen and I prided myself on my work ethic. I grew up with Mom and Pop saying you gotta work for what you want in life, there's no free lunches, and I accepted that. I think I spent half my childhood doing homework, helping Pop on his boat, helping Mom with dinner… or flat on my back from allergy treatment, but that's another story."

"So if this was how kids were brought up in your family, how do you explain Chelsey?"

"I don't."

Laurie propped herself up on one elbow.

"Speaking of your family, I have a question," said Laurie. "You keep talking about the problems you're having. Money problems."

"And health problems in the case of Pop-pop. And Chelsey's problem."

"I remember you telling me that diamond start-up girl used to be your best friend when you were little."

"Sort of part friend and part babysitter, yeah. See, she was born in New York, but her dad left when she was a baby and her mom came to Talbot County—"

Laurie gave a little wave, as if shooing a swarm of irrelevant details away from her brain. "Either way, these days that girl is richer than fuck. Can't she help you guys out?"

"We haven't asked."

"You haven't? Why the hell not?"

"Because she actually *is* our friend. We don't want to be hitting her up for money."

"Oh, come on!" said Laurie. "If you were friends, there's gotta be at least one favor she owes you."

"Other way around," said Isabel. "I owe her. Big." She paused. "She saved my life once."

Laurie let out a low whistle. "You never told me that."

"Well, you never seemed all that interested in my stories of growing up on the Bay."

"No, this story I definitely want to hear."

"Okay," said Isabel. "I was six years old. Mrs. Symcox—Sandy's mother—was visiting. I was out on the porch with Chelsey. I can't remember what we were playing, but Chelsey kind of had her back turned. Sandy was there watching us. I think she was trying to read a book, but part of her must have been paying attention, because…

"I felt something land in my hair. I didn't know what it was, I just reached up and suddenly there was this iron grip on my wrist yanking my hand away from my head." Without thinking about it, Isabel caressed her right wrist a little. "It was Sandy. She looked white as a sheet. Then with her other hand she snatched whatever it was out of my hair—really fast, *bam*, like a snake—and sort of squeezed it between her fingers.

"I was like, *ow*, Chelsey saw what was happening and said 'Hey, what are you doing?' Mom and Mrs. Symcox came out to see what was happening… and then Sandy let go and opened up her other hand."

"A bee?"

Isabel nodded. "The porch was screened, but somehow it must have gotten in. And it stung her in the index finger before she killed it. Mrs. Symcox took her into the kitchen and covered her finger with wet baking soda so it wouldn't swell up too bad… after that, Mom ripped out every flower on the property and started me on allergy therapy. Every Friday after school I'd go to the doctor's office and get injected with a teeny tiny little dose of bee venom, and then I'd spend all night and the next morning feeling like I was weighted down with a hundred pounds of *bleah*. It got better after the first five months or so… the point is, she saved my life and she let herself get stung doing it. How many eleven-year-olds could do that? I mean, even knowing it was the right thing to do, how many of them could?"

Laurie nodded. "Yeah, that's… pretty awesome."

"It doesn't end there. She's the one who got me interested in science, and that's what led me into STEM in general. So she's a big part of the reason I'm doing as well as I am."

"When was the last time you met in person?"

"Her mother's funeral," said Isabel. "See, her mom was killed by a drunk driver a few years after she left, so she came back for the funeral. And I'm telling you right now, this story does not make me look good.

"First off, I didn't realize until we were in church that I'd left my cell phone on, and I couldn't turn it off without it letting out this beep. I couldn't even figure out how to set it on silent without taking it out and looking at it. The whole service, I was terrified somebody was going to call me and make me look like the world's biggest asshole.

"Second, I was wearing these new dress shoes that weren't comfortable. I said they were uncomfortable when Mom bought them, but she said it was okay because they were dress shoes and I was never going to walk far in them.

Well, the day of the funeral, we parked on the edge of town, we walked six blocks to the church, we walked four more blocks from the church to the cemetery, we walked I forget how many blocks from the cemetery to Mrs. Fluharty's—she's one of the other teachers—for a little reception with food, and then we walked back to the car."

"Ouch," said Laurie, caressing her own feet.

"So all through the service, not only was I thinking about my cell phone, I was thinking, 'ow ow ow my poor feet I think my little toes are about to come off…' which is not what you're supposed to be thinking at a time like that. One of my closest friends had just lost her mother right out of nowhere, and I kept getting distracted by my own problems."

"Is that why you never wear good shoes?"

"I always wear good shoes," said Isabel, gesturing to the neat line of well-worn sneakers, work shoes, and boots that rested against the bedroom wall. "If they're not fashionable, they should be."

Laurie laughed. "Anyway," she said, "from what you say, it sounds like this woman has a track record of helping you."

"That's the problem," said Isabel. "Somebody once said—I think it was John Wayne—'If you help people when they're in trouble, they'll remember you when they're in trouble again.' I can't be one of those people. Really, I can't. I don't think I can face her again unless I'm giving something back."

"Why not?" Laurie rested a hand on Isabel's arm. "Seriously, what's stopping you?"

"It's sort of… this is going to sound crazy."

"Let's hear it."

"It's this sort of voice in my head."

"Oh… kay."

"I told you it was going to sound crazy. It's like my conscience or something, only it isn't always right—I've caught it in a contradiction more than once. It's weird, because it's not consistent at all. Sometimes it sounds right-wing and sometimes it sounds left-wing. Sometimes it sounds like Pop after a bad day. Sometimes it sounds like my least favorite teachers. Every once in a while, it sounds like Martelle Sherman."

"That girl you knew back in school?"

"Yeah. My beloved co-Valedictorian. But you know who it sounds like most often?"

"I'm gonna take a wild guess," said Laurie. "Me."

Isabel nodded. "It's not your fault," she said. "I had this problem long before I ever met you. But that was why I kept getting so mad at you. You were basically broadcasting enemy propaganda in time of war."

"I never knew about it... so does this voice ever have anything nice to say?"

"No."

"Even when you do something good?"

"No."

Laurie rolled onto her back and thought for a moment, then sat up and looked at Isabel squarely. "I'm going to give you some really bad advice, and I hope you'll take it to heart," she said. "I say it's bad advice because it's always bad advice when somebody who isn't a medical specialist gives you advice on medications."

Isabel leaned forward. *She sells medicinal roach turds, and* she *thinks this is bad medical advice? This I gotta hear.*

"I used to have the same sort of problem," she said. "Only I didn't have a voice in my head." She paused for what Isabel suspected was dramatic effect. "The voice in my head had *me*. You've been at war with yours—I just accepted mine."

Isabel reached over and held Laurie's hand. "I didn't know."

"Why do you think I was such a cunt, anyway?" Now there was a word Isabel had *never* imagined hearing from Laurie's perfect lips. "I couldn't stand being the only one in the room who felt bad about herself. Just as well I didn't know about your little problem. I would not have put that knowledge to good use." She sighed.

"Losing you was kind of a wake-up call," Laurie said. "I mean, you're not perfect, but you have the patience of stone. If you decide you've had enough of somebody, there's got to be something wrong with that somebody. So I talked to some therapists. Got some shit sorted out. Only it wasn't the sort of thing you can fix just by talking about it. So I... well, I started taking Suiamor."

For a moment, Isabel's muscles tensed themselves and her eyes pivoted to the exit. Then she forced herself to relax. *So. I'm naked in bed with a sweehead. That's... okay, that's bad, but it's not necessarily an emergency. She's just as naked as I am. And unarmed. And about half as strong. With no aptitude for physical violence.*

Yeah, but I gotta sleep some time.

So does she.

"Yeah," said Laurie, watching her reaction. "This is why I don't go around telling everybody. See, here's the thing about swee—it doesn't change your basic desires. If you don't want to commit rape or murder, if you don't want to molest children, you won't want to do it on swee." Laurie turned her back on Isabel and leaned back into her. Isabel gave her a hug, partly for the physical pleasure of it and partly to make sure she had the other girl under control.

Laurie crossed her arms and brushed Isabel's upper arms with her fingertips. "Now I remember why I stayed with you so long," she said. "You've got that peasant-woman bod."

"Is that a compliment?"

"Yes, it is. Strong with just the right amount of softness. Perfect for cuddling."

I should have known something was wrong when she ate the chicken. Back when we were dating, she really cared about that whole vegan thing. I should have asked myself why she stopped giving a shit, and what else she might have stopped caring about.

But you didn't, because all you could think about was how this made you more comfortable. Now you're cuddling a sweehead and you have no one to blame but yourself.

Speaking of pharmaceuticals, take a chill pill. She has a legitimate medical, psychological reason for taking swee.

Unless of course she's lying. Which sweeheads are known to do.

She didn't have to say she was on swee at all. It's not like it fell out of her purse right in front of me. She volunteered that information.

"Can I ask you a personal question?" said Laurie.

"Shoot."

"When was the last time you actually did something that was wrong? I mean, really, seriously wrong?"

Isabel was silent for a moment. There were times enough when she'd felt guilty over something she'd thought, or something she'd failed to do, but as for things she'd actually done...

"This is one of the things I learned in therapy," Laurie said. "That thing inside you—that little voice that's always finding fault with everything you do and think and feel—maybe for some people, that's their conscience. But not with you. Your real conscience is built into your behavior. You hardly even know it's there, because it never really says anything in words. You just sort of do the right thing naturally.

"And Suiamor has no effect on that. The only thing it affects is that little clot of… internalized negativity inside you that pretends to be your conscience. That you can do without."

OCTOBER 25:

ISABEL WATCHED AS LAURIE'S LITTLE electric car pulled out from the curb.

One night. That was the deal. She's just passing through. But it was going to be hard going back to being alone. *Just let me finish the specs on Conowingo. Then maybe I can start dating.* Now that Group 77 was gone, and its lawyers were running around screaming they hadn't done anything illegal, Marshpower was back in business and the Conowingo Project was a go again—in fact, Alpert wanted construction to begin in February and be done by the end of August. That would take either a miracle or a whole lot of money.

One night. That's all. And it's not like I can even trust her. Not after that little gift she left me. A few individually wrapped doses which Laurie "didn't plan on using." *Because it's totally normal to go around with drugs in your purse that you don't plan on using. Yeah. I'll buy that for a Red Ron.*

They were sitting in her bathroom medicine cabinet now, three little packets the size of postage stamps. Suiamor. The drug for people who thought discount Jellicoe treatments were too damn safe.

You need to throw it away. Right now. Today.

Do you have any idea how much that stuff costs? Even the generic version of the antiautechthic cost about two hundred dollars a dose. It seemed wrong to throw away such an expensive gift.

What are you going to do—sell it on the black market?

Actually, if I knew anybody on the black market that wouldn't be a bad idea.

For the next hour or so, Isabel did some research online. She read the testimonials of people who'd gotten a new lease on life from it. And she read about other people whose lives had been ruined by it.

Suiamor was, basically, a painkiller. But it only blocked certain kinds of pain—fear, guilt, shame, and self-loathing. It was a blessing to people who had survived abuse or suffered from social anxiety. The trouble was that there was a technical term for people who didn't feel fear, guilt, shame, or self-loathing. It was "sociopath."

And those who took it without really needing it sometimes found that the things it blocked were themselves blocking other things—dark impulses, desires never meant to be acted on. Swee opened doors inside your head. Sometimes they turned out to be doors that should have been left shut and locked.

The effect lasted three to four days, and you weren't supposed to take it more than once a week. If you took it all the time, your brain would respond by rewiring itself in an attempt to rebuild the blocked connections, and would probably do it wrong, resulting in some really spectacular neuroses.

It was no more habit-forming than anything else that produced a temporary pleasant sensation—which is to say, it was habit-forming. And if you did or said something really bad under the influence that you regretted when it wore off, of course you'd want to take it again as soon as possible... and possibly do something equally bad, leading to what they called a "swee spiral." And since it didn't affect the brain in the same way drugs like heroin or cocaine did, a Jellicoe treatment wouldn't work. *If Laurie's trying to get me hooked so she can be my dealer, I'll kick her perfect ass so hard she'll shit through her ears.*

What are you waiting for? Throw it away!

Suppose I throw it away. Will you thank me? Will you fill me with the warm glow of having done the right thing? Or will you just yell at me for having taken so long to do it?

You're using yourself as a hostage. I don't negotiate with terrorists.

You don't negotiate, period. The swee stays. I'm not using it—not today—but it stays.

NOVEMBER 4:

IT WAS THE MORNING AFTER the midterm elections. If it had been the morning after a night of heavy drinking, the assembled men and women could not have looked worse. A lot of them had been up late last night, and had been rewarded for their diligence with very bad news.

For this occasion, Henry Pratt was acting in his capacity as leader of the Republican Party, not as President of the United States. His wife was sitting at the far end of the table, small and silent. Slender, goateed Vice President Quillen was at his right hand, and at his left was RNC chair Meredith Grimes, middle-aged and so colorless she almost vanished into the upholstery. The rest of the guests were, for the most part, Republican senators who hadn't been up for reelection this year. All of them were sitting in front of plates of five-star-restaurant-quality eggs Benedict. None of them were doing more than pick at it.

Well, there was no point putting off this discussion. "Last night was one of the worst nights our party has had in a long time," said Pratt. "Even considering the incumbent party often loses in the midterms, it was bad. We're down six seats in the Senate, twenty-three seats in Congress and at least five governorships—possibly six. Graves would know the figures on state legislatures better than I. Does anyone have anything to add to this?"

"I do," said Sen. Bryce Wilkinson (R-AL) a note of anger in his old-fashioned drawl.

Pratt gestured for him to speak. Wilkinson pushed himself to his feet with a mighty effort, scooting his chair backward to give his gut room to clear the rim of the table. His face was red, and his jowls were ornamented with a white goatee in a failed attempt to not look like Boss Hogg from *The Dukes of Hazzard* in a navy-blue suit.

"Mr. President," he said. "You say we're down six seats, but in fact we lost eight seats. Eight seats! And seven of them should have been safe! One of them the Minority Whip! Six of those seats we never imagined losing in our worst nightmares, and we lost them! And the only reason we lost them was because of voters who were put there by FEMA!" The other senators were nodding and looking angry.

"I don't even know what to say," Wilkinson said. "Mr. President, you are the worst thing to happen to the Republican Party since... since the *last* Republican president! Or the one before that, even!"

"Before I accept the blame for this," said Pratt, "I want the answer to one simple question. Why didn't anybody in our party try going into the camps and campaigning for votes?"

"We thought we had a chance in court!" Flecks of spit leapt from Wilkinson's lips and landed on the white tablecloth. "We honestly thought we could fix it so they wouldn't be allowed to vote at all. And once you start down that road, you are committed. If you lose the court battle, you can't just turn around and say, 'I fought like hell to make sure you people would never get a vote that counted, but I lost, so please vote for me anyway.' We've tried that in other places. It does. Not. Work."

"Haven't we gained a couple of senators? Illinois, Michigan? I know it's not enough to make up our losses, but..."

"You're right, it's not. It still leaves us with only forty-three senators. Also, Patterson and Izenberg aren't exactly Republicans as we understand them."

"The same has been said of me." There was an awkward silence. The same had in fact been said of him by people in this room.

"Well, yes," said Wilkinson, "but between them and three Democrats—that I know of—Morgan's got her own little bipartisan voting bloc in the Senate. Does that concern you, Mr. President?"

"As a matter of fact, it scares the hell out of me."

Grimes spoke up for the first time. "Speaking of things that should scare the hell out of you, have you heard the latest from Oklahoma City?"

"Is the recount still going on?"

"Yes," she said, "and it doesn't look good for us, but that's not the bad news. The bad news is, Diggins has already said he's not going to concede. He says he doesn't give a damn what the courts say—he's not going to let Oklahoma get taken over by 'foreign invaders.' And Lofton is backing him up."

"Does Lofton have any power?"

"Nope. He's term-limited out."

"So what are they going to do? Move to Texas and form a government in exile?"

"Something like that, actually. I don't know the exact details of what they think they're planning."

"What's Haralson saying?"

"He's saying he'll respect the will of the voters, that if the count comes out in his favor he'll work for all the people of Oklahoma with lots of emphasis on 'all' and he 'trusts Gov. Lofton and my opponent to honor the norms of a democratic society.'"

"Do they have to be so goddamned self-righteous?" muttered Sen. Turgeon. "'Ooh, look at us, we're the Democrats, we're *nice*, we Honor the Norms, unlike *those* subhuman animals—"

Pratt coughed. "Time to get back on track," he said. "As I see it, there are still some parts of our agenda that we'll be able to move forward with next year."

"With all due respect, Mr. President," said Sen. Brearley, "what I think you mean is that there are still parts of *your* agenda you can move forward with. *Our* agenda, on the other hand"—he gestured around the table—"for at least the next two years, it's deader than King Tut's nuts." That was a phrase he used a lot. It hadn't caught on yet. But judging by their expressions, most of the people around the table at least agreed with the sentiment. The agenda Pratt had run on in the first place—more drug law reform, getting started on sentencing reform—was a lot more popular with Democrats than with his fellow Republicans.

"And don't try blaming all this on the so-called 'Monsoon,'" Brearley continued. "We could've had our tax cuts during the first hundred days if you'd been willing to fight for them. The weather was fine then. But you just had to do drug law reform and currency reform and everything to save taxpayer money except *not taking their money!*"

"And if we had cut taxes," said Pratt, "where would we be now?"

For six or seven seconds by the clock, no one spoke. They just sat there glaring at him or each other and poking at their eggs in a desultory way. Maybe half the people around the table genuinely believed that if you cut taxes, the resulting economic growth would bring you more revenue than if you'd left them where they were. The other half knew this was nonsense, but regarded cutting government revenue as an end in itself. And by acting as though he'd somehow anticipated the disasters of the last two years, Pratt had just offended all of them.

"There is one good piece of news," said Grimes in a tone of deliberate cheer.

"What is it?" said Wilkinson.

"We're finally rid of Darling," she said. "They voted him out. No more playing games with the ShameList, no more unsolicited opinions on Israel… I never thought I'd be glad to see the last of a Republican, but he's a special case." The other Republicans nodded in agreement.

DECEMBER 1:

GOVERNOR ALPERT, IN THE INFINITE depths of his mercy, had decided to wait until the day after Thanksgiving to evacuate the last families from Smith Island. That Thanksgiving had been a hard one, with nine people sharing what might be their last meal together in a house that two of them had lived in for the better part of fifty years and six others had moved into this summer after having to leave their own home.

The day after Thanksgiving, the day they moved everyone and everything into a house in a new development in St. Mary's County (and why there? Why not Somerset County? Only Alpert seemed to know)... that had been a worse day.

Today, however, broke all records. The authorities, having no record of the Bradshaws as part of the population of Smith Island, chose this rainy morning to evict every member of her family but her maternal grandparents from the housing development. The police herded them onto a shuttle bus and sent them... nobody seemed to know where.

Mr. Roberts took calls and texts from them all day, trying to keep track of where they were while also trying to get hold of the state agencies and find out what was happening and why. Isabel, meanwhile, drove around Maryland in the rain in her father's old gas-guzzling, no-self-driving, not-even-any-GPS truck, having no plan other than to find her family, bring them back to her apartment for the night and find *somewhere* for them tomorrow.

Now she was seated in the office of a Mrs. Dew, whose exact title she was uncertain of. Mrs. Dew was small, black, wore heavy bifocals, and looked closer to seventy than sixty.

"First, I went to St. Mary's City," she said, glossing over a three-hour drive with a couple of rounds of heavy traffic. "I spent about an hour in town trying to find out where they were and getting the runaround. Finally Pop called and said they were headed for Annapolis. So, another hour and forty-five minutes to get to Annapolis and right when I'm right in the middle of town, I get a call from Mr. Roberts saying whoops, the place I want is actually in Lanham." To avoid sounding whiny, Isabel decided not to go into detail about her adventures navigating downtown Annapolis, which would have been a time-consuming task even with GPS and was next to impossible without it. She'd heard it said that people in Annapolis live twenty to thirty minutes longer than the national average because the Grim Reaper keeps having to stop and ask directions. "So..." *after another fucking hour on the road...* "here I am. And here they apparently aren't."

"Well, no, they wouldn't have been sent here," said Mrs. Dew. "Let me see…" She consulted her computer.

"It looks as though your parents had a talk with DHR yesterday," she said, "They were looking to see what kind of public assistance would be appropriate."

"Only out of desperation," said Isabel. "The last thing any of us want is to be asking for any kind of help. All Pop needs is a roof over his head at night within walking distance of a dock and he can start earning money again and we won't be any more of a burden."

"Is that all?"

"Well, Pop-pop still needs his medication, so there's that."

"It looks like they were turned down," said Mrs. Dew. "I'm trying to find out—wait, your father has a *boat*?"

"Oh, for fuck's sake!"

Mrs. Dew gave her a disapproving look over the tops of her bifocals.

"Sorry. But the boat is a business necessity. He's a waterman. You need a boat for that. It's not like it's a yacht or something."

"I understand that," she said.

"Here's the thing," said Isabel, pulling a printout out of her purse. "The state already owes us money. They said so themselves. Pop is the legal owner of the Bradshaw property—the bank made that very clear. When the state took that property, they were supposed to compensate him. Instead, they sent us this IOU basically saying, 'We'll pay you the fair property value as soon as we can afford it.'"

"Plus interest."

"Right. But you know what that means, right? They're going to wait until coastal property values hit rock bottom, then pay us off with some loose change they found in the sofa. Plus interest."

"Do you think the state would be doing that if we had a choice?" said Mrs. Dew. "You have any idea how many miles of coastline we're talking about?"

"Well, it depends on how you measure it and whether you're at low tide or—"

"That was a rhetorical question, Ms. Bradshaw. Now, when your older sister and Mr. Freitag broke up, the house got sold. What happened to the money?"

"Rod got half, and God only knows what he did with it. Chelsey's half went straight into a trust fund for Jourdain's education. If we tried to get it out of there and use it for ourselves—which we would not do—Mr. Roberts would be legally required to stop us. It's not money we can spend." Isabel sighed. "Look, I'm trying very hard to keep my temper, but what the… what exactly is the problem? My family has been paying into the system all their lives, and now they need a little bit of help and you're all acting like they're trying to rip you off."

"Ms. Bradshaw. I believe you. If it were up to me, I would help your family. I'm just trying to understand why somebody else said no." She folded her hands, set them on her desk and looked at Isabel squarely. "Are you looking for somebody to blame?"

Isabel could feel her face getting hotter. Her fingernails pierced the cheap upholstery on the armrest. *If you're going to suggest this is somehow MY fault…*

"Blame anybody who ever worried that somebody out there was living high off the hog on taxpayer expense," said Mrs. Dew. "I would really like to help your family, but I don't have a lot to work with. This system was built by people whose worst fear in the whole wide world was somebody taking advantage of it who might not really need it. That's why people have trouble getting off welfare—as soon as they start earning a little money, they get dropped from the rolls and lose a lot more. That's why you have to be just about broke to get public assistance. Especially these days, when the whole state's running on a shoestring. Any excuse to say no."

Okay… that's fair. And it did kind of remind Isabel of things her parents had said—especially back during the debate over UBI. Which was why she tried not to talk too much about politics with them. Chelsey wasn't like that, but only because any mention of politics made her eyes glaze over. Kristen wasn't like that either, because she seemed to think real Christians ought not to be that way. *She's probably right.*

"All right," said Isabel. "Apart from personally overthrowing the government and society, what is it I should be doing right now? I mean, forget economic assistance. I just want to know where they are."

"Why don't you just call them yourself? One of them's got to have a phone."

Oops. Isabel kept her armphone turned off while she was driving unless the vehicle could at least partly drive itself. She'd forgotten that was an option. It wasn't like the state was taking them prisoner… probably. She hurriedly selected the first family number to come up, which happened to be Kristen's.

Kristen's face appeared on the screen. "Hi, Isabel," she said. "How're you doing?"

"Never mind me—what about you? What happened to you after Pop called?"

"We stopped in Annapolis and some homeless people got on," she said. "Or I guess I should say, some more homeless people. We stopped in Baltimore and half the bus filled up." She held the phone up to let the camera pan over the bus, revealing what looked like a large group of extras in a post-apocalyptic movie. "Then we stopped in Frederick, Hagerstown, Cumberland…"

"Cumberland?"

"Mmm-hmm."

"Are you still there?" *If they get off the bus and I get started right away, I can meet them there in… two and a half hours? Three? And what the hell are they even doing in Cumberland?*

"No, we crossed the border into West Virginia a couple minutes ago."

WHAT.

"They say we're going west," she said. "But I guess that's pretty obvious. I'm sorry I can't be more specific."

"Do you know who's running the bus?"

"No. They came when the police called, if that's any help."

Isabel made a noise of frustration in her throat.

"Didn't Mr. Roberts say the state was supposed to help us with relocation costs?" said Kristen. "Maybe this is how they're doing it."

"At this point, that wouldn't surprise me."

Kristen held the phone up to the rain-streaked window, giving a blurry glimpse of mountains. "I don't know why we never came out here before," she said. "This place is beautiful. Too bad about the weather."

"Is everybody okay?"

"We're a little nervous, but nothing's actually gone wrong yet. Jourdain's taking a nap. Chelsey's conscious, alert and oriented times three, as they say." In the nursing lingo Kristen had picked up, that meant she knew what was going on around her… or as much as any of them did. "I hope you haven't gone to too much trouble on our account. We're going to be fine."

After the call was over, Isabel just stared blankly at the screen for a moment. *Homeless.* Once you didn't have a roof over your head, there was nothing people couldn't do to you, and not much they wouldn't do just to get you out of their hair. Isabel had always thought of this as one of those social problems that somebody ought to sort out one of these days when the country had some money again. Suddenly it seemed a lot more urgent.

Judging by the look on Mrs. Dew's face, she'd heard every word. "I'm sorry that happened," she said. "But it's quite likely that the state they end up in is going to be better able to take care of them than we will."

Isabel got up. "Mrs. Dew, thank you, you've been very... um..." Isabel's brain spent a couple of seconds buffering. "Honest. Anyway, I won't take up any more of your time."

The drive back was the hard part. The rain splattered against the windshield, and the brakes were making alarming noises. Every instinct Isabel had told her she was going in the wrong direction, that she ought to chase down that bus and find her family and bring them back to her apartment... where there wasn't room for them. She had no money to put them anywhere else, unless they went to live in the storage locker she was renting—and even that was getting to be a noticeable expense.

Okay, now *can I ask Sandy for help?*

Don't even think about it. She's your friend, not your piggy bank.

If she's my friend, she'll want to help?

What if she doesn't want to hear from you? She could have called any time. You shouldn't intrude on her. She doesn't owe you her time and attention.

As she headed east along Route 50 on the way to the Bay Bridge, Isabel wondered if the real reason Annapolis was such a labyrinth was to make it harder to hunt down state officials and strangle them. Those people actually did owe her their time and attention. She distinctly remembered having paid her state taxes back in April.

IN CANADA, DECEMBER ONCE AGAIN brought several feet of snow over the whole nation west of the Rockies, and heavier snow on the northern slopes of the mountains. In the United States, FEMA struggled to bring supplies into the Monsoon-stricken area before winter began in earnest.

Russia, Scandinavia, and the northern British Isles were hit with the same sort of heavy snowfall as Canada. Yevgeny Nardin, his status as president freshly confirmed in a special election, took this opportunity to shut down the airports to all but emergency flights. Those involved in Group 77—or alleged to be involved—who had not already escaped would find it much harder to do so in time.

In China, the work of rebuilding from Typhoon Haiyan was underway. Unfortunately, with so many refugees crowded together in so many places, some sort of disease outbreak was inevitable. No one ever pinned down where it first emerged—cases emerged almost simultaneously in the area of Qingdao, Weifang, and Tianjin—but this was the month of the first recorded cases of a form of H5N1 influenza that spread rapidly from human to human.

Saudi Arabia collapsed into civil war, as a vicious cult of extremists seized the capital without warning. The war in Nigeria simply continued.

In Mexico, if you drew a line from the Rio Grande de Santiago through the city of León to Cabo Rojo, the government more or less controlled everything to the south. To the north, former drug kingpins turned warlords held sway. In the heart of the city of León, one of the warlords had created a fortified area covering several blocks with over one thousand armed men and five times that many civilian hostages.

Government forces surrounded the block, but did not attack. The attack was left to a recently-formed specialist unit of the U.S. Army, equipped with experimental weapons that Pratt wanted to see tested in real-world fighting conditions.

DECEMBER 17:

TRYING TO THINK ABOUT SOMETHING other than her work or the situation her family was in, Isabel turned on the news feed. In Mexico, León had just been liberated. The Mexican army and the U.S. Army were both being very closed-mouthed about the details, just showing footage of thousands of freed hostages and maybe fifty or so surrendering gangsters. *You'd think it would take more guys than that to shut down a city. Are we missing something?*

Maybe there just aren't that many criminals. Which would be good news for places next door… like, say, Texas.

There was no way she could keep her mind off it for very long. Her family was in a FEMA camp—specifically, Texas Foxtrot, down near the border with what used to be Mexico and was now basically no-man's-land.

She hadn't heard from them in more than a week. Depending on which crazy rumor you chose to listen to, that meant they'd either been converted to Islam or converted to biofuel. More reliable voices said that it was hard to keep cell phones charged out there. If anything absolutely terrible had happened to any of them, Isabel liked to think the others would have found a way to let her know, but the sheer absence of information was driving her nuts.

It was dinnertime, but Isabel couldn't make herself eat. She tried to concentrate on the Latania Project. It was still in the conceptual/early design stage, but it would make the Conowingo Project look like something she'd built with her old Lego set. When was the last time anybody tried to create a whole new city from scratch?

While you're sitting here in this apartment sketching out an imaginary sewer system, your family is going through God knows what.

What am I supposed to do? Move in with them? The one thing that would help is the one thing you keep telling me is a terrible idea.

Next year was looking promising. Conowingo would be under construction by then, and there would still be Latania to finish designing. Also, the new governors of Ohio, South Dakota, and Wisconsin had said they would only be giving contracts to American citizens. So at least with them, she might be able to demand something close to what she was worth. Assuming they kept their promises. Isabel wasn't betting her financial security on that, but she was allowing herself a little bit of hope.

You're planning to take money from racist governments.

Why, yes. Yes, I am. And if everything works out, the racists will end up with less money, I'll end up with more money, and the things I design will help people of all races, or whatever races happen to be in the area. Win-win-win.

That can't possibly be how it works.

Also, do you know for a fact that they're even racist? They might just be biased in favor of American citizens. American citizenship isn't defined by race. The only people who think it is are racists. Are you a racist?

There was no answer. *I'm getting good at this.*

ALL EVENING, ON INTO THE night, Isabel kept working. She had a lot of projects to work on, and she wanted to get them done in the next four or five days. She was hoping for a chance to get out to Texas Foxtrot and visit her family.

Visiting them is all very well and good, but it won't help. The only thing left to do is—

No.

Is talk to Sandy Symcox and ask her for help. I don't like the idea, but I'm out of options.

No.

Do you have any better ideas?

Not my job.

She's my friend. Don't you think she'll want to help?

If she were really your friend, wouldn't you have tried harder to keep in touch?

You told me I should wait until she got back in touch with me.

Who says I have to be consistent?

I do. If you don't like it, go hang out in somebody else's head.

You're not making that call.

Isabel put her work aside for the moment and picked up her armphone. She could send a text directly to Sandy without it getting intercepted by a secretary. Come to think of it, there were probably very few people in the world who could do that. Unless Sandy had put somebody else in charge of that number.

Isabel's finger hovered over the screen. And hovered. And hovered. She knew why she needed to do this, but… she couldn't escape the feeling that this was *wrong*. How long had it been since the two of them had actually talked? Was she really going to start things up again by asking for money?

And now Isabel needed to go to the bathroom. *This is ridiculous. I'm wasting time. I don't want to do this. But I need to do this. Why can't I do this?*

While she was washing up afterward, Isabel looked in the mirror. Behind the mirror was the medicine cabinet. Maybe Laurie hadn't been planning anything sinister. Maybe her little gift had been a sincere kindness—a way for Isabel to get around her own hang-ups.

Oh, no. You are NOT doing that.

She knew how to take swee—she'd looked it up online about a month ago, just out of morbid curiosity. *Just once. Just to see what it's like.*

As she was opening the cabinet door, Isabel had a realization. It wasn't just her guilt holding her back from calling Sandy. It was her pride. She was strong, she was smart, she was self-reliant, and she was going to get her family out of this by herself... except she wasn't. Not in any reasonable amount of time.

Isabel had always wondered why pride was considered a sin. It was one thing if you thought you were better than everybody else, but simply thinking *there are people in this world who take more than they give, and right now I'm not one of them, and that makes me happy...* what could possibly be wrong with that?

Now she knew. What was wrong with it was that it was getting in her way. It was stopping her from asking for help when she needed it.

Would swee do anything about that?

Only one way to find out.

Don't you dare.

YOU ARE NOT THE BOSS OF ME.

Says who?

Better do this quick before I change my mind. Isabel took out a packet. Ripped it open. Pulled out something that looked like a small strip of black tape, less than an inch long and less than a quarter of an inch wide.

Stuck it under her tongue.

It didn't taste of anything, but it felt strangely warm.

Spit it out! It's not too late! The active ingredient couldn't survive a trip through the stomach. You had to hold the strip in your mouth for a couple of hours and let it soak through the soft tissues directly into the bloodstream. It took several hours after that for it to make its way through the blood-brain barrier and reach the place where the effect began.

No. I'm going to see this through.

But what if I wake up tomorrow and I don't care about my family?

Then I just won't do anything for them. Which I wasn't doing before, because I couldn't. So things wouldn't be all that different, would they?

Isabel went back to work. She kept working until midnight.

Then she got up and spat out the strip into the trash. It had faded to white.

She went to bed, wondering who she would be when she woke up.

DECEMBER 18:

ISABEL'S ALARM CLOCK WENT OFF at 6:30 a.m. It might have only been her imagination, but even before she'd showered and had her chyq, her thoughts felt clearer and colder inside her head.

Maybe not colder. But definitely clearer. As if all her life, her mind had been a band playing for an audience that kept holding little conversations or talking on the phone or outright heckling... and for the first time, the audience had decided to shut up and listen.

And yet she still felt slightly guilty about what she'd done last night. Which shouldn't have been possible if it had worked properly. But then, like a lot of modern pharmaceuticals, Suiamor was sold in doses tailor-made for individual patients. That dose had been formulated for Laurie, who weighed somewhat less than she did.

Isabel had a protein shake for breakfast. *My family needs help.* The problem seemed... still there, but a lot more distant and abstract now.

She was an engineer. She didn't need to feel bad about a problem to solve it. And this was a problem that needed solving, the sooner the better. People who were on her side, who had helped her before and might do so again, needed her help now.

As far as you know, she's still a friend. You're asking for her help as a friend. So do what a friend would do. Make an appointment to talk. Get caught up with her. Spend a little time. If you tell her what's happening with your family, she might volunteer to help of her own accord. It's almost Christmas. If ever there's a time for her to feel giving, this is it.

Isabel sent the message.

I've been thinking about you a lot lately. How've you been?
Is there a chance we could talk face to face sometime soon?

Either she wants to hear from me, or she doesn't. If she does, I move on to the next step. If she doesn't, then the friendship is already over. It's possible that she has a new social circle she feels more comfortable in. Her fellow geniuses. Her fellow billionaires.

If this is so, it isn't my fault, and I'm no worse off than I was before. This was nothing she couldn't have thought before. It was just that now she felt a lot... calmer about it.

DECEMBER 21:

IT WAS EARLY AFTERNOON. ISABEL was trying to do two things at once—finish the last project, and prepare her mental defenses. People who took antiautechthics for medical reasons said that you had to use the time the drug gave you to prepare yourself for when all the negative feelings came back.

She hadn't heard back from Sandy in three days. That bothered her. *Either she doesn't want to talk to me, or she's busy. Either way, sending her another message won't help.*

There was a knock at the door. Isabel looked through the peephole. It was Mr. and Mrs. Comegys.

"Come in."

They were a few years younger than her parents. Mr. Comegys' hair was getting thin on top, but not going completely bald. He'd once been a heavy, burly man, but he'd lost a lot of weight lately. He had that warm, friendly look that more than substituted for conventional handsomeness. Mrs. Comegys was a thin little woman with a face that always looked worried and hair that was probably dyed black. They had a cooler with them.

"We were getting a little worried," said Mrs. Comegys. "We missed you at church the last couple weeks." Isabel didn't go to church out of any fervent belief. She went because her family had always gone, and because that, and a board game club that met on Thursday evenings, and helping with the lighting at a community theater, were the whole of her social life.

"Sorry. I've been really busy with work." *Also, I'm not sure I should be interacting with people until the swee wears off.* "And I've got a trip to get ready for."

"You're really going to Texas for Christmas?" said Mr. Comegys.

"Yeah." They looked impressed. Interstate travel was either a lot harder or a lot more expensive than it used to be, depending on how you went.

"Well, I hope they're doing all right," he said. "It's a damn shame what happened to them."

"Have you heard from Mr. Roberts?" said Mrs. Comegys.

"Yeah. The state is still trying to drag this out in court."

"Damn shame," said Mr. Comegys again. "Well, I've got something you can serve for Christmas dinner." He opened the cooler, took a good-sized chunk of red meat wrapped in tinfoil and handed it to her.

"It's nutria," he said. "Hindquarters and saddle. I got rid of the glands without breaking 'em, so it should be good."

"Well, thank you," said Isabel, "but I can't possibly carry this all the way to Texas. Not on top of all this." She waved a hand at the assembled bags of canned vegetables she was planning to bring.

Mr. Comegys shrugged.

"Eat it yourself," he said. "Bring 'em some extra cans."

Isabel nodded. That made a lot more sense.

And in all honesty, she was glad to have it. Muskrat was rich and delicious—like the dark meat on a turkey, but much more intense. Nutria* wasn't as good as muskrat, and was terrible if you ruptured the scent glands while dressing it out, but it was in season all the time—the sooner the invasive species was hunted to extinction in the Chesapeake, the happier everyone would be.

Being handed a chunk of game woke up something weird and primitive in the bottom of Isabel's mind: *This man is a good provider. Attach yourself to him. He will bring you more meat.* To which the rest of her mind responded *he's already married, stupid. His wife is standing right there. This is not the Neolithic. Shut the fuck up.*

"We've got some beans and stuff in the cupboard we can give you," said Mrs. Comegys.

"Don't do that. Seriously. See, I'm limited to what I can carry in one load." Isabel opened her freezer, moved some stuff around to make room and inserted the nutria meat with a feeling of gratitude. You couldn't say people around here didn't give a rat's ass.

LATE THAT NIGHT, ISABEL WAS finding it hard to concentrate on her work. She could already feel the swee starting to wear off. It wasn't a sudden crash, like what she'd heard coming off a drug high was like. It was more like a part of her had fallen asleep, like her arm if she slept on her side all night, and now the feeling in it was slowly starting to return. She readied her mental

---

* For the uninitiated: The nutria, or coypu (*Myocastor coypus*) is a large, fat, hairy aquatic rodent with orange teeth and a ratlike tail. It's native to South America, but was introduced into the marshes of Louisiana and the Chesapeake Bay area in the twentieth century in the hope that its fur would be of value. It proved highly destructive to wetlands and has been the subject of eradication efforts ever since.

defenses. *I have nothing to be ashamed of. I have done nothing to feel guilty about. I wouldn't have done it for my own sake, but I've got my family to think about. I did the right thing.*

If getting in touch with Sandy was right, why'd it take you so long?

Excuse me? Weren't you telling me not to do it? And aren't you still telling me that?

Like I said, I don't do consistency. You weren't trying to do the right thing. You were trying to avoid shame.

If that was a mistake, then I stopped making it already. That's your cue to shut the fuck up.

Don't I get to—

No. No you don't. I'm wise to you. You're not my God, not my conscience, not my teacher, not my friend.

If I do something that looks like it'll turn out well, you tell me I broke the rules. If I obey the rules, you question my motivations. If I do something with good intentions, you tell me it'll all end in tears. I'm done listening.

All you have is words, and your words are lies.

All you have is feelings, and a headache *is a feeling.*

You have no power over me.

You have no power over me.

You have no power over me.

The feeling of shame began to retreat, but a new feeling arose—embarrassment at doing this. As far as mental health went, it wasn't a good sign when you were sitting alone in the dark repeating something to yourself over and over again.

It's okay. Mental health is like physical health—nobody's ever at 100 percent. Everybody's a little crazy. The important thing is to stay functional.

I won't take swee unless there's no other choice, but I am never *letting this thing stop me again.*

DECEMBER 24:

IT WAS JUST BEFORE NOON, on a hot, dry winter's day at the train station in Del Rio, Texas.

Isabel's journey here was the sort of thing best glossed over for narrative purposes. Given the choice, she would rather have glossed over it herself than gone through every single moment. The eastern and western halves of Amtrak's network had once been joined together at Chicago and New Orleans. The tracks around Chicago were still being repaired or re-repaired, and New Orleans was an abandoned city. So in order to get here from Maryland in a reasonable amount of time, she had to take the train from Union Station to Hattiesburg, Mississippi, transfer to a bus to get to Houston, then transfer back onto the train and head further west. And she had to do all this while schlepping around two bags of groceries, a load of Christmas presents, and her own small personal luggage. And all while trying not to think about the hundreds of dollars all this was costing her—still cheaper than plane tickets— or how much she missed Hunter, who had also left Union Station by train.

Anyway, she was within reasonable driving distance of Texas Foxtrot, and she had summoned a rental car to the train station. She put the presents in the back and got in, putting the canned goods on the passenger seat… or rather, the other passenger seat.

It was Isabel's first experience with a purely self-driven car. There was no steering wheel, no gearshift, no pedals. There was only a screen and a microphone. The microphone was for telling the car where you wanted to go. The screen was for watching videos or reading books, which Isabel couldn't do in a moving vehicle because it always made her carsick. She felt like there at least ought to be a human set of controls in case something went wrong with the computer, like one of those early steamships that had masts and sails so if the engine broke down in the middle of the ocean, they wouldn't all die.

As soon as Isabel had fastened her seatbelt, a message appeared on the screen.

Hello. Where would you like to go?

"Drive me to FEMA Emergency Housing Center Texas Foxtrot."

I don't know where that is.

This was going to be complicated. The camp wasn't on the list of destinations and there was no street address, so Isabel found it in satellite photos on her armphone and patiently recited the GPS coordinates of the front gate.

I'm sorry. I can't go there.

It's not accessible by road.

Pick another destination.

Just to be helpful, it began listing what she assumed were sponsored businesses and tourist destinations within a fifty-mile radius.

"Fuck you," she said. *I'm trying to get to my family for Christmas, and you want me to go to Walgreen's instead? How is that supposed to help?*

I'm sorry. I didn't mean to make you angry.

And like that, the list of suggestions was gone.

You hurt its feelings.

It doesn't have feelings, you fucking liar. It was programmed to recognize words and phrases that signify irritation before somebody loses their shit and breaks the dashboard.

Isabel looked at the manual. It told her to check and make sure she had entered the correct location in a clear voice, and then to call the help number. She called the help number. It told her that all lines were currently busy. *Surprise, surprise.* It also said to check the manual and be sure the answer wasn't in there.

Think. It says the place is not accessible by road. That means it's running on map data, not satellite data... "New destination." She found the GPS coordinates of the spot on the road nearest the front gate. This time, the car started without a problem. Guided by muscle memory, her hands flailed around in the empty spaces where the gearshift and wheel would normally be, and her feet drummed against the floor. The car pulled out of the parking lot and headed down the street.

But before Isabel had gone two blocks, a warning message appeared. A dust storm was coming out of the west. It would be on top of her before she made it to the camp.

I can't drive in this weather.

Pick a place to stop.

A map appeared on the screen. *Somewhere with food,* thought Isabel. *God knows how long I'll have to stay there.* She directed it to the parking lot of a restaurant just outside town.

Wrap me up and keep me safe.

This cutesy message was accompanied by a series of diagrams showing how to take the tarp out of the trunk and cover the car with it so that the front grill and exhaust pipe were both protected. It was supposed to be a two-person job, and the wind was picking up, so Isabel had to plan ahead a little—tying the tarp into place at the windward corner first and letting the wind blow it over the rest of the car before she tied it down. It wasn't that different from getting the tarp over Pop's old skipjack.

By the time she was done, there was a roiling cloud of burnt-orange across the western horizon. There were other cars pulling off the highways, people looking for any place they could take shelter. Isabel decided to go inside while she still had a chance of ordering a meal.

The restaurant was a Cabratería, one of a new restaurant chain in Texas that had the odd ambition to be the Chick-fil-A of goat meat. They offered a small but tasty selection of Mexican-style entrées, all of which included goat. Isabel had only heard of them because they'd run a series of targeted ads online and there had been a mix-up at the ad agency. An ad reading "You've Earned It! Take Advantage of Cabratería's Senior Discounts" was shown at a Fear of the Onyx fan site, while another ad exhorted AARP members to "Feast on the Flesh of the Goat." Isabel ordered a medium burrito and a cup of chyq.

As she ate, Isabel considered the ingredients of the burrito—goat, salsa, tortilla wrap, cheese—where they came from, and how long they were likely to remain affordable. The goat meat was no mystery—goats could live just about anywhere. And it seemed to be all meat, which was worth noting. Go to almost any fast-food restaurant these days and they'd be bragging—*bragging*—that their burgers were "50% Real Beef." For about ten dollars more, you could get "75% Real Beef." Only high-end restaurants served burgers made of pure bovine muscle and fat.

As for the salsa, you could grow tomatoes and onions almost anywhere. A little research on her phone told her garlic and chili peppers were pretty adaptable too. Isabel wasn't sure about cilantro, which turned out to be another name for coriander, but it wasn't like they needed a lot of it. You could probably grow it in greenhouses.

The tortilla wrap had an odd sweetness to it. Probably they'd mixed in some potato and cassava flour to keep the price low. The cheese... was the government still subsidizing and stockpiling it? It didn't seem like the sort of thing Pratt would do, but it wasn't like he was king.

Isabel kept one eye out the window. Now the storm was a wall of dust-colored cloud that stretched out beyond the highway and reached higher than she could see through the window. It wasn't obvious when the storm engulfed the restaurant—the parking lot gradually grew hazy, and the sky turned orange. At the table next to her, an old man who'd been a small child in 1940 was telling his grandchildren, or possibly his great-grandchildren, about seeing the last of the big dust storms blow through, the sky going dark and everything getting covered with grime. Some people were still driving out there.

The sky darkened to red. Isabel thought about what she'd read about the original Dust Bowl. It had been an agricultural screwup—during a decades-long wet spell, farmers had started planting wheat in places wheat was never meant to grow. Then a terrible drought hit and all that plowed land dried out and started blowing east. Eventually the drought ended, and the land in question had become pasture, which it should have been from the beginning.

The sky darkened to brown. Only the dim outlines of nearby buildings were still visible.

The sky, and everything else outside the window, darkened to black—but not like night. Isabel could see the lights over the parking lot peeking through the torrents of dust and sand, but they did nothing.

If I have grandchildren and great-grandchildren, she thought, *I'll tell them about this.*

Then she thought *if I have grandchildren and great-grandchildren, they'll probably think this is normal.*

EVEN AFTER THE STORM, THE drive the rest of the way to Texas Foxtrot was a lot slower. There was so much grit everywhere that in places, it was like driving on dirt roads.

Isabel's car finally approached the camp, which didn't look any better on the ground than it had in the satellite photos. First there was a line of fence topped with barbed wire that ran perpendicular to the road and stopped a few feet from the ditch. Then there was a line of what looked like portable classrooms. Then came trailers and shabby-looking cabins in neat rows, with alternating wide and narrow gaps between them. The strange thing was that Isabel could definitely see fences in the distance, on three sides, but no fence at all on the side facing the road. It made the camp look both evil and half-assed, as if built by a totalitarian regime that couldn't finish anything without getting bored and wandering off.

The entrance was dominated by a crowded parking lot with a portable classroom beyond it. There were cars parked on the side of the road near the entrance. The rental car pulled over and came to a stop just before the entrance.

We're here.

"Do you see the driveway up ahead, to the right?"

Yes.

"Enter that driveway." *That's where I wanted you to go in the first place*, she thought, but there was no point saying it.

"Look for a parking place."

The parking lot is already full.

Of course. She wasn't the only person wanting to visit her family on Christmas.

"Pull over to the side." It did, but the engine kept running.

I'm sorry. I can't stay here.

This isn't a legal parking place.

"Not a problem," said Isabel, grabbing her overnight bag and groceries. "Once I'm out, you're going back to the car rental. Come back *here tomorrow* at *eleven a.m.*" She made sure to put extra clarity into her voice for the key words and phrases.

Isabel took her bags out, closed the driver's side door and took one step toward the back of the car—but that was all she had time for before the car pulled forward, went past her and turned to go out the same way it had come in. Apparently it thought she wanted it to go back right now.

"No, wait!" she shouted, but it was too late. The car took to the road and disappeared into the distance with the presents still in the trunk. Isabel spent a moment cursing quietly, but at least nothing in there was perishable, and she had the groceries with her. Whatever else, her family would have something for Christmas dinner.

An electronic signboard out front directed everyone to get in line at the entrance, so she did. About an hour later, Isabel's arms were aching from carrying the groceries, and she was glad she hadn't tried to carry them and the presents into the camp all at once. This place had looked so small on the map. Barely two miles square.

But at least now she was at the head of the line. "No, this is *not* a concentration camp," someone was saying in weary tones to a white-haired man. "I don't care what the news told you. Seriously, look around. You see any guard towers? Or guards, for that matter? Machine guns? Big mean dogs?"

Isabel had to admit this was a fair point. There were no towers or guards, and the only dog in sight was a harmless-looking puppy that a little girl was clutching in her arms.

"But the fences!" said the white-haired man.

"Yeah, the fences kinda throw people when they first get here. If you look closely, though, you'll notice they're not all one fence. That's because we didn't set them up. Local landowners set them up on their side of the property lines. Which they had every right in the world to do."

"And do they surround this camp?"

"Well… most of it. But everybody here is free to leave."

"Then why would they stay here?"

"Where would they go? Nobody here has a car, and the nearest town's nine miles down the road. Cops on the road see you walking, they'll pick you up for hitchhiking even if you got your hands in your pockets. And if you do get to town, you'll last about five minutes before you get arrested for loitering. Then they'll dump you right back here. But none of that is our fault." *True*, thought Isabel, *but it does kind of stretch the definition of "free to leave." God bless America, the only country ever to create a gulag archipelago by accident.*

"I can help the next person over here!" came a man's voice. *That's my cue.*

There were two people at the open desk—a white guy with a narrow face and a fringe of dark hair on an otherwise bald head, and a tiny Hispanic woman in a white lab coat whose face was half hidden behind the tablet. Their nameplates read Lawrence Bardwell and Ashley Natividad.

"Hi. My name is Isabel Bradshaw. That's B-R-A-D-S-H-A-W. I'm looking for my family. Same name."

"The Bradshaws?" Lawrence asked. "That would be… a couple in their late seventies, a couple in their early fifties, a sixteen-year-old boy, and a four-year-old girl?"

"That's some of them," said Isabel. "There should also be two women, ages twenty-five and nineteen."

Lawrence shook his head. "No sign of them. Just the others."

WHAT. "But… they should be here. They should have arrived with everybody else." Isabel took a couple of slow, deep breaths to keep herself from panicking.

"Hold on a minute. Let me check the entrance logs."

"They arrived on the third of this month, if that's any help."

"Yes, it is. Thank you… you're right. There they are, Chelsey and Kristen."

His face brightened, then clouded over. "Okay, I think I've figured out what happened. See, you can't have more than six people living in a residence at the same time. It's against the rules. My guess is, those two were held back until they could be relocated and then we lost track of them."

"You lost track of them." *A teenage girl. And a woman who can be roofied with chocolate. You lost track of them. I'm not asking you to go around defending fair maidens with sword in hand, but aren't you just a tiny bit embarrassed right now?*

"Yeah. Either they were assigned somewhere else and it didn't get recorded or they went off on their own looking for an unused residence."

"What do you mean, assigned somewhere else? Another camp?"

"We don't do that. It's disruptive and it wastes fuel. I'm almost certain they're somewhere in this camp. I wish I could tell you where."

"I wish you could too," said Isabel, in lieu of grabbing him by his pencil neck and shaking him until he agreed to grow a competence.

"Try to understand," he said. "This time last year there were 600,000 people in this camp. Four months ago, we were down to 84,000. Now we're up to just over 500,000. Ideally, we should still be able to keep track of everybody, but with that kind of turnover, with a system that was slapped together in a rush over a year ago and the state refusing to provide any resources... you see the problem."

Isabel sighed. "Here's the thing," she said. "Chelsey can only sort of take care of herself. She got a bad Jellicoe last year."

"I'm so sorry," said Lawrence. "We do make a special effort to keep tabs on people with disabilities. What about the other one—Kristen? She have any issues?"

"No." *Apart from being too nice for her own good.*

"Then it's probably for the best if they're together. She can look after Chelsey better than we could. I'm sorry I can't tell you where they are, though.

"I can tell you where to find most of your family." He took out a paper map and unfolded it to show the whole camp. He took a red pen and drew an X on a residence about two thirds of the way to the northwestern side. Then he drew a path from the front to the residence. It took only two turns, and looked walkable even with armloads of groceries.

"I think this is your best bet," he said. "You don't have to follow it exactly. If you stick to the main paths, you'll be all right. If you get thirsty, these buildings with the little wave markings are the water distribution centers. Oh, and this area right here, south of the western health center? You might want to stay out of that."

"Why that area in particular?"

"You know about sex offender clusters?" said Lawrence. "Those neighborhoods where you get a lot of sex offenders 'cause it's the one place around they can move to?"

"What about them?"

"A lot of cities have found ways to break them up—find some place in the middle of the cluster and designate it as a public park or something. Morgan's pretty much cleaned them out of New York State. I'm sure it boosts the property values, but all those creeps have gotta go somewhere, and…"

"Let me guess. They ended up here."

"Yeah. They're kinda concentrated right here." Lawrence tapped a spot on the map.

"No, they're not," said Ashley. "They had to move back in September. They're in the western corner now."

"You sure? I didn't hear about it. Anyway, this is the straightest way to get to your family, and I'm pretty sure it's safe." There were several questions Isabel wanted to ask at this point, such as *You're "pretty sure" it's safe, but why the uncertainty? And if the sex offenders had to move, who made them move?* But the line behind her was getting really long. She couldn't stay here all day.

"Have you had booster shots?" said Ashley.

Isabel paused. Had she ever gotten around to getting booster shots? She couldn't remember, but she suspected not. There always seemed to be something else to take care of. And she certainly hadn't brought her medical records here.

"If you're not sure, you can get them now," the nurse said, opening a small refrigerator by her desk and taking out a box. "You're not anti-vaccine, are you?"

"No. Why?"

"Some of the other residents… they don't have a sense of humor about that. They heard about the outbreak in Texas Charlie and they're afraid. You'll notice the graffiti when you go out that way." She approached Isabel and took a set of needles out of the box. "You want to look away?"

"Why?" There might have been a time in Isabel's childhood when she was bothered by needles, but that had been many years and allergy treatments ago. She got out of the way of the line and rolled up her sleeve.

Seeing Lawrence's desk from this angle, she noticed the photo of two children on it, and the ring on his finger. This guy had a family, and here he was on Christmas Eve making at least some kind of effort to help an enormous mob of strangers. And it seemed like when he failed to help, it was the system's fault, not his. And for all she knew, Chelsey had gone off looking for a cabin on her own, and Kristen had followed her. It was the sort of thing they'd do.

But if they ended up in the middle of the sex offenders' ghetto, I'm going to beat his pointy little face into the back of his skull as a statement of principle.

AS SOON AS SHE GOT through the rear door, Isabel saw the graffiti Ashley had been referring to. It was in huge red letters sprayed on the side of a trailer, and it said MATAREMOS A LOS ANTIVACUNISTAS SIN PREVIO AVISO. Isabel's Spanish was pretty rusty, but she couldn't help noticing that the first word in this sentence was a form of the verb "to kill" that looked kind of first-person-plural, and the final phrase was "without prior notice." Trying very hard not to look like an anti-vaxxer, she ventured into the camp.

If you focused on the people rather than the cabins and trailers, it didn't look so bad. Every fifty feet or so, Isabel passed somebody else visiting family and friends, bringing gifts and exchanging hugs. *Well, it is Christmas Eve. Probably this place wasn't so great back in July.*

The only thing about the people that was odd was the ones wearing white armbands with the letter M on them. They were all adults or older teenagers, predominantly male, and all armed—but not all with the same weapons. Isabel saw a woman with a small handgun in a holster next to a man with what was obviously a hunting rifle slung over his back. Their weapons were openly displayed, but not held in their hands. They didn't seem to be doing much— just standing around like crossing guards, watching everybody. Sometimes somebody waved at them, or stopped and said hello.

When Isabel looked toward the places where all these people were living, that made her feel a lot less Christmassy. The homes ranged from new trailers, to old worn trailers, to relatively well-built cabins, to cabins that didn't look fit for human habitation. A lot of the cabins had bright blue FEMA tarps stretched over boards in place of a roof, which explained why the people living in these camps were called "tarpies." They couldn't be all that safe, either—on every third block, there was a trailer or cabin that had been gutted by fire. Her family had come here not too long ago, and well after the influx of refugees from the Monsoon. They wouldn't have gotten first choice. And God only knew where Chelsey and Kristen had ended up.

It got worse. The residences were arranged in blocks. When you looked at the blocks, you noticed that they tended to be kind of monolithic. There were blocks where everybody was Hispanic, blocks where everybody was black, blocks that were mainly white with some Asians and South Asians, and blocks where everybody was white. *Has this place been taken over by gangs? Like prison or something? Please tell me Kristen and Scott didn't have to get swastika tattoos. That would make it really hard for them to find a job.*

Isabel wondered if the whole camp was self-segregated like this. For whatever it was worth, the mysterious White Armband Guys were drawn from every race and ethnicity, and mixed freely. That was a good sign. Unless it wasn't. After all, the only area that was guaranteed to be multiracial was the Pervertopia Lawrence had mentioned—sex crimes weren't the exclusive province of any one group.

Relax. People don't look afraid of the White Armband Guys. They seem comfortable around them. You should be too.

THE BRADSHAW CABIN LOOKED MORE or less okay, but it had a tarp for a roof. Mom-mom answered the door when Isabel knocked. She looked thinner than Isabel remembered her, but her face still brightened up.

"Isabel! Come in! It's so good to see you! What have you got there?"

"Just some food. I'll get you the presents tomorrow." Isabel looked around. "Where is everybody?"

"Out helping fix up the Tuplin place. Did you carry all this here yourself?" Isabel nodded.

"I'll put it away, then. You go keep an eye on Jourdain."

What followed was half an hour of Isabel reading books aloud to Jourdain. She had the feeling she wasn't doing it right—Kristen was much better at giving different voices to different characters.

Once her niece had curled up next to her and fallen asleep, she spent the next hour listening to Pop-pop tell some of the old stories from Tilghman Island—

the terrible shipwreck of '79, the night of the 75-ton catch. She'd heard these stories before, but Isabel wanted to get them straight in her mind. There was something about triumphs and tragedies on a small, human scale that had a strange appeal for her right now. In a world that went through human life and fortune like it was so much fossil fuel, it was all the more important to listen to those stories and try to remember them.

Then the rest of the family came back. "I understand Chelsey and Kristen are living somewhere else," said Isabel. "What happened there?"

"The guys at the front desk were supposed to assign them somewhere," said Pop. "They never got around to it. The girls waited until it was starting to get dark, then they went looking for a place on their own."

"They said they figured it was what you'd do in their place," said Scott.

Rather than wait around all night, I might do that. And at least now I know the rest of the family hasn't lost contact with them. Still, it alarmed Isabel a little to think that other people were using her as a role model. That was a lot of responsibility.

"So where are they?"

"There's a cabin right near the middle of camp. It's pretty bad, but nothing's happened to them."

"Okay," said Isabel. "Wait—there's already six of you here. Does this mean I need to spend the night with them?"

"I hope not," said Mom. "I don't think it's safe where they are."

"I don't want to get you guys in trouble." *Also, I kinda gave up on the whole safety thing when I came here. And I'd hate myself if I were any safer than Kristen.* "And I really want to see them."

"It's not that bad where they are," said Scott. "There's people looking out for them."

"Who's doing it?" said Isabel. "Who's in charge around here, anyway?"

Scott looked at Pop. Pop sat down and told her the story.

As Isabel listened, she realized that this camp wasn't nearly as bad as she'd thought it would be. Her mistake had been comparing it to prison. Take a bunch of young males, mostly unmarried, raised in dysfunctional families and bad neighborhoods, unemployed and self-selected for violence, and throw them together in a crappy place, and they organized themselves into gangs. Do the same thing to men and women from every age group, every walk of life, whole families, and they organized themselves into… churches. Or rather, some of them did. The rest joined later out of a need for mutual aid and some kind of community.

Which was why the Bradshaws were living on this block—this was a Methodist community, and that was the church they'd grown up with. Probably nobody but the pastor could have said how Methodism was different from other branches of Christianity, but that hardly mattered. It was a familiar name, and in a place like this that was more than good enough. People got together for worship, and then stayed to see who needed what and who was available to help. They weren't waiting for God to step in and fix this place up. Instead, they seemed to have gotten the idea that the Lord helped those who helped themselves, and even if He didn't, hey, at least you'd just helped yourself.

And not all the groups were churches. There was an American Legion, a bikers' club, and a gaming group. Scott took her map of the camp and added to it, showing her the various churches and other groups and over which blocks they held sway. Isabel would have felt better about the human race in general if one of them had been "The Organization of People who have Agreed to Assist One Another on a Regular Basis out of Mutual Self-Interest."

So that was how individual neighborhoods were organized within the camp. There was also a handful of teachers and medical personnel among the displaced, who'd gotten together to help FEMA provide a certain limited amount of education and health care to the residents.

But what was really holding the whole thing together was the camp militia—something Isabel hadn't even known existed until this conversation. It consisted of everybody in camp that had weapons and was trained to use them, or wanted to be trained. They held exercises twice a week. They had no guns beyond the ones they'd brought, and their only uniform was the armbands Isabel had seen. But they were the ones who had strong-armed the sex offender community into moving out to the western corner of the camp, well away from anyone with children. Also well away from her sisters. *One less thing to worry about.*

FOR ALL HIS ASSURANCES THAT this camp was really pretty safe, Scott accompanied Isabel to Chelsey and Kristen's cabin. According to the map, it was right on the border between "Iglesia Catolica" and "some kind of Muslim thing." The neighborhood looked… it wouldn't be fair to say *bad*, because all the neighborhoods in Texas Foxtrot looked equally bad. This particular one looked like somebody else's bad neighborhood.

Racist.

Shove it. In College Park, Isabel had gotten used to being in a minority, and sometimes the only white girl in the room—the others being immigrants from all parts of the world. Not only that, other white students tended to be from white-collar, upper-middle-class backgrounds, and she felt like she had only slightly more in common with them than with the kids from Brazil, Mongolia, Pakistan, or Liberia. But of course at College Park, there was really only one ethnic group… students.

"We're here," said Scott, gesturing at a cabin between two trailers. It looked worse than Pop's. Not only were the roofs made of tarps, but parts of the walls appeared to be backdrop panels from a theater set. "Listen, I gotta go. I promised the Burchams I'd help get their place wired and I'm already late."

"See you tomorrow." Isabel knocked on the door—not hard, but the door shook a little in its frame. "Chelsey? Kristen? It's me."

From somewhere inside came Kristen's voice: "Isabel! Great! Come in!" Isabel tried the door and found it either locked or stuck—she couldn't tell from the feel of it. She was about to start rattling it when Chelsey said "Careful— you'll break it. Let me get that."

Also not a good sign, thought Isabel. She was starting to forget what good signs looked like. There was a click of a key in a lock, and Chelsey opened the door for her. Her dark-blond curls were hanging in her face. She was wearing pajama bottoms, no makeup, and one of Isabel's old College Park sweatshirts. The disparity between her bust and Isabel's was such that the sweatshirt only came down to her belly button.

"Before you come in," said Chelsey, "there's something I have to tell you. We kind of have a bedbug problem."

"You're shitting me, right?"

"I shit you not."

Isabel stood there for a moment. This would explain why they hadn't moved Jourdain in with her mother.

"Fuck it," she finally said. She stepped through the door and shut it behind her. That done, she drew Chelsey into a hug.

"Merry Christmas, blondie." Isabel would never be able to explain to anyone outside the family why she called Chelsey "blondie" when Kristen was even blonder.

"Same to you, chunkybutt."

"So how bad is it?"

"We covered the bedroom in bean leaves," said Kristen, pulling out a chair for Isabel. "Those are supposed to work. They've got these little hairs and the bugs sort of get their legs stuck on them."

"Where'd you get them?"

"There's a farm east of here. It belongs to a Mr. Williams. We trade with him sometimes, but he gave me the bean leaves for free. He says with winters so mild, he can grow things over the winter now. He's a very nice man." Kristen paused. "You know, I keep hearing how the locals don't get along with us as well as they used to—especially since the midterms—but I don't see it. The few people I've talked to have been very friendly."

"She bats her pretty blue eyes at 'em and tells 'em Jesus loves 'em, and they'll give her anything," said Chelsey. "And don't worry. If Mr. Williams decides he wants something in return, I'll take care of it." Isabel was pretty sure she didn't mean money. This seemed like a great time to change the subject.

"I know this family doesn't do begging," she said, "but under the circumstances… has anybody heard from Sandy?"

"Nope," said Chelsey. "Not a word. You really all that surprised?"

"Well… yeah. I mean, we're still friends. At least, we used to be."

Chelsey laughed. "You're supposed to be the smart one, chunkybutt," she said. "Girl spends half her time getting sued by people she used to be friends with. Did you hear she even screwed over her pop?"

"No… I didn't." Isabel had never met Sandy's father, or heard much about him.

"Him and her used to be co-owners of the diamond business—it started out in his garage. A couple years later, she bought out his share for ten million dollars."

"Unless he gave her eleven million to begin with, that sounds pretty darn good."

"His wife didn't think so. A little while later she sued Sandy for like a billion dollars, but it got thrown out of court. You know… rich people."

"That sounds like a story I want to hear the other side of."

"Anyway, I never liked her," said Chelsey. "Nobody did. She was such a know-it-all. But after the thing with the bee, Mom and Pop just had to keep her around. Like a good-luck charm." She sighed. "All that time she spent hanging out with you, telling you about stars and planets and shit… you really think a girl would spend her free time with somebody five years younger if she had friends her own age?"

I never thought of that. Why didn't I ever think of that? But that left Chelsey open to an obvious response. "Excuse me—you married somebody twelve years older."

"Yeah, and look how that worked out."

"You want something to drink?" said Kristen.

"What have you got?"

Opening the little fridge, Kristen found that they had two beers left, which was awkward. If there'd been three, they all could have had one. If there'd been one, Isabel would have been given it as the guest. If they'd had some glasses, they could have poured two-thirds of a beer into each glass. To resolve the situation, Chelsey drank one, and then she drank the other.

There were no tablets or other computers here, apart from their phones and Chelsey's e-reader. (Which was just as well. This wasn't a place Isabel would have wanted to keep anything expensive.) Once dinner was out of the way, there was nothing much to do except talk. And for once, Isabel had to do more than her share of the talking—Kristen wanted to hear her stories, and the beer had hit Chelsey's Jellicoed brain, so her reception wasn't clear enough to take part in the conversation.

Isabel tried telling them about the biofuel plants she'd helped build and the trouble with Group 77, but there was a limit to how technical she could get before Kristen's eyes started to glaze over. Chelsey's eyes were already glazed over—the Jellicoe again.

It turned out that Kristen had actually been having some adventures of her own. Texas Foxtrot was full of schizophrenics and other people who needed regular medication but weren't getting it any more. So when they got violent or suicidal, somebody had to come along and either physically restrain them, talk them down, or both. Kristen was turning out to have something of a knack for the latter. "A woman I met last week said we were better than police," she said. "She always used to be afraid to call the cops because she'd heard of mentally ill people who got shot by them. We always go in unarmed."

"You're kidding," said Isabel. "Unarmed. In a room with a crazy stranger."

"Yeah. The idea is, if… things go wrong in there, that's when they send in somebody armed."

"So you find out if these people are really dangerous by… going in there and seeing if…"

Kristen shrugged. "Is there another way?"

Isabel took her by the hand. "Damn, girl, you… some time when I wasn't looking, you grew an *awesomeness*." Part of her wanted to tell Kristen to stop doing this, but the rest of her knew she had no right to make such a demand. Tomorrow she'd be headed back to Maryland, Kristen would still be here, and everyone here would still have the same problems. And Kristen wasn't a little girl anymore.

"I just tell myself it's what you would do," she said. Isabel wanted to say that this was not what she would do, but then she remembered that she'd knowingly spent the night in bed with a sweehead two months ago, so she decided to keep her mouth shut.

"And I pray, of course," said Kristen. "Can't go in without backup."

The thought of Kristen doing anything dangerous, even with backup from the Supreme Being, still seemed wrong to Isabel. Her little sister was one of those people that other people were supposed to put themselves in harm's way on behalf of, not one who went there herself. Or so she'd always seemed. It looked like there was more to her than anyone had realized.

And at least this meant that her sisters were somewhat more likely to be safe here. In a place like Texas Foxtrot, being useful to the community was probably better protection than a lock on a door. But then, all sorts of things were better protection than the lock on the door to this place.

AFTER FIVE, IT STARTED GETTING dark. Over dinner, three cans of reheated beans, which Kristen still managed to sound genuinely grateful for while saying grace, they started reminiscing about the good old days of five to ten years ago.

"It's the little things that get to you," said Kristen. "You know what I miss? Bananas*. Real, ripe bananas. The kind that tasted like… um…"

"Like bananas?" said Chelsey, who was starting to come back to herself.

"Well, I didn't want to say so, but yeah."

"I know what you mean," said Chelsey. "I miss cheap coffee—real coffee. Remember when you could get it at Royal Farms? Or 7-11?"

---

* The spread of Panama disease among banana plants has caused a severe shortage.

"Chyq tastes pretty much the same," said Isabel.

"Blasemphy and lies," said Chelsey, who never could say "blasphemy" but seemed to enjoy trying.

"That's what I love about you," said Kristen at almost the same moment. "You take everything in stride. You don't let things get to you." *How little you know*, thought Isabel.

Kristen rested a hand on Isabel's wrist. "It helps me face the future knowing you're still out there," she said. "That way I know whatever happens, one of us is always gonna be okay."

Isabel looked into Kristen's clean blue eyes and tried to smile. *No. Not good enough. If I'm okay and you're not okay, that's not okay.* She couldn't even relate to the thread of the conversation. For her, it had never been the little things. It had always been… everything.

ISABEL HAD TO STOP FOR a moment when she stepped into the bedroom. What she saw was one of those scenes that was so weird you couldn't take it all in at one glance. The stripped-down bunks, the naked women, the hammocks, the leaves—they didn't add up to anything the brain could immediately recognize.

There were six bunks, three on each side. All the pillows, blankets, and mattresses were gone. Scattered over the floor and the bunks were leaves— mostly green, but some of them starting to turn yellow. A sealable plastic bag, full of Chelsey's and Kristen's clothes, hung from a nail driven into the doorjamb. A small light sat on an exposed beam on the far wall, illuminating the room. A space heater, aimed at the middle of the room, sat on the floor. The wooden floor. Isabel suddenly remembered the burned-down cabins she'd seen.

Two wooden poles were resting with their ends on the middle bunks, lying across the aisle. Three hammocks made of nylon rope were hanging from these poles. Chelsey and Kristen were in two of them, leaving the middle one empty.

Both of them were naked, without even blankets. Kristen was lying on her left side with her legs tucked in front of her. She was already asleep, her left arm curled under her head and her right arm across her chest and draped over the side of the hammock, her pink fingertips hanging over the floor as if to taunt whatever bedbugs were already trapped on the bean-leaf cilia. Chelsey was lying flat on her back, reading an e-book by the light of that little lamp. Her breasts had flopped down to cover her armpits. It was like a porn scene made by people who'd forgotten how to porn.

So, these were the sleeping arrangements. The first thing Isabel did was to get one of the folding chairs from the other room and set the space heater on it. That would reduce the odds of the three of them waking up all brown and crispy on Christmas morning in this firetrap of a building.

Next, Isabel took off her clothes and stashed them in the bag with her sisters', then resealed it. She ducked under the pole and climbed into the center hammock, taking care not to wake Kristen, step on any of the leaves or get her hands and feet tangled up in the rope matrix. There wasn't really enough room for her between them, so her left shoulder pressed against Chelsey's right shoulder, while her right arm was pushing Kristen's left arm into her breasts. Isabel was now the middle bead in a Newton's cradle made of sisters.

The walls in this part of the cabin were so thin she could hear everything happening outside. The conversations of passing strangers were mostly in Spanish or something that wasn't Spanish—possibly Arabic. In the cabin next door, a family was singing something that, from what Isabel could understand of the lyrics, was a Christmas carol.

"You remembered to lock the door, right?" whispered Chelsey, who didn't even know any Spanish and probably thought they were singing about gang violence or something.

"Of course." She had indeed secured the lock that a slightly-stronger-than-average woman could break with one hand if she wasn't careful.

"Good."

Isabel lay there, staring up at the lath-and-tarp ceiling. There was no chimney, and although she must at some point have believed in Santa Claus, she couldn't remember when it was. The night felt chilly, but that didn't mean much when you were naked in midair—it was probably seventy degrees, or a little less. It was just cool enough to make her acutely aware of her bare skin, and how exposed it was to all the hungry little insect mouths in the room. Also, her butt and thighs were going to have some embarrassing net marks in the morning.

Isabel shut her eyes, listening to Kristen breathe. Her sleep was untroubled and peaceful. *She* was untroubled and peaceful. As if, somehow, despite everything she could see and hear, God was whispering to her *don't worry, I got this.*

She didn't belong here. And Jourdain didn't belong here, separated from her mother as well as her father. And Mom and Pop who had worked all their lives, and Mom-mom and Pop-pop who had worked all *their* lives, and Scott who had been such a good student until the money ran out… and what the hell, it was Christmas Eve, Chelsey didn't belong here either. *There has got to be a way of getting these people out of this place.*

Well, I'm not going to think of it tonight. Isabel slowed her breathing in the hopes of getting to sleep faster, and listened to the voices of the last few passersby.

"You know what I want to do right now?" whispered Chelsey.

"What?"

"Get out of this hammock… open the door… invite the whole neighborhood in and say 'Merry Christmas.'"

Isabel needed a moment to think of a response to that.

"Well, you can't," she finally said. "We've got bedbugs. And you drank all the beer."

Chelsey laughed—almost too loud. Isabel glanced over to her other side to make sure Kristen hadn't woken up.

"God, I've missed you," said Chelsey. "Never change."

DECEMBER 25:

THE BEAN LEAVES SEEMED TO have done the trick—Isabel woke up the next morning with one bite mark on her foot. Still, she and her sisters spent the first half hour or so of Christmas morning meticulously checking their clothes and themselves for any bedbugs that might be stowing away. The last thing any of them wanted to do was spread this problem around.

That done, they went over to Mom and Pop's cabin for breakfast. Kristen led them in saying grace. That would have been Pop's job, but by general agreement she was the one best suited to sweet-talking the Almighty.

"Amen," said Isabel along with everybody else, feeling like a hypocrite. She thought of herself as an agnostic, but she suspected that what she really was somebody who hadn't put much thought into the question. Given the role the churches had in making this place halfway livable, she felt like she owed God a favor whether He existed or not.

Once she'd said her goodbyes to the rest of her family, she ventured out toward the camp entrance with Pop and Scott behind her—not to protect her, but to carry the gifts back. Most people were still inside, but all through the camp Isabel heard Christmas carols and the excited shouts of children. For the first time, this place seemed something close to all right.

She meant to arrive in the parking lot at five minutes to eleven, just to be on the safe side, but Pop met someone in the militia and got drawn into a conversation. She arrived in the parking lot at 11:01 a.m.

The car wasn't there.

She looked around for some place it might be idling, or somewhere it might have parked. Had it left already? *Where is it, where is it, it's supposed to be here, if it's gone I'll never get out of here…*

Then she turned her phone on and noticed she had a message from her car, sent at precisely 11:00 a.m.

I'm on my way!
NO HEAVY TRAFFIC DETECTED
ESTIMATED ARRIVAL TIME: 11:44 A.M. CENTRAL
Merry Christmas!

Of course. She'd told it to *come back* at 11 a.m., not to *arrive* at 11 a.m. The computer's software still needed some work. Or maybe her software did.

DECEMBER 27:

THE NUTRIA HINDQUARTER WAS READY. Isabel took it out of the oven, put it on a big plate next to a still-hot baked potato, poured on the gravy, and set them down at her kitchen table. Since she didn't have a proper wineglass, she poured the Cabernet Sauvignon into a heavy glass tumbler.

The Cab had been a gift from the director at Marshpower. The wine guide said this wine was "angular" but otherwise well-balanced, with an aroma of "red and black fruits" and a flavor of ripe black raspberries, "cassis"—whatever that was—and "cigar box." *WTF?* There were also said to be notes of cherries, blue violets, smoke... leather... and "moist black earth." *Ohh... kay.*

With a certain amount of trepidation, Isabel sipped the wine. It tasted like wine. That was as far as her palate could go. Just as well, really. Drinking an angular cigar box sounded like a bad experience. And Cab was supposed to go well with game.

She sighed. It wasn't exactly that she was lonely. On the contrary—after the hours of conversation with her family, and the conversations with strangers on the train going both ways, Isabel was feeling drained. She desperately needed at least one night to herself.

At the same time, it was two days after Christmas and here she was with roast haunch of swamp rodent, potatoes and gravy, and a reputedly decent Cabernet Sauvignon, and nobody to share them with. That felt like a kind of failure. Hunter or Laurie or somebody ought to be here, even if they didn't say anything. That was something she missed about Hunter. The two of them had reached a point where they could be comfortable together in silence.

And even thinking about her personal problems felt wrong, considering what her family was going through. They seemed to have a relationship with the community that kept them more or less safe from other people, but that wouldn't help if Chelsey got careless with a space heater. And if Pop-pop's health took another turn for the worse, a place that couldn't get medicine to schizophrenics certainly wouldn't do him much good.

At this point, Isabel's phone gave a little chime to let her know she had a new message.

It was from Sandy.

Isabel! It's great to hear from you! I'm sorry it took so long to respond. I spent Christmas Day catching up on my personal contacts.

We've got to bring each other up to speed. Should we talk online, or in person? If you can spare the time to come up to New York, I'd be happy to pay travel costs. You can spend the night at my place. I've got all this room I'm not using. Come any time you like.

I'm mostly in my office these days—you should probably visit me here right after work hours. If nothing else, you've got to see the renovations they did on this floor.

Isabel read this several times. She'd missed social cues before, but she couldn't see any way it was a message from somebody trying to politely discourage somebody else. It sounded completely the opposite.

She offered to pay travel costs. So it literally costs me nothing to go up there and talk to her. And maybe she wants to help. Chelsey never got a response, but that was Chelsey. She and Sandy never did get along, and honestly, how much money would you give her? Things might be different with me.

Even if she's okay with this, do you really want to be taking her charity?

Why is it okay to accept nutria meat from the Comegys family, but not to accept money from Sandy?

Isabel responded with another message:

How about tomorrow?

DECEMBER 28:

LAURA BRONZINO'S LATEST ALBUM INCLUDED a song called "December 28." It was all about being alone between the holidays and trying to find things to do to fill up the time and missing someone who wasn't there. Isabel had liked this song a lot better when it wasn't about her.

You brightened up the time we shared in a thousand different ways
Baby, with you there were no empty days...

Needless to say, on the titular day itself every radio station in the country, with the possible exception of the weather stations Pop favored, played the song again and again until even Isabel was ready to stuff Laura Bronzino into a cannon and blast her over the horizon.

Just as well that she wasn't staying home on this particular day. She'd driven up to Wilmington and was on the bus to New York City. She had pajamas and a change of clothes with her, but that was it. As the bus got closer to the city, Isabel got her first look at the famous balloon turbines of New Jersey.

She wished the bus would make a stop, so she could go out and get a better look. Traveling through so much of America felt like a tour of a run-down version of the late twentieth century. This, on the other hand, looked like something from ten or twenty years in the future. The balloons hovered, vast and blue-tinted with distance, in a row that stretched from horizon to horizon. Their tops and sides were midnight blue, collecting solar energy to add to their wind power. The third of them between the lower vanes had color cells in their skin that showed ever-changing pictures of magnificent landscapes and cityscapes, wild animals, cute puppies and kittens, famous works of art, abstract and fractal patterns, and drawings by some kid who'd won a school art contest, all of course punctuated by one-second ads for Coca-Cola, Pepsi, Quesch, McDonald's, Burger King, Wendy's, Motel 6, Comfort Inn, and the new hit movie *Kobanî**. They managed to be both tacky and magnificent. *If we can build this, we can do anything*, she thought. *Only somehow, we can't.*

NEW YORK CITY. ALL FOUR of her grandparents would be horrified to learn that she was here. They'd formed their impressions of the Big Apple in some godawful decade of the twentieth century and never bothered to change their minds. To them, it was a bigger, nastier version of Baltimore. And now, of course, two of them were in a place that was more lawless than New York had ever been.

According to the map on Isabel's armphone, she was on West Street, just south of the Holland Tunnel. She looked around. There were two cabs on the street, but they were both black. Isabel spotted a yellow cab a couple of blocks up the street, but before she could do anything it pulled over, let in a passenger, and turned black to let everyone know it was taken.

Checking the map again, Isabel saw that the Freedom Tower was less than a mile away, an easy walk down West Street—and it was so much taller than everything else that she could hardly lose her way. She had time. She'd been hoping to see some of the sights, but there wasn't time for serious tourism, and what she really wanted was to go there and get this over with.

---

* About the 2014-15 siege of Kobanî, or Ayn al-Arab, by Daesh.

The sky was overcast. The air tasted like snow about to happen. The setting sun was peeking under the clouds, sending streams of gold light over the river against the flat faces of the buildings on her left.

Isabel had always liked to think of herself as someone who could get by either in a small town or the big city. College Park was as urbane and cosmopolitan as any place on Earth, but it wasn't *big*. It didn't tower over your head. It surrounded you with what looked like a cross-section of the world's population, but not in numbers like this.

For the first few moments, Isabel had the feeling that people were looking at her and thinking *what a rube*. This was soon crushed by the awareness that no one was looking at her at all, or was likely to. Heading south along the Hudson River Greenway, she knew deep down that she was tiny, broke, and one among millions. Here, there was no way you could pretend to yourself even for a second that you were a big deal.

Or possibly there was, if you actually were a big deal. She'd have to ask Sandy about that.

THERE WERE A LOT OF tourists in the elevator at One World Trade Center, but Isabel was the only one who got off at the ninetieth floor. When she left, she could see the renovation Sandy had been talking about. The halls were dimly lit, and the walls had been turned into video screens that showed a complex pattern of cirrus cloud over twilight sky. As she walked down the hall, the clouds nearest her glowed especially bright, as if the full moon were shining through them. Also, the recessed lights down the middle of the ceiling turned on as she approached, creating narrow cones of light for her to walk through as if she were the star of her own little noir movie.

Maybe this setup was meant to save energy after regular business hours, or to make visitors feel welcome. What it seemed to say to Isabel was: *Hello. We have buttloads of money and we know exactly where you are.* Isabel was suddenly acutely aware of the spot on her blouse where she'd had to hand-sew a hole back together. She had a very strong feeling that she wasn't supposed to be here. She almost wished she'd taken another Suiamor last night, although God only knew what would have happened if she had.

Isabel wasn't even sure how much money Sandy had. She'd found five different estimates online, the most recent of which was from back in February.

All of them were pretty far apart.

Except that all of them were in ten figures.

All of them except the newest one. That one was in eleven figures.

Was it really a good idea to approach her like this?

No. No. I asked to meet her and she said yes. She scheduled this appointment, not me. This is no intrusion.

The door to the office was open, but as soon as Isabel entered, the woman behind the desk said, "Office hours are over." She looked at Isabel with an expression of distaste. Her clothes looked expensive and impeccable, her hair was a shade of dark magenta that didn't occur naturally in mammals, and her face was about thirty years younger than her neck and hands.

"I have an appointment." The you-don't-belong-here feeling was so strong Isabel had trouble getting the words out. And at this point the secretary hadn't just noticed the mended spot on Isabel's blouse, she was staring at it like it was an infected wound.

"You're… Isabel?"

"Yes. I know it's not until five-thirty, but I didn't want to be late, so I showed up a little early." Isabel sat down.

"No, you can go back," said the secretary. "She said to let you in as soon as you arrived."

Between the reception area and the offices was a furiously glittering bead curtain. Mostly blue beads, with clear beads forming the De L'Air logo in a sort of hanging mosaic. It seemed a little too tacky for such a classy office, but just as Isabel was passing through it, she thought *holy shit this thing is made of real diamonds.* De L'Air diamonds, but still, *diamonds.*

And no sooner was Isabel through the curtain than she was face to face with the CEO herself. Sandy was wearing charcoal-gray slacks, a cashmere sweater the exact color of wet cement, and shoes that added maybe an inch to her height. At some point she'd traded her thick glasses for contact lenses, or possibly corrective surgery. Her hair still went down past her shoulders, but she wasn't wearing it in a ponytail any more. That bothered Isabel a little— years ago, she'd modeled her own ponytail on Sandy's and had never gotten around to changing it. But then, it looked decent and kept her hair out of her face.

"God, how long has it been?" Sandy hugged Isabel, then pulled back just far enough to look her in the face. Isabel had looked into Sandy's eyes many times during their childhood, but had never been able to decide on their color. Depending on the light, they might be pale gray, pale blue, or pale green. Mostly they were just pale. They looked so strange without thick lenses in front of them—kind of naked.

Isabel glanced around at the office itself. Midnight-blue wall-to-wall carpet. Ice-blue walls. Sculptures made of some kind of crystal, lit with beams of white light. The overall effect was cold, but with a couple of patches of warmth. One of these was right at Sandy's desk, which looked like mahogany and had a lamp on it with an amber LED bulb. Another was a pair of comfortable-looking red leather chairs with a small table between them and a light on overhead, set so they half-faced out the window and half-faced each other.

"Have a seat," said Sandy. "I'll get us some dinner." She stepped over to the entrance, then turned back. "You don't have any allergies, do you? Food allergies, I mean?"

"Nope."

"Anything else? Dietary or religious restrictions?"

"If it's food, I'll eat it."

"Good." She stuck her head through the curtain. "Olivia, would you call Dapur Emas and have one of those satay party platters sent up here? A Full Eight Combo with coconut water?" Then she turned back to Isabel.

"You didn't have to do that."

"Oh yes I did," said Sandy. "Maybe once a week I have time for a real dinner. The rest of the time I live on meal-replacement shit. Tonight I want to eat some critters that were killed on my behalf. And I don't want to eat alone."

Isabel nodded.

"Of course, basic hospitality says what I ought to be doing is taking you out to a world-class restaurant."

"Please don't do that." Isabel put a hand over the mended spot on her blouse. Then she changed her mind and stretched the fabric a little, so Sandy could clearly see it.

"Yeah, I wouldn't be doing you any favors, showing you off in front of this city's social scene in your current packaging. Not just the blouse—your boots, your hair… personally, I think you look great, but other people don't have my good taste."

Isabel smiled a little. This was good. This was putting off the moment when she'd have to beg for help.

"If it helps, people here aren't shallow so much as they are scared," said Sandy. "Ever read 'Masque of the Red Death'?"

Isabel nodded. She had in fact read it, back in school, many years ago. Either Poe or Hawthorne had written it. Something about a castle with all the doors locked, a big fancy crazy party going on inside, outside everybody around was dead from some kind of epidemic... her memories of it were vague, but she was pretty sure that was the gist of it.

"Things here aren't quite that extreme," said Sandy, "but sometimes it has that feel to it." No, Poe had definitely written it. Hawthorne had written the one with the black veil.

"See, New York has been really lucky the last few years," Sandy said. "Most of the crazy weather has passed us by. The river got a little high during the last Monsoon, there was that ice storm in January—that was pretty bad—but we got through it all right. We've been lucky, and we know we've been lucky, and of course the rich people here are the luckiest of all... and we're starting to understand just how fragile it all is. So when somebody comes into a party or something with anything about them that suggests they're at all down on their luck, it's like they're the bloody shroud guy in that story. Just standing there reminding us all of everything we're trying not to think about.

"Wait a minute—I'm doing all the talking here. How's Martelle?"

"Martelle Sherman?"

"How many Martelles do you know?"

"I haven't thought about her in a while," said Isabel. "I heard someone saying her parents are going to Oregon and moving in with her." Under other circumstances, being reminded of her co-Valedictorian would have irritated her.

"I was sure you two were either going to end up married or kill each other," said Sandy. "And how's your family?"

And here we go. Isabel opened her mouth to say something along the lines of *fine, only we've run into a little trouble...* but the words just wouldn't come. For the space of several breaths, she just stood there, biting her lip, desperate for anything to say.

"Look, I can't do this," she finally said. "They're in a FEMA center, and it's completely toilet. Worse than toilet. I'm gonna make a bonfire out of my pride here—help us out. Please. I'm begging. I'm not asking for much, and I swear I'll pay you back—"

"Sit down." Sandy hadn't raised her voice, but her smile was suddenly gone.

Oh shit. This is already going wrong. Isabel sat down in one of the two armchairs. Sandy stood in front of her and leaned in a bit, looking her in the eye. Right now her eyes were pale green like iceberg lettuce, and it took an effort of will for Isabel to meet her gaze.

"Three times," said Sandy. "Three times I called your dad myself and offered to help. Three times he said no. Two weeks ago I texted your sister—knowing she's a single mom, knowing there's no way she doesn't need help—and I got no reply."

That explained it. Nothing made people OOP angry like having their do-gooder impulses thwarted by the very people they were trying to do good to. *Chelsey, you lying... crotchburger. And why didn't you tell me, Pop?* "I didn't know," said Isabel. "I'm sorry."

"They didn't tell you? Shit..." Sandy paused. "Yeah, that would make me look kinda bad, wouldn't it?"

"Not really. It's not like you owe us anything. Hell, in my case—"

"Excuse me? Are we friends or are we not?"

"Would I be here if we weren't?"

"Then stop acting like I'm the fucking Godfather!"

Isabel sat there for a couple of seconds, biting her lip, looking at her feet. How could this be going so badly? How could she have botched the simple task of asking an old family friend for help? *She came to us and offered to help us out. She came to us three times—no, four—and it was us who turned her down. Now here's me coming into her office like Bob Cratchit begging for an advance from Ebenezer Scrooge, as if I expected her to say no. That would annoy almost anybody.*

"I'm sorry," said Sandy. "I'm making things worse, aren't I?" She sat down in the chair next to Isabel.

"I didn't mean to insult you. I just... wasn't sure how you still felt, and..."

"See, this is what I'm talking about. You're scared of me. You. The girl without fear is scared of me." She sighed. Isabel thought for a moment. She hadn't even realized she had that reputation. *The girl without fear... was that really how people thought of her?*

"For the longest time," said Sandy, "people in this town treated me like I was just this little bug they could step on any time they felt like it. I would have killed for some fucking respect. And now that I have it, now that people have to respect me…"

Isabel opened her mouth. Then she closed it again. Then she thought *no, she doesn't want me to be scared of her* and opened it again.

"When you were trying to talk to my family, why didn't you call me?"

"Because you were the only one who didn't need help," she said. "Sorry. I'm not used to dealing with people who need family members to run interference for them. And I'm really not used to dealing with people who *don't* want my money."

"Just out of curiosity—how much money have you got?"

"That's not an easy question to answer," said Sandy. "Most of it's in the form of assets whose value changes from day to day. And there's a lot of stuff I control but don't own. Like, ten percent of my earnings and salary goes to the Symcox Foundation. I'm pretty much the deciding vote in how that money gets spent, as long as it's spent making the world a better place, but it stops being mine as soon as it goes to them.

"My biggest single asset is De L'Air Diamonds—the original diamond company. I own that completely. It isn't publicly traded. I also own fifty-seven percent of De L'Air Capital LLC—that's the holding company that owns forty-two percent of De L'Air Graphene and Diamondoids."

"Which I'm guessing is a lot bigger than the diamond company."

"And you're right. I also own about ten percent of De L'Air G&D in my own name, and the Symcox Foundation owns another six percent. So between me, myself, and I, we've got the company well in hand."

"Forget what you control. Just tell me what you own. Give me a ballpark sum."

Sandy actually bit her lip and blushed at this point.

"Sixty-one billion," she finally said.

There was a long pause.

"Sixty-one," said Isabel.

"Yep. Billion. With a 'b'."

"No, I knew that much, I just didn't know… Jesus." Isabel was having trouble getting her mind to take that all in. Something small and stupid inside her was squeaking *SIXTY-ONE BILLION? I know we're a capitalist country and all, but do they seriously let you have that much money? That's like letting somebody have a nuclear bomb! Hell, you could probably buy a few nukes with that kind of money! Or build your own!*

Sandy nodded. "I'm officially the richest woman in the world. Richer than J.K. Rowling or the Walton heirs or the Queen of England or the Sultan of Brunei's favorite wife."

"That's... that's... sixty-one billion, I mean... sorry, I know I'm sounding really slow on the uptake."

"No, it's okay. Some days I don't believe it either." She smiled a little. "If it helps, less than one percent of that is liquid."

"Liquid?"

"Liquid meaning I can just take it and spend it, without selling anything else. I mean, I can't exactly go to the supermarket and say 'Hey, you got change for a holding company?' So if it makes me seem closer to human-scale to think of me as only having five hundred forty-two million, one hundred thirty-six thousand, nine... sorry. Keeping track of exactly how much cash I have on hand is a hard habit to break."

Because in case you've forgotten, five years ago she was poorer than you. Now look at her. And what have you accomplished? Isabel told the little voice inside her head to put a little sock in it.

"Let's get this part out of the way right now," said Sandy. "One way or another, I'm going to get your family some help—don't worry about that. But we've already established that it's not going to be simple. They're not going to let it be simple. You might've made a bonfire out of your pride, but your dad and Chelsey are a different story. They won't take anything that smells like charity, even now."

"I can't believe she lied to me," said Isabel. "Chelsey, I mean. She told me she'd tried to ask you for help. She did this big speech about how you forgot where you came from."

"Well, it's true I haven't been back since the funeral. I've just been so busy—first school, then Verdissimus, then De L'Air... but I bet I could still take apart a steamed crab with the best of them." She smiled, then was silent, staring out the window.

"You want to know the truth?" she finally said. "People like me—to the extent that there are people like me—aren't really *from* anywhere. There are places where we're born and raised, and sometimes those places are good to us, but we never fit in there. And most of what shapes us, growing up, is inside our heads." Sandy sighed. "I could just buy the damn island and be done with it, but as I understand it, your father doesn't own the property anymore."

"Nope. The state has the property and he has an IOU. Our lawyer is already on it, but the case is moving pretty slowly."

"Well, I can send you bigger and scarier lawyers, but that won't help right away." Sandy looked Isabel up and down. "You know what? I have a little one-time gig in mind for you, and the pay happens to be exactly seventy-five grand."

Isabel couldn't think of anything to say. That would do it. That would clear her own debts, get Pop and the family out of that damn camp, and at least get them a rental property until he could get back on his boat and start bringing in money again.

"Thank you," she said. "If there's ever anything I can—"

Sandy lifted a hand in a stop gesture. "This is a job, I said. You are doing a thing that will benefit me, and I am giving you money for it. Okay? One more word out of you about paying me back and I'll personally tie you up and sell you to a lesbian sex dungeon just so you don't feel like a freeloader."

Isabel chuckled. "That… would be sort of a solution to my relationship problems." That, of course, turned the conversation over to the subjects of Hunter and Laurie, which kept them busy until dinner.

Before she even heard the delivery person enter Olivia's little domain, Isabel noticed the smell. It was a delicious smell of spices and hot grease that pulled her up out of her chair. It was funny how hunger worked. You went through the whole day thinking about everything except food, no appetite at all, not even really seeing why you needed to eat anything today… and then the right smell hit your nose and your eyes opened wide and your mouth started to water and this *beast* woke up inside you, and went ARRRGH BLAARGH BRING ME BEEF AND BRING ME PORK AND BRING ME ALL MANNER OF MEAT. Maybe if you were a vegetarian it went ARRRGH BLAARGH BRING ME SALAD. Isabel didn't know. All she knew was, she'd had a protein shake for breakfast, nothing for lunch and not a whole lot yesterday, and she was ready to do some serious feasting.

Sandy took the tray and set it on the table between the chairs. It took up the table all by itself.

"We've got beef, lamb, blackened chicken, marinated chicken, duck, fish, shrimp, and tofu," said Sandy. "We've also got peanut sauce, cucumber yogurt dip, and some sriracha that'll burn the roof off your mouth. God, I love these things. Let's eat."

Feeling like a complete sponger, Isabel started with the duck. *Oh god it's got the skin on it and the skin is brown and crunchy all over but not burned anywhere and I think my mouth just had an orgasm…* It was so good she had to put it aside so she could eat some beef and marinated chicken and come back to the duck when she was ready to slow down and savor it. The rest of the meal was a succession of exquisite experiences washed down with coconut water.

Finally, they were both getting full. "I've got a fridge in the office," said Sandy, "but we should finish the fish and shrimp. They won't be so good tomorrow." Isabel was a little surprised at how much was left. This hadn't looked like such a massive amount of food at first glance. But if every satay stick contained four ounces of whatever, and there were eight groups of five sticks, that was ten pounds of rich food for two women, one of them quite small. No wonder they couldn't finish it.

The last of the satay eaten or put away, Isabel discreetly took a paper napkin and wiped the peanut sauce off her face. Sandy got up, walked over to the window, and stood there for a moment, just looking out. Her arms were folded behind her back.

"To really appreciate this city," she said, "you have to see it from the ninetieth-floor window."

"Good thing we've got one of those," said Isabel, getting up.

"Actually, the observation deck has a better view, but here we've got a little more privacy."

Isabel stood next to Sandy and looked out the window. The view really was spectacular, especially on a night when the snow was just starting and was creating haloes around all the different lights of the city and the sky had that purple-orange urban glow to it, but she had the uncomfortable feeling that Sandy was about to say something like "tell me what you see" and she wouldn't have anything insightful to respond with.

"Try clasping your hands behind your back," said Sandy.

Isabel did so, straightening her back and letting the knuckles of her left hand rest on the slope of her butt.

"There you go. Now we're rocking the power look."

"Too bad nobody's watching."

They just stood there for another moment. Isabel was about to sit back down again when Sandy said something completely out of the blue. "Ever think about… prepping?"

Isabel had to think for a moment.

"Prepping?" she said. "You mean those guys who stockpile food and ammo and stuff?"

"Yeah."

"Well, my family always kept some supplies and a generator on hand in case we lost power for a few days. Being prepared for two to three weeks without basic services… I don't see anything wrong with that. Especially these days. In fact, I think you'd have to be a fool not to make a few plans." Isabel hesitated. "Are you thinking about getting ready for a more… long-term crisis?" Considering how smart Sandy was and how much information she had access to, if she thought the world was headed for a major breakdown, that was enough to scare the hell out of Isabel.

"I considered it," said Sandy. "For about five minutes. Long enough to see the problems.

"Suppose I buy a farm out in the country. While I'm learning how to farm, I build up a huge stockpile of canned goods, guns, ammo, medical supplies, whatever else I need to get by on my own.

"Then civilization collapses, but I'm doing all right. By the time I run out of canned food, my farm will be producing its first crop. So I kick back and laugh… right up until the horde of armed and starving refugees shows up outside my place. What do I do then? Try to fight them all off by myself?"

"Good question," said Isabel, "but why would you want to do anything so small? I mean, right now you could use forty or fifty million dollars to buy a whole bunch of something that would come in handy in an emergency. You'd never miss the money, and if shit got real, you'd be richer than ever. You could buy much better defenses. Or you could pay off the starving refugees."

"Makes sense. What do you think I should buy?"

Isabel shrugged. "Medicine? Gold?"

"I invested a few thousand in gold a few years ago, back when I knew bad shit was going down with the climate but it wasn't here yet. Sold it at a pretty good profit, too. But even when I had it, it wasn't literally in my possession. What I had was a certificate saying someone else was holding onto the gold in my name." Sandy chuckled. "Yeah… I can definitely see myself trekking across a lawless post-apocalyptic wasteland, fighting off attacks by the cast of *Mad Max* the whole way, reaching the front door of the vault, waving my little certificate in front of the security camera, and saying, 'Hey, you in there! Gimme my gold or I'm calling the police!'"

Isabel laughed. "Now that I think about it," she said, "if law and order really did break down, the last place I'd want to be is sitting on top of a giant heap of gold. Scratch that off the list."

"Exactly," said Sandy. "And no matter what you stockpile, you're going to run into the same problem. Food… antibiotics… if it's valuable to you, it's valuable to others, and there's nothing much to stop them from coming and taking it."

"Even if it's guns and ammo?"

"Especially guns and ammo. The thing about guns is, you can have a hundred of them, but the only one you can rely on is the one in your hands right at the moment. All the rest of them are just sitting around waiting to be stolen."

"What about drones?"

"Drones need maintenance, which I don't know how to do. I'd have to hire some guys to staff my own private repair shop and hope civilization rose again before their tools wore out."

"For that matter, you could hire guys with guns."

"Yeah, what I'd really need is an army of henchpersons. The trouble with henchpersons is, you've got to pay them. And what could I pay them with when money isn't any good? Canned goods? Seed corn? Fertile… members of the opposite sex? What could I give them that they couldn't just kill me and take?"

"I guess you'd just have to make sure everybody was loyal to you first." Even as Isabel said it, it sounded stupid.

"Exactly," said Sandy, smiling a little. "And how about that. In the absence of a working central government, the only thing worth hoarding, worth stockpiling… is loyalty. Bone-deep, irrational, inarguable, literally *in-value-able* loyalty. The one thing nobody can steal. And also the one thing I can't buy and have never been that good at earning.

"So at this point I realized the only good way to prepare for the apocalypse— the only way that really makes sense—is to not let it happen in the first place. To keep it all together. To sustain civilization as a going concern. And I think a lot of the people who prep—the smarter ones, anyway—they realize this. Trouble is, they personally can't do anything about it. They don't know how to save the world, and even if they did they wouldn't have the resources."

Isabel looked at Sandy with newfound awe.

"But you do," she said softly. She'd known in an intellectual way how rich Sandy was, but she hadn't really understood it until now. "Billionaire" was just a word. "Multibillionaire" was a slightly longer word. The power Sandy had, and the apparent scope of her ambition… it was staggering. Her old babysitter was literally trying to save the *world*. It was too much to take in all at once.

"Well, up to a point," said Sandy. "But I have to really plan ahead. I mean yes, I have an enormous amount of money, but… the U.S. government has passed economic stimulus packages larger than my entire net worth. If I want to accomplish more than they did, I have to be smarter than the government. The whole government, not just the stupid parts that get in the news." She turned to Isabel. "And I can't do it alone."

"Um… you think I can help?"

"I think lots of people can help, and you're one of them," said Sandy.

"Well, I'd love to help, but what can I do?"

"I don't know yet, but I've followed your career and it seems like you can do whatever you set your mind to. And I can trust you. I know you're not just after my money. You have no idea how special that makes you."

"Excuse me. Didn't I come here to basically hit you up for money?"

"Only out of desperation. Listen, if there's one thing I've learned over the past couple years, it's which of my old friends are motivated by greed and which ones are not. You're on the good list."

"Sounds like you're considering me for a job."

"I did mention that little gig. Do you have any plans for New Year's Eve?"

"No," said Isabel, "but my car's in a parking garage in Wilmington. If you want me to stay the next few days, I'll have to pay the garage." She took out her armphone. "And this is one expense I can handle myself."

IT WAS ONE OF THOSE towering, ultra-mega-upscale apartment buildings that overlooked Central Park. In addition to the two bodyguards inside Sandy's self-driving McLaren, there were several formidable-looking guards outside the building.

"This is Isabel Bradshaw," she said. "She's a friend. Remember her face. She has access." The guards looked at her as if to say *are you sure? If you need friends, we can get you some much classier ones.*

"Yes, I mean it," Sandy said. Then she planted a hand between Isabel's shoulders and gently escorted her in. The lobby was all white marble and polished ebony or some other wood that was about the same color. There was a guestbook Isabel had to sign.

Sandy's suite was on the forty-second floor. The living room, if that was what it was, looked to have as much space in it as the house where Isabel had grown up, and most of it was hardly being used. It was dominated by a glass wall that looked out onto the park, and a water feature was burbling away in the middle of the room.

"Well, what are you waiting for?" said Sandy. Isabel took a deep breath and stepped inside. She hung her hat and coat on a twisted-looking wrought-iron coatrack, heard a little splutter of suppressed laughter behind her and turned. Sandy was smiling.

"What?"

"Anton Felski," said Sandy. "One of the more famous artists working in New York City today. Last year he made an abstract metal sculpture called *Loneliness Number 4*. He said it represented 'the suffering of the human soul, torn between the need for privacy and the need for connectedness in an age which deprives us of both.'"

Isabel stood there silently, trying to figure out why Sandy was telling her all this.

"I was just picturing the look on his face if he saw you using it as a coatrack."

At this point, Isabel noticed the rows of wooden coat pegs on either side of the door. She looked back over her shoulder. Sure enough, that wrought-iron thing didn't exactly look like a normal coatrack. Some of the arms were twisted back as if covering a face, while others were reaching out in a way that did sort of suggest desperation. Her face flushed and hot with embarrassment, Isabel turned to take her coat and hat off.

Sandy touched Isabel's arm. "It's cool," she said. "Leave it. You found a use for the damn thing, which is more than I've done."

"I feel like such a hick." She looked around. The walls were painted white, with polished blond-wood trim. The furniture was white, upholstered in silk. "Why is everything so... white?"

"I think because so much sun gets in that it'd fade anything with color. Now if you ask why I need such huge windows... that I don't know."

Isabel nodded and looked around some more. There were a few other works of what she could only assume to be art, but the most interesting thing was the fountain. It was a bowl, about five feet wide and two feet deep, filled with smooth river rocks and flat slabs of slate in a pile, with a dozen streams of water playing over them and dripping down into the depths of the thing.

"Feel a little out of place here?"

"Yeah."

"Me too. I sometimes think the interior decorators in this city are part of a communist plot to drive rich people insane. I tried to strike a balance between things that are considered signs of impeccable taste and things I might actually want to look at." Sandy switched the fountain off. "I really shouldn't leave this thing on at night. It's meant to be looked at during the day. When I'm generally not here, of course."

ISABEL HAD THOUGHT SHE WAS going to be sleeping on the couch, but it turned out this place had a guest bedroom. It was small, but the bed was so comfortable she wasn't sure she'd be able to get out of it. Which made it a pretty good metaphor for the whole situation. Or possibly a simile. She couldn't keep those two straight.

It felt wrong to be questioning Sandy's motives when she'd done nothing but offer to help—repeatedly, as it turned out. If anyone needed to be questioned, it was her father and older sister. Especially her older sister. Not asking for help was one thing. Refusing offers of help was something else. Lying about people offering to help you... it was almost too bad they couldn't leave Chelsey to fend for herself in Texas Foxtrot, but she was Jourdain's mom.

But what was Sandy up to? She hadn't actually told Isabel much about her plans, except for the fact of their existence and the scope of them. Was there some elaborate multi-year strategy that Isabel was supposed to play a part in? Or was Sandy just winging it, trying to push the world in the right direction and reaching for whatever or whoever looked potentially useful? The latter seemed more likely, but with somebody that smart you couldn't rule out the former.

And what did Sandy mean by calling her "the girl without fear"? How had she gotten that reputation? From running away from a bear... and then turning around and dropping it with two tranquilizer darts while everybody else either hid under the deck or just stood there like cardboard cutouts. Getting her ass handed to her on Yuschak's show… and leaving the set in a more or less dignified manner. Oh, and the time she blew the whistle on her bosses while her bosses were watching. Along with the head of the Corps of Engineers. And the governor. And the president. At this point, maybe she did have something of a reputation. ("I just tell myself it's what you would do.")

But what does she want with me? She must already have a hundred better engineers than me working for her. What do I have to offer that she couldn't buy in bulk?

Put that way, the answer was obvious. Friendship. Loyalty. Sandy had told her as much. Hell, she'd practically been screaming it at the top of her lungs.

Suddenly this place felt like a trap. Isabel's instincts were telling her to get dressed again, run, not walk, to the nearest exit, hop a train or a bus back to Wilmington, get in her car and head for the hills. *Okay, instincts, I've about had it with your bullshit*, she said to herself. *You better start putting your objections into words, and you better do it NOW.*

Her instincts, naturally, failed to do so. All they had to offer was a general impression that friendship was supposed to happen a lot more naturally than this, without so much deliberate effort on the part of either party.

But we already are friends. It's not like she's mad at me. It's not like we parted on bad terms. We might have fallen out of touch for a while, but we were both busy. There was nothing wrong with Sandy. Her heart was in the right place, and her temper was under control. If she wanted to be closer friends with Isabel, why should that be a problem?

Because they weren't equals, that was why. They hadn't been equals when Isabel had blindly reached up to pull a foreign object out of her hair and Sandy had taken a bee sting to save her life. They hadn't been equals when Sandy had been teaching her more about science than she was learning in school. And they sure as hell weren't equals now.

Dear God, were they ever not equals. *Sixty-one billion dollars.* That kind of money had its own gravity, like a giant planet, and if Isabel's little asteroid wandered too close it might be pulled into Sandy's orbit and end up mooning her. Okay, that metaphor or simile or whatever it was needed to be taken out and shot in the back of the head, but the point was that with the best intentions in the world, a couple months of being around Sandy and Isabel would turn into a hanger-on, one of the entourage of borderline parasites that every seriously rich person seemed to collect. The one thing Isabel treasured about herself was her independence, and now she was supposed to just hang out and be pals with somebody who could give her everything she'd ever need or want in life as easily as paying for a cup of chyq. That was why, despite all sense and reason and personal obligation, a big part of Isabel wanted out of this deal right now.

But you're not independent, she thought. *You can look after yourself, but you can't help your family. To the extent that you care about them, which is a big fucking extent, you're not independent. Some women become prostitutes to support their families. You just have to be nice to somebody you like.* **And what does it say about you if you find that so difficult?**

But that's not the problem. The problem is, why doesn't she have any other friends she can talk to? She left Tilghman Island at fourteen—what about all the people she's met since then? The ones she was in college with, worked on Verdissimus with? Granted, she seems to have ended up in court battles with most of them...

Oh.

Sandy hadn't talked much about any of those people... but that was a clue right there, wasn't it? She hadn't talked about them because she hadn't *wanted* to talk about them, because it was still too painful. The closest she'd come was to drop a little hint—"If there's one thing I've learned over the past couple years, it's which of my old friends are motivated by greed and which ones are not."

She's been betrayed and hurt. She's lonely as all hell, but she doesn't know who to trust. She needs me.

And just like that, Isabel's instincts changed their minds. She suddenly felt sure she was exactly where she ought to be.

DECEMBER 29:

IT WAS JUST BEFORE SEVEN. Isabel was already showered and dressed. Sandy was in either a kimono or a bathrobe that looked like a kimono.

The kitchen was bigger than Isabel's apartment, and had equipment in it that she'd only ever seen in coffeeshops and the kitchen of Celebrazione. Every surface, tool, and appliance gleamed as if freshly polished and never used. A screen on the wall showed a restaurant menu. Another screen, on the refrigerator, was on a news channel showing the crisis in Saudi Arabia. The one thing this kitchen didn't have was the makings of an actual meal—only drinks, snacks, and protein shakes.

"What's for breakfast?"

"That's right, I didn't tell you," said Sandy. "This building has a private restaurant. I'll show you."

Sandy got up and tapped the menu on the wall screen. "Here's where you order," she said. "They bring you the food in just a few minutes. I think I'll have one of these Belgian Chocolate Waffles this morning."

"That sounds great."

About ten minutes after Sandy ordered, when they were both seated at a table near the silent fountain, the doorbell rang. Sandy escorted in a waitress pushing a large cart with a waffle iron, a wide thermos, and a variety of other things on it.

She took two small waffles off the waffle iron, put them on plates and set them in front of Sandy and Isabel. They were the color of chocolate brownies and smelled so good that Isabel was really sorry they were only about six inches square.

Then she picked up the ice cream scoop, opened the thermos and put one scoop of dark chocolate ice cream on top of each waffle, where they immediately started to melt. She then covered the waffle and ice cream with blueberry syrup, then added a layer of whipped cream. On top of the whipped cream, she arranged raspberries, blueberries, and a single plump strawberry in a complex pattern with precision a neurosurgeon might have respected. Then she picked up a pepper grinder and dusted the whole thing with what smelled like ground hazelnuts.

No wonder Sandy's still so thin, thought Isabel, trying to savor hers instead of wolfing it down right away. This thing was delicious, but she could have eaten both and called it a light meal.

"Should I leave a tip or something?" whispered Isabel as soon as the waitress was out of the room.

Sandy blinked. "I'd forgotten people still do that out there," she said. "Anyway, no. She makes twenty-seven fifty an hour."

After breakfast, Isabel was about to take the dishes to the kitchen, but Sandy stopped her and took them herself. "I'm afraid I'm going to be a terrible host," she said. "Work to do, the big fundraiser to organize… no time to hang out today. This is your first time in New York, isn't it?"

"Yeah."

"Then go forth and see the sights." Sandy placed the dishes in the sink and left them there. Isabel assumed she had somebody come in here to wash up for her. "We'll take in a show tonight and tomorrow we go shopping. You're definitely going to need a new outfit for what I have in mind."

"Um, just out of curiosity…"

"Shit, I never got around to telling you, did I? The Symcox Foundation is holding a charity event on New Year's Eve to raise funds for Monsoon victims. We did this last year, and I hired a model to come with me wearing advance copies of the spring/summer line. This year, I would like that model to be you."

"You're kidding."

"The pay is seventy-five thousand dollars, plus you get to keep the outfit. Not the diamonds, of course."

"I'm… not exactly built for modeling."

"First of all, your face is awesome, and your body is better-looking than you think. Second, plus-size models aren't even a new thing anymore. Third, you're modeling diamonds, not swimwear."

Isabel wanted to argue, but… this was something she might have done as a favor to a friend, even if she didn't already owe that friend more favors than she had any hope of repaying. And she was being paid for it—paid more than what she'd gotten for any of her "real" work, which was completely unfair.

Life is unfair. Sometimes that works to your advantage.

DECEMBER 30:

IRENE J. HARRIS'S SHOP WAS small, but—as far as Isabel could tell—tasteful. An Asian woman about Sandy's age came out from behind the counter. "Sandy! I wasn't expecting to see you again so soon. How are you?"

"Hi, Lynn," said Sandy. Or it might have been Lin—the woman wasn't wearing a nametag. "Is Reenie in?"

"She's away for the holidays. Can I help you with something?"

"This is Isabel. She needs a black velvet dress to present the spring collection on."

"For tomorrow, I take it?"

"Afraid so. I'm sorry—I know this is kind of last-minute."

"That's all right. I've got a pretty simple pattern that should work. I'll have it delivered around five p.m. tomorrow."

Nobody had ever made a dress just for Isabel before. She'd hardly ever worn dresses. Lynn took her into a back room, and she stripped to her undies to let the assistant take her measurements.

Lynn was very professional, noting Isabel's hips and thighs without a hint of reaction. Which was good. Isabel wasn't bothered by her weight, but the reactions of other women tended to send her into spiny mode.

Lynn worked quickly. The only thing slowing her down was that she kept having to use a stepladder—everything was on the top two shelves. This Irene J. Harris had to be just about the tallest woman in the city. Isabel was sorry to have missed her.

Sandy came in while Isabel was pulling her pants up. "Trust me, Isabel," she said, "you're going to be a hit."

ON MOST OF THE PLANET *it was the last day of the old year, at least according to the Gregorian calendar.*

In San Francisco it was just past midnight. A very important man was disembarking from his business trip to Hong Kong. He was not important enough that we need to go into the details of his business, or even mention his name, but he was important and wealthy enough to have a private plane— old, heavy, diesel-guzzling, and swift—which let him cross the Pacific before the virus in his lungs had finished incubating.

In Dhaka it was early afternoon. The next national election was a week away. Over one million people were demonstrating in the streets in support of a political party which demanded that "the perpetrators of crimes against humanity and the world be brought to justice."

In Ürümqi the time of day didn't really matter. The city was just north of the Tien Shan range, and had hardly had a chance to recover from the floods of the Monsoon. Now it was in the process of being buried under five feet of snow.

In Riyadh it was still the middle of the morning. For the past few days, the city and its suburbs had echoed with the sound of gunfire, artillery, and air strikes. Now it was silent. A strange black banner was flying over every government building. The new regime was already taking steps to reassure the population that the lives of the truly righteous would be spared.

But the real story was what was happening down south…

DECEMBER 31:

IT WAS ALMOST TIME TO go to the fundraiser. Sandy and Isabel were in the apartment with a hair stylist named Isidore, a makeup artist named Loretta, and a massive guard whose name no one seemed inclined to ask. He stood over the case of diamonds, as still as a gun on a nightstand, his eyes quietly taking in everything in the room.

Sandy took out a large box with the name "Irene J. Harris" signed on it in big, florid letters. "Take a look," she said, opening the box. "This is what I'm wearing tonight."

Isabel lifted the top part of the dress out by the shoulders. It was white and glossy without a hint of translucence. It was embroidered around the edges and over the left shoulder in a sort of frost-fern pattern of deep blue and purple. There was something odd about the pattern that made Isabel look closer.

When she realized what it was, she had to fight the urge to let go and step back a pace. It was definitely embroidered in fine thread, not printed, and the pattern didn't repeat anywhere. No loom could have made it. Someone whose time was worth thousands of dollars an hour had spent more than a few hours hunched over a sewing machine… or possibly doing all this by hand.

"Are the sleeves supposed to be different lengths?" said Isabel.

"As a matter of fact, yes," said Sandy. "It'll look a lot better when I put it on. Let me show you what arrived for you this afternoon." She opened another, unsigned box and took out a black velvet dress. Then she stepped behind a partition with Isidore and Loretta.

Putting the dress on, Isabel found that it was very tight around the waist—it almost seemed to have a built-in corset. It was low-cut in front, but had tight sleeves coming up from under the roomy shoulders.

Isabel put the shoes on, looked in the mirror—a real old-fashioned mirror, not one of those screen-mirrors—and blinked in surprise. She had always thought of her looks as okay, but not gorgeous. Maybe it was the dress and the shoes doing things to her posture, but she seemed to have gone up several steps in attractiveness without warning.

Isidore emerged. "Black is so slimming, isn't it?" he said. Isabel wasn't sure if that was a general remark or a veiled insult, so she just nodded and let him start arranging her hair. Then Loretta started working on her makeup. When they were done, Isabel took another look, and blinked. This time the woman in the mirror was downright beautiful. Not exactly familiar, but beautiful.

And then... Sandy stepped out from behind the partition. It was an appearance that deserved to be preceded by an ellipsis.

Isabel couldn't tell if her shoes were high-heeled or platform or some combination of the two, but she'd definitely gained at least one more inch in height. She still wasn't as tall as Isabel, who was already five foot six barefoot, but she was definitely taller than before.

And then there was the dress. It left her right arm mostly bare and her left arm mostly covered, but the asymmetry somehow worked in its favor. The line of embroidery ran over her torso like a sash, and for the first time it was clear how many little details in the frost pattern drew the eye up toward her face. Isabel knew nothing of the history of women's fashion, but the lines of the dress put her in mind of Greek and Roman illustrations she'd seen. It wasn't quite the same, but the overall effect was timeless, like a universal symbol for "very important woman."

Then there was her face. Isabel's first thought was *why is she wearing so little makeup, and how did she suddenly get so pretty?* Then she realized the source of the confusion. She had just never seen makeup applied that well before.

Finally, there was her hair, tied back into a single braid that was intertwined and wrapped with long strands of gold ribbon as thin as rice paper. Not gold-colored ribbon. *Gold* ribbon. That combination of malleability and ductility was only found in one metal. And then there was the sort of lace hairnet on top of her head, made of cobweb-fine wires that had to be platinum. Put it all together, and the whole ensemble set off some ancient warning system in the hindbrain—*this isn't just money, this isn't just power, this is* royalty. *Start showing deference NOW.*

"Open up the case," said Sandy. "Let's get this girl good and stoned." The guard opened the case. Sandy took out the various bits of jewelry and started decorating Isabel with them. They were turquoise, periwinkle, and shades of blue ranging from sky to electric to an indigo just above black. Isabel had already committed the names of the different colors to memory in case anybody asked her, but there is no need for the reader to do the same.

Isabel put on her new coat, covering all the diamonds except for the earrings. It was a fur coat that cost as much as a year's rent on her apartment—one more thing Sandy was footing the bill for.* It was summer and winter ermine. The different strains of skin cell that produced the chocolate-brown and white furs had grown together in unique and complex fractal patterns, like a drop of ink or watercolor paint falling into a glass of water.

Sandy's coat was similar to Isabel's, but its pattern was one of white marbled with slate-blue. "Arctic fox, white and blue phases," she said. "I'm helping save the species—I figure they can spare me a few skin cells." Catching a glimpse of the two of them in the mirror, Isabel was reminded again not only how much money, but just what kind of rarefied environment they were headed into. Not even in Texas Foxtrot had she been so far outside her comfort zone.

Sandy started talking business as the car drove itself to the hotel. "One of the keys to making smart decisions," she said, "is to think of what you'd do if you were stupid, and then do something else.

"Here's what I'd do if I were stupid. I'd pick some loser candidate whose campaign was hard up for money, set up a PAC, spend millions of dollars advertising this candidate, and then tell him or her, 'Okay, now I own your ass.' Then I'd stand around rubbing my hands with glee and cackling evilly at how awesome I was because I had the power to turn this bag of hair into a major political player. I'd dream of the day when he or she was in the White House and I was pulling the strings from behind the scenes. Then my candidate would lose anyway, because he's still the same schmuck he was before, and I'd basically have spent a big pile of money to cackle and rub my hands with glee for a few months. Which I would normally do anyway for free.

"What I'm getting at here is that the sort of person I'm interested in supporting is the sort of person who might benefit from my help, but doesn't

---

* If you're wondering how many animals died to make this coat, the answer is… none. The same technology that can turn an ounce of tuna muscle into thousands of tons of *oke-maki* can turn a tiny sliver of live skin cells from an ermine or mink or other well-upholstered critter into hundreds of square yards of coat material. Over the past few years, this has revolutionized the fur industry. (PETA is still protesting it, but nobody knows why.)

absolutely require it. Which means they're also the sort of person I can't control. I try to choose these people carefully, because I have to treat them as equal partners. You're about to meet some of these people."

"I promise to behave myself."

"Relax."

Isabel took several deep breaths as the car approached the hotel. She had half expected the front of the hotel to be crowded with paparazzi and lit up by flashbulbs going off. For all she knew, it was. The car pulled into a parking garage built into the hotel, so it didn't really matter.

The elevator ride to the penthouse seemed somehow longer than the trip to Sandy's ninetieth-floor office. *I have no idea what to say or how to walk or how to do this. Help.*

"When I enter the room," said Isabel, "should I smile, or go for that pissed-off model look?"

"Whatever feels natural."

As they left the elevator, Sandy put her hand on Isabel's arm. Under other circumstances, this might have bothered her a little, as if the other woman were somehow claiming ownership of her. Now it was like a message to everybody—*It's cool. She's with me. She belongs here.*

They stepped through the doorway. Isabel half expected there to be some kind of announcer at the door saying "LADY SANDRA SYMCOX! And guest." In lieu of that, somebody near the door just said, "She's here!"

Sandy nodded. "And this is Isabel Bradshaw, wearing next year's spring collection," she said. "If you have any questions about them, you can ask her." Sandy gave her a little pat her on the back. Isabel strutted into the middle of the room, trying to manage a relaxed and friendly smile that on another occasion might have come naturally, and also trying not to wobble on her new shoes. She took off her coat and handed it to somebody who would presumably put it somewhere safe until she needed it again. *God help me, I am starting to get used to this lifestyle.*

Not so easy to get used to was the dozen women of various ages, all obviously rich, who immediately gathered around Isabel like buzzards around a deer carcass and started talking about the diamonds. They didn't engage Isabel in conversation except to ask her the names of the various colors. A couple of them called their husbands over to point out various colors of diamond. "Look at this one." "Doesn't this look nice?" They never actually asked for anything, but they were dropping massive hints. Mayor Lopez and his wife showed up and said hello to everybody. His wife had just enough time to cast a meaningful glance at Isabel's right armband before they left to grace some other gathering of notables with their presence.

After a few minutes, Isabel was starting to get really exasperated. She couldn't talk to anybody, get a drink or even be alone with her thoughts. Then it went on for another few minutes. And then another few. *I agreed to be a walking display counter. This is no time to start complaining.*

Then they started talking about other things—mostly gossip about friends of theirs who didn't happen to be here. One of them was complaining that her husband was on the ShameList over some editorials that used to appear in a publication he owned. The other women nodded their heads sadly.

Somewhere nearby, Sandy was going on at length about a deal she was working on. "Between the typhoon and the flood, the Chinese government needed some money really fast, so they sold a bunch of U.S. Treasury bonds for around two hundred seventy-five billion. Thing is, they should have gotten more. But you know how it is—when you're hard up for cash and everybody knows it, suddenly you're not doing so well in the negotiations.

"When Congress heard about it, they thought it was on purpose. They were all like 'Oh no! We're under attack! This is a plot by the crafty Chinese! They're selling our bonds cheap to undermine our finances!'" Sandy snorted. "Now as it happens, I know a thing or two about being under attack by the Chinese— specifically the Tanqiji Group—and if those guys were any craftier… they'd *invent* some shit instead of just ripping off my patents, and let me tell you, Congress was no help there.

"But now they think China's declared economic war on us, so it's a different story. Now they're ready to treat De L'Air like Beijing treats Tanqiji, as a national asset. Between that and the fact that Tanqiji lost half its physical plant to the typhoon, we were able to buy out their contract with Boeing. Our product's better anyway. So there's your stock tip of the day, if you're looking for one."

"Really, Sandy," came a voice from behind. "Shop talk? On a night like this?" About that time, the women around Isabel started retreating like buzzards when an eagle shows up.

Isabel turned around, and almost gulped. She could count on her fingers the number of politicians she could recognize by sight, but *holy shit this was*

Morgan.

The governor had gone for a simpler outfit than Sandy's. There was a shawl wrapped around her shoulders. It was made of silk, or something like it—white, but rippling with purple and silver shadows like mother-of-pearl. Underneath that she had on a unitard made of fabric even blacker than Isabel's velvet, so dark it hurt the eyes a little. The effect was to make her seem slightly unreal, like a woman-shaped hole in space. Between the second and third fingers of her left hand she was holding a gold-plated Respier, a complex little vaping device about a foot long and the width of a pencil.

Sandy and the governor both stepped toward Isabel. Morgan fiddled with a couple of the minuscule valves on the Respier, making some slight adjustment in the proportions of whatever herbal cocktail was in its compartments. Then she brought the end to her lips and drew a deep breath.

"Still in trim, I see," said Sandy. "What's your diet this year?"

Morgan paused to finish inhaling before she spoke. "Carbs first thing in the morning, protein the rest of the day, nothing after six p.m. Why change a winning formula?"

Sandy turned to Isabel. "Brooke used to be vegan, back when meat was cheaper," she said. Isabel nodded. In a world of meatless Mondays, and for most people one or two other days of the week as well, a vegan diet wasn't much of a status symbol any more.

Paying no attention to this, the governor leaned in to look at the diamonds. Her gaze moved from one earring to the other, passing over Isabel's face like it was a blank spot on the wall. Isabel noticed that she was wearing light-blue diamond studs in her ears—probably more of Sandy's work. "So this is your spring line," she said, sounding none too enthusiastic.

"Yes, indeed," said Sandy. Isabel had been expecting her to start gushing about the colors again, but for the moment she was keeping her cool.

Morgan took off her shawl and draped it over one arm. Then, without hesitation, she lifted the necklace off Isabel and put it on her own shoulders. Isabel glanced nervously at Sandy, thinking *can she do that?* Sandy seemed calm, so it was probably okay. *Of course it's okay—what do you think, she's going to steal them in the middle of a party? And by the way, have you noticed that these two don't seem exactly friendly?*

The governor looked at herself in a nearby mirror. Her lip curled. "I liked the ones you introduced in spring—the Horizon and Snowshadow," she said.

"They were subtle. Just a hint of color."

"This year I'm feeling more confident."

Morgan nodded. As she was putting the necklace back where it belonged, her breath brushed over Isabel's face like warm feathers. It smelled of whatever was in that Respier—marijuana, mint, lavender, clove, and some things Isabel couldn't identify.

Isabel felt her face turning pink and her heart speeding up. Supposedly, Morgan was around fifty, but even up close she didn't look older than forty-five. Less than that, really. If she'd had plastic surgery, it had been really good plastic surgery. Even her hands didn't show her age—Olivia in Sandy's office could have learned something from her.

And it had been years since a woman had turned Isabel on this much.

"Well, I'm sure they'll be very popular."

"That is the name of the game."

With that, Morgan was gone. Isabel shut her eyes, forcing herself not to stare longingly in the governor's direction as she went to go look bored at some other people.

EAST ANTARCTICA HAD CHANGED VERY little over the last few years. The East Antarctic Ice Sheet had lost a little here and there around the edges, at the Totten Glacier and other places, but in the center, it had grown thicker, offsetting the losses of ice elsewhere in the world. In the heart of Antarctica, rising temperatures— typically rising from minus twenty-five centigrade to minus twenty at the height of summer—only meant slightly more snow.

The West Antarctic Ice Sheet was a different story. The coming of summer had brought unexpected warmth to this portion of the continent, raising the temperature above freezing almost everywhere north of the 80th parallel. To the satellites above, the perfect white sheet appeared to be spattered with flecks of impossible blue, as pools of meltwater formed and expanded. Some of these pools expanded downward, forming the bore-holes called moulins as they melted their way down to the bottom of the ice sheet.

SANDY LEARNED IN CLOSE TO Isabel and smiled. "You can go off duty now," she said in a low voice. "I think everybody here who wants to look at the new diamonds already did. If anyone wants a second look, you know what to do."

With that taken care of, Isabel didn't really know what to do with herself. Everybody here seemed to know everybody else, and they were all engrossed in conversations with each other. It was like every party she'd ever been to where she didn't know anybody, only worse because everyone's social standing was about ninety stories above hers. The only person in sight who even looked to be within ten years of her age group was a tall, spectacularly built redhead in a red dress who Isabel didn't dare to approach or even look at too long.

When in doubt, get something to eat and drink. As if sensing her thoughts, a waiter came up and handed her something called a "rambutan mimosa." She had no idea what this was, and it looked like a glass of champagne that a couple of guys had ejaculated into after catching a glimpse of the ginger goddess over there, but it tasted all right.

Once she'd finished it, she handed the glass to another server and headed for the snack table. Whoever was in charge of deciding what foods were fashionable had chosen niçoise salad with aioli this year. Only now there were certain rules to serving it. You had to make it with garden-fresh tomatoes and herbs, you had to make the aioli good and strong with plenty of puréed garlic and concentrated lemon juice, you had to chop the olives and red onion extra fine—and be careful with the red onion, a little goes a long way—you had to arrange it artfully on little bite-size toasted brioche buns and top each one with a whole seedless grape, and—this was important—you had to remember to put the thing under the "c" in "niçoise." Otherwise it didn't count.

"Is this real tuna?" said a man in front of her.

"I can't imagine Sandy would serve anything else—especially not to *her*," said the woman next to him. So, most people here were on a first-name basis with Sandy and a She-Who-Must-Not-Be-Named basis with Morgan. Good to know.

As Isabel was loading up a little plate with edible-looking stuff, she heard a voice at her side.

"Excuse me—don't I know you?"

Isabel turned and looked up at a forty-something woman, taller than her, with a broad, friendly face. It was Governor Camberg. Or former Governor or ex-Governor or however you were supposed to say it. Isabel had last seen her more than a year and a half ago. She'd lost a lot of weight since then, and the gray streak in her hair had unmysteriously disappeared. She was apparently a much more conservative dresser than Morgan, wearing a wool pantsuit so dark Isabel wasn't sure what shade it was in this light, other than not quite black.

"I know I've seen you before somewhere," said Camberg. "Don't tell me… don't tell me… you worked on the Norfolk Plan, didn't you?"

"I did." *But how the hell did you remember? We spoke once for one minute.* Then she thought *she's a politician. Remembering people is part of the job.* "I'm… sorry about what happened in Congress."

Camberg shrugged. "It was too much to hope for that it would succeed the first time. Anyway, now we have a chance to update the Plan and get it to the new Congress. There's going to be another conference in April, and this one's going to be in an actual conference center. No more making everybody stay in a wrecked naval base."

"I hope I can make it."

This is actually going okay. It might have been shop talk, but talking about her family would feel like asking for help from yet another rich and powerful person, and conversationally, Isabel couldn't think of much else to bring to the table. Unless Camberg happened to be into rhust or a big fan of the Ravens, neither of which seemed likely. Also, she was the first person Isabel had met tonight who'd looked at her rather than her bling.

"So how'd you end up doing this?"

Isabel explained her connection with Sandy.

Camberg turned. "Thel?" she said. "Come over here."

And now, because this night was not nearly crazy enough, here came the redhead. When she stepped into the light, Isabel got a good look at her and realized that she couldn't be older than eighteen, and was probably a year or so younger. Then she remembered reading that the governor had a teenage daughter.

As Camberg did the introductions, Isabel's salivary glands felt like they were trying to make up their minds whether to go dry or start drooling. Thel had a face that belonged on a fashion magazine cover, freckles and all. Her auburn hair was in a choppy sort of shag that almost reached her shoulders. She smiled, showing teeth so white and even they must have put her orthodontist's kids through college.

Thel leaned in close to get a better look at the diamonds. *MUST NOT LOOK DOWN CLEAVAGE. MUST CONCENTRATE ON FACE.* Her eyes were the same color as Isabel's.

"These are awesome," said Thel. "Hey, did you get that dress from Harris's?"

"Yes, I did." Thel's dress was fire-engine red, pleated in the skirt and made for somebody six inches taller, but otherwise it was much the same. But if the dress had been designed by Irene J. Harris, the contents had apparently been designed by a teenage boy.

Thel touched the necklace, then one of the Alpine diamonds. "I know I want some new earrings," she said, "but I can't decide what color."

Since her fingers had brushed the base of Isabel's throat, she was having a little trouble finding her voice through all that tingling. She finally managed to say, "Well… they're coming out in April. You've got plenty of time to decide."

All that Isabel knew about Thel Camberg was that she'd gone with her mother on some trip to the Mideast and some crazy religious extremists had chucked a rock at her. That sort of thing was why Isabel stayed out of the Mideast. Thel looked okay now, though. Actually, "okay" was putting it mildly. *What is wrong with me? First the governor, now this girl who probably isn't even legal and whose MOTHER is watching. I swear I wasn't this horny the last time I was having actual sex. Come to think of it, I haven't thought much about sex since Laurie left. Is it just that I've been spending so much time worrying about money and my family? And now that we're all more secure, my libido is coming back?*

"So," said Thel, "what kind of music do you listen to?"

"I'm into rhust. Also Laura Bronzino, Epifania…"

"Cool!" This gave them something to chat about for a minute or so. It turned out they had both been at the Rodomontade concert in June, although of course Thel and her friends had had much better seats. Meanwhile, Thel's mother was sending a long, complicated text.

Finally Camberg looked up from her phone. "You know what?" she said. "I'm going to bring somebody here and let him introduce himself. Just wait here a moment and he'll show up."

Thel rolled her eyes. "It's that guy, isn't it?"

"Excuse us," said Carrie.

Then Camberg and her daughter went up to talk with Morgan. What happened next might have been Isabel's imagination. For just a moment, it seemed that Morgan's too-cool-for-any-emotion-other-than-mild-disdain mask slipped, and what was under it was a look of raw hate... directed at Thel, of all people.

THE DEEPEST OF THE MOULINS was in the stretch of West Antarctica called Marie Byrd Land, midway between the Crary Mountains and the spectacularly unpoetic Executive Committee Range. Without warning, and seemingly without cause, the ice around this moulin began trembling as if in an earthquake. A satellite captured the sudden rippling of the water in the melt ponds within a twenty-mile radius.

When the shaking stopped, the moulin was at the center of a starburst of narrow crevasses down which the water had vanished. From above, the ice looked like someone had hit a sheet of glass with the point of a chisel.

Glaciologists and cryologists the world over had new questions to ponder: What just happened? Is it likely to happen again, and if so, how often and on what scale? Some twenty feet of potential sea level rise was locked up in the West Antarctic Ice Sheet, waiting to be unleashed on the world. Any sign of instability in it was a harbinger of disaster.

ISABEL TURNED HER HEAD AND saw someone new coming through the coatroom—a slender young man in a tailored navy suit and red tie. His hair was parted on the left and buzz-cut on the left in what Isabel assumed was the latest style. He was about six feet tall, and handsome in a thin-faced way. He walked up to her with the cold, confident swagger of a man who'd watched an online video tutorial called *How to Swagger with Cold Confidence* and practiced in front of a mirror several times a week.

"Hello there," he said, looking her straight in the eye with hardly a glance at the jewelry she was wearing. "You must be the notorious Isabel Bradshaw. Am I right?"

"Uh... only if I'm notorious." *Am I? Shit, I probably am at this point. I'm not even sure what for.*

The thin guy nodded. "I am Jerome Ross, the greatest political aide of my generation," he said, taking her hand and shaking it. "They call me Rome, in honor of my many conquests. I've served with the Morgan campaign in

New York, and this year I masterminded the victories of seven different upset candidates in Senate races." Isabel tried not to look impressed, but that sounded... impressive. Assuming she could take his word on the importance of his involvement. Which would be a really stupid assumption.

"I am the right hand of Carrie Camberg and the pimp hand of God above," he said, "and now I'm going to introduce you to my friends. Damn, you're wearing a lot of sparkly shit." He beckoned her into the coatroom. Isabel followed him, desperately trying to think of something to say in response. Thel was right. This was definitely... that guy. He might well be the thattest guy in the history of thattitude.

"This is a little lounge the cleaning staff uses," said Rome, gesturing to the door at the far end of the little room.

"Where's the staff now?"

"Downstairs somewhere."

The lounge was small. There was a collection of comfortable but mismatched chairs in it, and a small table with a bucket of champagne and a plate of tuna niçoise bites and other fancy nibbles on top of an assortment of print magazines. There were nine or ten other people in the room, none of whom looked older than thirty.

I swear, thought Isabel, *I could find the uncool kids' table in a thousand square miles of trackless wilderness.* Still, at least she had a remote chance of finding something in common with some of these people.

"Everyone!" said Rome. "Your attention please. This is a personal friend of our host, and as such is a woman of status and consequence. Do not grope her. That goes double for you two." He gestured to a couple of tiny young women sharing an extra-wide chair near the door. "Isabel, meet Rosencrantz and Guildenstern."

"Hi," said Isabel, reaching out to shake their hands. "I'm guessing those aren't your real names." *And how does Rome know this much about me already? Just how much did Camberg tell him in that text message? Or does he have other sources of info?*

The one on the right stood up, the top of her head about level with Isabel's lower lip. She had light-brown hair almost the same shade as Isabel's, but cut short. She wore square-rimmed glasses and a black pantsuit. "Call me Gabrielle," she said, shaking Isabel's hand.

The other one was probably Hispanic, but with her hair dyed a shade of canary yellow that matched her long-sleeved dress. She just reached out instead of getting up, exposing enough of her arm that Isabel could see it was covered in tattoos of winding roses. "Lexi," she said.

A deeply tanned guy with conspicuous earrings and a touch of eyeshadow stepped up. "I'm Tyler," he said. "If Rome gets too fresh, just hit him in the face with a rolled-up magazine."

"Ignore him," said Rome. "He's just sad 'cause he wants to have sex with me and I only think of him as a friend."

"In your dreams, fool," said Tyler. "Your ass looks like two postcards fighting under a blanket. If I tried to fuck it, I'd probably miss."

"His mouth, on the other hand, is huge," said Guilden—*no, Gabrielle*, thought Isabel. *Keeping track of new people's names is hard enough when somebody isn't giving them cute nicknames too.*

"But enough about my body parts, which apparently even the lesbians are obsessed with," said Rome. "Tell us all about yourself, and what brings you to this assembly of the great and the good and these guys."

So Isabel spent a few minutes introducing herself and explaining her connection to Sandra Symcox, while being repeatedly interrupted by Rome's flirting or self-promoting or whatever it was he was doing. She wondered what the point was of bringing all these people to a party like this if they weren't allowed to mingle with the really important ones. She also wondered why Carrie Camberg thought that what she really needed was an introduction to this guy. He was cute in his own way, and at this point Isabel really wanted to get busy with *somebody,* but he was apparently addicted to... on second thought, no, there wasn't a drug on Earth that did this.

Isabel tried to keep the talk on the diamonds relatively short, since it didn't seem likely that any of these people were prospective customers and she didn't want to be a bore. Gabrielle nodded respectfully, Lexi looked unimpressed... actually, a lot of them looked unimpressed. Maybe it was because they worked for Morgan.

"I like them," said Isabel, feeling strangely defensive. "I mean, I might not have the world's greatest taste—"

"Well, I think they're awesome," said Rome, "and I do have the world's greatest taste. Seriously, I tried everything I like and it all turned out great! What are the odds?"

"Heads up, guys," said Tyler, gesturing at the coatroom. From somewhere beyond it, someone was tapping something against something or doing something else to make a ringing noise loud enough to get everybody's attention. Only Sandy, or possibly the governor, would have dared do that in this crowd.

"Ladies and gentlemen," said Sandy, "from the bottom of my heart, thank you all for coming. There's only one New Year's Eve every year, and there are many events, many causes of equal worth. You chose to be here and to help this effort on behalf of our fellow Americans.

"Are we doing this just to be nice? Are we doing this to make us feel good about ourselves? Okay, maybe a little. But mostly we're here because deep down, we know that our fates are intertwined with those of the least fortunate among us. We, and they, are all in the same country, all in the same world. And we here in this room are blessed to be in a position where we can be of assistance to others.

"Even for us, it can be easy to lose heart. From our lofty perches, we have looked down on a world fighting a losing war against chaos, dreading the day when it blights our own lives and fortunes. Some of us have already been affected.

"But the year is over, and here we are. This city, this nation, this world—*still here*. Stronger. Wiser. And ready to turn the tide of this war in the new year."

As she listened, Isabel couldn't help looking around her, seeing where she was and in whose company, and being overwhelmed by the strangeness of it all. *Is this actually my life? A week ago I was trying to sleep naked in a hammock in a bedbug-infested firetrap in the middle of a FEMA camp. Now I'm here, wearing a big load of diamonds, doing this.*

And six weeks ago my parents had a home. And three months ago I had a boyfriend. And four years ago nobody had ever heard of the Northern Monsoon. Isabel was starting to understand how that polar bear must have felt— swimming and swimming through an endless gray void, desperately looking for something solid, something reliable that wouldn't melt away under her feet just when she was getting used to it.

The big difference was that she wasn't hungry. In this world, that meant she was already ahead of the game.

It was 11:59 p.m. The last seconds were ticking away. Somewhere a few blocks away, the ball was dropping.

"To the New Year!" came Sandy's voice.

"The New Year!" said Rome, a split second before everybody else.

To the New Year. May the next bunch of changes be for the better.

Where will the Northern Monsoon strike next?

Will Carrie Camberg's presidential campaign ever get off the ground?

Will Isabel and Rome have sex?

Yes, I meant Jerome Ross—what did you think I meant?

If so, are we going to have to watch?

What is this "ShameList," anyway?

When do we get to meet this "Martelle Sherman" person?

Or what's-his-name, that brother of Rome's?

And isn't anybody going to give Walter Yuschak
a good swift kick in the junk?

And is this story ever going to get an actual villain,
apart from the frigging weather?

Find out in the forthcoming

ALTERED SEASONS
AGE OF CONSEQUENCES

ACKNOWLEDGEMENTS

This story began as a short timeline, called "The Day the Icecap Died," in the "Future History" section of alternatehistory.com, where it won an award. The encouragement of that community inspired me to share it on my own Web site.

Information on how communities are already confronting rising sea levels came from the documentary *Facing the Surge* (2016) directed by Diogo Castro Freire, Jorge Castro Freire, and Martha Gregory.

Much of the information about the Old River Control Structure came from the writings of John McPhee and can be found in *The Control of Nature* (New York: Farrar Strauss Giroux, 1989). I am indebted to *A Paradise Built in Hell* by Rebecca Solnit (Penguin Books, 2010) for observations on community formation in time of crisis.

The carbon fee and dividend proposal alluded to comes from the Citizens Climate Lobby. If you're curious, the details are these:

- A fee of $15 per ton of carbon is placed on carbon-based fuels at the point where they become a part of the U.S. economy. This fee rises by $10 per ton per year.

- The money from the fee is distributed to all U.S. households on a per capita basis.

- A border adjustment would place a tariff on imports from countries that do not price carbon themselves.

ABOUT THE AUTHOR

PAUL BRIGGS learned to read and write when he was two, the same time he was learning to talk. He spent the next twenty years learning that nobody talks the same way they write, or vice versa.

He lives in Easton, Maryland, has a master's degree in journalism from the University of Maryland, College Park, and is the author of two middle-grade science fiction novels, *Locksmith's Closet* and *Locksmith's Journeys*. He is working on the concluding volume of the trilogy, *Locksmith's War*. Paul has also written several short plays, two of which (*The Worst Super Power Ever* and *The Picture of Health*) have won awards.

Find him online at:

WWW.PAULBRIGGS.COM